SEARCH THE SEVEN HILLS

Formerly entitled: The Quirinal Hill Affair

Barbara Hambly

BALLANTINE BOOKS • NEW YORK

Library of Congress Catalog Card Number: 82-17051

ISBN 0-345-34438-3

Manufactured in the United States of America

First Ballantine Books Edition: November 1987

For the Magic Christian—
Dr. Jeffrey Russell

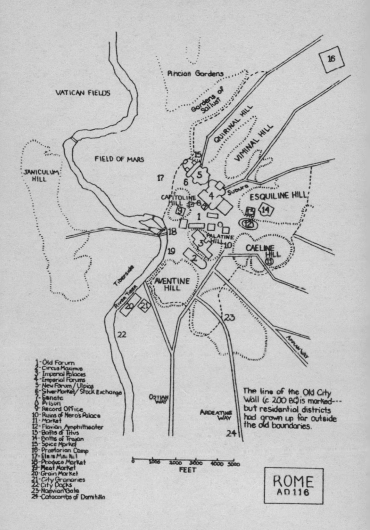

VATICAN FIELDS

Pincian Gardens

Gardens of Sallust

QUIRINAL HILL

VIMINAL HILL

16

FIELD OF MARS

JANICULUM HILL

17

15

6

5

4

Subura

ESQUILINE HILL

CAPITOLINE HILL

9

1

12

14

18

PALATINE HILL

3

10

CAELINE HILL

11

19

2

Tiberside

AVENTINE HILL

River Tiber

20

21

23

22

OSTIAN WAY

ARDEATINE WAY

24

Appian Way

1 - Old Forum
2 - Circus Maximus
3 - Imperial Palaces
4 - Imperial Forums
5 - New Forum / Ulpia
6 - Silver Market/ Stock Exchange
7 - Senate
8 - Prison
9 - Record Office
10 - Ruins of Nero's Palace
11 - Market
12 - Flavian Amphitheater
13 - Baths of Titus
14 - Baths of Trajan
15 - Spice Market
16 - Praetorian Camp
17 - Meat Market
18 - Produce Market
19 - Meat Market
20 - Grain Market
21 - City Granaries
22 - City Docks
23 - Naevian Gate
24 - Catacombs of Domitilla

The line of the Old City Wall (c 200 BC) is marked --- but residential districts had grown up far outside the old boundaries.

0   1000   2000   3000   4000   5000
FEET

ROME
AD 116

I

He [Nero] inflicted the most exquisite tortures on this class well hated for their abominable practices and called Christians by the mob. Christus (who gave them their name) was put to death in Tiberius' reign by the procurator Pontius Pilate; but the mischievous superstition, though momentarily checked, broke out again not merely in Judaea, but in Rome itself, where all things foul and shameful find a welcome and a home. So arrests were first made of all such as pleaded guilty; and then, on their evidence, a vast number were convicted not so much on the charge of incendiarism as of hatred for all mankind.

Tacitus

Distantly, the slap of sandals and the miscellaneous jingling of leather and brass echoed in the canyons of the narrow streets. It was the quiet time of evening, the eleventh hour of the day when most people were finishing their suppers and the few shopkeepers still open were putting up their shutters for the night; here among the elite shops and wealthy homes on the Quirinal Hill it was quieter still. The noises of Rome's center seemed to lie far off, like a noxious sink of sound.

The young man leaning in the deep-set doorway of a modest apartment building could hear the approach of the litter quite clearly. It was still early enough that they might not have the usual entourage of torchbearers and an armed guard. If they were coming from somewhere close—this side of the Forum, for instance—they wouldn't, but the gods only knew where she'd been. Had he been less of a philosopher, he would have prayed for this to be so, but as it was, he stoically prepared to accept whatever circumstances for the meeting Fate should choose to lay upon his bony shoulders.

Fate appeared to be in one of her pleasanter moods this evening.

At the curve of the twilit street, the chair came into view, pale curtains fluttering in the summer gloom. The houses were tall at this point, and the brilliant gilding of the sunset had faded from their brick-red roof tiles some quarter hour ago. Somber dusk filled the lane, azure and smoky purple, but even so the chair was recognizable as belonging to J. Tullius Varus, prefect of the city of Rome and, now that the emperor Trajan had resumed his campaigns in the East, one of the most powerful men in the city. It was borne by two sweating Arabs and followed by a middle-aged Greek slave laden down with parcels, but it was otherwise alone.

From his hiding place, the young man watched it approach, prey to overwhelming shyness. He wondered if she'd even deign to speak with him, or if it was she at all—he'd look tremendously silly if he hailed the occupant and it turned out to be her mother. He wondered why a perfectly adult philosopher of twenty-two should feel this helpless dread of a meeting with a girl of sixteen; a girl, moreover, whom he'd known since they were both children. It also occurred to him, absurdly, that he'd forgotten to comb his hair.

It was with a curious feeling of exposure that he stepped from the shadows of the doorway and stood, paralyzed and mute, in the gloom of the lane.

The white silk of the chair curtains moved. The chair came to a halt at his side.

Miraculously, he found his voice. "Tullia?" He cleared his throat. "Tertullia?"

The curtain slid back on its gold rings, each ring the perfect curve of a leafed tendril of vine. Vines were worked into the white silk, too, and the pattern of them laid a soft moiré of shadows on the small, rather elfin face of the girl within. He saw she'd been crying, but she said in a perfectly calm voice, "Hello, Marcus."

To a philosopher, grief and joy, fortune and death, should all be equally acceptable. But the red eyes and puffy nose evaded his philosophic armor and pierced his heart like a javelin. Forgetting his carefully prepared congratulations, he blurted helplessly, "I'm sorry! I came as soon as I heard!"

Her breath caught in a laugh that was perilously close to a sob. "Oh, Marcus, the betrothal was announced a week ago! You must be the only man in Rome who hadn't heard."

It was a fair hit, and there wasn't a thing he could say. He looked so forlorn that she reached out her hands to him. "My poor Professor, I should have known you'd be so wrapped up in your books that you wouldn't hear about it. But I'm glad you've come. I'm so glad."

He clutched her hands to his breast, but the technical difficulties of embracing someone positioned in an unstable vehicle slightly higher than one's own center of gravity defeated him. Besides, there were the bearers to think of, who might or might not know Latin, and the slave, who certainly would. "Tullia, I heard about it yesterday. I came to see you that same evening. Your father was gone . . ."

"He's in Sicily," she whispered, her fingers tightening over his hands suddenly, as though she feared he would run from her. Then she broke off and looked around quickly. "Hylas? Why don't you take that on home, please?"

The slave bowed. "Of course, mistress." He trotted away up the street, his wide shoulders briefly washed by the light that fell from the windows of the apartment houses on both sides of the street. Then he turned a corner and was gone. All about them the lane was still, the last of the shopkeepers having bolted up their shutters and gone inside. From the little lofts above the shops the ubiquitous scent of porridge and onions floated, mingling with the cooling dust smells of the lane. From the rustling gardens farther up the hill and the trees around the spacious town houses of that old and elegant neighborhood came the sleepy twitter of nesting birds. In that blue deepening light Tertullia Varia's face looked fragile and pointy, as though she had not slept, and very young in spite of the sophisticated masses of symmetrical curls that framed it. Earrings in the shape of bronze lilies twinkled among that dark profusion like autumn flowers on the forest floor.

"Father will be back at the end of July," she continued softly, "when the new city officials are appointed, for the inaugurations and the last meeting of the Senate."

"So nothing can be done until then?"

She was silent for a moment, her slim fingers light on his, then tightening suddenly, as though to feel the shape of his big awkward bones. "Exactly what do you think can be done?"

Taken off-guard, he could only gape.

"Chambares Tiridates is rich," she went on. "Your offering for my hand won't make him any poorer. It won't make you anything other than a penniless philosopher who spends all his time between the library and the schools of philosophy in the Basilica Ulpias."

He gulped and found his voice. "Your father can't seriously contemplate marrying you to—to some fat Syrian shopkeeper!"

"Tiridates isn't a shopkeeper. He's the wealthiest importer in Rome," said the girl gently. "And more than money, he has political power, power among the Syrian and Persian merchants—"

"Your father has all the political power he could possibly want!" cried Marcus. "He'd have to be a megalomaniac to want more!"

"Power's like milk," Tullia said in a tired, ironic voice far too old for that thin elfin face. "It goes bad quickly. Father needs money; he needs popularity; it isn't enough that a man be good at his job. You know that. To keep power, a man has to put on a good appearance, have clients at his beck and call, give splendid dinners for his friends, sponsor games—"

Outrage made his voice squeaky. "Stupid, bloody, vulgar spectacles—"

"Marcus." She released his hands, caught his face between her palms, her fingers fragile and cold among the soft curls of his light-brown hair. He gazed up at her helplessly for a moment, remembering suddenly that even when they were children, Tullia had been the one to handle the logistics of their scrapes.

"My poor Professor," she whispered. "Don't you know how things are done? Don't you know that men who have power will keep it, no matter what it costs? Don't you know that power is based on the masses, and that the masses are crude, and vulgar, and stupid, and vicious? Don't you know that no matter how perfect, how beautiful were the ideals of the ancient republic, our wealth comes from Empire and that empire is mostly Persian and Syrian and African, and we can't afford to ignore that? Don't you know we must move with the times, or die?"

"I know it," replied Marcus unhappily, taking her hands again, "but it doesn't mean that I cannot fight for the philosophic ideal."

"Father would never let us wed."

"He's a Roman," Marcus said simply. "For all he's a politician, wouldn't he rather see his daughter marry a Roman, rather than a—a—"

"As of last year," pointed out Tullia, "Tiridates has been a Roman, too."

"Bought citizenship!"

"And in any case it might be different if the Roman were wealthy, and powerful, and could maintain a wife in the princely comfort that Father expects for his only child. It wouldn't be some"—her voice took on Tullius Varus' rich rolling accents in an uncanny mimicry—"some worthless wastrel whose very father has banished him from the ancestral roof."

"That isn't true! I left of my own accord!"

Tertullia only looked at him, pity in her dark eyes.

"And besides," continued Marcus lamely, "my family's wealthy enough to suit him—or it should be."

"But you yourself live like a pauper. Marcus, I know why; I know it's by your own choice. I know you're committed to a life as a philosopher, and that's what you care about." Her voice shook, and she tightened her full, too-sensitive lips, as though to control it. "He wouldn't understand."

"Do you understand?" He gazed pleadingly up into her face. Both of them had entirely forgotten about the two chair-bearers, who stood with the patient stoicism of slaves in the uneven pavement of the street that was now almost wholly dark.

Her face was almost invisible in the shadows of the chair curtains, but her earrings glinted as she turned it aside. "No," she said in a flat voice. "I don't understand the life you lead. And anyway we shouldn't suit. I'm glad to have had the opportunity to speak with you—"

"Stop it!" he cried despairingly.

"I mean it," she insisted, her voice breaking.

"Tullia, please, I'll mend my ways. I'll go back home, I'll leave Timoleon's classes, I'll learn to manage the family lands . . ."

The chair swayed under the angry jerk of her body. "Don't you dare, Marcus Silanus! Don't you dare go crawling back to that—that selfish little shriveled-up raisin of a father of yours! What kind of philosopher are you? I'd never speak to you again if you did that, and I don't care how rich you became!" She wrenched her wrists free of his grasp, and he was too startled by this outburst to hold them.

He began, "We could wait . . ."

"Wait for what?" she sobbed. "I'm sixteen already! All the girls I went to school with are married and some of them are divorced! Marcus, it's no good," she went on, her voice cracking and raw. "Tiridates wants the wedding to go through as soon as Father gets back from Sicily. I've spent the day with his horrid sister buying my bride things and it's no good, Marcus."

She was crying again. His heart torn with compassion, he

reached to embrace her, calling her by her childhood nick-name, "Tullia, no, there has to be some way . . . Tell them to put down this wretched chair, by the gods!"

"No," she gulped, drawing back, "No. You know he won't listen. What good would it do us if he married me to Tiridates by force? And he'd do it, Marcus. With the elections and the new appointments coming up, and he's already planning to give games next year . . . I think he'd do anything." Her voice had turned suddenly thin and forlorn, her tears shining like quicksilver in the deep shadows of the white curtains. She whispered, "Marcus, do you love me?"

Thwarted of an embrace, he kissed her fingers passionately. The slaves continued to stare bleakly off into space. In the blue darkness of the summer evening they were alone, but for the bearers and another slave, whistling his way along on the other side of the street, bound on some errand of his master's. If he noticed the scene at all, he had the good manners to pretend he didn't.

"Marcus, listen." Tullia's light, soft fingers touched his uncombed hair. The silk of the litter curtains stirred in the breeze and touched his cheek like the kiss of wind-spirits. "We can't do anything now. But I can send for you—after the wedding." Her voice was low, excluding the chair-bearers (who might not have understood much Latin anyway). "Will you come?"

"WHAT?" At her furious signal he dropped his voice to a hoarse whisper. "What? You mean you're cold-bloodedly planning to deceive your husband . . ."

"Oh, don't be such a baby!" she hissed furiously, thrusting shame and sorrow aside by the more convenient emotions of anger and scorn.

"Baby?" he whispered back. "You say 'baby' when you sit there, practically on the eve of your marriage, plotting an affair before the knot's even tied!"

"Don't pretend you don't know that it's done! Everyone does it!"

"That's no reason for you to swell the ranks of adulteresses!"

Her hand lashed out at him in an inexpert slap that all but

overset the litter. Marcus caught her as she swayed; the bearers compensated for the sudden swerve without a flicker of expression. Tullia pulled violently away from his steadying grasp. "Take your hands off me, you—you philosopher!" she raged. "You'd put your own stupid priggish morals before our happiness . . . *Our* happiness! Your happiness, I should say!"

Marcus could only gape at her in inarticulate outrage, his hand to his cheek, which was not stinging nearly so badly as was his self-esteem.

"You'd cause trouble with my father about my marrying a foreigner, which is something that can't be helped, but just because of some silly vows . . ."

"No vow is silly if you're going to have a workable human society!"

"Human society!" cried Tullia, weeping afresh, though not, if either of them had been old enough to know it, with anger at him. "My own father is selling me as a slave, practically, to some fat Syrian who'd sooner cuddle you on his wedding night than me, and all you can do is prate at me about human society! I hate you, Marcus Silanus!"

"Tullia . . ."

"Move on!" she sobbed wrathfully to the chair-bearers.

"Tullia!"

The bearers had begun to move off with their loping, professional stride. Tullia slued around in her chair and screamed at him, "Go away! Go back to your dirty old books! I never want to see you again!" And with a jerk she pulled the curtains shut.

"Tullia, listen!" Marcus broke into a run to catch up and tripped over the flapping ends of the toga that marked him as a Roman citizen come of age. He landed in a patch of mud and fruit peelings, and by the time he'd scrambled drippily to his feet, the litter was turning the corner with practiced neatness, into the street that led up the hill to Consul Varus' town house.

Marcus was gangly for all his height, and a bookish boy-hood had given him no great turn of speed. By the time he'd reached the corner, the Arabs were far up the street with their burden, and where the street turned, at the crest of the hill, he could see the walls of the house, creamy white against the gloom, the dark trees of the gardens spangled with light from the courts below, like firelit smoke. Even at this distance he could make out two forms in the gold rectangle of the open door: the slim dainty shape of Tullia's mother, Lady Aurelia Pollia, and, dark and blocky behind her, a big man in the purple-bordered senatorial toga whom he knew for the praetor Priscus Quindarvis, Consul Varus' adopted cousin and political running dog.

They would be waiting for her, having evidently expected her back earlier than this. In fact Quindarvis had said something of the kind when Marcus had spoken to him earlier in the afternoon, when he'd first come inquiring for Tullia. He had had some notion of running after the litter, of calling to her to stop, not to become one of those sleek worldly women whose loveless marriages were sweetened by cheap and changeable loves. But he couldn't do it, not with her mother listening—not to mention a problematical uncle and an unknown slave and the chair-bearers (if they knew Latin). So he could only stand, panting, at the corner of the street, as she receded from him. He thought, *I have lost her,* and despair closed over his heart.

When the gang of men emerged from an alleyway halfway up the street, blocking the litter's progress, Marcus' first thought was only a kind of mild surprise that so many would be abroad so late. The litter-bearers stopped, expostulating; then in the lamplight that filtered from the distant open door Marcus saw that the men carried clubs.

One of the bearers dropped his end of the poles and ran; men emerged from an alley on the opposite side of the road, surrounded him, and clubbed him unconscious. The chair had heeled drunkenly, then fell as the other chair-bearer went down. In the thrashing mill of the white curtains, he could see Tullia being dragged out by the ambushers, struggling desperately, her dark hair tumbling down around her shoulders.

Then at the top of the street he heard her mother scream,

and with an incoherent yell he grabbed up the flapping ends of his toga and plunged into the fray.

He tripped over the body of a fallen bearer, scrambled up, and went sailing into the man nearest him, swinging his fists and shouting. He had no idea how to go about attacking a man, having never struck anyone in anger in his life; he got a brief glimpse of the man's face, swarthy and grinning, white teeth gleaming in a coarse black beard, a gold ring flashing in one ear.

The battle was humiliatingly short. Somehow he was abruptly on the ground, Tullia's screams ringing in his ears. Beyond the litter and the milling bodies he could see her white limbs flashing in the tangle of her gown, brown greedy hands holding her, lifting her off her feet. He sought to rise and a boot thudded brutally into his ribs. His sight blurred, and he tasted mud and wetness and the welling sourness of vomit in his throat. As the world reeled into darkness, he heard the screams muffled, and the clattering welter of fleeing feet.

By sheer force of will he heaved himself half-upright, in time to collide with another young man—the slave who had passed them earlier and had come leaping out of nowhere to run to the rescue. They tangled and fell, the slave cursing him in British. There were other voices, shouts ringing off the high walls; a flicker of white and struggling movement in the mouth of an alley. The slave writhed free of Marcus' entangling toga and was off after them again, to catch them before they were lost in the maze of lanes downhill; Marcus tried to follow, tripping again, fighting a dizzy blackness that clutched at the edges of his mind. He reached the black canyon of the narrow lane at a staggering run, hearing something falling and, in the impenetrable shadows before him, the clatter of footsteps and a horrible smothered squealing. Without pausing for thought, he plunged after the sound. Something white and blurred danced elusively among the twisting alleyways.

Then his feet were hooked from beneath him, and he hit the pavement again, the stones of the wall beside him ripping at his flailing hands. A body lying half under his feet twisted to a sitting position, and he had a brief vision of the dark angular face of the slave as powerful hands caught his shoulders and slammed him unconscious against the wall.

The goddess Persephone had been raped by Pluto, lord of the underworld.

It had all happened in the ancient days of the gods, he knew; and Timoleon, the Greek philosopher at whose feet he had studied these last three years, had explained to him once that the myth was, in fact, an allegory of the union of the elements in a single godhead.

But through the gold fog that seemed to surround him, he thought for a time that he lay in the grasses of an ancient Greek meadow, the scent of flowers thick in his throat. He saw the coming of the death-god, the girl taken by surprise; saw the white struggling body in the reeds beside the stream, and the brown hands of that inexorable assailant gripping at the girl's clenched, protesting thighs. He struggled toward them, trying to call out, but his body felt heavy, as though he were half-asleep or very, very drunk. He saw the girl's mouth part in a scream, stretching wider and wider; and turning, looked into the horror-stricken eyes of Demeter, Persephone's goddess mother.

Through the foggy blurring of his senses he thought he heard the philosopher Timoleon's voice as he lectured. "What we have here is not the disgraceful behavior of God toward God—for how can there be violence of one element of the Godhead toward another?—but an allegorical figure of life and death as united emanations of the One. Earth, and the commonplaces of human affairs, are here represented by the goddess Demeter, whom we may take to understand . . ." The voice seemed to fade, to change into other voices. Marcus thought groggily, *No, it isn't that! No measure—no godhead.* Only the rape of innocence, blind and random injustice, the thrashing pale reeds whitening to a froth of torn white silk, the bronze lilies tangling in the helpless girl's hair. *All the philosophy in the world will never reconcile me to that.*

"My dear boy . . ." Something shockingly cold against

the side of his head made him flinch, and blinking, he saw
Pluto's face melt into the square, anxious countenance of
Priscus Quindarvis as the big man bent over him, a dripping
rag in his hand. "Are you all right?"

The bright haze of the dream blurred the features, and the
lights stabbed at his eyes, so that he twisted his head aside to
escape burning.

"It's the lamp," said another voice—Nicanor, he identified it, Varus' Greek physician slave. The dazzling glare
shifted.

Somewhere a woman was screaming, a moaning animal noise
of grief. His eyes opened suddenly, he said, "Demeter . . ."
Then, as consciousness devoured the last fragments of
the vision, "Lady Aurelia!" He tried to get up and sank back
with a nauseated groan.

"Are you all right?" asked Quindarvis again, daubing
worriedly at his face with a rag, and Nicanor demanded
brusquely, "How in the name of Apollo would he know if
he's all right? Lie still, Professor." It was an old nickname
that dated back to his bookish schooldays; even Tullia's
father's slaves used it. He supposed it was better than what
the other philosophy students at the Basilica Ulpias sometimes called him—Silenus, after the Greek god of drunken
poltroonery, a pun on his family name of Silanus. The physician's light swift fingers turned back his eyelids, then felt at
the cords of his neck. Gradually his senses cleared. The
softness of the dream's grasses turned to rocks beneath his
smarting ribs, though rolling his head painfully to one side,
he saw that he was actually lying on one of the dining-room
couches in Varus' house. Someone seemed to have filled the
sockets of his eyes with sand; his mouth tasted as though it
had been carefully stuffed with Egyptian cotton.

A night breeze wafted the scent of honeysuckle through the
open archways from the central court. A single bronze standing-
lamp threw titan shadows over the marble pilasters that lined
the painted walls. In the courtyard a fountain murmured; there
was a muted bustling, a distant blur of frightened voices, and
from far off, the rattling din of cart traffic from the stew of

sound that was Rome. Lady Aurelia's sobs were a distant, broken jarring in the night.

"You'll do," grunted the physician, "though Asclepius only knows how."

Quindarvis swung around, his dark cynical eyes brooding in the lamplight. "Wretched, dirty, filthy beasts . . . How're the other ones?"

"I've already sent the bearers home—they were Tiridates' men . . ."

"Why in the name of the gods didn't she have her own slaves to carry her chair?"

Nicanor shrugged impatiently. "The bearers who took her over there came back this afternoon—one of them had a fever or something . . . That damn Syrian has so many slaves he could easily spare a couple. No harm done, they were only stunned."

"What about the man who was supposed to be with her?" continued the senator in an outraged voice. "The man should be put to death, and if he was mine he would be."

"She sent him away," protested Marcus feebly.

"He shouldn't have left." Quindarvis came pacing back to his couch, despite his square chunky build and puffy, unhealthy skin, giving the impression of latent power, like an overweight tiger. On one thick hand a massy gold signet flashed like a mirror. "Great gods, man, we're not talking about a pilfered winecup! How's the other man, the slave?" he added.

"I'll live," said a younger man's voice. Limping steps halted up to the side of the couch, and Marcus found himself looking up into the dark face he had seen just before the wall came rushing up to smash him over the head. "Young master," said the slave, who couldn't have been much older than Marcus' twenty-two years, "I beg you to forgive me for—for tripping you. I thought you were the last of those scum. Indeed I did."

In spite of the brand on his cheek and the simple dark tunic of a rich man's slave, there was pride in him—a barbarian, thought Marcus, taken young in war. He remembered how he'd dashed to Tullia's rescue, charging up the alleyway after her kidnappers, and to judge by the smear of crusted blood down the side of that angular face, he had doubtless been felled by an ambush the minute he'd turned the corner. But in spite of that he'd come up fighting. Which would cost him his life, Marcus realized, if he was charged with all but bashing the brains out of a Roman citizen.

He blinked stupidly for a moment and nodded, though the effort brought a blinding pain to his neck. "It's all right," he managed to say. "I—I'm glad you were so ready to fight, even for a total stranger. To go against them unarmed."

No slave was ever armed.

The young man shrugged. "They only had clubs."

Marcus managed to touch the tender swelling at the back of his head. "So I learned." The quick, silent gratitude that flickered in those dark eyes embarrassed him, so he turned to Quindarvis and asked, "Did they catch them?"

The praetor was silent for a long time. Lady Aurelia's cries had faded to a muffled undercurrent of sound. Among the grotesque looming shadows of the room it seemed that the only noise was the hissing of the oil in the lamps. After a moment he said, "Naturally, there's a hue and cry throughout the Quirinal Hill. All the men in the household are out— we've sent to the watch—it's early yet to hear." Those little black stone eyes slid to the young slave. "What's your name, boy?"

"Churaldin," he returned quietly. "My master is Claudius Sixtus Julianus."

Marcus had never heard the name before, but the praetor, who made it his business to stand among the fashionable and the great, looked at him with renewed interest. "Really?" His manner perceptibly warmed. "I thought he was dead."

"No, sir," replied Churaldin, with the manner of a well-behaved mastiff under an unwanted caress.

"Well," said the senator, "he'll doubtless be worrying for you, boy. Some of the prefect's men will go with you . . ."

"It isn't necessary, it's only a little way farther up the hill."

"Well, if we find you in the morning eaten by the pigs in the street, don't blame me," grunted Nicanor, returning to the group beside Marcus' couch. "Here, I'll show you the door . . ."

Quindarvis followed them as far as the curtained doorway that led into the hall; Marcus could hear the murmur of their voices there for a time. He stared up at the ceiling, where the three shadows clumped like harpies awaiting their prey, remembering how on the hot afternoons of other years he and Tullia and his younger brother had played chase and leapfrog over these very couches. The linen couch cushions had been white then instead of red, he recalled, but the dark polished surface of the ebony table was the same, the oiled claret-red gleam of the lion's-foot couch legs, the frescoed frieze of horsemen around the wall. He remembered the priceless vase that had used to stand in the niche between the lampstands, that Tullia's father had beaten her for breaking.

The Tyrian curtains fell shut behind Nicanor and the departing slave. Quindarvis turned back toward the couch, his head bent in thought, his thin, ungiving mouth drawn into a single hard black line. He had something in his hand. "Did you see the men who did it, Marcus?" he asked abruptly, standing over the couch again.

Marcus blinked up at him for a moment. "Yes, one of them. A—a sort of brown man, Cretan, or Carthaginian . . ."

Quindarvis held out something in his fingers, small and flame-shaped, that caught the light like a slip of mercury. Gropingly Marcus held out his hand for it; it was scarcely longer than the joint of his thumb.

It was a stylized fish, flat-cast in pure silver. A hole near the head showed where a chain had passed through. It was smooth and polished and bore little nicks and marks of wear. Turning it over he saw the initials inscribed on the back.

ICTHYS

"What is it?" he asked stupidly.

"I picked it up from the mud," said Quindarvis slowly.

"It must have been torn loose from the neck of the man you struggled with." He paused, the tiny muscles jumping suddenly in his thick jaw. "It's a Christian medal."

"Christian?" whispered Marcus, and the horror was like the touch of cold fever on his bones.

"I'm afraid it's they who've taken her."

II

Details of the initiation of neophytes [into the Christian church] are as revolting as they are notorious. An infant, cased in dough to deceive the unsuspecting, is placed beside the person to be initiated. The novice is thereupon induced to inflict what seem to be harmless blows upon the dough, and unintentionally the infant is killed . . . the blood—oh, horrible—they lap up greedily; the limbs they tear to pieces eagerly; and over the victim they make league and covenant, and by complicity in guilt pledge themselves to mutual silence. . . . Their form of feasting is notorious; . . . they gather at a banquet, with all their children, sisters, and mothers, people of either sex and every age. There, after full feasting, when the blood is heated and drink has inflamed the passions of incestuous lust, . . . the tale-telling light is upset and extinguished, and in the shameless dark, lustful embraces are indiscriminately exchanged.

Fronto
(quoted by Minucius Felix)

"What do you know about Christians?"

Morning had come, after a night of hideous dreams. Clothed in a borrowed tunic, Marcus sat before a little table set up in the garden, unable to touch the thinned wine and white bread before him. Across the table Priscus Quindarvis was talking

17

with a man named Arrius, a centurion in the Praetorian
Guard.

When Quindarvis didn't answer, Marcus ventured, "They're
a sect of the Jews, aren't they? Who caused the great fire?
Wasn't there some kind of general arrest of Christians about
three years ago?"

"About that," grunted Arrius, and those shrewd greenish-
hazel eyes narrowed in the dappled light. "It was hardly a
general arrest. On the whole the Christians keep pretty quiet,
and the emperor's been fairly tolerant of them."

Quindarvis looked up, his square, dissolute face clouded
with rage. "And look where it's got him," he snorted. In
contrast to Marcus' crumpled and unshaven state, the praetor
looked oiled and sleek, having availed himself of Varus'
private baths and barber. He did not look as though he had
slept, but he was dressed in fresh clothing and smelled of
balsam. "They should have stamped those lunatics out from
the beginning."

The centurion cocked one long, curling, sun-bleached eyebrow at him. "You ever try to find a Christian? We thought
we'd gathered in the lot three years ago. But you'll still hear
rumors of them from time to time. Marks chalked on walls.
Hymns somebody hears as they walk down an alley at night
in the Tiberside or the Subura districts. Sometimes you'll hear
of a child disappearing."

Marcus looked up with a jerk, his throat seeming to con-
strict. "It's true, then? They eat babies?"

The soldier frowned in thought. "I don't know how true it
is. A woman friend of my cousin's had a neighbor whose
little girl disappeared, and she claimed the Christians got her.
But there are others who steal children for other reasons."
His eyes shifted to Quindarvis. "What do you know?"

He took a sip of his wine, and his mouth tightened distaste-
fully though the vintage was excellent. "Only what everyone
knows. They're scum, mostly, Jews and dirt-poor Greeks that
somebody's managed to delude into thinking their morbid
superstitions and filthy rites will render them immortal. They
abhor the empire as ritually unclean; they'll work to destroy

both it and the city of Rome in the hopes of winning Jehovah's approval. That was the reason behind the fires, you know.''

"You think they set the great fire, then?''

"I didn't think there was any question,'' retorted Quindarvis. "Why would Nero have done such a thing? He was the emperor. His cousin Caligula had had islands made in the deepest part of the sea, cities built on boats stretched across the Bay of Naples. Why would he have had to resort to a subterfuge like burning the city to get ground for his building projects? He could simply have ordered the land cleared. No—the Christians set the fires and threw the blame on him to discredit him, and they evidently found enough people sufficiently discontented with their lot to believe them.''

He glanced up irritably as Varus' butler appeared in the garden, a Carthaginian Greek with smooth manners and in general an absolutely chilling demeanor. He looked haggard now, and more than a little frightened. Quindarvis listened to his murmured words and made an impatient gesture. "Send them away. I haven't time to waste on a pack of good-for-nothing sponges who have nothing better to do than clutter up the prefect's doorstep. Certainly Aurelia Pollia's in no fit case to see them. Damned clients,'' he muttered, turning back as the butler bowed his way from the arbor. "What a price to pay for consequence! To support a bunch of second-rate sycophants who hang around your door hoping you'll further their ambitions or at least invite them to dinner . . .'' He shook his head, like a bull goaded by flies.

"But the Christians!'' cried Marcus, horrified that anyone could be so calm in the face of such hideous events.

"Christians!'' spat Quindarvis, his eyes smoldering with fury. "You ask me what I know about Christians, centurion. Unfortunately I know too much. I know that they hold everything in contempt that's good and decent. They hold their women in common; I gather sexual abominations of various sorts are a regular part of their rites. Their rituals include the sacrifice of children—babies, usually, but I've heard of cases of boys and girls up to the age of seventeen or eighteen being killed, their flesh eaten and their blood drunk.''

Marcus whispered, "No!" and the centurion looked thoughtful, folding his brown, broken-knuckled, soldier's hands on the sun-dappled marble. He was a medium-size, sinewy man who reminded Marcus of something braided out of leather, relaxed within the weight of his chain-mail shirt, the transverse crest of his helmet brushing the curling tendrils of the vines above his head. Like an animal, thought Marcus; a cold-blooded and bony-faced outsider to whom this anguish is only another problem to be solved, another body to be found.

Marcus lowered his head to his hands, his eyes aching, his skull throbbing even with the diffuse green light beneath the grapevines. Quindarvis' voice went on, "That isn't the worst I've heard, either. I'm told the Christians raid tombs and eat the flesh of the corpses after burial. Maybe the emperor hasn't been able to come up with confessions from them, but they're murderers, centurion. Children mean no more to them than sacrificial doves."

He heard the centurion grunt. "You been down to the Flavian Amphitheater lately, praetor? I've seen ten-year-old girls fed alive to bears there, and a hundred thousand people cheered."

"That's a little different," pointed out Quindarvis. "They were the children of criminals, or criminals themselves—cutpurses, whores, bait to lure drunks to their death in alleys."

"Maybe," agreed the soldier. "But I don't think all those people were cheering because they were seeing Roman justice in action. My point is that a lot of people will spend their festival days watching children die, for whatever reason."

"But that's the whole point!" cried Marcus, raising his head again. "The city *is* filled with vulgar, vicious, uneducated mobs. Only most people know the difference between what happens in the games and what is lawful for them to do or not to do."

"Do they?" murmured the centurion, regarding him with thoughtful eyes. "It's interesting that you brought up that incident three years ago, though," he continued after a moment. "Do you remember it at all?"

Marcus shook his head. "I heard about it. I suppose everyone did.'' If Timoleon hadn't mentioned it peripherally in a discussion on moderation and excess, he doubted he would have been aware that there were Christians in Rome at all.

"I was in the lawcourts at the time," said Quindarvis. "I was pleading a case at the other end of the Basilica, but I remember the din was such that we could scarcely hear one another speak."

"Well, I was there," said Arrius dryly. "They called in the Praetorian Guard to keep order, and by Mithras we were needed. I don't think I've ever seen such a madhouse in my life. Christians screaming curses against the emperor at the top of their lungs, people coming in from the Forum and throwing things, the Christian women shrilling and keening like a pack of harpies. We had to clear the court . . ."

"Then you've actually seen Christians?" said Marcus, and the soldier chuckled grimly.

"Oh, I've seen them, all right, and a bunch of dirtier, smellier, more vicious ruffians you aren't likely to meet this side of hell. Their priest was like a mad sibyl, with a great mane of dirty gray hair streaming around his face like fire. When they were sentenced to death he broke from his guards and jumped up on the table before the judges and shook his fists in their faces. And I remember he cried to the head of the tribunal''—and here the centurion's voice grated suddenly harsh—'' 'The Lord Jesus Christ will avenge upon you what you have done to us today. He will smite thee and all thy children, and bring you down in sorrow to your grave.' And then, as now," continued Arrius quietly, "the head of the tribunal was the city prefect, J. Tullius Varus."

". . . thee and all thy children," repeated Quindarvis softly.

"That's what he said."

"And were they executed?"

The centurion nodded. "They were smeared with pitch and torched. That was at the games of Ceres in April of that year; Varus was up for reappointment to the prefect's office. He was out to win friends. Maybe he took advantage of the situation and condemned them to death for the sake of the show—but he's still city prefect."

"Now, that I *do* remember," smiled Quindarvis reminiscently. "He must have laid out three hundred talents in gold, enough to support his entire household and all his slaves for three years, on three days' worth of games. An enormous investment," he added, with a wry grin, "as I have call to know—but worth every sesterce of it." His brow darkened suddenly. "But I see your meaning."

Marcus straightened up, though the effort made him sick and giddy. "But we've got to *do* something," he groaned. "Close the roads out of the city . . ."

"We've had men watching them since last night," said Arrius, "for all the good it's likely to do us. There's too many places for them to be keeping her in Rome itself. We've alerted all the watches of all the city wards, but they're untrained men."

"But what can be done?" cried Marcus. "They're fanatics— lunatics! We don't know what they'll do."

"No," agreed Arrius equably. "But we can make some guesses. They didn't kill her on the spot. If revenge is their game, it's unlikely they'll do anything before Varus returns to town. Did you send for him?"

"Last night," said Quindarvis. "He's in Sicily, on his estates. He should be back within ten days."

Arrius nodded. "Good. As city prefect, he'll have the authority to undertake a major search; but with luck we'll have her back before then. If we can get just one Christian . . ." He mimed the turning of a screw.

Marcus lowered his head to his hands again, feeling as though his skull would split open if not held tightly together. He fought to retain a philosophic calm—*Remember that anything that can happen*, he told himself, *can happen to you.* He groped feebly for Timoleon's precepts. *It is not the event that is evil, but only my opinion of the event . . . I'm not the first person in the world to suffer grief and loss. It must be a thousand times worse for her mother than for myself. I should be comforting her . . .*

But the thought of speaking to anyone, much less offering comfort out of the crying blackness of his soul, was physically nauseating to him. Around him, the blurred voices went on.

"What about the mother?"

"Nicanor's given her poppy. I have business down at the treasury, not to mention all the arrangements that must be made for the games tomorrow. But I shall return this evening. I can't simply leave her with the slaves."

Marcus opened his eyes to see the centurion raise his head. Through the parti-colored green of the arbor leaves a maidservant was visible, flirting in the shadows of the columned breezeway with a handsome Spanish boy whose chief duty it was to carve game birds at Varus' feasts. "Don't," said the soldier quietly. "Don't leave her alone, and make sure there's someone you can trust with her. What about you, boy?"

Marcus looked up, blinking and startled, to find the centurion's remote lynx eyes resting thoughtfully upon him.

"You're looking pretty seedy. Where do you live?"

"In the Subura, near the Neptune shrine. But I'll be fine, I—"

"I'm going back that way myself," said Arrius brusquely. "I'll see you home."

Marcus felt too ill to protest. He somehow got to his feet and stumbled after them to the atrium; the Syrian underbutler brought the centurion his crimson cloak and deftly draped Marcus in his rather soiled toga. After the cool of the arbor, the atrium already felt rather stuffy. Half a dozen of the city prefect's clients were still hanging around in the blue shadows among the Ionic columns by the pool there: pettifogging lawyers or men whose sole occupation was to form a court around any wealthy man, applaud his lightest utterance, and hope for an invitation to dinner. They cast covert glances at Quindarvis as the butler arranged the purple-bordered folds of his toga, hoping to have it remembered in their favor, when Varus returned, that they had not deserted his household in its hour of need.

Quindarvis was saying, "Remind me, centurion, and I'll

get you seats at the games tomorrow. They're in celebration of the emperor's victories in the East''—he chuckled suddenly—''and, fortuitously, just in time for the elections next month. If I do say so myself, they're going to be quite fine. We've got sixty pairs of gladiators lined up, the cream of the best schools, and we've arranged for a hunt of wild boars and a beast-fight, tigers against crocodiles. And''—he lowered his voice impressively—''there's going to be a special beast-hunt. About thirty captives from the Persian front are going to be hamstrung, each given a short knife, and have a pack of hyenas turned loose on them. Pretty good, eh?'' He smiled cynically. ''The crowds will love it.''

''It should make an impression,'' said the centurion in a colorless voice.

''I'll get you a ticket, too, Marcus,'' promised the praetor. ''Since I'm footing most of the bill, the least they can do is give my special friends privileged seating.''

''Thank you,'' said Marcus queasily, privately vowing to pass the ticket (if Quindarvis remembered to produce it) along to his brother.

A doorman appeared—also Syrian, his dark-green tunic sprigged with leaves of embroidered gold—and bowed them into the vestibule. Blinding sunlight smote Marcus' eyes as he stepped out into the street.

''When I was serving in Germany I broke my leg on patrol and had to lie out all night fending off wolves till the rest of the patrol could track me in the snow,'' remarked Arrius, as the door shut behind them. ''After that I never cared much for those man-against-beast shows. Some people can't get their fill of them, though.'' They turned along the narrow street, the high walls of the big houses of the rich already trapping the morning heat. As they passed the mouth of the alley down which the Christians had dragged their struggling victim, Marcus shuddered.

''Can't anything be done?'' he demanded. ''Is all anybody going to do is just talk about the Christians? Can't a search be made? A—a general arrest?''

They turned into the lane that ran along the ridgy backbone

of the Quirinal Hill; a litter passed them, the feet of the
bearers throwing a choking cloud of dust over them. Arrius
regarded him with amusement in those cool greenish eyes.
"Oh, give us time," he said tolerantly.

"Time for what?" protested Marcus angrily. "Time for the
Christians to—to—" He stammered to a halt, his mind shying
from the possibilities.

"Time to make a round of my informers," returned the
centurion, unruffled. "See what and who I can smoke out."

They turned down another street, plunging steeply down
the side of the hill. The walls of the tenements loomed up
around them, the noise and the dust far worse. The lane was
crowded, the voices of the idlers in the street striving against
the shrill cries of hawkers in the shops and the din of mallets
from a sarcophagusmaker's shop. Soldiers in their leather
armor pushed past them, Syrian immigrants in bright robes
and oiled lovelocks, Jews in somber gray. Slaves on their
way back from the markets on the other side of the Forum
jostled them.

Marcus stumbled along in Arrius' wake, down streets that
grew narrower and narrower. The sky vanished behind a
clutter of outthrust balconies, fluttering clotheslines, and plank
bridges thrown across the street at the fourth or fifth story.
Like canyon walls, the high tenements trapped and held the
sound and threw it back in a million roaring echoes; voices
shouting in Latin, Parthian, Celtic, Greek, Aramaic. It was
like one of the beast-hunts held periodically at the circus—the
roaring and screaming of bears, elephants, tigers, crocodiles,
lions, ostriches, wild asses, all trapped in the narrow walls,
and all condemned to die.

Arrius yelled over the din of a clattering forge, "What
about you, boy? How long have you known Tertullia Varia?"

"About ten years," Marcus yelled back. Across the street,
a harried-looking teacher in a storefront school was screaming
declensions at his students. "We used to play together as
kids. Her mother and mine are—well, not exactly sisters. My
mother was a sort of poor relation; her mother's mother
married my grandfather Pollius—my mother's stepfather—after

he divorced Grandmother. But my mother was really the daughter of C. Drusus Cato, who was proscribed; Pollius was her third or maybe her fourth husband. But in any case Aurelia Pollia and Mother grew up together in Grandfather Pollius' household, and they remained friends for, oh, years.''

''Are they still friends?''

''No,'' said Marcus. They edged their way around a group of men surrounding a Vespasian memorial—a public urinal, of which that emperor had built hundreds throughout Rome. ''When my father was aedile in charge of city roads he had a falling-out with Varus, and after that he forbade Mother to speak to Lady Aurelia again.''

''But you were talking with her daughter just before she was kidnapped.''

Marcus said stiffly, ''As I no longer live under my father's roof, I don't consider it any of his business.''

Arrius cocked an eyebrow at him. But he only asked, ''And in all the years you've known her, did Tullia Varia ever mention the Christians?''

Marcus shook his head. ''Only in passing.''

''Did she know any Christians?''

''Great gods, no!''

The green eyes narrowed. ''You sure about that?''

Marcus hesitated, pulling together bits of the logical process out of his foundering horror and grief. ''No,'' he said at last. ''No, I'm not sure—but I am sure that if she did, she did not know they were Christians.''

The centurion nodded. ''And that,'' he said, ''is the chief problem with Christians. You don't know. A few of them don't trouble to hide their faith—often those are the crazier ones, the fanatics, the kind we're likeliest to round up. But they're not the planners. For the most part they keep quiet and keep to themselves, and the emperor isn't about to hunt them down as long as they don't make trouble. But they're a proscribed sect. Their membership is secret. You can't know who's a Christian.''

They followed the windings of a particularly foul and narrow lane among a labyrinth of six-story tenements, buildings that leaned against one another like tired and shabby drunks. In the shops below them, half-naked men and women worked at their trades, calling out to one another in Syrian or Greek, while naked children played in the dust outside. They were in the Subura proper now, and though it was scarcely the fourth hour of the morning, all the wineshops were open, and bedizened whores had begun to parade in their cheap finery. One girl called out gaily, "How're they hangin', Professor?" evidently sheerly for the pleasure of seeing him blush. She was not disappointed.

Arrius went on, apparently without noticing, "That's one reason I wanted to speak to you outside that house. Slaves hear everything—not that I blame them. Sometimes it's life or death to a slave to know which way to jump. But Christianity's largely a slave's religion. And I'm virtually certain there's at least one Christian in Varus' household."

Marcus felt himself blanch with shock.

"Think about it," urged the centurion. "Do you know the religions of all your father's slaves? Or their names, even? The ambush had to be set up somehow. It was only their ill luck that you were there at all. But Quindarvis said there were half a dozen of them, waiting in alleys on both sides of the street. It was planned."

"But— That close to her father's house! It would be too dangerous!"

"It was the only place they could be sure of finding her," replied Arrius. "This your place?"

Marcus nodded. They started the long climb up four flights of pitch-black stairs that swarmed with roaches and stank of grease, stale urine, and cabbage. Arrius went on, "They knew her father was away; they also knew of her upcoming wedding. This might be the last chance they had to strike at her father through her. Now, I'm taking a risk telling you about all this, because I know nothing about you and you could be a Christian yourself, for all I know. But it's unlikely. You'll very seldom find a philosopher who has anything to do with that cult."

"I should hope not!" cried Marcus, with a vehemence that

made the centurion grin. "Have you read their tracts? Vulgar grammar, rotten construction, not to mention holes in their logic you could drive a laden hay-cart through! And as for that—that emotionalistic nonsense—drivel . . ." Words failed him.

They made their way down the stinking, Stygian hall to Marcus' single room. Its one window faced south onto the building's central court; the whole place was hot as a baker's oven. Marcus leaned in the doorway, exhausted by the climb and suddenly giddy; the room began to blur before his eyes.

Arrius' voice seemed to come from miles away. "Professor?"

"Hunh?" he said faintly.

"You see me all right?"

Marcus blinked at him and nodded.

The soldier dumped two scrolls and a couple of apple-cores off the wobbly-legged sleeping-couch, took Marcus' arm, and steered him to it, kicking aside a pair of discarded sandals, a dish, and several more apple-cores.

"You'll have to excuse my housekeeping . . ." mumbled Marcus.

"You have someone to look in on you?"

He lay back gingerly on the couch, paused, and ejected an empty cup from among the tattered sheets. "Don't waste your time sending for my family," he said, with faint defiance. "They certainly won't waste their time coming."

Arrius looked around him at the squalid little chamber. Though he made no comment, Marcus felt called upon to add, "I couldn't live a lie. And my father couldn't live with a philosopher for a son."

The centurion peered under the upended pot that kept Marcus' bread safe from the local rats. "But he sends you money for your keep?" he surmised.

Splitting pain lanced through Marcus' head as he tried to sit up. "If he didn't, I'd still live as I do," he flared. "I'd find work of some kind—copying books, or teaching . . ."

He felt himself being scrutinized again and fell silent, feeling exhausted and a little absurd. But in the hot sunlight that fell through the window he saw the calculating expression on the centurion's face, not mocking him, but gauging what sort of a man he was.

"I expect you would," he said after a moment. "And I daresay the old man only sends you money to keep his friends from tattling about how he cut off his only son without a quadrans."

Marcus lay back again and closed his eyes, wondering how he could have become so angry. His whole soul seemed to be a single raw wound, sick and dizzy, exhausted but dreading the dreams that he knew would come with sleep. He said, "And anyway, I'm not his only son. I have two brothers."

The soldier made a little growling noise of approval. "Well, that explains why he let you go instead of keeping you for stud."

It was a hideously accurate representation of his father's opinions about young men who fribbled away their responsibilities to the House of Silanus rather than wedding and setting up their nurseries, and it surprised a chuckle out of him that caught him under his cracked ribs.

Arrius went on, "You study with the philosophers in the Basilica Ulpias? What's your teacher's name?"

"Timoleon of Athens. He's usually there around noon. But if he's busy . . ."

"If he's too busy to see one of his students who's been slugged by the Christians, he has no business setting himself up as an arbiter of the good life," retorted Arrius equably. "I'll send one of my men to tell him you're ill."

Marcus opened his eyes a slit, dazzled by the reflection of the sun on the bright rings of the hauberk. "But . . ." he protested, knowing he shouldn't be lying here doing nothing, but feeling too sick to do anything else.

"But nothing. Take care of yourself, boy. You'll be hearing from me."

A few moments later he could hear the man's hobnailed boots on the rickety wood flooring of the hall and feel the jar of his body weight as he descended all those flights of stairs. Then abruptly he fell asleep and, contrary to his expectations, slept like a dead man, dreaming nothing.

III

If you love an earthen vessel, say it is an earthen vessel which you love; for when it has been broken you will not be disturbed. When you are kissing your child or your wife, say it is a human being whom you are kissing; for when the wife or child dies, you will not be disturbed.

Epictetus

Grilling and oppressive, the heat of afternoon seemed to strangle him out of unconsciousness instead of into it. He lay for what seemed like hours, staring at the stained, cracked boards of the ceiling over his head, wondering if all last night and that morning had been some kind of insane delirium. Though he was sure he had lain down fully clothed, he was now naked, and the bedding of his narrow sleeping-couch was damp with his sweat. From across the room he heard voices, the philosopher Timoleon's, slow and dry and deliberate, laboring over the commonplaces of the Forum and the market, against the high nattering counterpoint that Marcus recognized with surprise as belonging to his brother Felix.

"Of course, one hears all manner of gossip," the teacher was saying, "and one sees these orgiastic processions wending their way through the very heart of Rome; these mincing priests of Cybele and Attis, with their dampened locks and affected gait. As Juvenal says, the mire of the Orontes has spewed itself into the Tiber . . ."

"Oh, quite, quite," agreed Felix's voice. "Fact is, though, can't expect all them easterners just to drop their ways when they come to Rome, now, can we? I mean, we conquered 'em, and all."

"No," sighed Timoleon. Opening his eyes, Marcus could see the deliberate shake of that leonine head. "For the gods made all states and degrees of mankind, as they created different varieties of animals, each for their different task. And as horses, and asses, dogs, and wolves were each separately made, so the minds of the different races were each cast to their own mold . . ."

"That's just it, ain't it?" said Felix. "Can't blame a dog for sniffin'—though, mind you, all that philosophy gaff is a sight beyond me. Always was."

Marcus closed his eyes again, blotting out the afternoon sunlight and wishing he could silence those disparate voices as well. He wondered how he could possibly have slept, when the gods only knew what was happening to the girl he loved—except, of course, that he had the suspicion that the centurion Arrius would not have permitted him to do otherwise.

He sat up, stifling a groan as his cracked ribs pinched him, and Felix said, "Hullo! It's Silenus himself!" Felix, as was to have been expected, had brought wine (and cups—he'd called on his brother's lodgings before). He and Timoleon faced each other across the makeshift table, and Felix had clearly been doing his unsuccessful best to keep the dignified rhetorician entertained until Marcus could awaken and explain himself. With great presence of mind, he reached into the satchel that lay on the floor at his feet, produced another cup, and slopped it full from the wine mixer on the table without spilling a drop. "Thought I'd bring my own dishes," he added brightly, carrying it over to the couch where Marcus sat gingerly probing the bruise on his side. "Save us grubbin' around for yours and havin' to haul the water up to wash 'em.''

Marcus let this perfectly justified slur on his housekeeping pass and sipped at the watered vintage. "So that meddling centurion told you after all," he sighed. "I asked him not to.''

"Nor did he that I've heard." He looked down at his senior, his head on one side, rather like some ungainly bird of exotic plumage. "Some slut who lives downstairs sent me word you'd been brought in by the watch at all hours of the morning with a cracked head and the looks of a prize brawl printed all over your noble frame, so I thought I'd push along and see what a philosopher looks like after a night on the tiles.''

Marcus sighed and lowered his tangled head to one hand. "Gods, if only it were that," he whispered.

"The centurion Arrius was good enough to send one of his warriors to the Basilica Ulpias, where I had repaired, as is my custom, to teach," Timoleon informed him kindly. "Hearing that you had been somehow injured, I was greatly distressed and, dismissing my other students, came here with all speed, to find your brother already in possession of the field, if not of the facts. I enlightened him insofar as I was able, from what I had myself learned at third hand from the soldier who first brought me the news.''

Felix's gentle vacuous eyes filled with admiration. "I say, Professor, will you talk like that when you become a philosopher?''

Timoleon looked down his long elegant nose at him and made no comment.

Not being a citizen, Timoleon was not entitled to wear a toga and garbed himself instead after the fashion of the Athenian philosophers in a simple Greek chiton, which left his right arm bare. He was a tall, graceful man, Jove-like in his grave dignity, his tawny hair fading in streaks from russet to straw to white. He reminded Marcus at times of a statue of the god, wrought in old ivory and worn gold, an oracle of times past, imbued with the wisdom and dignity of former ages.

Beside him Felix looked hot and overdressed, the white toga his father insisted it was his duty as a citizen to wear contrasting absurdly with the blue and scarlet birds and grapes embroidered on his cream-colored tunic. Felix himself was a ridiculous caricature of his older brother, having the same long, narrow face, in which all the features were exaggerated: the nose beakier, the chin weak instead of square, the wide, gentle brown eyes blinking, lamblike, and heavily painted with malachite and kohl. On his head Marcus' unruly brown curls were a carefully wrought confection of perfumed ringlets. The scent of balsam and depilatories breathed from the folds of his elaborately wrought toga as he fished among them for a handkerchief and carefully blotted his brow.

"Say, I was badly rocked to hear about this, you know?" he said after a time. "Tullia bein' snatched, and all. No word?"

"Not yet," said Marcus, in a voice cracked with exhaustion and anxiety.

"Lady A. takin' it all right?" For all his ludicrous appearance, there was genuine concern in his tone. "Awful for her, of course. She was always kind to me."

"Not well," said Marcus quietly. "She's been given a sleeping draft, but she'll have to wake up sometime."

"May the gods endow her with the strength to endure this misfortune with philosophic mind," said Timoleon gently. Shrill and distant as birds, the cries of children rose from the court below, along with a man's voice, free and lazy and clear, singing in Aramaic. Marcus thought of the sound of Aurelia Pollia's tortured animal weeping, and said nothing. Tullia was somewhere in Rome, in the hands of vengeful terrorists; there was no way to find her, nothing that he could do. Yet he felt that if he remained in this airless room all day he would go mad.

"I should see her," he said finally, half to himself. "Even if she's asleep, or drugged, she'll need someone. I can't do anything . . ."

"At all events, you can offer her the inestimable consolation of philosophy."

"Dunno about the consolation of philosophy," put in Felix, "but havin' your hand held for a bit never goes amiss."

The philosopher's rebuttal to this was a frigidly polite silence. Felix, unaware of having committed the gross philosophical solecism of comparing the lowest usages of the emotions with the highest ones of the mind, was busily picking through the heap of clothes in the corner in quest of a clean tunic for his brother.

"Tell you what, though," he continued after a moment, "if you're going to visit Lady A. this afternoon, you really ought to wander by the baths first, elder brother."

"What?" blinked Marcus, jerked abruptly from his misery by the mundane. He looked down at himself and rubbed at his stubbly jaw. "I suppose you're right."

"I'll even lend you the tin, if you're short the price of a shave," added Felix handsomely. "Where'd you get this tunic, brother? It's miles too big for you."

"I don't know," said Marcus impatiently. "It's Varus' —they lent it to me . . ."

"Should have known. Dashed sight better than anything you'd wear. Clean, too."

Disgusted with such trivialities, Marcus turned away. "Timoleon, could you—could you spare the time to walk along with me to the baths? I need to talk. I feel desperately in need of wisdom."

"Ah," cried his brother, "be toddling on my way, then— come to the wrong shop for that. Good to see you're not dead, though, Professor. Bit of a blow to Mater, what with the cost of funeral masks, and all that." He smiled, and Marcus realized the absurdity of being angry with him for any length of time.

"Does Mother know?"

"By Castor, no! She'd never keep it from the old paterfamilias, and then we'd have the whole triumphal procession again about your hanging about with freethinkers and lowlivers and associating with Christians—though why if you was asso-

ciating with 'em they'd half-brain you beats me. Fine mind,
Father," he explained aside to the philosopher, "no logic,
though." And with that he finished his wine, collected his
winecups, and pattered on his way.

"But what can we *do*?"

"Do?" Timoleon's fine brow deepened. He leaned his
shoulders against the brisk rough friction of the bath-slave's
towel, and considered his student gravely. "In the face of
tragedy, Marcus, the most that a man can do is school his
heart to bear the worst, and face Fate with courage."

Down at the other end of the long drying room, a fat
gentleman was fussily directing half-a-dozen liveried slaves to
blot him dry, rather than rub him; through the open archways
that led to the pool deck Marcus could hear the racket of
men's voices echoing in the vaulted mosaics of the ceiling.
For a long time he could make no reply.

Timoleon continued, "As Epictetus has told us in his
Enchiridion, a thing is what it is. Willing it to be otherwise
not only hurts you, but makes you slave to the whims of
Fate."

"But they have her prisoner," whispered Marcus helplessly. "They could be doing anything to her. Isn't there
anything that we can do?"

He looked pleadingly at the philosopher, who sat beside
him on the black marble bench, his faded reddish hair lank
and dripping from the warm water of the baths. All around
them was the quiet bustle of men coming and going: wealthy
men, surrounded by clients who all but fell over one another
to be the first to laugh at their patron's jokes; senators emerg-
ing pink as lobsters from the steam rooms, still dictating away
to their pink and sweating secretarial slaves; wealthy sports-
men returning from the training room, bronze as statues under
the oily dust of the track and trailed by a string of slaves
carrying hardballs, towels, strigils, oil. Despite his present
mode of life, Marcus was enough of a rich man's son to place
baths above food, and to patronize only the best.

Timoleon rose as a bathman appeared, carrying their two

neat piles of clothes. He rested a white slender hand briefly on Marcus' shoulder. "Torturing yourself will not lessen another's pain," he said quietly. "This young girl is in the hands of Fate. Comfort yourself with Plato's assertion that no true evil can befall a truly just person, and cultivate the detachment necessary to see both good and evil as necessary parts of this earthly existence."

Marcus was silent as he dressed; silent as the well-trained slaves draped his toga; and in silence he followed the Athenian through the vast hall of the indoor swimming pool, where slanted sunlight flickered on the sparkling water. They passed through an enormous vestibule, where fig-sellers and book-stalls displayed their wares between columns of rose-red Samian marble, and out into the dusty brilliance of the square outside.

"Marcus," said Timoleon quietly. "Please believe that I am not insensible to the grief that you feel—with justification —at this shocking event. You are young in your philosophy, and this makes it difficult for you to understand that to a true philosopher all events, good and bad, are like ripples upon the sea. They are not the sea itself. This horror that has befallen your friend is less than the horrors that happen in war. You must prepare yourself to meet waiting and anxiety, and possibly greater horrors, with a calm and equable mind. As Plutarch has said, we are all the sport of the gods."

In the square before them a few groups of people had stopped to watch a religious procession, winding its way to an imposing columned temple opposite the steps of the baths. The priests walked with heads covered in the folds of their togas, lest they should see an inauspicious omen; the obligatory flute players followed, piping to drown out any profane interruptions that would cause the entire ceremony to have to be repeated again from the beginning. A hot drift of breeze blew the words to Marcus—they were in archaic Etruscan, memorized by rote, an unfailing ritual to a god whose very name had been forgotten in the course of the centuries.

Gods like those? he wondered.

He raised his head, his heart a sounding hollow of misery within him. Over the roofs that shut in the square he could see the towering walls of the Flavian Amphitheater, high even from the hilltop beside them, and glittering like sugar in the sun. Through a break in the buildings where a wide street ran down the hill, he could see the forest of columns that marked the various forums; the glint of the gilt roof of the Vesta temple; the smoke that rose from the multicolored pillars of red and green Egyptian porphyry on the porch of the temple of Avenging Mars. Far off he could discern the marble woods around the newest imperial forum, flanked by its libraries, its temples, its deep-cut curves graven into the bones of the shouldering mass of the Quirinal Hill itself; and above and behind it all, rising like a solemn finger, clean as a sword blade in the sun, the emperor's column with its lacework of embroidered stone.

Timoleon's hand rested lightly upon his arm. "I'm sorry," said the philosopher gently. Then he, too, was gone, moving down the steps of the baths, erect and aloof from the troubles of a filthy world.

For a time Marcus only stood, staring sightlessly before him. *Why not accept it?* he asked himself. *There's nothing you can do. Even if you were to rescue her, she'd still be betrothed to someone far richer than you, someone who hasn't been cast out by his own family.*

Arrius said you'd hear from him. Shouldn't that be enough? School your heart to accept what must be.

But the consolation of philosophy was ashes in his mouth.

He moved slowly down the steps, exhausted and light-headed, wondering what he would say to Lady Aurelia Pollia. Maybe Felix was right, and he could give her only his presence, to wait at her side until Arrius brought them news.

The centurion's words returned to him, that it might be a slave within Varus' own household. How could he ever tell her that?

Who? he wondered. The sleek Syrian doorkeepers? The boy who carved game birds at the feasts and, as far as Marcus knew, didn't do much else? One of the secretaries? Varus' personal barber? Nicanor? Which one of them had relayed the information, through such swift channels as only slaves can know, that Tullia Varia would be coming home at such and such a time?

Which of them was a Christian?

And abruptly, bitterness over the evils of the world vanished in the sudden thought: *Churaldin might know.*

If he were a slave himself, he might have picked up information, rumors of other slaves.

If he's a slave he might be a Christian himself.

Not if he ran to her rescue, he wouldn't be.

Wild elation went through him, and desperate hope. A slave's testimony was useless in a court of law, of course, but he might be able to give them some kind of lead . . .

There was neither despair nor the quietude of philosophy in his heart as he hastened across the square, dodged past the affronted priests at the tail end of the procession, stumbled over the flapping ends of his own toga in his haste, and hurried on down the hill.

Churaldin had said that his master's name was C. Sixtus Julianus, and that his house lay somewhere close to that of Consul Tullius Varus. On his way through the crowded lanes north of the Forum, Marcus tried to remember such a person, or at least hearing mention of the name. Back in the days when he, Felix, and Tullia had run wild like a pack of ill-assorted wood-sprites through the aristocratic upper slopes of the Quirinal Hill, he had been familiar with the names of the owners of all the big houses there, and the name was unknown to him. But as he passed the sidewalk booth of an astrologer, gaudy with painted signs and bronze amulets, and heard the crier there advertising cut-rate horoscopes and conversations with the dead, he remembered Quindarvis' words, "I thought he was dead."

And it occurred to him that Sixtus Julianus was probably the owner of the haunted house.

As children they'd often scrambled up adjacent trees to get a look down into the overgrown jungles of its gardens. Once they'd seen a slave moving about, but that was all. Nevertheless the run-down walls had exerted a kind of fascination on them all. Tullia, who had followed the brothers in and out of scrapes with a stubborn courage remarkable in so young a girl, had surmised that the owner of the house was a sorcerer who kidnapped children and made magic with their bones: this despite the utter dearth of evidence of anything of the kind. In spite of his more adult awareness that the master was a retired general turned scholar, Marcus had still thought of the place, when he remembered it at all, as a kind of haunted house whose ghost had not yet died, and it was with an illogical feeling of trepidation that he knocked at those bronze-bound doors.

In the harsh light of late afternoon, the house was no longer mysterious. It simply had the dilapidated air of a place whose owner no longer concerns himself with keeping up any semblance of a position in society. Yet to have a house at all, instead of spacious apartments on the bottom floor of a multiple-family dwelling, argued considerable wealth; certainly to have a house in this quiet tree-grown quarter did.

When the door was finally answered, it was by a breathless, chubby slave who had obviously run all the way from the kitchen, and Marcus' first impression was confirmed. The place was run by a skeleton staff. He asked, "Is this the house of Sixtus Julianus? Is he in?"

"Of course," smiled the scullion, wiping a hand on his apron. "He's always in." And he bowed him into the vestibule. "Not been out of these doors in five years—the crazy old coot," he added affectionately. "Can I tell him who's here?"

"Uh—C. Marcus Silanus. He doesn't know me. But if he isn't busy . . ."

"Oh, he's always busy," said the slave cheerfully, as they emerged into a shadowy atrium whose only light was that which fell through the skylight above the pool and whose floor of old, yellowing marble was thick with dust and scattered with brown leaves. "But take a seat. I'll tell him you're here." And, still wiping his hands on his tunic hem, he trotted off between the slender decorative pillars and down a hall, leaving Marcus alone in the semi-darkness under the ancient, knowing, haughty eyes of the sculptured Egyptian cat in the wall niche.

After a few moments the man returned, puffing and out of breath. He led Marcus down the hallway, past priceless frescoes faded by time, out into the green still jungle-riot of overgrown willows and uncut vines, where the fountain trickled through bulbous cankers of moss and the lichened bricks of the few paths still visible were being relentlessly thrust apart by the weeds. The colonnade around the garden was so badly choked with vines that only a small entrance remained. Through green filtered light he led him down a kind of tunnel of stone and leaves, to a sheltered bay that had once been a workshop looking out into the garden. Marcus had the curious impression that he had wandered into a hill cave, inhabited by a scholarly hermit and stocked with scrolls and tablets and curiosities, strange stones, and a globe of the stars.

Sixtus Julianus rose as Marcus was ushered in. For all the apparent frailness of his build, Marcus' first impression of him was of a kind of latent toughness, coupled with a kingly dignity. He was an aristocrat of the most ancient traditions of a long-vanished republic, clean as bleached bone, his plain tunic the color of raw wool and his short-clipped hair and beard fine as silk and whiter than sunlit snow. The burning demons of sun and wind, sand and enemy steel had carved his face; from the webwork of lines, blue eyes regarded him, fierce and pure and serene as the desert sky. His hands, resting among the scholarly confusion of the table, were heavy and powerful, the white-furred forearms crisscrossed by old pale scars. *A soldier's hands*, thought Marcus, *like those of the centurion Arrius.*

He said, "Please be seated," in a voice deep and rich as bronze. Someone brought up a chair, and turning, Marcus met Churaldin's eyes.

The slave asked, "Is it about the girl?"

Marcus nodded.

Churaldin turned to his master. "Sir, this is the man whom I—tripped—in pursuit of the kidnappers last night. Are you well?"

"No thanks to you," grinned Marcus wryly.

"Have they found her?" asked Sixtus, reseating himself and clearing aside part of the welter of scrolls that lay between them.

Marcus shook his head. "Not yet." He fished in his purse. "But they found this." And he laid the silver amulet of the fish on the table between them like a coin. "It was picked up from the mud near the litter. I must have torn it loose from the neck of one of the attackers in the struggle."

The old man picked it up carefully, and turned it over in his fingers. His eyes met Marcus'. "Do you know what this is?"

"Yes," said Marcus quietly. "Yes, I do. We have to rescue her, and rescue her quickly. I need Churaldin's help to do that. I—I came here to ask your permission to speak with him."

Sixtus nodded and rose to go. Churaldin, who had also seated himself at the other side of the table, glanced up and met his eyes, and Marcus saw, with a curious sense of shock, the trust and understanding between the young slave and the ancient master. "Will you stay, sir?"

"If you don't object, Marcus Silanus," said the old man. Marcus quickly shook his head. Sixtus moved back to his chair, steadying himself on the edge of the table, and Marcus saw then that he was lame. "Now, how can my wild Briton be of help to you?"

"The men we're looking for are Christians," began Marcus, looking from that haughty old man to the slave who sat at his side, proud and forbidding as a black hawk on his master's fist. "The centurion Arrius—the centurion of the Praetorian Guard who's in charge of finding the men who did it—believes they had a confederate in the household. He says the ambush couldn't have been planned any other way."

"Oh, it could have," remarked Sixtus. "But I'll admit that having a confederate in the household would be one of the easier ways of doing it, particularly if it is a large household."

"Not overly large," said Marcus. "Fifty or sixty slaves, I think. But I wondered if Churaldin had heard anything, any rumor, about one or more of them being Christians?'' He turned to look at Churaldin and was surprised at the anger that flushed that dark angular face.

''You're asking me, in effect, to turn informer,'' said the slave, his voice harsh for all the quietness of his speech. ''In spite of the fact that, as a citizen, you must know there's only one way they have of examining slaves.''

Marcus felt his cheeks scald. ''Well—I mean—that wasn't exactly what I meant—''

''It was what you said,'' he lashed at him. ''What if one of them happens to be a Christian who knows nothing about it?''

''But in any case,'' cut in Sixtus smoothly over the slave's anger, ''even if you did know anything, Churaldin, it would probably be better to let the authorities know than to have the Praetorian Guard embark upon a general hunt. But the question is academic, I believe. Had Churaldin been aware of any Christians in any of the households upon the Quirinal Hill, he would have told me. When you are a crippled old recluse such as I, it pays to know your surroundings.''

Churaldin was still regarding him with a smoldering resentment, and Marcus was philosopher enough to know that although no Roman citizen is ever obliged to apologize to a slave, he owed this man an apology.

''I'm sorry,'' he said quietly. ''I really didn't mean . . .''

''Oh, I think you did,'' said Sixtus, in a tone of great kindness. ''Or at least, I don't believe you thought much about what you meant. And it all comes under the heading of civic duty anyway.'' He turned the amulet over in his blunt fingers, and experimentally nicked the soft silver of the tail with his fingernail. ''And Churaldin, for all his other faults, isn't one to screen criminals of that nature.''

At the mention of his other faults, the Briton looked up quickly, his eyes meeting his master's in a flash of amused connivance, less master and slave than father and adopted son. But he only murmured, ''No, sir,'' in a humble voice, and turning to Marcus he said, ''I shouldn't have lost my temper. You've probably never witnessed a judicial examination in your life.''

"I'm far more certain," continued the old man, to cover Marcus' confusion, "that information could be gleaned from the chain that this hung on. It's pure silver, you see. An expensive trinket for a slave."

Marcus shook his head. "There was no chain found, sir."

"Indeed?" One white eyebrow went up. "Interesting." He turned the amulet over in his fingers again and angled it to the light. "But what is far more interesting is why the Christians would put themselves to the trouble of kidnapping the sixteen-year-old daughter of so formidable a father in the first place."

Marcus swallowed, trying to keep his voice steady. "Sacrifice."

The blue eyes looked into his, kind but very grave. "Children are cheap."

"And revenge."

"Ah." He laid the amulet down. "But I thought that the Christians were opposed to violence in any form?"

"Are they?" asked Marcus, considerably startled.

"Of course." The old man folded his hands among his papers. "That's why they refuse to enter the legions. They have placed themselves in the hands of their god. They will not struggle against his will."

"But I thought—I mean, I don't know much about it, but I have heard stories of Christian soldiers, even Christian gladiators. And the man who kicked me sure didn't have any scruples about violence."

The bright blue eyes widened at him. "It would hardly be the first time that a man believes one thing and performs the opposite. Under stress, the most stoic Stoic has been known to curse Fate and even try to meddle with its outcome."

The look the old man shot him was so knowing, and yet so teasing, that Marcus had to chuckle. "But I've been told I'm very young in my philosophy," he apologized.

"I venture to say," returned the old scholar, "that you are merely very young. For all his own philosophy Plato almost grieved himself to death over the murder of Socrates—thereby demonstrating that he placed far more importance on the event than did Socrates himself. But as for the Christians . . ."

"Wait a minute," said Marcus. "How did you know I was a philosopher at all?"

"I didn't," smiled Sixtus. "You told me."

"Yes, but . . ."

"Why else would a rich man's son leave his father's house, to live like a pauper in the Subura; and where else would any man get that lamp-oil pallor and bookish stoop?"

Marcus stared at him blankly for a long moment. Sixtus pointed to the stained hem of his toga. "Mud that color isn't found elsewhere in Rome. The stains are all ages; you obviously spend considerable time there and just as obviously don't have slaves to keep the garment properly cleaned."

"Yes, but . . ." Marcus halted, those twinkling, impish eyes daring him to ask another question. Instead he said, "Have you ever thought of going into soothsaying, sir?"

"Frequently, but not only would I lose my citizenship, but the incense makes me sneeze. I suppose if I hadn't been coerced into a military career by an arrogant and well-muscled father, I might have made a fair lawyer, but even that would have been a blot upon the name of the House of Julianus; what he'd think of me now I can't imagine. No, what a man is and does marks him, body and mind. It only takes reading the marks and a modicum of the logic with which, believe me, I was inundated during my days as governor of Antioch."

Marcus had to grin. The Syrian capital was famous for the wranglings of its metaphysicians. "How long were you governor there, sir?"

"At the time it seemed like forever. It's less of a social nuisance than other things one can acquire in Antioch, but in the long run I'm not sure it hasn't been more troublesome. Why revenge?"

He was beginning to wonder how Churaldin kept pace with the old man's lightning changes of subject. "Because Tullius Varus was responsible for the deaths of a group of Christians three years ago."

There was momentary silence. "Yes, he was, wasn't he? As prefect of the city he would be able to order such things. And he was, I believe, giving games?" Sixtus leaned his chin on his hands; chips of white light outlined the stretched skin over the cheekbones, the delicate fretwork scoring around the eyes. Then he glanced back at Marcus again, the tips of milky lashes glinting like silver. "But I can hardly imagine the Christians themselves would be so united as to prepare an organized revenge. I am given to understand that of the several groups of Christians in Rome, no two are on speaking terms with each other."

"Several groups?" The scope of the problem widened, suddenly and alarmingly.

"Yes, of course. I gather that Christianity, unlike the other cults based on irrational acceptance of some central mystery, puts a high premium on acceptance of the correct beliefs—on the correct interpretation of the mystery. Unfortunately, opinions differ on what is correct. And since all Christians, whatever their belief, are passionate believers, tomcats in a sack are nothing to it. This doesn't even include offshoot cults, Gnostics and Black Gnostics and the worshippers of the other Jewish prophet John."

"You know a great deal about it," said Marcus slowly.

"I should hope that I do," remarked the old scholar dourly, "Antioch was alive with them, fighting and cursing and denouncing one another and forever hauling one another into court over the most trivial litigations. Since I've returned to Rome I have spent most of my time in seclusion, but I'm using my time to compile an encyclopedia of eastern cults." He gestured at the room around him, which, Marcus could see, as his eyes grew used to the subaqueous light and deepening shadows, was heaped with scrolls, wax writing tablets, and stray leaves of parchment and papyrus. From the gloom of the corners idols peered with agate eyes from crude shelves made of stacked boxes, on which Marcus saw clay baals, bronze votives to barbarian deities of unimaginable age, a tiny gold image of the Slayer of the Bull, and a minute jade of a little man with an enormous bald head, sitting cross-legged amid a swirl of draperies. "My researches have taken me very far afield," continued Sixtus' deep voice. "I probably know as much about Christianity as any man in Rome.''

''Do you know any Christians?''

For a long moment he did not reply, only toyed with a stylus on the table before him, tracing the pale grain of the waxed table with its blunt end. Finally he said, ''I know people who have been suspected of being Christians. I have taken care, however, never to ask them directly if they were, in fact, followers of Joshua Bar-Joseph, for the simple reason that if asked, they might speak the truth. Then I should be in the intolerable position of having to decide whether to abet them or denounce them.''

''It's a fine distinction to make,'' said Marcus hesitantly, ''between lying and truth.''

''A year governing Antioch,'' returned the old man in a dry voice, ''would make a semanticist out of anyone.''

''But—why would you screen them at all? Why would you screen anyone who does the things they do?''

His shock and disgust must have carried into his voice, for Sixtus looked down for a time, rolling the stylus slowly between his fingers, as though struggling with something within his own mind. At last he looked up and said, ''I did a lot of killing when I was a young man. Soldiering in Africa I must have killed hundreds of men personally—nobody I knew, of course—and caused the deaths of literally thousands more. Generals do that, it's their job. And later, as military governor of Antioch, I was responsible for law within the city. I saw a lot of very untidy dying, and I learned the painful fact that once one has been accused, if the crime is heinous enough it does not greatly matter whether one is in fact guilty or not guilty. Perhaps I am merely philosopher enough to try and make a distinction between general and specific guilt.''

''But they're all guilty!'' argued Marcus. ''I mean, they're all guilty of abominations, of sacrificing children to the ghost of a dead fisherman—and besides I thought the Christians hated philosophy, along with just about everything else.''

Sixtus smiled wryly. ''They do. But that is hardly reason for philosophy to hate them back. After all, one doesn't return the compliment when an ill-mannered child throws stones.''

"But that isn't the same thing!"

"No," sighed the old man, "perhaps not. But then, the Christians hardly have the monopoly on the killing of children. Quite aside from what goes on at the Flavian Amphitheater— Have you heard of Atargatis?"

"Well—of course, I mean—everyone has. There are rumors . . ." He glanced up, to meet a blue gaze turned suddenly hard as chipped ice.

"The practices of the cult of Atargatis," said Sixtus, "are hardly rumor. They were pursued in Rome until the beginning of the present reign; every emperor from Augustus down winked at them." He got to his feet and limped to the mazework of boxes in the back of the room, to remove a small brass image from a shelf. "Pretty, isn't she?"

Marcus averted his eyes. The idol was obscene, fishy, and crudely done; even in that small size the Syrian goddess was depicted with her arms outstretched over a wide and slightly hollowed lap. "Did they really sacrifice children?" he asked queasily.

Bitter memory edged the deep voice. "Yes." He set the baal back in its place.

"Did you see them?"

Sixtus didn't answer. Though he looked still at the shadowed figure of that many-breasted mother, it was clear he did not see her.

"Here in Rome?" he whispered.

Sixtus turned away. "In Antioch," he replied unwillingly.

Churaldin, who had remained seated in silence all this while, looking out into the dark dappled tangles of the vines, asked, "And what were you doing in the Temple of Atargatis in Antioch while services were being held?"

"Looking for a child." He turned back to them, an ancient anger deepening the lines of his face. "Meddling in what wasn't my business. I saw their faces then, you see. And they were men and women I dealt with daily, in the market, or the lawcourts; some of them were relatives of the child who had been kidnapped. People I thought I knew. I had thought up until that time that—that such a thing would be written upon the human countenance, so that it could not be hid. Maybe they didn't even consider it wrong to roast a three-year-old girl alive; maybe they were so sunk in their trance that they weren't aware of what they did." He limped back to his worktable, his movements restless and halting; the baals watched his back. "But it taught me that you cannot understand human motivation, or human need. Every rock has two sides, and only one of them is exposed to sun and washed by air. I have never been sure," he continued, his voice low, as though he spoke half to himself, "whether that was the starting point of my philosophy, or whether it crippled me in its study forever."

Marcus was silent, feeling suddenly very young and unfledged. Darkness had deepened in the gardens; the cavelike workroom had slipped imperceptibly from cool shadows to a thicker gloom. Churaldin said quietly, "I hadn't known that."

The old warrior relaxed, as though wakening from a half-trance, or an ugly dream. His voice in the semi-dark was amused and kind, "There's a great deal about my evil past that I'm at pains to keep from everyone—including my well-meaning meddler of a body servant." He limped to the corner, where a six-foot staff of iron-shod hardwood leaned against the wall. "Have the lamps lit, if you will, Churaldin," he continued. "I shall show this young man out."

Leaning on his staff he conducted Marcus through the murmuring twilight of the dark garden, through the hall and into the dusty atrium, where the last gleams of evening quivered like quicksilver in the waters of the pool.

"The question, Marcus, is not entirely one of guilt or innocence," his deep voice said out of the faceless gloom that surrounded them. "To undertake a general persecution of the Christians is one matter, and one that is entirely within Arrius' sphere. But it will hardly serve to restore this girl to her family. To follow a single trail—to affix specific, rather than general, guilt requires judgment on your part, and at least a temporary tolerance of things that you might consider quite abominable. Don't confuse the two.''

They paused in the vestibule, a dark silent room as black as the anteroom of Pluto himself. No lamps had been lit in the front part of the house for many years. Evidently if this courteous, old-fashioned scholar had ever had clients, they had long since gone elsewhere for their patronage.

''Socrates always opened an investigation of any truth by demanding that people define their terms,'' mused Marcus after a time. ''Once you understand the question, sometimes you don't need to seek very far for the answer. I think you're the only person I've met who's done that.''

''Recreational hysteria relieves the feelings,'' replied Sixtus, ''but it is seldom of use in achieving the best solution to what is not, at bottom, an emotional question. What you need is an unclouded mind, my son, and an unflinching capacity to confront unexpected truth.''

''It isn't all I need,'' said Marcus quietly. ''I need help. I realize it's an imposition to ask it of you, when you've been retired for so long from the world, but do you realize that you're the only person I've ever met who actually knows anything about the Christians? Can I—can I count on your help? I don't know where to start, or what to do.''

''Leave that to me, for the moment,'' said Sixtus. ''There are other ways to utilize Churaldin's particular talents without forcing him to spy upon his acquaintances. In the meantime—''

''I know,'' sighed Marcus. ''School myself to accept the dictates of Fate.'' Relief, exhaustion, or the release of what had felt like an unbearable burden put a cracked, gritty edge to his voice that he had not intended; Sixtus raised one white bristling brow at him.

''We should all learn to do that, of course,'' he replied mildly. ''Or at least learn to identify them. I was going to say, in the meantime, keep your wits about you. You may see one of your kidnappers in the street at any time, you know. If you do, don't rush up and seize them—follow them, and see where they go.''

Marcus laughed shakily. In the warmth of the distant gardens he could hear the crying of cicadas and the sweet voice of a woman singing a love song in Greek. Throughout that empty and time-haunted house, there was no other sound.

After a time Sixtus sighed. "When I returned to Rome fifteen years ago, it was with the intention of retiring from the world, and in that I feel that I have been happy. In the last eight years I have scarcely gone out of the house; my world has been encompassed by my books, my meditations, my friends, my research, my little statues. I hardly thought to embark upon a Christian-hunt at this stage of my career." He straightened his shoulders a little, folding his blunt warrior's hands around his staff. "Come back, when you need advice. I fear you will generally find me at home."

And in the absence of a doorkeeper, Sixtus Julianus, former commander of the Imperial Armies, former governor of Antioch, opened the doors for him and bowed him graciously upon his way.

IV

Kindly remember that he whom you call your slave sprang from
the same stock, is smiled upon by the same skies, and on equal
terms with yourself, breathes, lives, and dies. . . . I do not wish
to involve myself in too large a question and to discuss the
treatment of slaves, toward whom we Romans are excessively
haughty, cruel, and insulting. . . . As often as you reflect how
much power you have over a slave, remember that your master
has just as much power over you. "But I have no master," you
say. You are still young; perhaps you will have one. Do you not
know at what age Hecuba entered captivity, or Croesus, or the
mother of Darius, or Plato, or Diogenes?

Seneca

"See any of them?" Priscus Quindarvis turned from the
smooth mirror of polished brass with a startled growl; the
slave who was holding it up for him bowed and effaced
himself. "Great gods, boy, by the time I'd summoned the
men of the house and come running to the scene those
murdering scum were long gone." He paused in his pacing,
the folds of his toga settling into graceful lines around his
heavy shoulders and massive arms. Marcus, who generally
looked as though he'd been rolled in his garments like a piece
of fish, regarded the effect with envy.

"Did you notice anyone—well, hanging about the place earlier in the day? I know you were here when I called at the ninth hour . . ."

Quindarvis gave the matter some thought, then shook his head. "Well, aside from the usual sycophants cluttering up the atrium, and beggars in the streets, and those infernal shopkeepers down the road. But then, I was here in the garden, with Aurelia Pollia and my cousin Varus' steward."

There was an awkward silence. Outside, dew still glittered on the banked lilies of the garden, visible through the fluted columns that separated the drawing room from the court. Marcus had called early, on the way back from doing some necessary shopping in the markets by the river; an alternative, in the gray hours before dawn, to lying awake contemplating the familiar lines of the ceiling. There was a telltale puffiness about Quindarvis' eyes that made him wonder how much sleep the praetor had had. But then, on the night before his games, that was to have been expected.

"How is Aurelia Pollia?" he asked after a moment.

Quindarvis shook his head. "She slept all yesterday," he sighed. "I've told Nicanor to look after her—he's trustworthy enough, for a slave. You know Aurelia as well as I do, boy. She isn't very strong, and this has been a hideous shock to her. If she drinks more poppy and sleeps today through as well, it would be for the best." He prowled to the open line of columns that let into the garden. They were red porphyry from Egypt, to go with the red of the painted walls. Against them his toga had the whiteness of marble.

"I wish I could remain here with her," continued Quindarvis. "I'm late as it is— You sure you don't want a ticket to the games? They'll be having the march-in in an hour."

"Thank you, no," replied Marcus, trying to hide the distaste in his voice.

"They're going to be very fine," continued the senator persuasively. "Since the emperor isn't in Rome to give his own games, more than usual latitude has been allowed the praetors in charge. Over one hundred fifty—"

"No, really." He made himself smile. "I apreciate your offer, but . . ."

"I know," chuckled the big man. "Your philosophic principles." He slapped Marcus genially on the shoulder. "Well, here. In case your philosophic principles wear a little thin." He handed him a slip of fired clay, inscribed with a seat number.

"I'll look in on Aurelia again this evening," he continued. "I spent last night here, you know. It isn't good to leave her alone, with just the slaves. And by the way, I sent a suitable reward to that boy—that Briton boy, whatever his name was, Sixtus Julianus' slave—for attempting to help." He frowned to himself. "Perhaps I should pay a call on Julianus one of these mornings myself, to thank him personally."

Marcus smiled, trying to picture this highly polished portrait of elegance among the blown leaves of that dusty atrium. But he only remarked, "He's supposed to be some kind of an eccentric, isn't he?"

The praetor winked. " 'Crazy' I think is the word I've heard. But he's one of the ancient aristocracy. They've bred among themselves too long. But the power's there, and the wealth, from all I've heard. This might be the opportunity I've been seeking, to get to know him." He frowned again, giving the matter consideration.

From the hallway a slave's voice bellowed, "It is now the beginning of the second hour of the morning! It is now . . ."

"Jupiter Capitolinus, I'll miss the march-in! Baccus!" At his roared summons, Quindarvis' Greek secretary came hurrying in from the atrium, followed by an undersecretary to carry the wax note-tablets and a page to run errands. Ignoring them as if they had been so many flies, he continued, "Look in on Lady Aurelia if you can, boy."

"I was going to come back a little later, if it would be all right." Marcus gestured with his woven cane basket, which contained leeks, part of a squash, and a quarter of a skinned hare that was inclined to drip. "I've been shopping."

Quindarvis regarded it with wrinkled nose. "So I see. More of your philosophic principles, I suppose. Oh, that reminds me. That centurion of the guards, whatever his name is . . .''

"Arrius."

"Just so. He left word with us that he wanted to see you; he has some Christians down at the prison.''

"What?'' squeaked Marcus. "When?''

"Oh, his man was here this morning. They said they'd looked for you at your lodging. . . . What would your father say about you turning police informer . . .?'' He strode back toward the door to the atrium, Marcus and the string of slaves trotting at his heels.

"The police are servants of the city and the emperor,'' retorted Marcus quickly, stung at the imputation. "They represent order and peace. Does a man scorn his own faithful servants?''

"No, but he doesn't offer to help them clean out toilets, either.'' Quindarvis brushed through the embroidered black curtains and into the atrium. Half-a-dozen clients sprang to their feet. "Get them out of here, tell them to drown themselves . . .''

"Yes, sir,'' murmured the Syrian underbutler.

"Is my chair ready?''

"Certainly, sir.''

A hand touched Marcus' shoulder. He turned, startled, and met the eyes of the Greek physician Nicanor, who drew him quietly into an alcove that contained the statues of the Varus clan's ancestral gods. "May I have a word with you, sir?''

Marcus glanced back at Quindarvis, who was dispensing an arrogant tongue-lashing to the frightened butler amid a crowd of eager clients. The praetor had clearly forgotten his existence.

"The other slaves asked me to speak with you, sir,'' said the Greek quietly. "You're a friend of the family. Are you going down to the prison, to help that centurion who's looking for Mistress Tertullia?''

"Yes, I'm on my way there now,'' said Marcus, suppressing his annoyance with Quindarvis for not having mentioned the matter to him earlier, and wondering if Arrius would have given up on him already in disgust.

"Is it true that the centurion thinks there's a Christian in the household?"

Marcus blinked at him, startled afresh at the speed with which news traveled among the city's slaves.

"Because it isn't true, sir." Those dark, intelligent eyes grew intent, and Marcus saw suddenly at the back of them a lurking dread. "By Asclepius I swear it isn't." He gestured toward the group in the atrium, the fussing praetor and his little court. "Does *he* know what was said?"

Marcus shook his head.

"Then don't speak of it to him, sir. Please." Nicanor's office had protected him from many of the indignities of a slave's life—there was a stiffness to his voice that spoke of a man unused to pleading. But the curtain of the archway at his back moved; Marcus wondered how many of the others were listening. "If he thought such a thing, it'd be the rack for all of us, you know it would. He's had poor Hylas locked up . . ."

"Who?"

"Hylas. Mistress Tertullia's footman. The one she sent away with her packages. The poor man's half sick with grief that he left her to begin with, and he's in terror of what will be done to him."

"But it wasn't his fault!" protested Marcus. "It wasn't any of your fault."

Nicanor shrugged fatalistically. "The law says when a man is murdered, every slave in his household can be put to death as well for not preventing it. Even the questioning is more than many can stand."

Churaldin's words returned to him, "You must know there's only one way they have of examining slaves." It came to him how monstrous it was that this slim, gentle-handed man, with all his skill and talent, would have to beg like a scullion or a concubine to be spared torture. He was a man of full life, thirty-five or so, and handsome in his way, with his close-trimmed beard and wary dark eyes. It was monstrous, thought Marcus, that he should have no more rights than a child, who at a father's whim can be exposed upon the hillside for the wild dogs to eat.

He supposed in his place someone else might have felt powerful, or magnanimous, to receive such pleading. But in his shabby toga, clutching his shopping basket in both awkward hands, he felt embarrassed and ridiculous. The noises in the atrium faded as Quindarvis and his train boiled through the vestibule doors. "All right," he said quietly. "I won't mention it to him, or to Lady Aurelia, and I'll—I'll do what I can to help Hylas. He's not Quindarvis' slave, after all; he can't do anything to him."

"No," said the Syrian doorkeeper, coming across the echoing marble of the empty hall. "But may the goddess Cybele help him—and all of us—when the master returns." He took Marcus' shopping basket from him and added to its contents a little bundle containing bread, some cold meats, and several sesterces; the usual handout a wealthy man gave to the clients who hung around his anterooms all day. "They'll never miss an extra one," he confided. "Thank you, sir."

From behind the curtain, Marcus heard a murmuring chorus of "Thank you, thank you . . ."

The thanks embarrassed him, and the gift still more. As he hurried down the hill toward the Forum, he wondered at the terrible injustice of it, that these people should have to beg for safety, not from a judge or a lawgiver, but from a twenty-two-year-old dilettante philosopher, and not a particularly good one at that. They had shown their thanks in the only way they could, with goods pilfered from their master, and to Marcus' eternal and acute discomfiture, he was aware that he could not have afforded to turn them down.

For many months his father, faced with his stubborn desire to pursue a philosophic career, had refused to send him money, merely stipulating that he should come and ask for it when he was in need. He had done so, hating it, hating the old man, starving in his ramshackle room in the Subura tenement until Felix had persuaded their oldest brother Caius to change the arrangement. Caius had understood neither the philosophy nor the pride, but he was pragmatic enough to realize that with an income of ten sesterces every few weeks and a rental of a denarius per month, and no surety that that might not be raised (not to mention fluctuations in the market prices of various commodities), if his brother did not starve himself to death he would in very short order undertake disgraceful means of remedying the situation. "Didn't know whether he meant crime or trade," Felix had remarked, dropping the small wash-leather purse onto the plank table in front of Marcus one afternoon. "But the old paterfamilias nearly had a stroke at the thought of it. He'll send old Straton over with one of these every quarter day. Mind you don't blow it all on fast women and slow horses."

It was an improved situation. But not so improved, thought Marcus, as he pushed his way through the crowds in the spice markets that clustered at the rocky end of the Quirinal Hill, that he could afford to turn down free food, no matter what its source.

The mob around the offices of the city bread dole was far thinner than usual at this hour of the morning. Most of them had got their tickets to the games in yesterday's basket and would be at the Flavian already, defending their places against all comers. He passed a poster inked on the base of the statue of some defunct emperor, advertising them as being given in honor of the emperor's victories by the praetors of the city, headed by Priscus Quindarvis, that most generous and popular of all good fellows. He noticed that there were more of the Praetorian Guard in the city, too, an obvious precaution if most of the population was going to abandon their shops and houses for the day. He thought of the centurion Arrius, and the Christians in the jail, and his normally mild blood stirred with sudden hot anger.

Among the imperial splendor of marble columns and gilded shrines in the Old Forum at the bottom of the hill, the buildings that housed the Senate and its archives looked small, old-fashioned, and a little dowdy. The usual racket in the bookshops and the silver exchange in Caesar's forum just behind had quieted. The doors of the Senate house were closed. Everyone was at the games.

At this hour of the morning, the main guardroom of the prison on the Capitoline Rise was still cool. It was a brick building, and small. Somebody—Juvenal?—had been very proud of the fact that Rome had only one prison. But it had been Rome's prison for time out of mind. The structures above the ground came and went, the present one dating from some forty years back; the cells of its pits were eternal. Marcus felt his flesh creep as he stepped into the bluish shade of that whitewashed guardroom. The place stank of bad death.

Contrary to his expectations, the soldiers dicing in the guardroom were quite civil. At his question one of them directed him to the inner door, and pushing it gingerly open, he found himself in a small, grimy cubicle occupied by several officers, including Arrius himself.

"Silanus." The centurion looked up from the scroll he held. "I hoped my message would catch up with you somewhere." He set the scroll on the table; it rolled itself together, and Marcus could see that it bore the stamp of the Imperial Archives.

Surprised, he remarked, "I didn't know people were allowed to remove records from the archives."

"They aren't. We've made some arrests . . ." With a faint jingling of mail rings the centurion leaned on the arm of his camp chair. "There's an off-chance you may recognize one of them; in any case we'll see what we can find out. I warn you, it might not be much." He pushed the scroll toward Marcus. "See what you think of that."

Arrius had marked the place in ink, an offense to Marcus' whole bookish soul. With some effort, because the scribe's hand was poor, he read the account of the last trial of Christians in Rome, three years before.

It was a simple and straightforward account, written by a clerk who could afford to waste neither time nor paper. In answer to a complaint by local magistrates, the watch had broken into a house near the Temple of Mars. Three men and two women were arrested. Charge: professing the worship of Joshua Bar-Joseph, called Christus. Put to torture, one of the men had given the names of two other women and two men. They had been arrested the following day. Tullius Varus, prefect of the city, had acted as judge.

One and all, they had refused to burn incense to the genius of the emperor. They had also disrupted the court, cursed and threatened the life of the emperor, and behaved in a gross and unseemly manner. (Marcus wondered what was defined as "gross and unseemly." He knew his father defined it as singing in public, a habit Marcus had had as a child until it had been beaten out of him; or, latterly, the study of philosophy.)

In any case their actions had not found much favor with Tullius Varus.

Sentence being passed, Nīkolas, called priest among the criminals, did break from the guards and spring upon the table in the face of his judges, and cry out that this same Christus would take his vengeance upon them, and upon all of their families. These same criminals were then sentenced to the amphitheater, where the men were tarred over with pitch and bound to stakes, and there lit, to illuminate the arena while the women were first raped by the beast-catchers and then devoured by lions. This was at the games of Ceres, Tullius Varus, prefect of Rome, presiding.

Marcus let the scroll roll itself shut, feeling just slightly ill. Had the priest known what was going to happen to them when he had shrieked his curse upon his judges?

He himself had avoided the games for years. Even as a youth they had shocked him. But worse than the shock, he unwillingly knew, was the fascination, the shivering horror of watching the helpless desperately struggling against inexorable and hideous fate. When he was fourteen and fifteen he had gone again and again, and only his later priggishness, he supposed, had prevented him from acquiring the habit of it.

Maybe, he thought, tying the tapes of the scroll together, if he had been more accustomed to the games the image conjured by that dry account would be less vividly horrible to him. Maybe such things were common usage to Arrius. He remembered what Sixtus had said about the temple in Antioch and cast a swift, unwilling glance across at the centurion, who was calmly paring his fingernails with his dagger.

He glanced up at him and stuck the dagger point-down into the scarred tabletop. "So there we are," he grunted. "Nine people who might or might not be related to those lunatics downstairs, or whose families might or might not have decided to have a fling at revenge. That's two possibilities. There's a third."

"A third?"

Arrius nodded. "Yesterday I took a little walk up to the Aventine, where Chambares Tiridates has a villa. You know anything about Tiridates?"

Marcus shook his head, mystified. "Only that he's Phrygian or Syrian or something, and that he was betrothed to—is betrothed to—Tertullia. He's supposed to be stinking rich and powerful."

"He is," growled the centurion. "I've had more civil treatment from members of the Senate than I got from his assistant doorkeeper. After one hell of a long wait in a vestibule that smelled like a high-class whorehouse, I finally saw him and asked him if I could talk to those two chair-bearers who brought Tertullia home that night. The ones the Christians slugged. I'd put the wheels in motion to round up our friends downstairs and I thought I'd give the bearers a look at them, too. Which reminds me—"

"I already spoke to the other man, Churaldin," said Marcus. "He knew nothing—I don't think he even saw them clearly."

A slow grin spread across that harsh bony face. The lynx-green eyes glinted with approval. "For a philosopher, you have a nice grasp of essentials, boy."

Marcus flushed with an odd pleasure at that backhanded compliment, but he only asked, "Did you ask if the bearers would come down to have a look at your Christians?"

"No," said Arrius. "Chambares said he'd sold them."

"SOLD THEM!"

"He said he was angry for their carelessness at letting

someone make off with his betrothed. He said he sold them the same day to a galley shipping out for Egypt.''

"Dear gods,'' whispered Marcus, appalled by the callousness of the act, its cruelty, and its utter injustice. The bitterness in Nicanor's voice came back to him, his own shocked disgust that a cultured, talented physician should have to plead with a family friend nearly half his age to intercede for his life.

"Oh, come on!'' said the centurion roughly, reading the horror on his face. "At two hundred fifty sesterces for an untrained bearer do you think he'd really let good men go like that? He just didn't want me talking to his slaves.''

"But why not?'' protested Marcus. "What does he have to hide?''

Arrius worked the knife point free of the wood and turned its blade to catch the thin sunlight from the window. "That question,'' he said dryly, "did cross my mind.''

Marcus was silent for a moment. "Maybe he just didn't want his slaves put in that kind of danger? If their testimony was required in court . . .''

"It wouldn't be,'' shrugged Arrius. "We have a freeborn witness. Now, I know there are men who would rather cut out their slaves' tongues than have them talk to anyone without their leave—and I'm not speaking in hyperbole, by the way. But from what I gathered, Tiridates is eager for the match, in spite of the fact that he had his hand up his wine-server's tunic before I was even out the door. For a poor boy from Syria, marriage with the daughter of the city prefect of Rome is a big step. So yes, I'm inclined to be suspicious. But Tiridates has seen me now, and he has enough political power to make me hesitate about bringing in one of my men— always provided I could find a man in the Praetorian with the wits not to haul off and break the jaw of the first man who addresses him as 'boy' while he's passing himself off as a slave.''

He was silent for a moment, and Marcus had the uncomfortable sensation of being weighed and judged by that aloof, gray-green gaze. He felt suddenly very naked, like a raw recruit being inspected: revealed in all his thin-shanked inadequacy as being not much good for anything but the ideal pursuit of Beauty, Truth, and the Good.

But to his intense surprise Arrius asked, "You think you could pass for a slave?"

Marcus hesitated. "I don't know," he said finally. "I've been told I couldn't pass for anything but a philosopher."

The long, curled eyebrows dived suddenly down. "By whom?" There was an edge of excitement in the centurion's voice.

Marcus grinned at the memory. "By a former governor of Antioch, believe it or not."

"I'll believe it," said Arrius eagerly. "Not Xystes Julian?"

"It's the Latin form of the name—Sixtus Julianus?"

The centurion gave a great shout of laughter. "The Falcon of the Desert himself! I thought the old madman was dead years ago! Where did you meet him?"

"Churaldin's his slave."

Arrius was still laughing. "And I'll bet he told you where you lived and who your father was." He leaned his elbows on the desk, the rings of his chain-mail shirt glinting in the thin sunshaft from the window.

"How does he do that?"

"Mithras knows—I certainly don't. But when my father was serving him in Africa and I'd been up to any mischief in the camp, old Xystes could pin me with it just by looking at me. He was a strange old coot," he added, "but his men worshiped him—more than they worshiped the current emperor, which is why he ended up being shipped off to Antioch. My dad said he could outthink a demon and outtalk the gods. Half the men were dead scared of him. The only things you could know—according to my dad, I was only seven at the time—was that he wouldn't fail you, and he probably knew more about the situation than you did." He stood up, looked around, and put on his burnished helmet, with its cross-roached centurion's crest. "You think, since his slave was mixed up in it, the old lunatic might give us a hand?"

"I asked him to," said Marcus, as he followed him out

into the guardroom. "He's retired from the world, practically turned hermit. But he said he'd advise me."

At Arrius' signal the guards were moving the cover from what had looked like a wellhead in the flagged floor. But a rickety ladder was revealed, leading down into a dismal pit below. "You couldn't have made a better choice," he said, with a sideways glance at Marcus. "If we can't get any sense out of this lot below, we might need him even to find a starting place." He put his feet on the ladder and started down.

"What do you mean, 'get any sense out of them'?" Marcus looked around hastily, set his marketing basket on a bench, and gathered up his soiled toga around him in order to descend behind him. "Aren't you going to question them"—he flinched from the memory of the slave Churaldin's bitter jeer, from Nicanor's anxious eyes—"in the usual way?" he finished.

Below him in the darkness Arrius laughed. "You ever try to question a Christian?"

V

Now I beseech you, brethren, by the name of our Lord Jesus Christ, that ye all speak the same thing, and that there be no divisions among you; but that ye be perfectly joined together in the same mind and in the same judgment. For it hath been declared unto me of you . . . that there are contentions among you.

Saint Paul
Letter to the Corinthians

On one side the wall of the corridor was brick, like its low-vaulted roof and its floor; old, uneven, cracked brick, slimy with moss and rank with the smell of evil. On the other side the living stone of the Capitoline Hill had been cut into four cells. All the doors were bolted, but only one boasted a guard. In the smoky glare of the single oil lamp the place looked clammy, dirty, loathsome; foul with the smells of excrement and fear. As he trailed in the centurion's footsteps, Marcus found his own soul prey to an unreasoning terror and an illogical desire to flee from this place.

The guard slapped out his arm in salute as they halted before the door. Faintly, voices could be heard within, babbling and confused. Arrius cast a questioning glance at the soldier, who shrugged. At his signal the man undid the door bolts and opened the door to the Christians' cell.

Out of the dimness, the voices grew suddenly louder.

". . . nonsense," a woman cried, her voice deep and husky and cracked like an old wine jar. "Our priest says that a god would never defile himself with a—a—a filthy earthly body, much less that any man could bind and slay a god! He says that in the Book of Peter it specifically states that what appeared to die on the cross was a substitute!"

"*Your* priest?" rasped a man's voice, harsh and angry. "And what, pray, would *he* know about it, or you either, you ignorant bitch? The whole point of Christ's descent to this world was that he take on the appearance and substance of humanity. 'For the Word was made flesh and dwelt among us . . .' "

"Now, wait a minute," chided another man. "You say, 'appearance,' but *our* priest has assured us that the entire meaning of the sacrifice of Calvary was that the Christ take on the true nature of a human being. That he was, in fact, a man, and not a god, at the time he died."

"Your priest is a fool!" screamed a shriller voice. "Who consecrated him, anyway?"

"Apollodorus . . ."

"That heretic? Only an idiot would ever believe that the Christ was ever a mere man. He was the Christos, the God-Made-Man, 'of a single substance with the Father' . . ."

"And therefore he couldn't have suffered and couldn't have died!" shouted the woman's voice. As the forms became clearer through the murk, Marcus could distinguish the speakers; the dark forms like the damned awaiting judgment, the white stirring of dirty limbs, the glitter of moving eyes. The woman speaking was tall and fleshy, standing with her hands on her hips, her dark hair lying in unbound waves over heavy breasts. She wore a dark-green stola stitched in some kind of lighter pattern, and her face showed the remains of a dark husky beauty. "You're no better than a bunch of Orphics," she was yelling at the others. "You believe the suffering of the god somehow saves his worshipers! If you want suffering go down to the Flavian! It's the Word, the message, the Logos embodied in the temporary spiritual illusion that saves us all from our lives of sin and filth and misery!''

A tall rigid shadow in the darkest corner of the room broke in. ''Just because he shared in the divine nature of the creator by no means indicates that he was not also a participant in the human nature common to us all.''

''Blasphemer!'' shrieked the woman.

''Heretic!'' screamed the shrill-voiced man.

''What in the name of the gods?'' Marcus murmured. The two soldiers, armed and armored, had been standing in the doorway of the cell for some five minutes, and not a Christian had so much as turned his head.

''It states in the Acts of John . . .''

''That Gnostic tripe!'' stormed the tall man in the corner. ''In his letter to the Hebrews the apostle Paul specifically states that Christ is Lord—not similar to God, not proceeding from God, not a mere result of the Divine Demiurge. Moreover, in the Gospel of Matthew and elsewhere in Luke, by providing his corporal nature to his disciples after his resurrection from the grave . . .''

In a bored voice the guard called out, ''Telesphorus!''

''. . . which they doubted, suspecting, as you do, my sister, that he was a ghost or spirit . . .''

''I'm no sister to you, you heretical limb of Satan!''

''TELESPHORUS!'' bellowed Arrius.

Silence fell. The guard lifted his lantern to shed a wan light into the drab and filthy chamber, and a gleam of it reflected from the high bald head of the tall man as he turned around, his gray eyes like a hawk's under the jut of gray-shot black brows. He stood up, gawky and rawboned in a laborer's coarse brown tunic. ''I am Telesphorus.''

Arrius jerked his head in summons. Telesphorus picked his way from among his quibbling brethren and walked to the door with his head high.

From the same corner a wiry little man sprang to his feet, like Telesphorus bearded, like him balding, but only across the top of his head. He flung himself hysterically to his side. "Be brave, my brother," he exhorted in that same shrill, grating voice Marcus had heard before. "The gore of martyrdom is nobler than the purple of the bastard emperor. The fire, the cross, the struggle with wild beasts, the cutting and tearing of the flesh, the racking of the bones, the mangling of the limbs—these are but the steps to the throne of Jesus Christ! God will give you strength to meet it."

"Let's hope God will give you forgiveness for your heresy," snapped a young man's voice. "And all of you, you scheming Oriental bitch and you bunch of cowardly prevaricators who won't understand that unless you renounce all matters of the flesh, the eating of all meat, the sin of fornication—"

"Whining Jew!" shot back the woman.

"Stinking whore!"

"Only possession by a demon," screamed the woman, "could excuse your perverse stubborn ignorance of the truth about the holy progressions of the Divine Demiurge . . ."

The shrill little man dropped to one knee and kissed Telesphorus' knuckles. "In the few hours that are left us," he whispered, "I shall preach to them the truth. Go with God, my brother."

The others were far too busy screaming imprecations at one anothers' theology to notice their brother's departure.

The examination room contained, at one end, a small table, a chair, two stools, and a lamp set on an iron lampstand. At the other end of that long narrow chamber was the rack, and with it a brazier and a tableful of implements. The walls were horribly stained. Marcus took one look and turned his eyes hastily away.

Arrius took a seat behind the table, paying no more attention to Marcus than if he had been a clerk. Since he realized this was the idea they were trying to convey, Marcus meekly took a stool in the corner, as far away from the other end of the room as possible. Telesphorus remained standing. In spite of his ragged clothes and dirty body, he retained the dignity of a doomed king.

The centurion glanced up at him. "Your name is Telesphorus, son of Dion," he informed him in a bored voice. "You're an Alexandrian Greek by birth. You're now a copyist, but you used to operate a school in the Publican Rise. Why did you close it?"

"Other demands entered my life, to which it was necessary that I accede." Despite the smoky oil lamp the room was almost pitch black. The walls stank of blood and pain and terror. Marcus knew he'd never have been able to reply that calmly.

"And what demands were these?"

The upright back stiffened slightly. "The demands of my church, of my priesthood. The demands of my god."

"Are you a priest?"

"I am a priest of the Lord Jesus Christ," said Telesphorus proudly, "as you knew, Roman, when you had me arrested."

Arrius picked up a little piece of equipment that lay among the parchments and wax tablets on the tabletop. He fiddled with it idly, twirling its bolts—Marcus saw that it was a kind of small thumbscrew. "How long have you been a priest?"

"It is twelve years since I received baptism at the hands of Evaristus, who was then the Bishop of Rome. For seven years I have served Jesus Christ, and my people."

"Did you know Nikolas, the priest who was killed about three years ago?"

Telesphorus hesitated. "No."

"Oh, come on, do me more credit than that," snapped Arrius impatiently. "You were priests of the same religion in the same part of town and you never met?"

The hard mouth under the dirty beard seemed to lengthen, the lips compressing into a solid line. The priest said nothing. Arrius watched him in silence for a moment, spinning the little clamps of the horrible thing he held. The smutty orange of the lamplight shone like oil on the nicks of old scars, the rock-hard ripple of muscle and the broken line of his nose, and looking at him, Marcus shivered involuntarily. For all his easy friendliness, the centurion was a stranger to pity.

Without a glance at Marcus, he ordered him, "Send for the guard."

There was not another sound in the room as he obeyed. A sentry came in, grinning and sweaty and jovial.

"Put this one in the next cell," said Arrius briefly. "Is the hangman around?"

"I think he's at the games this morning, sir, but he can be fetched."

"Maybe later. There's time. One more thing, old man," he added, as the guard took Telesphorus' thin arm in a hand like an iron shackle. "How did you happen to become a Christian?"

The priest drew himself up to his full height, sweat gleaming on the curve of his high forehead and in the hollow of his throat. "The Lord called me," he said, "and I answered. It is all I have to say to you, Roman."

Arrius' eyes flashed dangerously, but he only said, "Take him away. If he gives you any trouble, skin his back for him."

"What are stripes to me?" demanded Telesphorus. "Each stripe is a brand of victory, an emblem of my love and loyalty for the Christ, the living God. I welcome your flogging."

The sentry grinned, showing cracked and missing teeth. "Shall I oblige the man, centurion?"

"Don't bother." He glanced over at Marcus as the priest was led away. "He knows," he said

"About Tullia?"

Arrius shrugged and spun the bolts of the thumbscrew idly with one finger. "About the priest Nikolas and his group, anyway."

Marcus swallowed queasily. "Will you—will you use that thing?"

The hard face twitched into a wry grin. "I doubt I'll need it," he said, standing up. "What'll you bet me the woman'll break?"

Marcus blinked at him, confused. "What makes you think that?"

"Her kind mostly do."

In the darkness of the cell that thick husky voice was declaiming ". . . and Plato has proved—*proved*—that the fiery emanations from the Divine World-Soul crossed this intermediate world, becoming entangled in the gross and putrid flesh. These fiery emanations are our souls, which could only be released by the teachings of the Divine Demiurge . . ."

"You talk like a Mithraist," spat an older man's voice. "Yes, our souls are trapped in our filthy bodies, but it was the original sin of Adam, as Paul has taught us—"

"Paul!" screamed the youngest boy there. "That scabby faker! Rotten traitor to the cause of the Son of man!"

"Arete!" called out Arrius.

"Son of man, hell!" cried the shrill-voiced man wildly. "Son of God, and God Himself . . ."

"Now you can't be yourself and somebody else, too," yelled the first man, leaping to his feet.

"Who are you to say what God can and cannot do or be?" yelled the other woman, who up until this time had sat in her black corner saying nothing. "Telesphorus says . . ."

"ARETE!" roared Arrius in his best parade-ground voice. And when the babbling rose louder around him, he bellowed, "BE SILENT, ALL OF YOU!"

To Marcus' surprise, they were.

"Arete, widow of Simeon the baker?"

Marcus saw the woman's face turn chalk-white in the gloom. The shrill-voiced little man sprang to his feet and shrieked at her, "Fry in hell, you Gnostic whore!"

She whirled on him. "You scabby dung-picking monkey—" She lunged for him, hands opened to claw. Arrius reached her in a stride and seized her wrists, forcing them down behind her while the little man ducked behind the other woman.

"What have you done with Telesphorus?" he cried.

Arrius spat out a stray trail of hair; the woman had begun to struggle like the Old Man of the Sea, kicking at his booted shins with her bare toes. As he shoved her toward the door he answered viciously, "I fed him to the lions!" Marcus' last glimpse of the Christians, as the prison door closed upon them, was of the little man with his palms upraised in prayer, and all the rest of them arguing furiously around him.

Once outside the cell the woman Arete ceased to struggle, but as she stumbled along in the iron grip of the centurion's arm, Marcus could see the rim of white that showed all around the pupils of her eyes, like those of a frightened horse. She was saying, "Haven't you rotten pimps of Caesar got anything better to do than to persecute the Lord's anointed? Aren't there criminals enough in Rome without . . . ?"

"Be quiet, woman," sighed Arrius.

"Because in the long run the Lord will look after his own. You don't understand that when the sheep are separated from the goats—"

"I said be quiet." He pushed her ahead of him into the interrogation room. She whirled, as though she would try to flee, when she saw the rack there, waiting. But Arrius filled the narrow door, with bone and muscle and mail; Marcus had the impression that she did not see himself at all. Her breasts heaved with her thick frightened breathing; her dark eyes shifted, seeking a way out. Arrius kicked the door shut behind him. "Your name's Arete; your husband's name was Simeon. That right?"

She nodded and swallowed hard.

"Formerly an initiate of the rites of Cybele, formerly a worshiper of Isis, formerly connected with the cult of Moloch. When'd you turn Christian, Arete?"

"Can you blame a traveler who has found the right road for straying down many paths? This entire empire has come to grief because—"

"How long have you been a Christian?" he demanded, and her eyes flashed briefly with anger.

"Does it matter . . . ?"

"Yes, it matters." Arrius' voice was harsh. "When I ask you a question it's because I want an answer, not because I want to hear a bunch of drivel about the Christ."

"You speak of drivel when you talk of the One True Word!" she protested furiously. "I know the true path, the true knowledge, and I shall never recant it!"

"That's good," purred the centurion. "Because I'm not going to ask you to recant."

Her eyes widened with shock. "What?"

He stepped over close to her and rested his big hands on her shoulders. Though she was a tall woman, and strong, the mail-clad body with its crested helm seemed to dominate her, as inhuman and faceless as the implements of torture that surrounded them. His voice was soft, intimate, and utterly without warmth. "I don't personally care how much incense anyone throws on Caesar's altar, or who you sing your hymns to. It won't keep you off the rack."

Her eyes were huge, pits of horror staring into his. "You can't do that," she whispered. "My husband was a Roman citizen . . ."

"But you're not, are you?" he murmured. His gripping hands turned her, thrust her deeper into the hot blackness of the back of the room. She stared at the rack in a kind of horrible fascination, the stained boards, the long pale hollows worn by countless digging heels, the filthy leather and the dark iron shining with oil and grease. The gears and cogs and levers, stronger than any human flesh. He held her against his mailed body, so she could not turn away from the sight, but Marcus did not see that she even made the attempt. What Arrius said to her he did not hear, for the centurion's voice was as low as a seducer's, murmuring in the woman's ear, but once he heard her groan, "I'll recant! I'll burn the incense," and he said quietly, "I'm not asking for that, Arete. Now—how long have you been a Christian?"

She stammered, "Three years—almost four years."

"And did you know the priest Nikolas, who was executed?"

She raised her head a little. "That dolt? They were all scum, they weren't even true Christians at all, just a bunch of superstitious heretics who followed Paul's letters as if they'd been handed down by God himself. Butt-headed and ignorant as a corral full of jackasses. They—"

"I'm not interested in their faith," murmured the centurion through his teeth. "Who were they? What were their names?"

She hesitated, looking into his eyes and evidently finding

nothing there to give her hope. Then, with a kind of defiance, she rattled off a list of names, accompanied by abusive commentary upon the morals, character, and faith of each. "But they're all dead, the filthy heretics, and good riddance," she finished. "I don't see what—"

"You don't have to see," grated Arrius. "Did any of them leave families?"

"I don't know," she said sulkily. He shoved her back against the rack, so that her buttocks pressed the edge of the worn wood; she tried to pull away, frightened, but he kept her there, his body pinning hers. "I don't know, I tell you!" she gabbled. "I wasn't in that group, or anyway not for very long, I didn't know them. And anyway if their families had sense they'd have left the city before they were pulled in, too."

"Were there any survivors?" he pressed her, and her breath caught. She tried to turn her face away, but he seized her by the hair, twisted her head brutally back to look into his eyes. "Who?"

"There weren't," she gulped, panic in her voice.

"Don't lie to me. You said a minute ago they weren't real Christians anyway."

"Yes, but . . ."

"You said you'd recant the faith. You still mean that?"

"If you . . ."

"You ever seen anyone racked, Arete? Ever seen what the joints look like after the bones come apart?" Moaning she tried to writhe free of him, but he held her, breast to breast like an iron lover, and past that unyielding mailed shoulder Marcus could see the gilding of oily sweat on her terrified face. "You going to let that happen to those soft limbs of yours, over a bunch of swine who don't really understand the faith at all?"

She whispered, "But they're . . ."

"They're what?"

With his hand tangled in the knot of her hair she could look nowhere but into those cruel wolf eyes. Her face changed; she said spitefully, "They're that superstitious lout Telesphorus and his whining jackal Ignatius. They were the only survivors."

"What about the Christians on the Quirinal Hill?"

Her eyes flared wider. "You know?"

"Who are they?"

She stammered, gulping, "There—there aren't any." And she cried out in pain as his grip tightened on her arm and her hair.

"You just said there were. Who are the Christians in the prefect Varus' household?" And when she only stared at him, he shook her again, bending her body backward over the rack.

She sobbed, "No, please, I don't know—I really don't—"

He said through his teeth, "That'll be too bad, won't it?"

"I—They—It's the physician," she gasped. "The physician and—and—the maidservant—"

He dragged her back up to face him. Tears were running down her face, her bosom heaving with terror. Marcus looked away, sickened, his whole soul crying out that it couldn't be Nicanor—not Nicanor.

Arrius' voice was a deadly rasp. "There must be a dozen maidservants in the house. Which one?"

"I don't know," she gasped; Marcus saw their shadows thrown against the wall jerk suddenly, and her voice rose to a shriek. "I don't know! I swear it! By God I swear it! It's a—a Greek name, Chloris or Chloe or Charis or something like that—please . . ."

The dark shapes on the stained wall moved in the fitful torchlight. He heard Arrius growl, "Where'd they take the girl?"

"I don't know what you're talking about!" sobbed the woman. "I don't know who you mean!" Her voice was thick and jerky with sobs; Marcus saw the shadows sway and turn, and looked around to see the centurion push the woman away from him. She collapsed, weeping, on the floor.

Arrius said impassively, "Lying bitch."

She made no reply, only lay there sobbing, her inky hair

spread round about her, gulping and sniveling incoherently not to be hurt.

"Aurelia Pollia really have a Greek slave girl?" he asked softly after a moment.

Marcus shook his head. "I think she used to have a Greek girl named Ledo, but right now her dresser's an Armenian—Maali—and both her maids are Africans, sisters, Priscilla and Prudentia."

The centurion nodded. "But I'd say three quarters of the wealthy houses in the city have some Greek girl in them named Chloris or Chloe or Charis or Corrinna or Core. And damn near every one of them has a physician."

Marcus looked up quickly "You think she was lying?"

He shrugged. "If she was, she was pretty safe. You know the physician?"

Marcus nodded wretchedly.

"You think he's a Christian?"

"I don't know," he replied, miserable with the truth that it was impossible to know. Before them on the floor, the woman groveled, sobbing, oblivious to their soft conversation. "I don't think so, but . . ."

"We'll hold him in reserve, and I'll cross-check with the others," said Arrius. "No sense crushing the poor bastard's finger joints on her word alone. Telesphorus and Ignatius, eh?" He stepped over to the door, pushed it open, and called, "Guard!"

The woman Arete got slowly to her feet. With her struggles her gown had come unpinned and gaped open over her bosom; her damp black hair hung down like a river, framing her blotched, tear-streaked face. She said slowly, "I want to recant my faith."

Arrius shrugged, the dim lamplight glittering harshly over his mail shirt. His eyes might have been something dug from a mine. "Sorry. We're not out for recantations. This is a civil case, and I don't give an old date pit who you worship."

"But you promised," she said desperately. "You said . . ."

He glanced over at Marcus. "You hear me promise anything, boy?" Marcus shook his head.

"You promised me," said the woman frantically, as the guard entered and took her by the arm. Her voice rose to a shriek. "You stinking beast! You filthy pimp! The Lord God will smite you as he smote Ananias, as he smote Judas the traitor, as he . . ." The door shut behind them.

"Whew." Arrius removed his helmet and wiped the sweat from his brow with his arm. "She may be right," he said after a moment. "If I was planning revenge or anything else, she's the last person I'd tell of it. Odds are she knows nothing of the kidnapping at all. There's ways of finding out."

Sullen silence reigned in the Christians' cell. Arrius called out "Ignatius!" and was answered by that shrill rasping voice.

"Oh Lord!" it prayed, "sustain me to the glories of martyrdom in thy Holy Name!"

"Shut up, you stinking heretic Sodomite," growled the young boy in the corner.

The little bald man scrambled nimbly to his feet and threw himself at Arrius. "Do your worst to me, imperial thug!" he cried, ripping open his tunic to bare an unwashed and rather concave breast. "The teeth of the beasts in the arena will be but the grindstones to mill my body, to make the pure bread of the Lord!"

The older of the two men remaining in the cell sighed. "Gag him when you throw him to the lions," he advised.

"That's it!" screamed Ignatius furiously. "Gag the truth! I should have known it of you, Doriskos! Any man who would champion the desecration of the holy Easter Sunday by making it a cheap Jewish movable feast . . ."

"The Passover has always been . . ." began the younger boy, and the room showed every sign of degenerating into new squabbles. But at that moment Marcus heard the creak of the ladder in the corridor, and one of the guards from the room above emerged from the murky darkness.

"Sir?" he said. "There's a woman here to see the prisoners."

Arrius glanced from the rising uproar in the cell to the sentry, and back again. He signaled to Marcus, and they retired into the hall, unnoticed by any of the combatants in the room. In the next cell Arete and Telesphorus could be faintly heard, screaming abuse at each other.

Arrius took Marcus by the arm and steered him back into the examination room. "Will you let her see them?" Marcus asked.

"Oh, yes." He shut the door and went to the rear of the chamber, stepping around the black crouching shape of the rack to the shadowed wall behind. "Here." There was a faint scraping sound. Marcus saw the shadows of the wall shift and a darker oblong appear among them, where there had been only dirty and bloodstained plaster. Coming gingerly at Arrius' signal, he saw a very small chamber, like a closet, concealed behind the hidden door.

"Through that knothole you can see everything that passes in the room," said the centurion. "The wall's thin, and the ceiling's pitched so you can hear a whisper. Will you do it?"

Marcus swallowed, suddenly repelled. *Beauty, Truth, and the Good,* he thought to himself: their very natures seemed to slither like reptiles through his cringing fingers. *Where did I go wrong in my search? How did I come into this hole of ugliness and death, lies and blasphemies, to sit like a greedy little clerk in the hole where they crouch to take down confessions wrung in agony?* But he looked up and saw that uncompromising cynicism in the centurion's eyes, mocking his courage without mocking his search.

"All right," he managed to whisper, and Arrius smiled, a brief, bitter grin that never touched his eyes.

"Good boy." He rested a brown scarred hand on his shoulder. "We'll make a soldier of you yet."

Through the knothole he saw the woman enter the room a few minutes later, escorted by the sentry. She was pale, and under her brown veil her thick black curling hair was dank with sweat, but between the leering soldier and the crouching shadow of the rack she maintained her calm. She was young, eighteen or nineteen. Her dress bore the stripe of a woman

with children. The lamplight glinted on a silver amulet of a
fish that lay on her large, upstanding breasts.

Hobnailed boots clacked in the passage. Marcus saw her
flinch and realized how much courage it must have taken to
come here at all. The door opened, and the sentry's voice
growled, "Make it fast, grandpa." Telesphorus stepped from
the shadows and met the girl's big dark eyes.

The door closed behind him, the wind of it making the
grubby lamp flame startle. Marcus shifted within his sweltering cubicle, the sweat-dampened wool of his toga unbearably
itchy against his neck and the walls too narrow for him to risk
making a sound by scratching.

Telesphorus' face was shiny with moisture in the dim
brown darkness of the room. The fear of the place was
growing on him, but his voice was still calm. "You shouldn't
have come, Dorcas."

She gestured to the small basket she'd brought. "I have
food for you."

"It's a costly meal at the price of your life. You think
they'll let you out of here?"

She swallowed hard, hiding her fear. "I told them I was a
member of your family. They let me in."

"You don't think they'll be after our families as well?" he
demanded harshly. And then, as those full, sensitive lips
tightened, he added, "They're asking names."

Marcus saw her eyes flicker down to his hands, then his
feet. She asked him, "Are you all right?"

"So far. They want to know about Nikolas' group, and
their families."

Dorcas frowned, her dark strongly drawn brows swooping
down over her nose. "But they're all dead. Dead or left the
city. You and Ignatius are the only survivors of that group. I
don't understand."

"It may be the only lead they have."

"But why?"

He gestured impatiently. "Do they need a reason? That
heathen spectacle of blood they call their 'games' is going on.
It may be we're cheaper entertainment than the gladiators.

But if it comes to the rack, somebody's going to break, and God alone knows where it will stop.'' He folded his long arms. His eyes were only a brooding glitter in the deep shadows of his overhung brows. ''The Church has picked up a lot of dross in the last twenty years,'' he said finally. ''I don't know what kind of person would join a proscribed cult simply because it's proscribed, but there are those whose strength I doubt. And some of them know more than they ought.''

''Who's with you?'' asked Dorcas, and he shot her a glance from under those heavy brows.

''Ignatius and Agnes. Doriskos. Martin from John's group. That silly bitch Arete from Dioscordes' bunch.''

Dorcas said, ''You'll have to be broken out.''

Telesphorus raised his head, like a brooding eagle at the turning of the wind.

''I'll tell Papa.''

''If we can get you out of here yourself,'' rasped the priest. ''If not, pray God to grant us strength. At worst he may be able to save some of the others.''

''How long do you think you have?'' she asked softly, and he shook his head. The heavy tread of hobnailed boots passed in the corridor. They both looked up quickly, the small muscles in the priest's jaw standing out in a sudden relief of oily gold and blackness in the lamplight.

''Not long,'' he said in a strained voice. ''Let him know how we stand. His doctrines may be pernicious, but . . .''

In the grimy shadows Dorcas' cheeks colored. ''Papa isn't a heretic.''

Telesphorus' eyes flashed. ''No. But he rides a close line to it. Beware of him . . .''

The bolts rattled at the door. Dorcas got to her feet, startled; their eyes met. Then she said, questioningly, ''Wicked uncle?'' and Telesphorus nodded.

For a moment the question, if question it had been, made no sense to Marcus. But as the sentry returned he saw the subtle shift in the expression of the priest and the girl, each becoming, not different, but only what seemed to be a differ-

ent aspect of the same. The tension in Dorcas' face changed
to a kind of innocent horror, as though none of this had or
could have anything to do with herself. Telesphorus seemed
to grow stiffer and more withdrawn, but the wariness in his
leathery face turned to a kind of sly self-righteousness and he
picked up the basket she'd placed on the table and began to
examine its contents. With condescending concern he said, "I
thank you for your helpful thoughts, niece, but what you did
was foolish. Let us take care of our own. We have put aside
our families for a greater family, the Family of Christ. Meddling in it will only bring you trouble."

What Marcus could have sworn were tears glinted in Dorcas' eyes. "You may have forsaken your family," she replied
shakily, "but that doesn't mean your family is going to
forsake you. I don't understand your doctrines, but I'm not
going to leave you to starve." She started for the door,
drawing her veil once again over her hair. The sentry made a
move to block her way, but in the same instant she turned
back and said, with trembling chin, "I'll see you again,
uncle."

Telesphorus glanced up from the food basket, like an interrupted hyena. "If you plan to, you'd better get your ticket
early," he commented, with deliberate brutality.

Dorcas stared at him for one moment in stricken horror,
then burst into tears and pushed past the outraged sentry, her
running footsteps retreating along the hall. A moment later
the ladder creaked; the sentry gasped, "You self-righteous
old sod!" and cuffed Telesphorus hard enough to knock him
back against the wall. The priest clutched his food and snarled
at him. He seemed a wholly different man from the one who
had met Arrius' questioning with such quelling dignity. Had
he told them that the girl was no messenger of his he would
have been disbelieved at once; as it was, he had left her free
to take a message to the other Christians . . .

To the other Christians? Marcus thought suddenly, as Telesphorus was shoved brutally into the hall. *Great gods!*

He pushed against the door of the hidden closet, frantic to
stop her before she got away. Arrius had closed it from the

outside; there seemed to be no latch on the inside at all. Furious, he sprang to his feet, knocking his head on the low pitch of the roof, cursing in a most unphilosophic fashion as he rattled at the recalcitrant catch. *You'll have to be broken out,* she had said, and then, with simple unshakable confidence, *I'll tell Papa,* as though the one would follow upon the other. But she'd have to act fast. With any luck it was her father she would now seek.

In despair he threw his whole weight against the door, tripping over the stool in the process and precipitating both it and himself violently onto the floor of the examining room. He scrambled to his feet (stepping heavily on the hem of his toga) and stumbled for the door. In the back of his mind, as he blundered down the passageway, was a kind of amazement at the fakement; having seen the Christians fighting among themselves in the cell, he would never have credited even members of the same group with such capacity for quick, concerted action.

He threw himself up the ladder. The guardroom was now broiling hot, the sunlight glaring in through the open door. A clump of guards were grouped around a slimy little man in an embroidered blue tunic, who was marking down bets on a wax diptych. "Where's Centurion Arrius?" he gasped, and one of the men looked up.

"Gone off with some informer. He'll be back."

"It can't wait— Did that girl leave?"

The man nodded and jerked his grimy thumb toward the outside door, adding, "Poor little kitten."

Kitten indeed! thought Marcus, pausing only long enough to snatch up his shopping basket, then dashing outside. From the higher ground of the footslopes of the Capitoline, he could see the brown veil, making its way quickly among the scattered groups in the Forum below. He spotted her position and direction from his vantage point—crossing through the line of the monuments to the Caesars and heading for the corner of the Julian Basilica—and plunged down after her, trying to keep his toga out from under his feet and at the same time to look as inconspicuous as possible.

On any other day at this hour he knew he would never have been able to follow her across the Forum. But today its cobbled expanse was nearly deserted, only a stroller or two idling in the shaded arcades of its closed lawcourts. The sidewalk vendors were gone; so were the acrobats, the beggars, the sword swallowers who performed for a gauping populace. Distantly Marcus heard the rising roar of applause, an animal bellow of approbation, like summer thunder over the deserted streets. Quindarvis' games were evidently a wild success.

There was no crowd to hide her, but neither could he conceal himself amid the usual mob in the Forum. Keeping as much distance as he dared, he trailed her among the statues of the Caesars—that ill-assorted family-party of deities whose spirits still guarded the city that had murdered most of them— and through the shadows of Augustus' great triumphal arch. They passed the tall portico and round altar that marked the spot where Julius Caesar's body had been given to the fire, and crossed to the monumental shadows of the Temple of Castor and Pollux. Here the crowds were thicker, coming and going from the New Way and the shops around the base of the Palatine Hill. Marcus found himself snared in a gaggle of men around a Vespasian memorial, his shopping basket catching on someone's elbow. He tugged at it, cursing, casting a despairing glance after the girl as she vanished into the narrow New Way itself. By the time he'd got it free he had to run to catch up; moreover, the hare he'd bought for dinner was beginning to leak through its saturated wrappings, dripping down his toga and drawing after him curses and flies.

Ahead of him the girl was moving faster, heading straight along the New Way, the shadows of the overspanning arches barring her in a flickering series of patches of gold and black. Once she glanced over her shoulder, and his heart was in his throat lest she see him. But she turned neither left nor right. She followed a path beside a ruined wall, past the broken columns and tumbled masonry that had been Nero's fabulous palace, turned along the main way under the shadow of that incredible gilded porch. They passed the towering marble

Colossus, a 110-foot statue by the greatest dilettante of all
time . . .

. . . And he realized where she was headed.

When anyone said they were going to the Colossus, they
were seldom referring to that staggering piece of frivolity.
Already people had begun referring to the Flavian Amphitheater by that name. As he came around the corner and into the
mobbed square before those towering white walls, Marcus
heard the baying of the crowd again, a deafening elemental
howl like the sea. He made a run to close the distance as the
brown head-veil and blue dress plunged ahead of him into the
throngs that surrounded the amphitheater as thick as porridge,
and found himself entangled in an almost inextricable morass
of sidewalk fortune-tellers, blanket dancers, fig sellers and
bookies, each with their attendant mob of idlers. Ahead of
him the girl was edging and darting her way through the press
like a fish through weeds, and turtlelike, Marcus swam after
her. His shopping basket caught on some woman's parcel; he
tried to pull it free and found himself engaged in a desperate
tug-of-war, the woman shrieking and striking him with her
cane as Dorcas plunged into the roaring vaults of the arcade
that surrounded the Flavian itself.

With a final determined wrench, Marcus saved his dinner
and went shoving through the mobs into the shadows of that
preposterous edifice. The shadows of the arcade seemed black
after the sunlight of the square; the bellowing of the crowd
was deafening. He glimpsed Dorcas as she turned in an
arched doorway that led inside, and this time their eyes met.
Then she plunged inside and out of sight.

Marcus darted after her into a vaulted stairway whose
gilt-and-purple ceiling rang with the noise of the crowds.
Someone caught him by the back of the toga with a grip that
all but lifted him off his feet—"You got a ticket, boy?"
growled a burly man with an ex-pug's cauliflower ear.

"But I have to . . ." he gasped desperately.

"I know, I know," sympathized the guard, "but youse
still gotta have a ticket."

Marcus fumbled in his shopping basket, dropping the leeks,

trickling hare's blood down his foot, while people crowding behind him cursed at him in languages he'd never heard before in his life. He slapped the grimy bit of clay into the man's hand and ran up the wide marble stairs, pushing past the crowds that blocked his way. Sunlight streamed through the vast archway ahead of him, blindingly white on the dirt-smutched marble of the walls. It flashed blue-black on Dorcas' dark hair as she reached the top of the stairs ahead of him, pulled off her veil, and vanished past the archway into the light. Cursing, Marcus struggled into the open air.

The slopes of the arena stretched before him like a reversed mountainside, the white of citizens' and senators' togas forming a solid block to halfway up the slope, and from there, the blues and browns and dull greens that marked the ranks of the poor, of foreigners, or slaves. Overhead the vast awning rippled in the wind; in the center of the ring, where the sunlight struck directly, the white sand glared like salt, blotched with crimson dabblings of blood. From this distance the half-dozen pairs of men still struggling there looked very small. Their armor and weapons were edged in sun-fire as they moved—Thracians, like men of leather and bronze, faceless in their bizarre helmets, the lighter-armed hoplites dodging their blows with sun and sweat and blood gleaming on exposed flesh.

He swung around, scanning the crowds on the benches behind. In the teeming mob it was hard to tell, but he thought he saw one figure climbing the steps between the tiers more swiftly than the others. Without the head-veil for identification he could not be sure. He struggled to follow, tripping over feet, murmuring a spate of "Excuse me's" over the snarled yells of "Hey! Down in front!" Then another roar smote his ears like a thunderclap; as one man, the entire crowd was on its feet, surging around him and trapping him where he stood, roaring, "Make him fight! Get the irons! Coward!" Below, Marcus could see what had happened: A burly man in Samnite armor had lost his sword to a trident-man's net. He had no other weapon; he had dropped his shield and fled. From the gates in the fifteen-foot marble cliff that rose above the sand, men were coming out already, with whips and a smoking brazier. The Samnite wheeled, tried to change the direction of his hopeless flight; the trident-man, light on his feet as a terrier, was before him, driving him back against the barrier. Light flashed on metal, the blood leaping out to splatter them both; even the food vendors were jumping up and down yelling, "Kill him! Kill him!" The whole arena was one tornado of noise, over which the thundering *oompah* of the Flavian band boomed in incongruous counterpoint.

The man was down, doubled around his spilt belly. Amid the shuddering roar of the crowds, if he had cried out in pain, no one had heard. Slowly he raised himself on one arm, turned a helmeted head as gold and shapeless as an ant's toward the stands where the praetors, the sponsors of the games in the emperor's absence, sat. Impassive, the trident-man stood over him, his short dagger in his hand. Marcus recognized Quindarvis when he raised his arm, even at that distance saw the haughty dignity, the power in every well-timed gesture. It was at his signal that the victor helped his beaten opponent to kneel, placed the razor point of the dagger against the hollow of his throat. As all good gladiators should, the Samnite, in spite of his ruptured guts, leaned into the deathblow; the cheering of the crowd rose to a deafening crescendo, drowning out the thunderous fanfares of the band.

Men around him were already sitting down, murmuring approval and anticipation. Marcus remained standing, scanning the stands above him without much hope. He reflected that even if Dorcas had been trapped by the surge of the crowd, she had less far to struggle to reach one of the stairways that led from the topmost tier. And she need not even have done that: His vision blocked by the mobs all around him, he had lost track of the precise place in which he had last seen her. She could be any one of hundreds of tiny moving figures; for that matter, she could have seated herself on the nearest bench. Marcus felt a sudden surge of sympathy for whatever worthy young heroine of legend it had been who had been required to separate a mixed bushel of wheat, barley, and rye.

"You gonna stand there all day blocking the view, kid?" demanded a hairy-eared Illyrian with grease stains on his toga.

"Sorry," mumbled Marcus. He tripped over a long succession of feet on his return journey to the stairway and pushed his way through the tide of ascending crowds. It was only when he reached street level again and stepped out of the shadows of the surrounding arcade that he realized that his much-abused shopping basket swung considerably lighter in his hand.

One of the local cutpurses was going to have hare and stew for his dinner.

Marcus uncharitably wished the food poisoned and went dejectedly on his way.

VI

Stick to the good old ways, my boy, and do as I tell you. I hate to see a good man corrupted by the filthy, perverted manners that pass for morality nowadays.

Plautus

"I was had for a chump—a fool. A child could have done it better."

"Don't be so hard on yourself," advised Arrius easily.

"But I let her get away! She might be our last hope!"

"Not with half-a-dozen Christians in the prison, she wasn't." The centurion leaned his shoulders against the tiled curve of the niche and looked out across the vast expanse of steaming water and pink, heat-puffed, naked bodies. His arms, resting along the rim of the hot pool, were brown as leather up to the line where his tunic sleeve usually fell; after that they were startlingly white. Through the steam his greenish gaze seemed softened, as though, like asphalt, his soul become more malleable with heat. "She did exactly what I would have done, if I were being followed. And if her father's a powerful member of the cult, she'll have learned caution from the cradle. Did you stay for the rest of the games?"

"No," said Marcus in distaste, and Arrius grinned.

The Baths of Aphrodite were far less fashionable than the more elegant premises Marcus usually frequented. The arcaded roof was lower, and the big room with its warm swimming pool and series of hot tubs was far noisier. The clientele seemed to be mostly soldiers, laborers, shopkeepers and their wives, with some of the higher-class prostitutes of the neighborhood. Unlike the more stylish baths, these didn't have separate facilities for men and women. During their soak in the hot tub his conversation with the centurion had suffered several momentary gaps.

"You said yourself there's nothing more to be got out of the Christians in the jail," fretted Marcus. "They've had her since the night before last!"

"And we haven't heard—or found—a thing," replied Arrius stolidly. "They're holding her, you can depend on that. As for this morning, while you were out chasing skirts around the Flavian I got in touch with another one of my informers, greasy little ghoul that he is. He says he has another Christian for me."

Marcus had ducked his head beneath the surface of the heated water to rinse the sweat from his cheeks, but the words brought him up like a dolphin. "Where?" he gasped, shaking his lank curls from his eyes.

"At the Flavian. He'd have gone to the lions this afternoon if he hadn't been sick. The lion-keeper refused to send him into the ring, though why the silly bastard thinks lions will get sick from eating a sick man's meat is beyond me. They live half the time on carrion in the wild. He wasn't arrested for Christianity, in fact nobody knew he was a Christian at all, till he started raving."

"What was he arrested for?"

Arrius shrugged. "He wasn't—not technically, anyway. He was supposedly philandering with his master's wife; his master's a pal of your friend Quindarvis."

Marcus started to reply and saw that his companion's attention had been momentarily diverted by a bountiful young redhead, passing by with a towel thrown casually over one shoulder.

After a moment's reflection the centurion continued, "In any case, this poor ass can't have had anything to do with the kidnapping. But he might give us some names. Care to come?"

Marcus shook his head. "I—I have something else I have to do tonight." In his heart he was not sure which brought him more dread—the thought of another visit to the amphitheater, or the scrawled message that he had found upon returning to his lodgings, summarily bidding him to his father's house for dinner. "Did you learn any more from the Christians you have?" he asked, to change the subject.

"Nothing of value. And if what your girl Dorcas said to the priest was true—and there's no reason to think it isn't, since they didn't know they were being watched—it's no surprise. It's possible the kidnapping was planned by another group of Christians entirely, or that word simply hasn't got around about it yet." He sat up and splashed warm water over his face. In the main pool beyond, a rowdy fight had broken out, men yelling good-naturedly, women shrieking and laughing, the noise bounding off the mosaic arches of the low roof.

"So what are you going to do with them?" Marcus hauled himself up, dripping, onto the edge of the sunken tub, and deliberately ignored a wink directed at him by a fat black Libyan girl across the room.

"They're being transferred to the holding jail across from the amphitheater tonight. They'll stand trial tomorrow and be sentenced in time for the last day of Quindarvis' games."

Marcus stared. "That's awfully quick."

"I didn't give the orders. The games only last three days; it'd be a shame to waste 'em."

"But what if they're not guilty?"

Arrius had emerged from the water and stood dripping, like a scarred Neptune, drying his hair with a towel. He looked quietly down at Marcus. "Boy, they're guilty," he told him. "They've broken the law that forbids the worship of their crazy Jewish god, they've been formally denounced before a magistrate, and that's enough, whether they practice abominations as part of their rites or not.''

"They're not the only ones who do,'' Marcus pointed out.

"No,'' agreed the centurion. "We're surrounded by abominations. I personally think any cult that requires its priests to geld themselves in a religious frenzy—with, I suspect, the help of drugs—should be looked into, but there are temples of Cybele all over Rome.

"But it isn't the abominations. It's the politics. When times get bad people get scared, and they want to know that at least in their own lifetime everything's going to be fine. They want to kill what's troubling them. And since you can't blame the system or blame hard times, you blame the stars— which you can't fight—or blame a bunch of people who are messing things up, personally, for you. That's the Jews and the Syrians and the Christians. But the Jews are too powerful in the government—I don't think there's a department in the treasury that doesn't have its little Jewish clerk looking after things—and the Syrians have too much money. The Christians are a cheap target, and they've made themselves a target. They could sacrifice their babies in the Forum, so long as they handed a slice of the meat to the priests of the genius of the emperor.

"But they won't.'' He slung the towel over his shoulder and offered Marcus a hand up. A great splash of water was thrown out of the pool, dousing a vendor of honeyed figs; the vendor added his voice to the general noise in terms that, while undoubtedly Latin, Marcus had never heard before. "They won't,'' continued Arrius, unperturbed, "and that's where they leave themselves open. They aren't persecuted because they're maniacs, boy. It's because they're traitors. There's a lot of them, maybe more than we know; they work in secret; and we have no idea where their loyalties lie. That's what makes them dangerous.''

The town house of the Silanus family stood on the Esquiline Hill, not too far from the great baths. It was a new neighborhood, and fashionable. Many of the big houses contained shops and apartments as well, but his father's was not one of these. It might be more expensive, but at least the place didn't smell of cooking in every room.

Straton greeted him in the atrium, a roly-poly, gray-haired Greek who had looked after the details of the Roman house since Marcus was a baby. "How goes the philosophy?" he asked—a question that a number of people asked Marcus, but not all of them truly wanted an answer longer than "Fine."

Straton's question, however, fell into the other category, and Marcus gave the matter some thought before replying. "I'm not sure," he said finally. "Yesterday I would have said it was going badly because I haven't had time to be with Timoleon in the Basilica in days, but . . . I'm not sure whether I'm turning into a better philosopher or a worse one."

The Greek gave him a curious look and said, "If you can ask that question at all, you're probably turning into a better one." He lifted the hem of Marcus' toga, blotched with stains of hare's blood acquired during his pursuit of Dorcas with the shopping basket in his hand. Marcus felt his face turn scalding red, like a little boy who has dirtied his tunic. "Not a cleaner one, though," sighed the slave regretfully and helped him out of it, folding the massive weight of the garment over his arm with a deftness that Marcus had never been able to acquire. Though he ran a critical eye over Marcus' plain tunic, he said nothing; it was clean, at any rate, though the dark-blue linen was badly worn and faded.

"Oh, come on, old toad," called a voice cheerily from the drawing-room door, "don't you know philosophers are supposed to look like that? Positively bad appearance not to have a few frays in the hem, and all." Felix let the embroidered indigo curtains fall shut behind him and came striding across the room, holding out his hands. "Good to see you on your feet, Professor."

Marcus caught him by the shoulders, holding him off at arm's length. "Do I clasp your hand or kiss you?" he demanded, laughing.

"I beg your pardon, this is not a dress I'm wearing, it's a Persian robe! It's all the thing!" Felix bridled like an aspersed cat, clutching at the folds of the offending garment as if he feared it would be snatched off. "B'Castor, it cost me close to five hundred sesterces! Y'see 'em all over the town!"

"I suppose you do," murmured his older brother, considering the long drape of the sea-blue silk, the peacock embroidery of the long, full sleeves, "in certain circles. Turn around, sweetcheeks, I'm dying to admire it . . ."

"Well, it certainly beats that short little rag you're wearing," retorted Felix defensively. "Anyone with knees like yours ought to cover 'em."

"Oh, I agree, I agree," purred Marcus, "and believe me, you look utterly ravishing! Why, only today in the Forum I saw the cunningest little green slippers that would go with that . . ."

Felix pulled back his fist, his face pink under the teasing; Marcus' eyes were sparkling. A battle that, in all probability, would have finished in the atrium pool was averted by a third voice, absurdly identical to the other two. "Your politeness in admiring our brother's finery is certainly to your credit," it said, "but I am constrained by propriety to point out that seeing you together, I must judge Marcus' raiment to be the more manly, though it be frayed."

And as Caius Silanus stepped through the door curtain Marcus stuck out his tongue at Felix like a schoolboy. The oldest of the three Silanus brothers was, like his voice, an imitation almost to the point of parody of the other two. He was fully Marcus' height, and before he had begun to put on fat he had had that same loose-jointed gangliness. His brown eyes were grave, his hair, which like theirs was soft brown and curly, was cropped uncompromisingly short, which made his face look even longer than it was. His plain white linen dinner suit was discreetly embroidered with a single border of egg and dart around the hem of the tunic and the edge of the cloak, a quiet rebuke against everything the others wore and were.

"And how goes the philosophy, Marcus?" he inquired politely.

"Fine."

Caius was already turning to Felix. "Was your luck good at the amphitheater, Felix?"

"Dashed rotten," declared the dandy airily. "Silly brute simply lay down and let the other chap carve him to collops! Don't know where they found him. Racking good beast-hunt to finish the show, though. Chap killed a leopard with just one of those little pitchforks—one of those trident things they use . . ."

An underbutler brought up a folding backless chair for Marcus, set it down, and changed his shoes for the plain blue house slippers Marcus had brought in a bundle under his arm. He then carried away shoes and chair in a wordless aura of disapproval that his master's son would have sunk so low as to not have a slave of his own to carry his slippers for him.

". . . had a side bet with Trimalcho— You remember Trimalcho, Marcus? Anatolian or Parthian or one of those sorts, made a pile of tin on silks or amber or something of the sort, and now he's into everything . . . city rents, share in the Blues at the circus . . ."

Caius had already turned to conduct them into the summer dining room, leaving Marcus to deal with the interminable answer to his question. He didn't mind. As Felix would say, it beat the daylights out of trying to talk to Caius.

Their parents and sister and Caius' cowed-looking wife met them in the doorway of the small open room, and with one accord, each of the three sons bent his knee to the thin, small, bitter man who was their father; a man who hardly came up to any one of their shoulders. He favored Felix with a single, silent glance of absolute scorn and turned away from him without speaking. His hard black eyes flicked over Marcus. "I see you weren't too sunk in your own amusements to bother to come to dinner."

Marcus raised his head and said in a constrained voice, "I got Straton's note."

"I'm surprised that Greekling had the brains to leave a

note. But I suppose he could hardly have gone to search for you among all the bathhouses about the circus.''

It was on the tip of his tongue to protest that he never frequented the lower-class baths in that neighborhood, but since it was exactly where he had been today, he held his peace. His father took his silence for an admission and turned away coldly, to greet his eldest son with a warm handclasp and carefully measured kindness in his words. Looking up, Marcus met his mother's eyes, wide and brown like his own, and desperately unhappy.

''Well, we have been kept waiting long enough,'' declared Silanus. ''Like as not, thanks to Marcus, we'll get the first course cold and the second burnt.'' He held out his hand for his wife's, a peremptory gesture. She laid her soft, long-boned fingers in his hard little palm like a dead bird; he led her to the supper couch like an auctioneer escorting a slave to the block. Caius, with ponderous formality, took his wife's hand on one arm and his sister's on the other. Marcus wondered if he should offer to take Felix's hand, considering how he was dressed, but decided that this piece of levity would only precipitate the scene he knew was brewing. *Don't start the battle until the women have been got to safety,* he told himself bitterly. *They may as well get a meal in peace.*

The town villa of the Silanus family had three dining rooms, of which the summer one was the smallest. It faced out into the central gardens, open all along one side into the pillared peristyle that surrounded the immaculate handkerchief of grass, with its thick borders of lilies and roses, its scattered statues and covered walks. The tabletop was pink marble from Samos, on a base of elaborately wrought Corinthian bronze; the slaves, who had no surety for the wizened old man's changeable temper, moved in swift and slightly apprehensive silence. Typically, Silanus Senior had arranged things so that he and his eldest son were able to talk most easily back and forth, which they did, disregarding their ostensible dinner partners.

Marcus had not eaten under his father's roof in nearly six months. He remembered why, now, watching how his sister

picked at her food in cowed silence, not daring to raise her
voice to conflict with those of the men. Caius' wife looked
even more washed-out than usual—she was pregnant again,
Marcus saw, and her strained face had an unhealthy color to
it—and did not speak at all. His mother only looked across
the table at him once, to ask him how his philosophy went, to
which he replied, "Fine." He was more than ever thankful to
Felix, who, having firmly established himself as the family
fribble, was not expected to make decent dinner conversation
or understand it. Instead he kept his mother, sister, and
sister-in-law entertained with a light inconsequential patter of
news from the marketplace and the games (which all of the
women had been forbidden to attend by the head of the
house), while he tucked away every morsel in sight. Marcus
picked at the mull of tuna fish and eggs among the sharp
sauce and lettuce of his plate, listening with half an ear and
wondering why his father had summoned him.

". . . Nubian chap, or African of some sort, anyway,
absolutely ripping with a trident, y'know. Never saw the like.
Leopards're quick, quicker than lions by far—know a chap in
the beast-catcher training school who says he'd sooner take
on a pair of lions than a leopard. Says lions're cowards;
unless they're specially trained or into the way of it, they
won't attack a man at all. Unless he's wounded, of course,
and they get the smell of the blood . . ."

And riding counterpoint over that light, flutelike spate of
trivia, Silanus Senior's harsh rasp ". . . man of substance,
with lands and money behind him, and none of this town-
bred, trade-bought money that can be wasted putting on stupid
and expensive games to amuse a vulgar and idle populace. I
think your sister's dowry is sufficient, and as Garovinus has
been married twice before he should have no objections to . . ."

". . . expensive, though, dashed if I know where he's
getting the money to pay for the things. Dippin' into the
senatorial till, most like, which'll make it rough if they audit
the books when they change praetors in July . . . They say at
the Flavian he's been all to pieces these two years and more.
It's not as if he were one of the big landowners—he's not,

y'know—though mind you his wife has gold comin' out her ears. She's the one y'want to watch out for. They say in the Forum she has her own seraglio of young men and boys, keeps 'em out in a villa in the country. One of 'em bust another's nose in a fight, and spoilt his looks; she had the attacker whipped, but the poor chap with the broken nose, she had his throat cut, 'cause his looks were gone . . .''

"Nonsense! Your mother was married at fourteen! And in a time of the disgraceful decay of the Roman family it's a necessity for a girl to marry young, so that she may breed healthy children . . . Though with two miscarriages your Cornelia has been grossly slack in her duty. Stop picking at your food and either eat or leave the table, Aemilia! Though on the whole I don't believe in divorce—it's the rot at the center of the fabric of Rome—I have a good mind to have you and that worthless woman divorced when her pregnancy's done no matter how it turns out. Child'll like as not be so sickly it'll have to be exposed in any case.''

Marcus glanced across the table at Cornelia, as the slaves brought in the second course. The women of the Silanus household were forbidden to wear cosmetics, and it may have been only that which made her look pale and yellowish as old wax. It did not help, he thought bitterly, that Caius was nodding grave approval of every word his father spoke.

Sitting upright at the foot of her husband's couch, his mother leaned across to him, seeing him about to speak. "It's been so long since we've seen you, dear," she said to him quietly. "Your sister's getting married, you know.''

"So I gather," replied Marcus dryly.

"Of course, your father says that times are hard," she continued, as though his father were not always complaining about their nonexistent poverty and the decline of the House of Silanus. "But I think we'll be able to dower her creditably. We do have the credit of the family to think of. And of course, Garovinus is quite a wealthy man himself.''

"Well, he won't be, if he keeps on as he is," declared Felix, aside. "He runs with a dashed fast crowd, the whole pearls-in-vinegar set; he's been said to have spent upward of fifty thousand sesterces on a single banquet, not counting the wine. My guess is he needs the dowry to bring himself about."

Their father looked up sharply. "That's precisely the sort of gossip you would pick up in the baths and perfume shops. Lectus Garovinus is one of the most fashionable men in Rome, and a scion of one of the oldest families. His political influence is such that he may end up praetor, or even consul, one day. If you cannot restrain your cattiness, exercise it on one of your own set."

"Well, dash it, the man . . ."

His father's thin black nostrils flared to angry slashes. Felix glanced across the table, to where his sister sat in silence. Her eyes were red-rimmed, but she was making a valiant attempt to obey her father and eat. Marcus guessed she would very likely throw it up the minute she was out of his sight.

Lamely, Felix finished, "The man's not the sort of man I'd like to see married to m'sister, is all." He returned his attention to his plate abruptly, picking restlessly at his spiced shrimp, his painted eyelids lowered and his face taut under the rouge.

His father added viciously, "With as little experience as you have with manliness, Felix, I would venture to say that you're hardly qualified to judge."

Felix said nothing.

Silanus slammed his cup down on the marble. "Answer when your father speaks to you, boy! What this house is coming to I don't know!" His wrinkled little face stained a sudden red; in it his eyes were like two burning coals. "In the days of the republic the House of Silanus was one of the most powerful in Rome, that even the House of Caesar sought to ally itself with. We ruled Rome! If the republic still stood, my voice would be heard in the highest councils, and my sons would have retained the manners and respect that I've tried to teach them.

"But what have I got instead?" He looked spitefully around him, daring any of them to speak. "A painted whore who does nothing but spend my money chasing boys. A worthless chattering Sophist who's worse than the Greeks he wastes his time with, since they were born what they are, and he deliberately made himself to be like them. An arrogant and disobedient trull of a wife . . ."

Marcus started to speak, and his father cut him off with, "That's what comes of marrying somebody's dowerless poor relation. There was bad blood in all your mother's family, and the rot at the core of Rome has made it worse." He turned suddenly, black malicious eyes glittering, to his wife. "You haven't said much for yourself, Patricia Pollia Cato." The tone was a command. Lady Patricia raised her bowed head and in gracious, rounded sentences agreed with his evaluation of Roman society and the degeneration of the House of Silanus. In her face Marcus could see what he had seen for a long time—her awareness that anything was better than to continue the quarrel.

He found he had lost what little appetite he'd had.

When the dessert dishes were cleared, Silanus dismissed his slaves and his women with a few curt words. A good-looking, rather shy boy of fifteen or so came around with a crater of wine. Silanus lay propped on his elbow, restlessly turning his winecup in nervous, prying fingers, and watched his middle son with hard penetrating eyes.

"What's this I hear about you getting mixed up in some disgraceful business with the Christians?" he demanded, when the boy had gone.

"It is a disgraceful business," replied Marcus in a low voice. "They've kidnapped Tertullia Varia."

"So I heard," snapped his father. "I'm not surprised. Aurelia Pollia is little better than a Christian herself."

"She is not!" said Marcus, stung.

"All those eastern cults are the same. Mewing mystagogues fawning over a bunch of dirty eunuch priests—bah! I said when she went over to whatever worship she's favoring this year nothing would come of it but trouble, and so it has."

"It was still no reason to forbid Mother to see her."

"You leave your mother to me, boy, and don't take that tone. I'm still the owner of this house and, I might remind you, I pay you an allowance you'd be hard-pressed to feed yourself without. If all your philosophy has taught you is disrespect for your elders, I can't say I have much regard for it."

Marcus took a deep breath and, as Augustus Caesar had once advised, began to tell over the letters of the alphabet to himself. At *L* he said quietly, "Yes, sir."

"How did you come to be mixed up in it?"

"Purely by chance, sir. I was talking to Tullia in the street when she was on her way home the evening before last. When her litter was ambushed I tried to keep the men from carrying her away, that's all."

"Hmph. If that was all, for what reason did you go with some soldier down to the prison? I'll thank you to remember that you were born a gentleman's son, even if you don't choose to act like one. Your actions reflect upon the house as well as yourself. I can't have it bandied about Rome that you've taken to hanging about the barracks like some cata-mite whore. Wasting your time and my money among your worthless philosophers is bad enough."

"They're not worthless," began Marcus, and his father cut him off with an impatient gesture.

"Not to themselves, surely, if they can persuade young ninnies like you to pay to speak with them. But beyond that they produce nothing. They can philosophize from one year's end to the next, and have not enough of anything at the end of that time to fill a thimble. But it's an occupation I've seen pursued by other sons of gentlemen, though they have the decency to remain under their fathers' roofs while they do it, and not live like paupers in the lowest slums of the town. But to hang around the barracks—"

"But they need me to help identify the Christians who kidnapped Tullia!"

"Fine things your philosophers have done for your man-ners, boy, if they teach you to interrupt a man who has just fed you, before the covers are even off the table! Those repulsive lapdogs your mother used to keep had better manners."

"Yes, sir," said Marcus quietly. "I'm sorry, sir."

The old man nodded grimly. "The Praetorian Guard is paid to keep order in the city. It's their business to do the dirty work that the watch can't handle; it's their business to round up criminals and perverts. There's no need for you to dirty your hands with it."

"But they need me to find the men who did it," argued Marcus, trying to keep his voice steady.

"They're all the same, aren't they? Christians, Jews—it's the same thing. And if they round up the lot of them and throw them to the lions, Rome will be the better for it."

"But we may not find Tullia."

"Stop prating about that stupid chit! They'll find her." And his eyes narrowed unpleasantly as he saw the unguarded look that flared into his son's face. "So," he said, his voice honeyed with scorn. "It's more than your civic duty after all, is it, that leads you slumming on a Jew-hunt? That's quite a bit of work, isn't it, to find her only to restore her safe to some Phrygian's bed—if he'll have her, after."

Marcus was aware of a hand gripping his arm and knew that he'd made an involuntary move to rise. Glancing sideways he met a wide, frightened, warning look in Felix's eyes. He had almost forgotten the presence of his two brothers. His world, it seemed, had compressed to the small cubicle of fading daylight, his father lying lean and withered on the crimson cushions with the dark wine sparkling in the cup in his hands.

"You little ass," said Silanus softly. "You really think even if you do rescue the little bitch her stiff-necked demagogue of a father is going to turn her over to you? Or that I'd let any get of that pandering politician Varus into this family, even if she hadn't been rutted by half the criminals in town? What'll you call your son—Christos?"

With a violence of which he had not thought himself capable Marcus wrenched his arm free of Felix's grasp. In a single quick move he rolled from the couch and blundered out of the room. Somehow he found his way to the darkened atrium, snatched the folded toga off the one-legged table by the wall. The lamps had not yet been lit; in the semi-darkness he heard his father's harsh voice echoing in the dining room, demanding that he return. The toga unraveled itself in weighty folds all around him. He fought and cursed at the unwieldy thing, sobbing with rage and frustration, and ended by flinging it off, determined to carry it through the dark streets in a bundle under his arm.

A voice from the hall door said, "Let me." Caius, with lumbering firmness, removed it from his grasp. "I may not possess Felix's elegancies of education, but I hope I may know how a Roman gentleman drapes his garments. And be sure to change your shoes. I won't have my brother padding about the streets of Rome in his house slippers . . ."

"Gods curse it, am I never to do anything without the approval of the entire house and all my filthy ancestors?"

His older brother paused in his work and laid a ponderous hand upon his shoulder. "I confess I consider our father's remarks uncalled-for," he said gravely, "but he remains our father. I am sorry to see you return his scorn with disrespect."

"What would you have me do?" demanded Marcus furiously. "Bow and kiss his feet like you do? Turn myself into a faded dishrag like Mother? Let him drink me like a vampire until I have no will of my own?"

Caius turned him around to face him and looked gravely into his eyes. "Lower your voice when you speak so of him in his own house."

Marcus was silent, his breath coming in thick fast sobs, the rage in him already burning down into slow smoldering coals of shame. *Timoleon would never so forget himself,* he reflected bitterly. *In Epictetus'* Enchiridion *he exhorts us to understand that an event will be what it will be—I knew this would happen. It always happens, with Father.* But these reflections did nothing to ease the slow familiar cold and sickness growing within him, the wretchedness of defeat by the little tyrant in the supper room.

In silence, Caius draped his toga, found his street shoes, and handed them to him. As he put them on Caius asked him, "Tell me. Would you say that Felix is his own man?"

"Felix," said Marcus shakily, "I would scarcely count as a man at all."

"Perhaps," agreed his brother. "But nevertheless he is enough his own person to wear a gown like that to dinner, and slide from under our father's wrath simply by not replying. Aemilia will not marry until she is fifteen, despite all my assurances to Father that negotiations are proceeding, and she will certainly not marry a man with Garovinus' shocking reputation for dissolute living. But I will never tell Father so."

Marcus wrapped up his house slippers without replying.

"Marcus, listen," urged his brother. "It does you no injury to say, 'Yes, sir.' And after, you may truly do as you please, for you are of age, and he surely would not parade the affairs of our house through the lawcourts trying to establish his legal rights over you. The most he can do is disown you and cut you from his will, which he has not done yet. But any politician may tell you that lies are the price of peace."

"But my vocation is truth! I'm a philosopher!"

Caius regarded him soberly for a moment. "What is truth?" he asked. "There is truth and truth. Whom does it harm?"

"I don't know." Marcus turned away, feeling suddenly exhausted and sick. "Maybe Truth itself. Maybe I'm only using it as a weapon with which to strike at him, because I can't fight him on his own ground. But I—I respect him too much to simply tell him one thing and do another. He's going to have to face truth—real truth—about something someday, and I'd rather he faced it about me now. And I have my own truth to find."

His older brother's face seemed to grow longer in the shadows, as their father's occasionally did when he saw his children joking and laughing, or speaking their own secret languages among themselves. "I cannot say that I understand this stubborn quest whose only end is words," he sighed. "But I wish you luck upon it nevertheless. And on your other endeavors as well."

Marcus turned away bitterly. Like a ghost from the shadows the Macedonian doorman had materialized to let him out—he realized the man, whose sleeping cubicle let into the vestibule, must have heard every word of the conversation. No wonder people said slaves knew everything.

A heavy hand stayed him. "Search for her, younger brother," said Caius kindly. "After she is found, we shall see what can be done."

From the supper room a harsh querulous voice rose again, telling Felix not to be a worse fool than he was and shouting for Caius and Marcus to return at once. Caius clasped his brother's hands and nodded to the doorman to let him out. As he passed under the smoky lamp in the vestibule, Marcus saw that while he'd been at supper, Straton had had his toga cleaned.

VII

Allow me to be eaten by the beasts, through whom I can attain to God.

Saint Ignatius
of Antioch

It was a long and bitter walk down the Esquiline Hill. Like an ugly specter, Truth stalked beside him.

His father had spoken the truth. What made him think that just because he rescued Tullia Varia from the Christians—if he rescued her—he'd be any closer to having her than he had been before? Whether or not that mysterious Syrian would have her—and he might perfectly well—why did he think that he himself had any chance at all? To return to his father's household and tutelage might give him sufficient prospects of wealth, but the doubled hatred of her father's politics and her mother's religion were enough to make his own father forbid the match. And what made him think that if and when she was found, she wouldn't accuse him of wanting to take her out of pity, even if his father would stand for it? In all their bitter quarrels through his boyhood and youth, he knew that tonight was the closest he had ever come to striking the old man.

104

For speaking the truth.

What kind of philosopher am I? he wondered desperately. *To so lose myself in a mere human relationship, especially with an impudent little vixen like Tullia? Why beat my heart to death against the wall of my mind that knows that I'm seeking to rescue her to have her become some other man's bride? And knowing this, why does the very thought of her turn my brains to mush and make my palms go damp? How can I call myself a philosopher if I react with fury when someone says something that I know to be true? Or even if they say something that I know is not true? Timoleon never would.*

I'm no more a philosopher than Felix is, with his racecourse gossip and his pointless bets. But Felix has enough of a grasp of his own truth to realize it, while I'm still clinging to what some other man has called true. Maybe that's what gives Felix his kind of silly integrity. He may not be much of a man, but he isn't all things to all men. He certainly doesn't live a lie.

A variety of shallow considerations drifted through his mind, from suicide to membership in a frontier legion. But he knew already that he would do no such thing. Almost without his conscious volition, his restive footsteps carried him down the dark streets, through the ruins and overgrown patches of parkland that had once been Nero's house, toward the white bulk of the Flavian, glimmering like the moon itself on the dark brow of the hill.

The show had been over for some hours, but the amphitheater itself teemed like an anthill. Though most of the shops in its arcades had closed down, the pillared shadows were alive with sweepers, cleaning up trash and date pits, broken clay tickets and lost articles of clothing; all around the corners of the little streets and squares in the dark looming shadows of the hills, wineshops poured their dirty yellow light out into the cerulean softness of the evening. As he walked along the arcades, Marcus was accosted half-a-dozen times by whores of various sexes, and twice by touts hawking the odds on tomorrow's races, which would be held over at the circus.

The wineshop across the square was lit like a stage in the darkness; he could see gladiators lounging at its marble-topped brick counter, big scarred men with buffed muscles that caught the sliding lamplight. He recognized one of them, the gangly trident-man he'd seen earlier in the day massacring his Samnite opponent, and wondered if after surviving a bout like that the wine tasted any sweeter. There were a couple of bandy-legged little charioteers at the counter as well. The corners of the wineshop were wreathed in heavy festoons of fruits and grape leaves and flowers, all twined in blue silk ribbons, a clear announcement that the drivers and grooms and stableboys of the Green, Red, and White charioteering factions had better steer clear.

From a huge dark archway to his right a man emerged, stinking of urine and sweat, like a dyer's shop, and scarred all over his body, like a dog-chewed piece of leather. Marcus caught him by the arm and asked if there was a centurion down below talking to a condemned man, and the beast-catcher, after subjecting him to a long scornful scrutiny, allowed, in language so foul as to be almost unintelligible, that there was.

Marcus went on up the dark stairs.

Though he had haunted the place as an adolescent, he had very little idea of how to get from the public portions of the Flavian to its underground mazes where beasts, prisoners, and props were kept. In the vaulted immensity of the passage, his footfalls echoed weirdly, and up ahead, through the arched and gilded opening, he saw the stars, white and cold and shining in the blue of the night sky.

It did not seem to be the same place as it had been that afternoon. The silence, the emptiness, changed it, the starlight on its thousands of concentric marble circles making each faint crack and shadow eerily clear. Below him the white sand lay in a round, oceanless beach, still smelling faintly of the raw feral stink of animals and blood. Round it the marble wall gleamed in a flawless ring of white, its gold rail gleaming softly under the uncertain light. From here the noises of the city seemed distant, attenuated, the rattling of the wheels of produce wagons on the cobbled streets softened to a rumble like the sea worrying the rocks on the shore. Beneath the ground a lion roared, a fauve and African sound in the milky Italian night. Somewhere iron creaked, and a man's voice rose in rich Greek and undying musical love.

A shadow appeared, small and black and wavering, upon the sand.

"Oh precious boy, your cheeks are like the roses,/ Those eyes the pools in which my love doth drown . . ."

Marcus walked down to the gilded rail. "Hullo!"

The man paused with his sand rake and shaded his eyes against the uncertain starlit distance. "Hark ho!" he called theatrically, "Walks Endymion by starlight?" The accent was a combination of Ionian Greek and Vatican wine.

"Does that door you came through lead down to the prisons?"

"Sweet nightingale in darkness, it does."

Marcus judged the drop for a moment, then slithered under the railing, lowered himself over the marble edge to the full length of his arms, prayed briefly for the best, and dropped. It was farther than it had looked in starlight, but the sand was soft. Like a man crossing a desert he trudged toward the black maw of the beast door and its tall loose-jointed keeper, who had begun to moondance with his rake.

As he had feared, the man ceased his dancing at his approach and pirouetted up to him. He stank of wine, but, Marcus supposed, if your job was to go rake up snippets of human bodies out of the sand at the end of a long day, perhaps it paid to be drunk to do it.

"Ah! And why sojourns sweet Endymion, lover of the faithless lady of the moon, to these insalubrious shores?" In the starlight the man's face was brown, claw-scarred, and foolishly smiling; he leaned on his rake directly in Marcus' path. "The fruits of the seas these shoreless sands do yield . . ." He held up something from the bucket that hung at his waist, two human fingers stuck together by a rag of skin. "Here's shrimp that'll never crawl into a gold-lined purse again."

"Very nice," said Marcus queasily, and tried to edge his way past.

"You don't like shrimp?" The man interposed himself before the door, leering good-naturedly. "They aren't to the taste of all, I fear. What toll shall you give me then, fair boy, to let you pass?"

"I'm afraid there's been some mistake," Marcus said politely. "My name is Orpheus, not Endymion. I'm looking for the road to hell, and I fear"—he took the rake from the janitor's hand, stood it upright like a sundial, and consulted the resulting shadow on the sand—"I fear I'm desperately late."

"Yonder lies hell all right," said the drunkard, his smile momentarily fading. "You've but a short little trek, Orpheus, and no goddess at its end, either." He leaned closer, surrounding Marcus in an affectionate arm and a vast reeking gust of stale wine. "But there! Now what's our toll?"

"You have your toll," said Marcus quietly, stepping back and holding up his hand to make a sign in the air as he had seen the priests of Isis do in processions. "I have set my music in your mind and heart, and my dancing in your feet. What more can sorrowful man ask of the children of gods?"

The drunkard bent his long supple body in an exaggerated bow. "Nothing, my lord."

Copiously leaking sand from every fold of his toga, Orpheus passed him by and plodded on into the maw of hell.

The passage stank of animals, the musky stench of big cats mingling with the sharper odor of jackals. He could hear their roaring somewhere quite close and remembered Felix's prattling voice from earlier in the evening, describing how the lions of the amphitheater were often trained to hunt men. The passage was pitch dark, and he wondered for a horrified instant if his drunken psychopomp had deliberately directed him into the cages themselves. But no—it was from this door that he'd seen the man emerge.

Other sounds reached his ears, shrill and confused. As he felt his way along the wall he remembered that on the last day of the games there was supposed to be a colossal beast-hunt, a mass slaughter of the most exotic creatures obtainable. Their voices dinned upon him from the darkness, a cacophony of screeches, growls, bays; the liquid slurp of water and the sudden booming belling of crocodiles, the wild frightened braying of wild asses. As he groped his way through the windings of those stinking tunnels, green or amber eyes flashed out of the darkness at him, the floor fouled and mucky under his feet. He blundered through the room where the Flavian band kept its instruments. Hunched like beasts themselves in the darkness were the gleaming rims of tubas, octopuslike groping shapes that turned out to be bagpipes, grinning monster teeth that were in actuality the pipes of the famous water organ. He turned a corner in the darkness and stumbled against the bars of a cage; there was a chorus of growls and swift sudden movement in the murk. A hand seized his arm, and he almost died of fright.

" 'Ere, wot yer doin', scarin' my babies?'' snarled a voice from behind him. By the greasy ocher gleam of the single corridor lamp, Marcus could see a horrible old hunchback, his head bald and laced with scars, one eye socket gaping red and empty, with a reek to him that would have done credit to any lion in the place.

"I—er—I'm looking for the holding area for the condemned prisoners. The—the centurion's a friend of mine.''

The hunchback sniffed and pointed down a corridor "That way. Still no call to go a-puttin' my lambs in a fret.'' Growling, he shambled to the bars of the lion cage; as Marcus hastened down the new gullet of blackness, he could see the little man reaching through the bars to scratch the lions' proffered ears. Presumably, he thought, they weren't going to put their good man-killing lions into the beast-hunt. A cheaper grade of lion, perhaps, or those who were sick or injured.

The big holding cell had, up until today, contained several dozen people, "dishonest persons,'' as the law called them, condemned for infamous or disgraceful crimes. Though slaves had raked out the filthy straw, the place stank of ordure, the smell overlain now by the sharper reek of sickness, vomit, and putrefying flesh. Only a tiny seed of light hovered above a hand-lamp, the gleam of it picking out the brazen edge of an armored body from darkness, the angle of a broken nose, the smooth line of a muscle rucked and broken where it was crossed by a scar. In the blackness beyond he sensed restless movement and the whimpering of a man in agony.

Arrius glanced up at the grating creak of the door. "So you decided to sit with the sick after all."

Marcus nodded wearily. "Have you learned anything?" He gathered his toga about him and seated himself on the damp clay floor at the centurion's side.

"Not much," said Arrius. "He was wounded when he was taken; gangrene's got to it, and fever. I doubt the lions would have touched him." He rubbed at his eyes wearily. The stink of the wound turned Marcus queasy and sick. He was glad the centurion had not asked where he had been that evening, or why he had returned here.

Arrius went on, "He's been pleading on and off with his father to forgive him for leaving the faith. He's a Syrian Jew: I guess there's enough of a difference between Jews and Christians for him to think he's betrayed his father by going over."

"Anything that causes you to leave your faith is evil to the Jews," said Marcus. "Your faith is your family, it's your nation; you're a traitor to everything if you leave."

Arrius raised his brows curiously. "Really?"

"Of course." He kept his voice low, though he was certain that the dying man was too far-gone to hear. "One of the other students with me at Timoleon's was the son of a strict Jewish family, and they raised a terrible dust when he turned philosopher. I remember his father used to come down to the Ulpias and have bitter quarrels with Judah, calling him traitor, Greek, apostate; accusing him of helping the men who razed the Temple of Jerusalem . . . It was terrible." He looked out unseeing into the cramped stinking darkness of the cell. "At least my father never did that. I remember afterward Judah would sometimes be sick for days. It's—it's more to them than it is to us. Maybe that's why he and I were friends."

He leaned around the centurion and looked down at that wasted brown Semitic face. The young man was white under his tan, his skin dry and his eyes sunk in black pits. On his heaving chest gleamed the silver emblem of the fish, its chain shining like a ring of sweat around the tight-corded muscles of the straining neck.

Amid a salting of black stubble his white lips moved, mumbling cracked words in Aramaic, "Abba—abba—" and a string of broken phrases.

"What's he saying?" whispered Marcus, when he had again fallen silent.

"Calling on his father. Says he was called—he had to follow. Something about the son of David, whoever David is."

"David was their great king," whispered Marcus in reply. "Judah—my friend—used to tell me there was a prophecy that David's son or descendant would reunite the Jewish nation, and they'd go on to conquer the world."

Distantly a lion roared, and at the sound the dying man whimpered pitifully, fumbling with dry hands at the bandages over his stinking wound. He began to whisper again, desperate.

"He says he was cheated," translated Arrius after a moment. "Cheated of the glory of God. He says the gates of heaven will be closed to him. His death was not in the Lord's name."

"Didn't the Christians this morning say something about that?" whispered Marcus, and the centurion nodded.

The dying man clawed suddenly at Arrius' hand, his eyes opening wide. "Papa," he gasped. "Papa . . ." His voice trailed off again in broken Aramaic. He began to sob weakly, clutching at his bandages, rolling back and forth on the heap of urine-saturated straw where he lay. Disturbed by his convulsions, a huge roach scurried indignantly across the grimy floor. Arrius carelessly crushed it with one hobnailed boot. Then, with no more ceremony, he pulled his dagger from his belt, reached across to take the Christian by the hair, and slit his throat.

Marcus turned his face hastily away, unwisely closing his

teeth on the rising vomit and getting it, burning, in his nose instead. Darkness and the harsh coppery reek of fresh burning blood closed around him.

Arrius slapped him roughly on the shoulder. "Come on, boy, let's go."

He helped him get to his feet, and led him through black stinking corridors and out of the abyss.

They did not speak until they were in the wineshop across the street.

"Interesting." Arrius poured wine from the jug a black-eyed Dacian slattern set on the table before them. "You hungry?"

"Quite the contrary," murmured Marcus weakly. "What was interesting? Besides the accommodations, I mean."

" 'Papa' was the only Latin word he used."

Marcus frowned. "But he was asking his father's forgiveness for leaving the Jewish faith."

"But he was speaking in Aramaic," the centurion pointed out. "He called his father *'Abba'*; probably as he had done in childhood. The only word in Latin was 'Papa.' Who's Papa?"

"Dorcas' Papa?"

"That was my thought."

Marcus set down his cup. To his great surprise the wine stayed down, and moreover made him feel better. It took the taste of straw, and human filth, out of his mouth and, with them, the taste of his father's bread. "Then he might not really be Dorcas' father at all."

"He probably isn't," agreed Arrius, removing his helmet and laying it on the bench at his side. "The Christians aren't the only ones to use a family terminology. The priests of Mithras are called 'father.' " He leaned his chin on his hand and stared thoughtfully out across the dark square, where lights were still visible in the gladiators' compound opposite the moonlit bulk of the amphitheater itself.

Others were filtering into the tavern now, as their duties freed them: janitors, cage-keepers, doctors. In the smutty orange glare, Marcus made out the shape of the drunken sand-raker, leaning on the shoulders of a doll-faced boy of ten or so. At the next table a couple of bovine gladiators were discussing technique, using their three-inch cloak pins for swords; across the room a trio of prostitutes, gaily tricked out in togas of blue and scarlet, were leaning on the marble-fronted bar, shrieking with laughter over the labored witticisms of a well-dressed young blood with gold dust powdering his hair and cosmetics that looked as though they'd been laid on with a plasterer's trowel. The voices grated on Marcus' nerves, brazen in the tawdry light; the place smelled like the changing room of a third-rate bath. He leaned his head on his hands, feeling suddenly drained and sick. His father, Felix pirouetting in his new robe, Dorcas in her brown head-veil, and the sand-raker moon-dancing with bloody hands—all blurred together in his exhausted mind. Soaking in the baths with Arrius seemed years in the past; wandering the streets in the predawn gloom to do his marketing, his cane basket slapping at his side, might have been an event that had taken place in distant childhood.

Arrius' voice cut through his weariness like a blunt sword through flesh. "So tell me about your friend Nicanor."

Marcus looked up with a start. "Hunh?"

"Prefect Varus' physician. The one our girl friend put the kiss on this morning."

He felt as though the wine had turned to poison in his belly. "But he's not a Christian."

Arrius drained his winecup. "You sure about that, boy?"

Marcus was silent.

"I'm going to spend tomorrow," he went on slowly, "with the city hangman and that pack of lunatics. I'm not looking forward to it. Of the two that woman said were connected with Nikolas and company, Telesphorus may be too tough to break and his pal Ignatius too crazy. And I don't know how much anybody else will know.

"Now that bitch could have been lying. But I'm not willing to risk Tertullia Varia's life on that. If I draw a blank tomorrow, I may have to start calling in my other debts. When did Nicanor enter Varus' household?"

Marcus said unwillingly, "About two and a half years ago."

"Who'd they buy him from?"

"Porcius Craessius, I think. A private sale. I don't know why."

"Can you find out for me, without rousing anyone's suspicions?"

A police informer, thought Marcus, feeling suddenly stained within. He nodded miserably, unable to meet the centurion's eyes.

After a moment Arrius said, "Why'd you become a philosopher, boy?"

He stared unhappily down at the dark surface of his wine. "To seek the truth," he quoted. "To find the good, and the beautiful."

"Of those three," continued the soldier, "what's the most important?"

Marcus looked up. "They're all the same thing. They're what is—that is, True, and Good, and Beautiful."

"What if you found out the truth was ugly?"

From across the square somebody yelled, "Baby-eaters! Corpse-fuckers!" There was a clamor of catcalls, the deep baying of the mob. Against the darkness of the New Way, torches swarmed, their light wavering over the dark teeming bodies, the hard brazen flicker of mail. A voice cried, "Have that one, you poxy whore!" and a woman's voice began shrieking curses. A double file of soldiers entered the square, their burnished helmets gleaming in the ruddy light, and like a dog pack around a garbage cart the mob boiled on all sides, jeering and laughing, bending down to pick up rocks and dung from the road. Between the soldiers Marcus could clearly pick out the Christians: Telesphorus with his high bald head flashing with an oily sheen of sweat, Arete stumbling, sobbing, her dark heavy hair like a cloak over bowed shoulders, Ignatius shaking his fists and screaming back at the mob. The other Christians followed in sullen, frightened silence. He saw a rotten fruit explode against Telesphorus' back, heard the shrill chorus of profanity that accompanied it, both of which the priest received in stony silence. He found himself thinking that this man—kidnapper, pervert, and cannibal that he might be—was above his revilers.

He turned to his companion and saw the centurion's mouth drawn together in a single hard line of distaste. "Do you think Papa will save them?" he asked him softly.

"It isn't my affair to speculate," replied Arrius in a dry voice. "My affair is to find out who he is."

"Who?" A staff was leaned against the wall beside Marcus, a second jug of wine set in the midst of the table. Looking up in surprise Marcus found himself confronting bright fierce blue eyes under white brows like a hawk's.

"Sixtus!" he said in surprise. "What are you doing—I mean, I thought you never . . ."

"The locks and bolts on my gates deceived you into thinking that I never emerged into the light of day," replied the old aristocrat easily. "Hello, Arrius. Did you learn anything from your miserable Christian?"

"How'd you know about him, you old devil?" grinned the centurion, reaching up to clasp the blunt scarred hand in greeting.

"Don't tell me there's another reason you'd pay calls in that lion-reeking den." The scholar took his place on the bench beside him and regarded him with mild challenge in his lifted brows. "So you did join the Praetorian after all."

"I did, and how you knew me after all these years is more than I'll ever figure out. And it's just conceivable," he added haughtily, "that you're wrong about there being a Christian at the Flavian whom I went to see. I could be having an affair with the head cage-keeper."

Sixtus studied him gravely for a moment, as if giving the matter careful thought. "Unless his taste has sadly declined, I hardly think he'd find you any rival for a handsome young lion. And as for how I knew you, you look a good deal like your father, you know. And a boy of your enterprising nature would be bound to end up in the Praetorian Guard."

Arrius sighed. "Don't you ever find it a little disappointing never to be surprised by anything?"

"Not really." The old man poured out a cup of wine for himself. "The last time I was truly surprised it was by a cobra under a rock in the desert, and since that time I have endeavored to avoid all occasion for it." He looked out across the dark square. The guards had formed a semicircle around the door of a brick building at the corner of the gladiators' compound, and among the crowding backs of the mob, the Christians could be seen entering the building under the escort of more soldiers from within. Most of the crowd from the wineshop had gone to join the fun; only the sand-raker remained, moodily pouring raw wine down his throat, oblivious to all else.

"So those are your Christians?"

"Prime bunch," agreed Arrius.

"If one isn't particular about one's entertainment, I suppose so. Is there really a tunnel from the holding jail to the pits beneath the amphitheater?"

The centurion nodded. "It runs under the square. There's another one to the gladiatorial barracks. The whole compound there is barracks—the stables of the Red chariot-racing faction lie just beyond. The whole quarter between here and the circus is like that, lodgings and stables and armories."

"It must be a joy to police. Have you learned anything from your poor Christian?"

"Not much. He was far-gone." Arrius poured himself another cup of wine; his fourth or fifth, Marcus thought. Perhaps there was more to that curious, complicated man than the brutality he had shown in the prison. "Only—who is it that the Christians call Papa?"

Sixtus frowned. "What do you mean, 'who is it'?"

"Arrius thinks they could be referring to a kind of archpriest."

"Possibly," agreed the old man doubtfully. "But that would imply some kind of overall organization, wouldn't it?"

Arrius laughed unexpectedly. "Have you ever seen a roomful of Christians? I thought we'd be taking up the bodies in the morning."

"Oh, yes," smiled Sixtus. "As I said to Marcus earlier,

Antioch was crawling with them, all of them preaching brotherly love and ready to scratch one another's eyes out over whether the Christ had one nature in two bodies, or one body with two natures, or one and a half natures or whether he existed corporeally at all. I suppose that is the remarkable thing about Christianity: that it is attempting to apply logic to mysticism, to make rational sense of what is essentially irrational.''

"The remarkable thing about Christianity," growled Arrius, "is the damn Christians. Do you know what that scrawny little monkey Ignatius has been doing all afternoon? He's been trying to bait the guards into killing him, so he can die for his faith and go straight to heaven. The poker-backed old priest finally told him not to tempt the judgment of the Lord, and that set the rest of them off again. Lunatics, all of 'em. I've never seen anything like it.''

"Oh, it's quite the thing to die for one's beliefs." The old man leaned his back against the wall behind him, his scarred hands resting at ease on the scrawled carvings of the filthy table. He looked as at home in that grubby tavern, with its crude paintings of gladiatorial murder and ill-assorted ruffians at the bar, as if he had spent the last five years here instead of in study and meditation in that leafy cave on the Quirinal Hill. "It's easier than living for them. And in any case where their Savior led, they are eager enough to follow.''

Arrius grunted and poured himself another cup of wine. "You'd think their god would have picked a better way to go than a punishment reserved for traitors and brigands. If he did die that way, that is.''

"Oh, he certainly did," said Sixtus. "Back in the days when I was an arrogant junior staff officer of the Tunis garrison I talked to the centurion who had been in charge of the punishment squad at Joshua Bar-Joseph's execution. In view of the fuss that was made over the execution itself, and the rumors that went around immediately after, he remembered it quite well.''

"So he actually saw Bar-Joseph die?" said Arrius.

"Oh, yes.''

"What was he like?" asked Marcus curiously. "Bar-Joseph, I mean."

Sixtus was silent for a time, his chin resting upon his knuckles, his eyes seeming to lose their focus as they turned inward, remembering another night, in perhaps another tavern. "He said he chiefly remembered Bar-Joseph as being very tall, and quite strong," he said at last. "He was supposed to be able to break a cornel-wood spear-shaft in his hands, but had that gentleness you often find in big men, who have seldom had to fight. Longinus said it surprised him that he died so quickly. A crucified man will sometimes die in as little as twelve hours, depending on how it's done, but others can hang on for days."

In the warm darkness beyond the wineshop lights a stallion whinnied. Faint, bitter arguments could be heard floating from the barred window of the jail.

"Of course, Longinus admitted that the garrison had used him very badly through the previous night." The old man's eyes seemed to flicker back into focus, looking sharply from Arrius to Marcus beneath their heavy lids. "It's always the late-night watch that catches all the bad squad, you know. And evidently there were a couple of real toughs in the Jerusalem garrison who egged the others on. They were all rather drunk, because of the festival, and after a week of Messianic agitation, and rumors, and threats of riot, the guards were keyed-up and dangerous. Jerusalem was always a bad station, and Pilate was such an incompetent governor that the men were ready to lash out at anyone or anything. Longinus said by morning the Nazarene could scarcely walk, much less carry the beam of a cross through the city and up a steep hill—they'd flogged him with a leaded whip, and I suspect he had internal injuries from the beating as well. Longinus said he never spoke a word to them, from first to last."

"And was he dead," asked Arrius softly, "when they took him down from the cross?"

Sixtus nodded. "Quite dead."

Most of the crowd had returned to the tavern by this time, joined by others, gladiators or soldiers of the watch. At the bar, amid whoops of encouragement, a black-haired whore was attempting to drain twelve winecups in succession; the smell of lamp oil and cheap perfume and spilled wine was everywhere. From somewhere close by, the beasts of the Flavian could be heard roaring and growling—you could probably hear them in the jail as well, thought Marcus, and remembered the dying man in the stinking cavern below the amphitheater again.

He asked, "Why a fish? Because Bar-Joseph was a fisherman?"

The scholar shook his head. "No, in point of fact he was supposed to have been a carpenter, though most of his followers were fishermen. The fish is from the anagram of the Greek words for Jesus Christ, Son of God, Savior—Iesus Christos Theou Yios Soter—ICTHYS—fish. And of course, the symbol of the fish itself is sacred to other faiths from that part of the world as well . . ."

"There," said Arrius suddenly, pointing. "There he goes."

Marcus looked up, startled. From the darkness of a street that led up the Caelian Hill a litter emerged, surrounded by its host of bodyguards, torchbearers, slaves, and hurrying clients; a splendid equipage liveried in the bright colors that marked an eastern taste. The litter itself seemed to be plated entirely in embossed gold, the lotus-buds on its handles glinting with jewels. The embroidered curtains had been thrown back to reveal an enormously obese Syrian, clothed in a bright primrose dinner suit whose hems were a handspan deep in sardonyx, bullion, mother-of-pearl. His black close-curled hair was cut short, like a Roman's, and glistened with unguents. Blue silk ribbons fluttered from the knot of emeralds that tipped his cloakpin. His sausage fingers were thick with rings, as though he anticipated a fight and went prepared with a cestus made of gold and gems.

"Who is it?" Marcus asked in distaste. "I've never seen anything so vulgar in my life."

"It's your rival in love, boy," grinned Arrius unkindly. "That's Chambares Tiridates, the pride of Phrygia and potentate of the East."

"East bank of the Tiber, anyway," commented Sixtus, referring to the location of the import warehouses that were the source of the Syrian's wealth.

The litter and its procession halted in the midst of the square; the man inside called out and waved. A charioteer in a gaudy blue silk tunic detached himself from the bar at the back of the tavern and went striding past the table where Marcus and his companions sat, and ran lightly to the litter's side. Gold curly hair glinted in the light of the surrounding torches; Tiridates was evidently wishing the man luck in the races tomorrow. After a moment the huge merchant leaned down to kiss the charioteer full on the mouth, a salute that was received with practiced enthusiasm. The bearers, resignedly, shifted their grip to compensate for the sudden list of the chair.

"That's them!" whispered Marcus. "That's the bearers—look, you can see the bruise on the nearer man's face."

"Sturdy brutes," murmured Sixtus appraisingly. "They'd have to be, of course."

"So he didn't sell them!"

"I never thought he had," mused the centurion. He glanced sideways at Marcus. "You think they'd talk to you?"

He shrugged. "I don't know. They might recognize me as a friend of hers, but nobody in Tiridates' household knows who I am. I mean, that I—that Tullia—" He broke off in confusion, and Arrius hid a grin.

"Think you could pass yourself off as a slave?"

"Not in a household," Sixtus objected. "Someone would notice. There's a thousand things that would give you away as a free man, you'd stand out like a vestal in a whorehouse. Find out where he's having dinner tomorrow night and slip yourself in among the other linkboys and litter-bearers on the doorstep or in the nearest tavern. People talk to anyone about anything when they're forced to wait."

"He'll be out at that supper-party Praetor Quindarvis is giving at his villa tomorrow night," supplied Arrius. "Because of the Christian problem we've been asked to put an extra guard on the Naevian Gate.'' He turned to look at Marcus. ''Think you can do it?''

He nodded shakily. ''I can try.''

''Would Quindarvis agree to pass you off as one of his slaves?''

''I don't think we can risk asking him.''

They both turned to stare in surprise at Sixtus.

''Think about it,'' said the old man. ''From all I've heard—and believe me, Churaldin is a spy network in himself—Priscus Quindarvis is a climber. Look at the crowd he habitually entertains. Lectus Garovinus. Porcius Craessius. Men who are all far richer than he is, and viciously dissolute—men he can prey on. He's supposed to spend a fortune staying in the running with them.''

''That's what I've heard, too,'' put in Marcus suddenly, as various bits of Felix's gossip fell into place in his mind.

''If he's courting Tiridates, would he want to risk it getting back to him that he's sent a police informer in to pump his slaves?''

Arrius bit his lip thoughtfully. ''You have a point. And if we ask his permission and he refuses, he'll be on the lookout.''

''Whereas ordinarily I doubt he's ever been in the slaves' courtyard of that country palace of his. No—I think the best course would be to pass Marcus off as one of my own slaves.''

''Yours?'' said Marcus, considerably startled.

''I admit he doesn't know me from Tiberius Caesar—yet.'' Sixtus rose and drained his winecup. ''But do you think that after I call on him in the morning to thank him for the handsome recompense he sent to my slave, I won't be able to secure an invitation?''

Marcus shook his head. He was beginning to come to the conclusion that there wasn't a great deal that this frail, formidable old aristocrat couldn't do.

VIII

. . . everyone there seemed to be completely drunk on aphrodisi-
acs. . . .

Petronius

"One thing you must remember." Sixtus held out one arm, and the burly old Greek who generally looked after his ruinous gardens draped the toga over it, arranging its folds in a simple elegant style some forty years out of date. "To be what you wish to seem is not only excellent philosophy, but also very good advice for spies. To pretend to be something you're not is not only almost impossible, but painfully obvious. You must put an element of yourself into your persona, and you must take elements of that persona into your own heart. Temporarily, you *are* a slave, and you have to think like one."

Marcus, seated on the foot of the narrow bed that was one of the few pieces of furniture the Spartan room contained, remembered Telesphorus and Dorcas at the prison, playing "wicked uncle" for the benefit of the sentry, with her life and freedom as the stake. "But all slaves don't think alike," he protested.

122

Sixtus shrugged with his eyebrows, so as not to disturb his valet in the midst of an accomplishment of one of the "great arts." "Of course not. But slavery affects the way anyone thinks. What sort of person would you be if you were a slave, Marcus?"

"I don't know. I hadn't really thought about it. Pretty much the same sort of person I am now, I suppose."

"Really? You must have an extraordinarily strong character. I'm afraid that had I grown up from childhood with the knowledge that I could be summarily punished, even unto death or several things a good deal worse, for things I didn't do; the knowledge that I had no rights whatsoever; the knowledge that my life, my education, my body, my friends, my wife were totally at the whim of persons considerably less intelligent than myself—I'm afraid I would have turned into a terrible rogue."

Marcus remembered Nicanor, pleading for his silence; Quindarvis saying, "The man should be put to death, and if he was mine he would be . . ." about a man whose only crime had been to do as he was ordered. As though he'd read his mind, Sixtus continued, "That old chestnut about the slave who's punished for obeying his mistress's orders to climb in bed with her is a situation that happens tragically often. Can you wonder that slaves are popularly credited with slippery morals and a propensity for telling lies?"

"I suppose under circumstances like that," he replied slowly, "a brotherhood, a solidarity—even if it was based on whatever abominable rites the Christians practice—would be almost understandable. I mean, a slave's life is forfeit anyway, isn't it?"

Sixtus stepped back from his valet and looked at Marcus consideringly. "I think you're beginning to understand," he said. "Thank you, Alexandros," he added. "I have always felt guilty about letting your talents as a valet atrophy; I'm pleased to see one doesn't get rusty at this sort of thing." He turned to view himself in the polished bronze of the mirror. The toga lay in the simplest possible drape, but the folds fell like carved marble, showing off the quality of the weave and the perfect shaping of the garment itself.

"You do get rusty, a bit," replied the big slave mildly. "That there drape's not hardly the style no more, but it suits you, sir, better nor what the double-crossed folds in the front would, that men are wearing now."

"I bow to your wisdom," said the scholar humbly. "Thank you."

"That hired chair's gonna be here pretty quick. I'll be back." And with the sketchiest of bows the slave departed.

"Yet I wouldn't call Alexandros a liar, or say that his morals are particularly bad." Marcus looked through the open door into the colonnade in the wake of the gardener. "He seems to be pretty attached to you."

"He's been with me a long time," admitted Sixtus. "I'd like to think that he trusts me. I've offered him freedom for him and his wife, or sale to some fashionable nobleman who would do his talents as a dresser credit, and he says he'd prefer to remain as he is—stubborn Greek. And I admit I should hate for Phyrnne to leave the household. I've become much addicted to her cooking."

Marcus looked around at the stark cleanliness of the small whitewashed room. Through the latticework of vines that walled in the pillared walkway, he could see into the jungles of the garden, silent and somnolent in the late afternoon hush, where the gray cat slept on a sundial mossed over with disuse.

"You don't have many slaves, do you?"

"Actually, I have over a thousand," replied the old warrior mildly, "but they're all on the estates. I suspect my steward cheats me," he added regretfully. "And as for this house . . . Well, I suppose I've rather let things slip. One does, I'm afraid." He looked around him at the chipped tiles, the overgrown garden, the great elegant house grown dusty and empty. "But what's the use?"

And for an instant Marcus heard in his voice the tiredness of an old man who has been dragged from the safety of his chosen retreat, the sadness of someone who is aware that he has gone badly downhill but is not quite certain where he took the wrong turning. He felt suddenly sorry for him, and ashamed of himself for dragging him back to the noise and brilliance of the world he had quitted, to be a stalking-horse for his own affairs. But as he turned, an apology on his lips, Alexandros appeared again in the doorway, carrying a couple of cold torches, cloaks in case the evening grew chill, and an ebony shoecase containing his master's houseslippers.

"The chair's here."

"Where's Churaldin, by the way?' inquired Marcus, as they emerged from the vestibule to find the hired chair and its six bearers waiting in the street.

Sixtus' eyes twinkled. "I didn't ask."

"Boy's pecker's too damn long for his own good," grumbled the huge gardener, helping his master up the step and into the litter. It occurred to Marcus for the first time that this was what Sixtus might have meant when he spoke of his slave's "other faults." With his dark handsomeness and that curious quality of aloof pride, the young Cymry must be enormously attractive to women. And yet he had never impressed Marcus as a womanizer; although, he reflected, his heart turning over at the thought of Tullia, sometimes there was no accounting for women.

He remembered that his father kept the slaves locked in their rooms at night. One night he'd caught the boys' pedagogue stealing out to meet a woman and had sold him next day to a broker bound for Gaul.

Marcus was coming to understand how a talented manservant like Alexandros would prefer to dig this man's gardens, rather than leave his house.

The villa of Priscus Quindarvis stood two or three miles from the outskirts of Rome, close to the Ardeatine Way. A walled parkland of many acres surrounded it, scattered with dark groves of cypress and plane trees, green rolling land rich in the lucid sunlight of the late afternoon. As the hired litter approached the wide steps of salt-and-pepper marble that led up to the tessellated pavements of the terrace, Marcus caught a glimpse of burnished peacocks spreading their gaudy tails in the shade of fountained arbors. Not far off through a belt of trees, zebras drank at a marble tank at the feet of an image of Pan.

An Ethiopian doorman in livery of red silk met his master's guests on the steps. As Sixtus stepped from the litter Marcus had a quick look at the front of the villa, the high walls white and brilliant as meringue in the slanting sunlight, the pillars of the two-story porch pink marble, their garlanded capitals basalt and gilded malachite. Statues of gods and heroes—Hercules, Venus, Mars, Helen, Alexander—stood among the shrubs that flanked the terrace, half again life size and carved out of black marble, with draperies of red porphyry so fluidly carved as to appear to be agitated by violent winds. Even the immortals, grinned Marcus to himself, wore the uniform of the household. In the dim shade of the pillared porch two guards, ex-gladiators by the look of them, in silver armor and crimson plumes, stood to attention as Sixtus passed between them and out of sight into the shadows of the house, with Alexandros padding humbly at his heels carrying his slippers. For all the notice the kingly old aristocrat paid them they might have been bootscrapers.

The bronze doors shut. Marcus was on his own.

There was a big courtyard at the back of the house where the litters were taken. Two or three were there already, including an equipage of gold and ebony that would have done for the pharaoh of Egypt and must have required at least a dozen bearers. Only one guest seemed to have come from town in a cisium, and the brightly painted two-wheeled sporting carriage was drawn up at one side of the gate, its shafts resting on an abandoned bench. Marcus, whose ribs still smarted from the kick he'd collected from the Christian kidnappers, tried to picture riding in the unsprung vehicle even under the best of circumstances, and felt slightly ill. Dead drunk, its passenger would be likely to die of seasickness before they ever reached the gates of Rome.

Marcus had a story ready that would account for his inexperience, but no one in the slaves' court paid him much attention. There were already upward of thirty assorted bearers, linkboys, and footmen lounging on the benches; many of them evidently knew one another well. (As they must, he reflected—as well as their masters and mistresses knew one another. Everyone in Rome went to the same parties.) Someone had already got up a dice game in the shade of the porch. A couple of men started flirtations with the maids who emerged from time to time from the steamy confines of the kitchens; one of the Nubian bearers, stripping off his gold loincloth and jewels, challenged all comers to wrestling, and soon the courtyard was a fog of aureate dust.

Someone called out a greeting. Another litter was coming through the arched gateway, its gilded lotus-blossom shafts borne on the shoulders of eight men. Tiridates had evidently turned out his whole fleet of chair-men to carry him in comfort to and from the party. Marcus recognized one of the men at once—the right-front corner man, with his bruised face and his white teeth flashing in a grin as he returned the greetings of his friends. The other man he wasn't so sure of—he thought he knew him, but like most Romans, Marcus was bad at recognizing slaves.

He started to move toward them, not to speak but simply to establish himself as part of the scenery, when a small, light-boned hand touched his arm, and a woman's voice purred, "Haven't seen you before, have I, pearblossom?"

Marcus turned, startled, gasping, "Uh—there must be some mistake . . ." and found himself looking, not at another kitchen wench, but at a woman who was clearly one of the guests at the feast.

She pursed painted lips at him, and murmured, "Oh, I don't think so." Insinuating fingers wound in the fabric of his tunic; gentle, insistent pressure drew him into the shadows of the porch. "My, but you're a good-looking one."

Marcus knew that this was patently untrue. But he returned the compliment, stammering, "Uh—you're very —very beautiful—er—too," although, as he was drawn closer to her, he knew that this was untrue, too. The makeup gave the impression of beauty, rouge blossoming delicately on a background of white lead, lapis and malachite painted around the rather protuberant blue eyes, the whole surrounded by a stunning coiffure of snailshell curls built up six or seven inches above that fair white brow. But closer inspection revealed the haglike lines buried under the cheeks, the disguised puffiness beneath the eyes; and all the pastilles in the world couldn't cover the wine reek on her breath.

"Do you think so?" she crooned.

Marcus hastily disengaged his hands from where she was guiding them. "I—er—yes, yes of course. But they'll be missing you at the banquet . . ."

"Oh, that!" She shrugged half-uncovered shoulders, and staggered slightly, falling against him. "You know, I've always preferred to take the first course in private . . . if you know what I mean."

Marcus backed hastily and bumped into the wall of the alcove into which she'd led him. She giggled thickly, her hands sliding down his body, "You be good to me," she purred, "and I'll be good to you . . ."

He gasped, pushing her away; aside from philosophic principles and the fact that he wouldn't have mounted a hag like her if he'd been the worst rake in town, they were virtually within full view of the rest of the slaves' court. She lunged at him, and he ducked aside, escaping into the porch that ran along three sides of the court. She staggered after him, her voice blurry with drunken anger. "I'll tell your master! I'll tell old Priscus . . ."

Wonderful, thought Marcus. He dove through the first refuge that presented itself, through a doorway into the steamy darkness of the kitchen. The place reeked of spices, oil, and sweat; down at one end the head cook was sculpting a gigantic boar from goose-liver pâté, at the other, a downtrodden-looking girl of about ten was resignedly stuffing dormice with a paste of honey, saffron, minced mushrooms and chopped cherries, and arranging them in concentric rings on a golden dish. There seemed to be about a hundred people crammed into the tiny space, stripped to their stained loincloths and yelling at one another in Sicilian: plucking swans, peppering flamingo tongues, and swatting roaches for all they were worth. Marcus ducked through the confusion, and out the far door as his ladylove's voice grated down the porch, "I'll tell them to have you cut, if you're not already, you . . ."

He slipped through the far door and out onto the terrace. The terrace on this side ran the length of the villa, paved in lapis tiles into which the zodiac had been worked, in mosaic of red and gold. He hurried cautiously down its great length, listening for sounds of pursuit. Though none came, he decided that perhaps it would be better to let some time elapse before returning to the slaves' court. A confrontation, for whatever reason, with a drunken Phaedra and an indignant Priscus Quindarvis did not bear thinking of. He reached the end of the terrace, swung over the low carved railing, and dropped to the ground below.

From his family's villas—one near Naples and two in Gaul—he knew the layout of country palaces in general. But those had been the centers of working farms, the source of the family income. They had as little to do with this green silent paradise as a plow horse has to do with a thoroughbred. After the unceasing din of Rome, the crowded, reeking, grilling days and the endless clattering insomnia of the nights, this place was like the heaven of the gods. The clear darkening air was fragrant of citrus, of water and shrubs; the very solitude was like a cool drink after long delirium. In the silence he could feel his grief lessen. His fears for Tullia, his misery over his helpless guilty hatred of his father eased like the loosening of a constricting bandage. From an oak-crowned hilltop some distance from the house, he could see the lights of Rome, but it was as though he looked on another world. For the first time in many days, peace descended on his soul.

Confident as children in the safety of their protected glades, dark-eyed Arabian gazelles stared at him in the twilight. On a turning of a woodland path a deer emerged from the ferns almost under his feet and stared at him affronted, like a king who has encountered a charwoman in his anteroom, then faded back into the invisibility of the myrtle. Through the trees the lights of the villa glowed amber in peacock-blue dusk. He could not have been more than a few miles from Rome, but surely, he thought, the Greece of the ancient legends had been like this. It would have caused him no surprise to come upon Diana, the moon tangled in her dusky hair and her white hounds about her feet, hunting supernatural prey in the evanescent woods.

He topped the crest of a hill as the wind behind him died, and found himself staring into the huge amber eyes of a black-maned Numidian lion.

The violence with which he started almost lost him his footing and tumbled him down the fifteen feet of separating cliff. He caught his balance against the bole of a beech tree, staring down in shocked horror at the huge carnivore. The lion stared upward unwinkingly, its eyes like firelit mirrors in the twilight, lashed its tail, and growled deep in its throat. A chorus of growls replied. From the brush that circled the bottom of what Marcus realized was a broad enclosed pit, two lionesses emerged, rippling and tawny in the near-darkness. Beyond them other shapes moved, prowling in the shadows of the round pavilion that stood in the midst of the enclosure. The change in the wind brought their rank sharp stink up to him, and he shuddered with the memory of the pit below the Flavian.

The little pavilion was dark, though through its open pillars he could glimpse the liquid blue of the twilight beyond. Silhouetted against the light among the black shadows of the encircling pillars he made out what he thought were supper-couches and a table, lampstands and statues; under the eaves of the domed roof he could see the pediment festooned with elaborate garlands carved in stone. In spite of himself he had to admit to a kind of fascination with the place—what a setting for an intimate supper! The floor of the supper room was on level with the lip of the pit, joined to it by a single narrow footbridge. The lower story would contain kitchens, or perhaps, thought Marcus, looking at the bronze door that was the only break in the sheer wall of the ground floor, lodgings for the keeper of the beasts. To be served the finest of foods and wines while the lions prowled below—it was the sort of contrast Quindarvis and his friends reveled in.

In spite of the sheerness of the wall around the pit, and his conviction that lions could not leap so high, Marcus found himself looking over his shoulder more than once as he hurried back toward the villa through the darkness of the scented woods.

When he returned, the banquet was proceeding full-swing. A series of curtained arches looked out onto the long eastern terrace; half-a-dozen men could have concealed themselves in the shadows of any one of the huge supporting columns. He identified his erstwhile attacker at once, on a couch at the far end of the enormous dining room. Whether she'd had her private first course or not, she and the man she shared her supper-couch with looked to be starting in on a second course of the same. The slaves, no doubt well-trained, ignored them; the others at their table seemed too busy gossiping to notice.

The din in the room was unbelievable. Flute players preceded the slaves who moved about among the tables, playing in the wine and accompanying the wiping-up of spilled delicacies with popular airs. At the head of the central table Quindarvis lay, different from that cynical, proper magistrate who was so welcome in the home of his cousin and political patron. The cynicism had turned to a kind of oily mockery, not only of the ills of society but of its virtues as well; the propriety, Marcus saw, was a kind of camouflage, a magnification of the keynote of whatever surroundings he happened to be in. In his dinner suit of midnight blue, its borders flashing with flames and stars of gold and amethyst and pearl, he was one with the prodigal richness of the room. The woman beside him might have been fashioned of gold and ivory, as was the couch they shared; her hard, rather round face was fair under its rouge, her massive frontage of curls bright as electrum, the thin tissue of her thread-drawn silk dress as white as the massive breasts jutting under it. She was feeding him the honey-dripping little dormice on a golden skewer and laughing at his surreptitiously groping hands.

They weren't the only couple already slightly gone in their

cups. A tremendous guffaw drew Marcus' attention; a big coarse-featured man whom Marcus recognized as Lectus Garovinus, his sister's betrothed, had seized the pretty young boy who was going around with the wine, holding him around the waist and kissing him amorously, while the hyacinths fell from the boy's dark curling hair and the wine spilled in his struggles. The comedian who was entertaining between courses with a cutting account of his latest amorous exploits paused in mid-story, turned his head like a lean black hound only deigning to notice the intrusion of a cat into its territory, and called out, "Let the kid go, Garovinus, some of these nice people ain't been served yet." This elicited a bellow of laughter from the room, and Garovinus obeyed with an owl-ish grin. The floor beneath his supper-couch was already heaped with eggshells, olive pits, and two spilled winecups. Marcus turned away in disgust and returned to the porters' courtyard.

He found the entertainment there hardly better. A fire had been lit; some of the kitchen girls had come out, wiping sweaty faces on the hems of their tunics; the talk drifted from sex to the amphitheater and back again. The day's chariot races received exhaustive postmortems, lap by lap and crash by crash, and were compared unfavorably to those given at the Roman games last year. Speculations on the honesty of the races and universal cursing of the bookmaking trade were aired. Someone passed around a big wooden bowl filled with jumbled leftovers of the last course served—blood sausage of bear entrails, fat mullet with sharp sauce, flamingo tongues stewed in pepper, dates, mustard, and wine. There were hardly any tongues left; Marcus found two, forgotten behind a leaf of sodden lettuce. Someone remarked on the dancers who were going to entertain after the next course. Someone else said, "That's nothing—you remember that party Porcius Craessius gave six months ago? That guy who'd trained a jackass to copulate with a whore? Never saw anything like that in my life."

"That's nothing compared to that broad who has the three mastiffs, what's her name? Lana? Alandra?"

"How about that time at the Neroian when they had all these dancing-girls on this fake island, and after the naval battle they sank the island, and all the crocodiles crawled up . . ."

"Yeah, I remember that, you never saw such a bunch of startled tarts in your life!"

"Or how about the time . . ."

"Hell, I'll tell you one," growled a grizzled little linkboy with a broken nose. "This was years ago, when Domitian was rounding up the Christians. I remember there was this one old woman—must have been sixty, seventy years old—practically throwing herself at the lions. You know how they do." He laughed, revealing brown stumps of teeth. "But the damned thing was, they were new lions, they'd never been in the arena before, and they were all upset by the noise and the sun, and they ran away from her! So here's this old broad out chasing the lions, the lions are running away from her, and finally one of the beast-catchers had to come out with a cleaver and hamstring her, so they could get the smell of blood and attack. I nearly wet myself, I was laughing so hard."

"Shit, I'd run away from a Christian too, if she was singing' hymns," grunted somebody else. "That caterwaulin' deserves death, even if they didn't eat babies."

"They really eat babies?"

" 'Course they do. They hold 'em up by their little feet an' slit their throats into a big cup kind of thing, then they pass it around . . . I got a cousin who married a Jew, which just goes to show, 'cause she'd screw anything that didn't have tits . . ."

"Yeah, I hear them Jews and Christians kidnap older kids, too . . ."

Marcus sipped at the thin sour wine, moodily watching the faces in the firelight. Between the slaves and their masters there didn't seem to be a great deal to choose.

He could see the two Arabs, sitting with the other slaves who wore Tiridates' livery. They were all Arabs or Syrians, hawk-faced and swarthy, their dark hair cropped close and their muscles shining in the red glare. Their heights had been matched to an inch. He saw one of the men—the man with the bruised face—look across the crowded dusty court at him and frown, as if trying to call his face to mind.

In time someone got up a game of knucklebones. The remains of another course were brought in great wooden bowls: the remains of peacocks and pigeons roasted with damsons and yellow with saffron, a scattering of oily, half-eaten artichokes, the butchered remnants of the pâté boar. The voices from the supper room were rising louder, audible even in this court, and shrieks of laughter and the drifting strains of music could be heard distinctly. Marcus caught the Arab bearer's eye. The man's brows dived down, startled, as he recognized him; he quickly rose from his place and slipped out the courtyard door into the night.

After a moment, Marcus followed him.

It was by now almost the sixth hour of the night, and pitch black. Pausing to let his eyes adjust to the darkness outside the court's bonfire-light, Marcus could see no sign of the bearer. He looked around doubtfully, then made his way back toward the terrace, hoping this was the way his man had taken. The noise grew as he approached the supper room, everyone trying to talk over the music, punctuated here and there by a shrill scream.

An androgynous pantomimist was dancing the courting of Venus by Vulcan with a hunchbacked, lame, and truly deformed dwarf. The men were shouting with laughter, roaring their approval as the golden-haired sylph slipped through those big hairy arms, danced away from the dragging steps. As Marcus watched, a candied date caught Vulcan squarely on his hump, and someone in the audience yelled, "Dead in the gold! Ten points for Plotina!" Marcus scanned the room quickly, glimpsed Tiridates soddenly stuffing himself on peppered thrushes' legs dipped in wine, ignoring his graceful, sloe-eyed dinner companion who was being uncontrollably sick over the foot of the couch. Another man rolled heavily to his feet, staggered toward the tiled arch of a discreetly curtained door, stopping only to collect a peacock plume from a silver vase that stood on a table outside it.

The feast, thought Marcus, was obviously a success. He stepped cautiously back from the shadows of the pillars that concealed him, cast a quick glance up and down the terrace for signs of movement. Something stirred in the dense bar of blackness cast by a statue at the top of the steps, and Quindarvis' voice floated to him, thick and annoyed in the mellow sweetness of the night air, with words he did not catch.

A male voice with all the quality of plum syrup replied, "My dear Priscus, anyone would take you for a tradesman's son, to complain of costs! The life of a gentleman is to expand himself, to taste the sweetness of the world, to live as befits a man. To do otherwise is to diet oneself at the banquet of life. And speaking of banquets, dearest, didn't you say there was a course entirely composed of little gamebirds coming up?"

He could see them, outlined against the moonlight. Quindarvis had changed his dinner suit for one that was mint green stitched all over with silver. A wreath of white roses was gummed by unguents into his dark hair. As a noise caught his attention he turned his head sharply, the flat planes of his face grotesque in the shimmering light of the summer moon. The smears of melting perfume made streaks in his rouge. "Who's that?"

Three men materialized from the stairway below. Marcus could see that two of them were the ex-gladiators the praetor kept as bodyguards, big men with slab-sided, bovine faces and the bodies of athletes run slightly to fat. The man in between them—a menial slave by his dress—was wringing his hands and weeping in terror, shaking so badly that his captors had to support him between them. One of the gladiators said, "We found him out behind the litters in the court, sir. Drunk as a sow."

"Oh," drawled the fruity voice in fading accents. "How utterly gross." The man caught his own balance unsteadily on the base of a statue. "If there's anything I cannot stand, it's a drunk slave. Take him away and drown him in the fishpond."

The gladiator glanced for confirmation at his master; Quindarvis nodded. "Do it." The slave collapsed, sobbing with terror and clutching at the praetor's knees, choking that he hadn't meant it, and begging for his life.

"What'd you mean, you didn't mean it?" asked the other man languidly, and hiccuped. "You did it, didn't you? Really, slaves have the most amazin' view of the world."

In the thickness of the concealing shadows, Marcus felt ill. *The boys throw stones in jest,* the poet Horace had once said. *But the frogs they throw them at do not die in jest—they die in earnest.* The sweet strains of heartbreakingly lovely music, flutes and cithara and the glittering tinkle of the sistrum, sounded from the supper room; the gladiators took their victim down the steps toward the green murky water and razor-sharp weeds of the fish pond, and Quindarvis and his dapper friend recrossed the terrace, passing within a few feet of Marcus without seeing him. ". . . I fear if there's another one of your excellent courses in the offing, my dear boy, I shall really have to pay a little call on the vomitorium before I can go on . . ."

He slipped from his hiding place, moved lightly down the deserted terrace. There was no sign of the Arab, so he doubled back, puzzled, to the slaves' court, wondering if the recognition he'd seen in the man's eyes had been a mistake, and he'd merely left the court to relieve himself in the bushes outside. But he was not there either, among the group of men still talking idly of work and the games and women, or among those who were lying resignedly down in the dust or on the pavement of the porch to sleep. And in any case he knew the man had known him. He must be waiting for him somewhere.

But he could find no sign of him in the whispering groves of trees that surrounded the house itself. Nor did he find him in the most obvious meeting place, a half-ruined shrine covered with rambling roses that stood in the midst of the gardens a dozen yards from the house. Annoyed with himself for not having tried to make contact with the man earlier, he returned to the terrace, determined to return to the court and have a try at the other bearer who'd carried Tullia's chair that night, provided he could recognize the man.

The noise from the supper room had risen to a crescendo of shrieks above the striving of the voices and the music. Through a fog of crimson lamplight, the room seemed to blaze with colors; even in the cool open air of the terrace, Marcus was sickened by the stench of wine, spilled food, and vomit. A troop of little girls was enacting a masque of nymphs surprised by satyrs in the forest, and either they had not expected to be truly molested by the goatskinned men who emerged from behind the screens of tubbed orange trees to attack them, or they were all consummate actresses. Those who could get away fled shrieking from their obscene pursuers among the supper-couches, while the guests roared with laughter and called out advice. He saw that his sister's betrothed, Lectus Garovinus, had rolled from his couch to lie in a drunken stupor among the deep litter of crab claws, snailshells, gnawed artichoke leaves and upset dishes on the floor; the entire pavement of intricately colored marbles seemed to be awash in spilled wine. Elsewhere a bald-shaved Syrian woman was fellating a senator who appeared to be far more interested in the platter of shellfish in honey he was devouring. At the head table Quindarvis had returned to his place as king of the feast, having changed his dinner suit once again, this time for one the color of dark Falernian wine. He was watching the room with a kind of drunken self-satisfaction, mocking his guests' excesses without disapproving of them, seemingly pleased at having set so perfect a stage. The woman beside him, thick and husky, was laughing, her blonde curls loosened to a damp aureole around her plump pink face. His hand was idly busy, working loose the diamond pins that held the shoulders of her dress; the sweat-damp tissue stuck momentarily to her rouged nipples, then folded downward over his thighs.

In the midst of the orgy Sixtus lay on his supper-couch, a half-finished winecup untouched in his hand; clearly sober, his white hair wreathed in violets. He was looking about him with an interested expression, but his blue eyes were hard under their heavy lids. At his feet sat one of the little nymphs, a child of seven or eight, holding the ripped remains of her veils about her body and huddling as close to him as she dared.

So paralyzed was he by disgust, and the horrible fascination that the obscene holds, that Marcus did not hear the blundering steps approaching from the terrace until someone all but fell into his back. He whirled, startled, wondering for a horrified moment what they did to slaves who spied upon the antics of their so-called betters . . .

. . . and found himself face-to-face with his younger brother.

Felix blinked at him, struggling manfully to focus his eyes. "I say—Marcus?"

Marcus shoved him aside and darted down the terrace. Waving his hand Felix tottered after him, calling out, "Here—you—hold on—" in a feeble voice, his feet, bare for the feast, slapping damply on the lapis tiles. From another archway leading into the supper room a man abruptly staggered, fell to his hands and knees almost under Felix's feet, and began to vomit mightily. Felix skidded to a stop, barely avoiding falling over him, " 'Scuse me—so sorry—thought I saw someone I knew . . ."

Taking advantage of the diversion, Marcus ducked through a narrow archway into a deserted serving-chamber used for dinners on the terrace itself, blundering into a table in the darkness and catching his balance with a deftness of which he had never before dreamed himself capable.

A moment later he saw Felix pass the entrance, looking vaguely about him at the empty, moon-washed spaces. He scratched his careful curls, dislodging the wreath of dark roses tangled in his hair. "Dash it," Marcus heard him murmur. "Must be drunker'n I thought." The sound of his unsteady feet retreated, wandering back toward the primordial chaos of the orgy.

Marcus had almost made up his mind that it was safe to come out when he heard other footsteps approaching: two men, talking softly, one barefoot and one wearing stout shoes. He shrank back into his dark covert as shapes loomed in the door. The stink of perfumed unguents, wine, and sweat assailed him; the shadow of a tree across the terrace hid their faces in an inky bar of blackness, but the bigger of the men was unmistakable. An enormous mountain clothed in sticky primrose silk, short oiled curls, a fat round hand leaning against the edge of the open archway with its knobbed, glittering cestus of jewels. By the moonlight Marcus could clearly see, tattooed small on the oily flesh of that corpulent forearm, a small and beautifully done fish.

He felt exactly as if someone had thrown a great drench of icy water over his head; as if he had seen his father give a gold piece to a beggar. The breath went out of his lungs in a kind of stupid gasp, which he barely had the wits to keep silent. He heard Tiridates whisper ". . . do not care why and am not interested in why. Take him back to town with you. It's obvious we're being spied on." A murmured query. "No. Don't go back to the house at all. I'll tell Roxanne where you are in the morning. The sacrifice is an important one, and doubly so now. We cannot risk stupid hitches now."

A second voice whispered in assent. A shadow detached itself; moonlight touched hawklike Arab features, the blue smudge of a bruise, as the bearer left his master and hastened away down the moonlit terrace. Tiridates stood watching him go for a long time. In the shadows Marcus heard the retreating tap of heavy shoes and, above it, the terrified pounding of his heart.

IX

You are a thoughtless fool, unmindful of sudden disaster, if you don't make your will before you go out to have dinner. . . .

Juvenal

He reached Rome, exhausted, a good quarter hour before Tiridates' two bearers, at the cost of grilling agony that seemed to fire through every muscle in his body. He knew the chair-bearers were professionals; once on the road, they'd move with that steady, ground-eating jog that he could never have hoped to emulate. They'd have outpaced him long before they reached the suburbs, and moreover, the brightness of the moonlight would have made it impossible for him to follow closely enough to do any good.

All this went through his mind in the few moments before Tiridates had turned and lumbered back to join the riot in the supper room, and he knew that his only hope of tracking them was to reach Rome ahead of them and wait where the Ardeatine Way ran into the city among the sprawling commercial districts around the south slope of the Aventine Hill.

Resolutely thrusting from his mind the screaming protests of his common sense about the distance back to Rome and the

140

speed he'd have to travel to beat them there, he set off at a jogging run from the villa. To pick up distance he went cross-country, through the woods, leaping like a frightened gazelle at every shadow. The lions were still unpleasantly fresh in his mind. He scrambled over the park wall among the roadside tombs that stretched for miles outside the city along every highway. In the eerie darkness under the trees, it was difficult to maintain a philosophic attitude and keep from breaking into a panicked run, but he managed it and heard up ahead the noises of the road—the creak of wheels, the clip of tiny hooves, the mutter of farmers' voices.

Though it was not long past midnight, the local farmers were already bringing their produce to Rome. As he jogged toward the city they were all around him: tiny donkeys laden with bundles almost double their size, wood-wheeled carts that raised a clatter like a troop of cavalry on the stones of the road, men and women and some very small children with bundles on their backs and heads. Some of them carried torches, but most relied on the brightness of the moon. As he loped between and among and past them, the night seemed filled with the murmur of their back-country dialect and the smell of onions.

In time the tombs gave way to small houses, with plots of cabbages and coops of chickens, which in turn became warehouses, three-story apartment buildings, suburban baths; then bigger warehouses, taller apartments, and the dark stink of the city, which seemed to rise before him against the starry darkness like the black all-devouring monster that the Christians called it. The small square in front of the Naevian Gate was crowded with farmers and carts, and blazing with torchlight like the mouth of hell.

As Arrius had said, the gate-guards had been increased on account of the notables who would be coming back later in the night. At present the soldiers were dicing on the raised platform that in the daytime was the center of the ranks of rented cisiums, and barely gave Marcus a glance as he stumbled, gasping for breath, through the crowds to the gate itself. *Philosophy may do wonders for the mind,* he thought wearily,

but it certainly doesn't prepare you for times like these. Every
muscle in his body ached, rather to his surprise—since like
most nonathletes he'd assumed that running is done with the
legs—and he vowed to himself that he'd begin a course of
exercise at the baths tomorrow, provided he wasn't murdered
in the meantime.

The court on the other side of the gates was much smaller
and, consequently, far more crowded. In addition to the
produce haulers there were construction workers with loads of
marble and brick for repairs on the aqueduct. The din of
voices was tremendous, the smell of brick dust and bodies,
the shine of torchlight on straining muscles and the black
relief of shadows. Marcus slumped down beside a public
fountain, doused a handful of water over his face (much to
the indignation of the oxteam already drinking there), and
settled down to wait.

At rest, his body was immediately assailed by cramp, and
his mind by doubt.

What if the bearers weren't returning by this gate? What if
they'd anticipated him and circled to enter by the Appian
Gate? What if they weren't coming back to Rome at all?

No, Tiridates had said, "Take him back to town with
you."

But not to the house.

To Papa, whoever Papa was?

Tiridates a Christian. And his sister Roxanne, evidently—a
woman Marcus had never seen but with whom he remembered Tullia had gone shopping that day. And been unac-
countably delayed, as a matter of fact. The bearers had been
switched, too. An accident? Or a touch of poison, and a
kindly offer of replacement. Marcus broke into a sweat, his
stomach hurting worse than even a three-mile jog could account for.

"Sacrifice," he had said. *Sweet gods, don't let us be too
late!*

*They know we're on their trail. The girl Dorcas—Tiridates—
word has been got to Papa.* Were they holding her for sacri-

fice at a certain time, or would the approach of capture make them abort the whole project?

What were the holy seasons of the Christians, if they had any? Like the ides of April, when the cows were slaughtered for Vesta?

Sixtus would know, he told himself. Why hadn't he tried to see Sixtus, tried at least to send him word, before leaving the villa? Not that the old man would have been much help to him, but at least . . .

The Arab bearers stepped through the gate. They were clearly recognizable as they passed under the torches and seemed to have barely broken a sweat. Marcus stood up as casually as possible and slipped between a farm cart and a team of oxen dragging a sledgeload of bricks, circled through the press of carts, and followed the stream of traffic along Ardeatine Street, keeping them in sight as best he could.

The street itself was wide enough to admit a broad streak of moonlight, and enough of the farmers and carters bore torches for him to see his quarry at a distance. He kept to the same side of the street, knowing he'd never be able to cross the crowd in time if they turned down one of the small pitch-black alleyways; they walked quickly, talking softly under the noise of the crowd, but seemed to be in no particular haste. It was only after they crossed under the black towering arches of the aqueduct that they left the main way, turning left into the crowded slums that surrounded the circus.

One of the men had a lantern, which he now uncovered; the grimy light bobbed ahead of him as Marcus slipped along at their heels. He had to close distance a little; if they turned a corner, he would lose them in the maze. What he'd do if they came upon one of the gangs of toughs that haunted these sightless canyons by night he couldn't imagine. It would be beyond bearing if he lost perhaps his last chance to save Tullia's life because he was being robbed or rolled in the mud by a band of drunk blue bloods.

From the darkness above him he heard a shutter creak and flattened himself against the wall just in time. A stinking shower splattered into the squishy stream that already ran down the center of the alley. Up ahead, he heard one of the bearers curse in Arabic.

They turned one corner, then another. They seemed to be making for the river; above him and to his right he glimpsed the white wall of marble with its statues standing eternal guard. The circus, where some poor sand-raker—or a team of them, considering the size of the place—would be sieving broken shards of wood and bronze dyed with the blood of men and horses from the sands. Tomorrow the games would be back at the Flavian again. Bound to stakes and wrapped in the bleeding hides of slaughtered beasts, Telesphorus and his little crew would meet the lions.

He wondered if Quindarvis, as sponsor of the games, had anything special planned for the women.

The Arabs muttered among themselves, evidently debating the way. Distantly Marcus could catch the din of the markets along the Tiber, a less exotic cacophony than one heard under the Flavian, but no less loud. The meat market was somewhere ahead, with its cattle pens and hog wallows, its coops of chickens and geese. Even at this hour hunters would be coming in with game from the woods and fields—hares, partridges, pigeons, the bounty of all those half-forgotten goddesses of the countryside, Flora and Fauna and Pomona. And beyond the meat market lay the river itself, and the bridges to the dense Tiberside district around the feet of the Janiculum Hill, like a suburb of Damascus or Antioch transplanted to the outskirts of Rome.

Marcus wondered if they were making for the river. The Arabs went on, after a momentary pause for consultation; but they halted several times more, the echoes of their footsteps erratic against the black walls that closed them in. They turned twice more and crossed a tiny square, where the moonlight flashed on a public fountain under the guardianship of a particularly gross bronze Priapus. Marcus almost lost them at the square, hanging back in the shadows of one street until they had crossed that small space of paving stones and moonlit mud, then hurrying as silently as he knew how to catch them up on the other side. Only by the reflection of the lantern light from the walls of the dark tenements was he able to follow them. He began to wonder how he'd manage if they did cross one of the Tiber bridges.

They reached a larger square, at the foot of the Publician Rise. The noise of the markets was clearer here, the bellow of beasts in terror at the smell of the shambles, the yelling of stevedores at the docks. Every window around the dark open space was black; there was no sign of life but the two shapes of the men and the gold puddle of light bobbing around their feet. Somewhere in the tangle of streets to his right, Marcus could hear a gang of rowdies beating on a door, yelling drunken words of love to the woman within. He huddled in the darkness, watching the light retreat across the square and into the black canyon of another street. As soon as it was out of sight he scurried forward, trying to muffle his own footfalls as he headed for the entrance to the Publician Rise . . .

The men were waiting for him just around the first corner. They'd doused the lantern; the first he knew of it was the brutal force with which a great weight slammed into his back, the rasp of breath in his ear, and the bone and muscle and leather that crushed his throat. His ears filled with a dim roaring, and his nostrils with the stink of sweat and mud; his knees gave way and he fell into a hole of ringing blackness.

"By the grace of Christ he's alive," someone whispered. The stench of mud and decayed fish and pig's offal wrapped him up like a winding-sheet. He wondered if he'd ever be able to swallow again.

He was turned on his back. Cold hands searched his face, his throat. From the inky darkness above him a woman's voice whispered, "Thank God—but Christ could only be a recipient, or at most the vehicle, of grace. Your priest must have told you—"

"Our priest has told us that that's an error common to those who *think* they understand the true meaning of Christ's words," hissed the first voice back. "But in point of fact, the God of the Books of the Jews is clearly a god of cruelty, imperfection, and repulsiveness—the god of this world, in fact.'' The cold hands, surprisingly strong, dragged him over something that oozed and stank horribly, and propped him up against a wall. ''The grace of Christ supplanted that old god with a new law, and the unknown god, as Paul proved in his first letter to the—''

''Paul!'' retorted another voice out of the gloom. ''That self-seeking little Pharisee's limitations of thought were the only things that his letters ever proved. John understood more about the emanations of the Divine Soul, and Plato . . .''

Wonderful, thought Marcus. *I have been rescued by the Christians.*

''Who were they?'' hissed the woman.

''Well, the Divine Father himself is known as Bythos and Chaos, and at his side sits Sigē, or Charis, the incomprehensible silence and grace of—''

''Not the emanations, you pox-ridden Gnostic, the men who slugged this poor fellow!''

''I heard them speak in Arabic,'' said someone else. ''But they could have been hired killers or just thugs out to rob him—not that he looks like he has anything to rob, poor little scruff. What do we do with him?''

Another group of Christians? wondered Marcus. Sixtus had said there were factions. Actually members of two other groups, by the sound of it . . .

''We can't leave him here,'' whispered Cold Hands.

''We can't take him anywhere, we haven't the time,'' replied the voice that had championed Plato over Paul. ''It's nearly the end of the watch, and Papa said it would be at the start of the third watch of the night. We have barely time to get there now.''

''Right,'' whispered the woman's voice. ''Anthony, Sulpicius, you stay with him . . .''

''I refuse to stay here and listen to that heretic prate about the letters of Paul!''

''Look, offal-brain . . .''

''All right, Josephus stay with Anthony! By the Three, I should have let you people find your own way there . . .''

"How can you heretics swear by the Three, when God is One . . ."

"Three or One, Papa's going to have all our hides if we're not on the spot with the blankets when the doors are opened!" Quibbling, the voices retreated into the darkness, among the squishing of many feet in the muddy lane. Marcus' dazed mind groped for some kind of meaning behind their speech, but found none. Did "stay with him" mean guard him until they could return to dispose of him properly? But in that case why not simply let their brethren murder him in peace? Had they had some kind of conflicting order from Papa? Were they going to take him prisoner, perhaps to where Tullia was?

But even that theory was dashed when the woman's voice called back from some distance off, "You'll see that he gets home?" Someone must have nodded—though how anyone could see in the absolute blackness of the alley was beyond knowing—for the footsteps faded moistly into the gloom.

He struggled to rise, and a firm hand pushed him back against the wall. "Are you all right?" asked the voice that had referred to him as a "poor little scruff." "You were set upon by robbers."

"Was I?" he mumbled. Against the lighter gloom at the mouth of the alley, he could see a group of dark flitting shapes, but here the shadows hid everything but the silvery glitter of eyes. "Who are you?" he asked, hoping they wouldn't think he knew too much.

"We saw you being attacked," replied the Christian's deep voice—not, Marcus noticed, answering his question. "The men who struck you down ran away. We'll see you get home, as soon as you're fit to walk. Whereabouts do you live?"

"In the Subura," he answered groggily, "near the Neptune shrine," and then realized how stupid it was to give away his lodgings to the Christians. If they ever learned who it was they had rescued, they could simply show up some night and murder him at their leisure. "But I'm fine now, I can get there alone . . ."

"Easy, boy," said a second voice, with a strong accent of

an Alexandrian Jew. "There's no need to be running, you've had a bad shock."

"I'm all right, I really am," he protested, struggling ineffectively to free his arm from the man's prodigious grip. He struggled to keep the panic from his voice. "I have to be going." To his surprise they helped him to his feet, as if they feared he'd collapse again. "I'm all right," he repeated groggily. "I wasn't hit on the head . . ."

"You've the earth's own lump," pointed out the Jewish Christian doubtfully.

"No, that's all right, that happened days ago. Really, I'm fine." He made a move to flee, missed his footing on the slippery cobbles, and all but fell into the Christian's arms.

"You make a habit of bein' assaulted?" He could see the wag of the Jew's gingery beard, silhouetted against the moonlight of the square. "Eh, well, none of my affair. Let's go, son."

Marcus felt too exhausted to make further protest. Whatever nefarious plots the Christians had in mind for him, he was too tired to flee; he stumbled along between them through the darkness of the alleyways, until they reached the relatively straight stretches of Tuscan Street. The lane was narrow, and the moon westering, and beyond the fact that the Jewish Christian with the gingery beard was the taller of the two, and that both were wearing the worn dark tunics of poor laborers or slaves (much like his own), he could see very little of them. He wondered if he could ask them about the feasts of the Christians, about the times of sacrifice, but knew it would be foolish to reveal to them that he even knew what they were.

The noises of the markets faded behind them. The dark looming mass of the Palatine on their right overshadowed the narrow street. Looking up, Marcus could see the last light of the sinking moon as it touched the gilded roofs, making slivers of electrum among the velvet darkness of the trees.

Discordant singing caught his attention; he turned, startled, as a gang of rowdies emerged from the darkness of an alleymouth opposite them, lantern light illuminating grinning distorted faces, slippery with scented oils and rouge. There were half a dozen of them, their elaborately brocaded dinner suits smeared with food and wine, leaning drunkenly on one another or on their staggering girl friends. They seemed to have picked up some unfortunate citizen in their inebriated wanderings; a little man in a plain toga was among them, wreaths askew on his balding head, anxiously casting glances left and right as if seeking escape.

One glittering youth yelled out across the road, "Hey! Wh're y'all going? Party—party at Shenat'r Shevr's housh—Y'know where we're all going?"

"To perdition, I should imagine," retorted the deeper-voiced Christian; a rash remark, thought Marcus, in momentary terror. But the bejeweled drunks went into gales of laughter, slapping their thighs and punching one another (and their distressed little captive) in the ribs, and went reeling on their way, falling in the mud and bouncing against walls as they went. The respectable citizen's voice drifted after them, helplessly expostulating that he didn't really wish to attend a party at all . . .

"And there's some as seeks to be rich," sighed the Jewish Christian, shaking his head.

They emerged into the Forum, magical in its empty silence. The pillars of its porches gleamed all around them like a monochrome forest of marble; the statues of gods and Caesars, their colors deadened and flattened by the silvery light, stood like guards on their plinths, staring ahead with somber, shadowed, agate eyes. The shorter, deeper-voiced Christian whispered to the Jew, "What time do you make it to be?" and the gingery beard moved in the moonlight as the man shook his head.

Then Marcus heard it. A faint sound, over the distant clamor of the market carts; noises that were almost drowned. Then the sound rose suddenly. A riot of voices, cries, curses, borne on the drift of the night winds; a shouting confusion and the sudden wild clattering of hooves from the direction of the Flavian Amphitheater. Not the sound of one chariot team, or even a dozen. A roaring surge of hoofbeats, echoing from the warren of close-seamed walls that surrounded the gladiator schools, the stable complexes, the wineshops and holding jails attached to that great arena. Marcus gasped involuntarily, and almost choked on the pain in his windpipe, "What's that?"

The Jew whispered, half to himself and half to the other Christian, "He's done it!" and in the zebra shadows of the porch where they stood his eyes were shining.

Marcus blinked for a moment, not comprehending. Then like the bits of a puzzle falling together he understood what the little bands of Christians had been doing, abroad in Rome at night—and what it was that Papa had done.

"He's very neat, I'll say that for him."

Arrius dumped a dipperful of watered wine into a cup and brought it over to Marcus' bed. Sixtus, perched on the windowsill, broke a chunk from the halfpenny loaf he'd brought with him that morning and threw it across to Marcus, who caught it wearily and began to sop it in the wine.

Though the Christians had seen him to his door with every evidence of concern for his health, Marcus had not slept much the night before. His neck felt even worse than it looked—the bruise across his windpipe had begun to blacken already. He was almost wholly unable to swallow. Past Sixtus' shoulder the big window was blinding with morning sun, and the cries of children at play floated up from the courtyard below.

"It was timed to the minute," went on the centurion, seating himself on the foot of Marcus' narrow cot. "The patrols were at their farthest from the holding jail when the stables were broken open, so naturally the guards from the jail itself ran to help round up the horses. Half the guards and grooms at the stables themselves had been drugged, it turned out later; they were found sleeping like dead men in the straw. Mithras alone knows what caused the whole herd of horses to stampede past the jail . . ."

"They were driven with blankets," whispered Marcus painfully.

"What?"

"Groups of Christians stood in the alleyways near the stables and flapped blankets at them, to run them past. I met a band of them—the Christians, that is. Two bands, really." And he gave a brief account of his adventures of the previous night, concluding with, "And they said Papa wanted them there on time, and by the gods they were. I have to say I was impressed."

"So was I," added Churaldin, who sat blinking in the sunlight like a satisfied tomcat at his master's feet. "I don't think I've ever seen such confusion in my life."

"Were you there?" asked Marcus in a kind of breathless croak.

"I was coming back from paying a visit on the Caelian Hill in time to catch the tail end of the show," smiled the slave. "I admit it beats any put-up beast-hunt in the amphitheater I ever saw."

Arrius growled deep in his throat, like an annoyed lion. There were blue smudges under his eyes, from a night badly spent. "What it does," he said after a moment, "is knock your theory over the head, Sixtus, about the Christians being too disorganized to take concerted revenge for the massacre of their comrades by Varus. Whatever their stupid quarrels are about, there's somebody who can make them act as a unit."

"True," sighed the old man. "In which case we may be up against more than we know." He leaned his elbows on his knees and gazed abstractedly into space for a moment. He looked nothing the worse for last night's orgy; in fact, Marcus would have bet everything he owned that the old man was the only member of the supper-party on his feet this morning.

"Sixtus," said Marcus hesitantly. "If—if they did kidnap Tullia to sacrifice, would it be at a set time? On a holy day, like the ides of April or the seventh of June? Because Tiridates spoke of a sacrifice . . ."

"I still refuse to believe that as cheap as children come in this city, the Christians would have gone to the trouble of kidnapping a sacrifice that could cost them all their lives."

"We don't necessarily know that Tertullia Varia is going to be the victim," said Arrius slowly. "Is there a Christian feast coming up, Sixtus?"

The old man shook his head. "None that I know of. In fact, as far as I know the Christians can't even agree on the date they celebrate the rebirth of their savior—they drew blood over it, at Antioch. I know that some of them celebrate his birth in December, like the Mithraists . . . Some say, *very* like the Mithraists. But I've never heard they celebrate the summer solstice."

"The summer solstice?"

"Midsummer Eve," said Churaldin softly, and there was a sudden glow in those dark Cymric eyes. "That my people celebrated with the pyre of the Green Man and the dancing among the standing stones. The shortest night of the year."

Arrius looked down at the Briton for a long moment; in the stillness, the heat of the little room was like a bake oven. "And when is the shortest night?"

The Briton said, "Tomorrow night."

Marcus gasped, tried to sit up, and sank down again with a groan. He had grossly underestimated the effects of a three-mile run upon a totally untrained body. Moreover his cracked ribs were smarting again.

Sixtus mused slowly, "I suppose that the Christians could celebrate the solstice. The part of the world they come from—Syria and Palestine—is heavily imbued with the effects of Chaldean astrology, though it tends to crop out in other religions far more noticeably. In which case—"

"In which case we have only tonight and tomorrow," whispered Marcus.

"We'll find her," said Arrius grimly. "I have informers out all over town. We've been watching Tiridates' house for him since he refused to let me talk to those two Arabs."

"For all the good it's likely to do you," commented the old scholar. Arrius raised an inquiring brow. "Oh, come! If there's a secret passage connecting the cellar to another cellar, or to the sewers, your men could sit all night watching an empty house. Don't you know you can cross Rome from the

Quirinal Hill to the Aventine without ever coming above the ground?''

The centurion was silent for a moment. ''In which case she could have been taken outside the city altogether.''

''It's possible, but I doubt it. The Christians are a city folk; whatever they'll do, they'll do in Rome.''

''It doesn't mean they'll hold her in Rome until it's time,'' returned the soldier. ''We've turned up no sign of her . . .''

''It hardly means she isn't here.'' Sixtus glanced sharply over at Marcus, who was following this conversation with anguish in his eyes. ''Who lives upstairs from you here? I've heard them walking back and forth all morning.''

Marcus shook his head. ''I know there's a Syrian family named Baldad and a—a girl named Delia, but other than that . . .''

''She could be up there, then. They could have rented a room, kept her drugged . . . What's that square building down the alley from here? The one with the black walls and the boarded-up porch?''

''I think it used to be an old temple of Dagon, before the cult was proscribed,'' said Marcus, puzzled. ''But . . .''

''Ever been in it? In its cellars?''

He shook his head, mystified.

''Rome is a city where you can do anything, centurion. You could kidnap the entire College of Vestal Virgins and conceal them all within a mile of the Forum and no one would be the wiser. Old buildings, warehouses, temples, caves in the banks of the Tiber . . .''

''But there would always be the risk,'' said Arrius quietly. ''But outside the city—in a place where fear will keep eight people out of ten away . . . I think they've got her at the catacombs.''

''The catacombs?'' croaked Marcus hoarsely. ''You mean the old Jewish burial grounds?''

''Christians bury their dead in catacombs as well,'' said Arrius. ''There are two that I know of, and Mithras knows how many more. One of my informers tells me there've been rumors of the Christians using the old one down on the

Ardeatine Way as a hiding place as well. It's where we're going tonight." He dipped out a cup of wine for himself and stood for a moment in the hot bright bar of the window light, gazing into distance.

"Arrius," croaked Marcus after a time. "Is it possible—do you think that Tiridates might be Papa?"

The centurion was a long time silent, thinking this over. At last he said, "It's perfectly possible. It would be the best reason I can think of for his attending Quindarvis' supper-party last night. When the Christians were broken out of jail, he was nowhere in sight. And that's exactly what he'll say if we make a move against him without red-handed proof. He could have given all the orders beforehand; in fact, he contrived to be on the spot when the Christians were transferred to the holding jail. We saw him there ourselves. Would he really have gone all the way down from the Aventine to the amphitheater, just to kiss his boy friend?"

"But then why did the other group of Christians rescue me?" asked Marcus, confused. "I would have thought they'd let me be killed."

Arrius turned back with a short laugh. "Never think it. They said themselves they didn't get a look at the bearers, didn't they? Communications can get crossed like that in any operation. In Germany I've fought tremendous battles in the snow against what turned out to be the other half of my own scouting party."

"But if Tiridates is the head of the Christians," protested Churaldin, "why would he attack the woman he was going to marry in the first place?"

Arrius shrugged. "Part of the setup."

"You mean the whole betrothal was to get her in his power?" demanded Marcus, aghast. "But why go to the trouble? Why not simply kill her?"

Sixtus' voice was deep, quiet against the clatter of pans, the rising babble of Aramaic and Celt from the courtyard below. "Perhaps because, like lovemaking, revenge is the sweeter the longer it is spun out."

Marcus met his eyes, blue as cold water in their shadowed pits, and looked away, slightly sick at the thought.

"Or perhaps," suggested Arrius softly, "her death isn't what they intend at all?" He drained his cup, set it with a small soft *chink* on the table, and turned around, the sun seeming to drench his soldier's cloak in new blood. "Have you thought of that?" His leather-hard face was as calm and detached as it had been in the darkness under the Flavian, when he'd cut the Christian's throat. "D'you seriously think any man in Rome will marry a girl who's been kidnapped by the Christians, Marcus? Who's been living among them for days—weeks, maybe, by the time she's found? Who's been subjected to every perversion from murder and cannibalism on down?"

Marcus looked away, staring fixedly into a corner of the ceiling, and did not reply.

The grating voice went on, "You think any man will have her? Or any man's family? Knowing old Varus, do you think even her own family will have her back?"

"Shut up," whispered Marcus.

"Some philosopher you are," snapped the centurion brutally. "Have a look at the truth for once. Under those circumstances Tertullia Varia would have no choice but to remain with the Christians—to become a Christian herself. And in that case, do you think as long as Tullius Varus holds prefectural powers in Rome he'd permit any kind of general persecution, such as they've been talking about for years, against the Christians?"

"Yes!" shouted Marcus, his ripped voice burning like Greek fire in his throat. "Yes, he would, the stiff-necked, jealous, dirty old bastard! He'd cut her throat with his own hands!" And he turned his face away, sobbing, his body aching as though he had been beaten.

A shadow crossed the glare of the light. The soft heavy wool of a toga brushed against his arm, and a strong hand pressed his shoulder. Sixtus' deep voice spoke quietly, "We'll find her."

Beyond him, Arrius rasped, "You're the gods' own optimist, old man."

Marcus felt him look up, meeting the centurion's cynical eyes; he felt the serenity flow from him, as warmth flows from a fire on a freezing night. "We'll find her," he repeated, and there was no question in his voice.

"You sure we want to?" And he heard the soldier's heavy tread pass from the room and tremble through every board in the rickety building as he strode down the stairs.

X

The practice was repeated annually at a fixed season. They [the Jews] would kidnap a Greek foreigner, fatten him up for a year, and then convey him to a wood where they slew him, sacrificed his body with their customary ritual, partook of his flesh. . . .

Apion

Marcus passed the rest of the day as though numbed. He slept, heavily and amid dreams of racking pain. Twice he woke, to stare hopelessly at the blot of sunlight where it had moved upon the wall, tortured by blurred memories of last night's opulent horrors and by the centurion's brutal surmise. Both times someone spoke to him—Sixtus or Churaldin, he wasn't sure which—and both times he drifted almost immediately back into a kind of stupor. The third time he woke it was late afternoon. The room, which faced east, was heavily shadowed. Through the window he could see the line of sunlight, yellow as summer butter, on the wall of the court. It was about the eighth hour. Sixtus still sat on the windowsill, reading Marcus' much-battered copy of the *Enchiridion*.

"You still here?" Marcus mumbled, and the old man looked up and rolled up the book.

157

"I thought I'd remain until I was sure you were well," he said. "Arrius sent a message about an hour ago—if you want to be part of the expedition to the catacombs, they will leave from the prison at a little before sunset."

"All right." He swallowed experimentally. The pain was not noticeably less, but his voice seemed to be coming back. "I'm sorry I deserted you last night—I thought if I followed them . . ."

"You did well," said the old man. "After hearing all that passed between Tiridates and his bearers, had you wasted time coming to me first I should probably have hit you with my stick. My only fear was that you'd managed to get yourself devoured by Quindarvis' lions." He set the scroll on the sill, rose, and came over to stand at the foot of the bed, his game leg dragging stiffly behind.

Marcus sighed and shifted his gaze from the corner of the cracked ceiling to the old man's face, which was scarcely less lined. "So you know about them?"

"Nearly everyone in Rome does. There are rumors that they are the reason for the extremely good behavior of his slaves."

Marcus shook his head tiredly. "I'm afraid the rumors are wrong. It's the fish, not the lions, you have to beware of." He wondered whether it was only exhaustion, or if, like Arrius, he was becoming inured to the world's horrors. For in truth, among everything else last night he hadn't even given the poor little drunkard's death a second thought. The noise of the music must have drowned out his screams, if he'd uttered any. "Other people must know about that," he said at last. "You'd think somebody would—would at least denounce him." But already he asked himself, *to whom?*

Sixtus shrugged. "On the whole, public opinion runs against that sort of thing; but there are ways and ways of dealing with public opinion. I knew a man in Antioch who was supposed to boil his slaves, but his feasts were never thin of company. He had an excellent cook, entertained lavishly—and one could never complain of the service. And then, in the crowd Quindarvis runs with—"

"Weren't you shocked?" Marcus interrupted weakly, recall-ing the old man reclining in the midst of that blazing firefall of vice, the rescued child huddled at his feet.

Sixtus replied mildly, "I am never shocked."

Marcus sighed and shut his eyes. His body felt like one vast ache, sinking slowly back into unconsciousness.

"Marcus," said the old man. "What Arrius said about Tertullia Varia . . ."

Without opening his eyes, he said, "I don't want to talk about it."

"The Christians would not do such a thing. Believe me, they would not."

At least the Christians Anthony and Josephus had made sure that he came to no harm. "But it makes sense," objected Marcus, feeling as though he spoke from a great distance away. With a bitter chuckle, he added, "It'll make sense to her father."

"That is why she must be found before he returns to Rome. Listen to me, Marcus. Do you love this girl?"

He opened his eyes, looked up at that robed white figure that seemed so tall against the light of the window; the sun-riven face and scarred soldier's hands. "Does it matter if I do?" he asked hopelessly. "Arrius is right. I'm a philo-sopher—or anyway that's what I've chosen to call myself. At least I can look at the truth. The least I can do is—is school my mind to bear it."

Sixtus asked him, "And what is the truth?"

He forced his cracked voice steady. "That she's dead. By their hand, or by her father's, after."

"That isn't truth," said the old man. "It's only the com-fort of despair, to keep your heart from hurting."

Anger flared into him at these words, but there was no reply that he could make to them. He lay back, deathly weary.

Sixtus went on, "Despair is so much easier to bear than hope, Marcus. The truth is that we do not know the truth. Do you truly love this girl enough to marry her?"

Marcus was silent for a long time, looking within himself

for the truth. Not any philosophical truth, but simply truth about himself. He finally said, "I don't know. I think so, but—I won't know until I see her. If she won't have me, if she thinks I'm taking her out of pity . . ."

"Would you take her out of pity?"

He started to deny it, then stopped himself. "I don't know that, either," he said after a moment. "I'd like to think I wouldn't so insult her, but—I don't know."

Sixtus nodded, not seeming to demand an answer, having once made Marcus aware of the question. He said, "It's still four days until the prefect is expected back. She may be found tonight, or tomorrow night— You will have time to think. The city prefect may be stiff-necked and intolerant, but if we can face him with his living daughter and some viable alternative fate, I doubt that he will be able to harm her in cold blood." He limped to the wall, and found his staff leaning in a corner. "Hold to hope, Marcus. In default of knowledge it is all we have; and in some cases it can be greater than knowledge."

Supporting himself on his staff, he limped from the room and was gone.

Though the siesta hour was largely past, Marcus remained where he was, his body aching so badly he wasn't sure he could have got up if he'd wanted to. He listened to the voices of the children in the court outside, the women arguing back and forth across their tiny balconies, the thundering gallop of periodic footsteps up and down the halls. He wondered if it was possible to hope.

"Do you truly love this girl enough to marry her?" Marcus looked around the broiling, dingy single room, with its single small chest, containing his precious philosophical scrolls, that a couple of planks had converted to a table; its narrow third-hand bed; its few rickety stools. The whole place looked dirty and sordid. No different from how it had always looked, of course, but now he felt impatient with it. *Whether I married her or not*, he thought, *I certainly wouldn't want to bring her here.*

When this is over, I'll have to do something about that.

Just what, he wasn't sure, but it was in the back of his mind that, if asked, Sixtus could help him somehow.

"Hold to hope . . ." It was hardly the counsel of a philosopher. The Stoics said, "Train your mind to accept what is, and unflinchingly meet Fate." Better advice, maybe; aside from being grossly emotionalistic and illogical, hope was exhausting. But altogether an odd sort of advice for a philosopher to give.

But then, Sixtus himself had admitted that before he had ever begun his studies of philosophy, he had been crippled in that pursuit by the knowledge that in every human soul lurks the potential for unknowable evil. No wonder the old man had become a hermit, thought Marcus, watching through the window as the sunlight moved slowly up the cracked stucco of the courtyard wall.

Tomorrow night was the summer solstice. If they could find her by then . . .

"The sacrifice is an important one," Tiridates had said to his slave. "And doubly so now."

Why doubly so? Because it would mark Tullia's initiation into their rites? Because having once sacrificed, there would be no way out for her?

Someone scratched at the doorframe. From the hall a hesitant voice called out, "Silanus? Marcus Silanus?"

He made a move to rise and instantly sank back again, his teeth gritted. Then he yelled back, "I'm coming," and levered himself very carefully off his bed, found his tunic, and pulled it stiffly on as he limped to the door.

The face of the thin, somewhat bent middle-aged Jew standing politely in the darkness of the hallway was vaguely familiar to him, but the memory was unclear. Maybe it wasn't that sharp vinegary face at all that he recalled, but one like it . . .

"Symmachus? Isaac Symmachus?" He stood aside, to let the stooping gentleman pass.

"You remember," he said, and entered the room with that same hesitant gait, almost a limp, that Marcus recalled from that one flaming scene he had witnessed in the shaded porches of the Basilica Ulpias. His voice, which had been little more than a screech of rage then, was bitter and husky. "I almost wish you didn't."

"You'll have to excuse my housekeeping," murmured Marcus—his usual apology to anyone who entered his lodgings—as he dumped piled clothes off his one backless chair. The man's diffidence so embarrassed him that he added, "I've had enough rows with my own father about my philosophy I don't think I should have been surprised to learn Judah had them, too."

"I daresay," murmured Symmachus. "But I misdoubt your father ever came storming up to you during one of your philosophical discussions and tried to seize you and drag you bodily back to his house. I—was angry," he added quietly, folding his pale thin clerk's hands, with their soft wrinkles and smutches of ink and chalk dust. Then he looked up again, his sharp dark eyes bitter, "Though why anyone expects their anger to excuse such actions I have never understood."

"Don't worry about it," said Marcus, seating himself on one of the other stools. "How is Judah? I haven't seen him since he—he left philosophy."

There was a moment's awkward silence, the elderly Jew staring down at his linked fingers, his oddly sensitive mouth thinned in an expression that reminded Marcus tremendously of his friend's. Finally he said, "Neither have I."

Marcus looked up quickly.

"Oh, he still lived beneath the ancestral roof, for a bit. He was seldom home. I should have known that ending his course of studies among the pagans wouldn't kill whatever worm it was that gnawed at his heart. A wicked and iniquitous generation, but—my son. They say, 'Do not rebuke the scorner, for he will hate you.' And in the end he left, of course." The skin over the fine knuckles paled momentarily. "I heard from him once. I only wondered if you had." He did not meet Marcus' eyes as he spoke. It was enough, thought Marcus, that he would have to be asking strangers—and gentiles, to boot—the whereabouts of his own son.

"No," he said gently. "But then—I knew Judah. I guessed, when he quit coming, that he wouldn't flout your will."

"You mean you guessed that his straight-laced, stiff-necked old father had succeeded in harrying and chivying a promise from him to give up the heathen delights of the philosophy of the Greeks? Something I daresay yours never did?" And the dark bitter eyes traveled slowly over the shabby room.

"It isn't quite the same," said Marcus, though in his heart he knew it was. He realized Caius had been right: There is truth and truth. He could hardly tell this grieving man that he had indeed been responsible for his only son's desertion. "For one thing, our circumstances are different. I'm not my father's only son. And I'm a Roman citizen. My father may consider philosophy unmanly, but not unclean. Judah told me once that the philosophy of the Greeks, to your people, was about one step above pork chitterlings for dinner."

Symmachus made a sort of hoarse squeaking sound deep in his throat, a bitter chuckle, or a desperate attempt to suppress tears. " 'A foolish son is a grief to his father, and bitterness to her that bore him.' And they say also that if you beat your child, he will not die, but if you beat him you may deliver his soul from hell. And to hell, I fear, he has gone, and will drag us all with him." Perhaps for concealment, he leaned his lips against his knotted hands. "He has become a Christian."

For a moment Marcus did not know if he wanted to weep or burst into uncontrollable peals of laughter. He wondered if his friend, the only other one of Timoleon's students to whom he had felt drawn, had been one of the men who had dragged Tullia from her litter the other night. He wondered if he would meet him that night in the catacombs.

When Marcus made no response to his words, Symmachus looked bleakly up again. "I understand his—his seeking of them. He was impatient with the Law, and angry with all things. He asked what our nation is, now that the temple is gone; what are we, now that our land is destroyed. To Jews, Christianity is something different than it is to those who do not understand the Law. To a Jew turned Christian it is flower and fruit, which justifies the long waiting of the vine. I understand Judah's impatience . . . but I'm afraid for him, Marcus Silanus. I'm afraid for us all.''

Startled out of the hellish irony of his reflections, Marcus heard the real fear in the dry thin voice. "Why?"

"You haven't heard? This girl who was taken . . ."

"What?"

"It is noised all over the town," said the Jew, his brows, thick and surprisingly dark, meeting suddenly over the hooked nose, "that the Christians stole a girl—that they'll sacrifice her to their dead god—which is absurd, since not even the most degenerate offshoot of my faith would admit of human sacrifice—"

"What? No, wait— How did it get all over town?"

The Jew sniffed. "My son told me a pagan story once, about a man who whispered a secret into a hole in the ground, and the very reeds that grew from the earth whispered it to the wind, who bore the disgraceful tale through the world. I found chalked on my door this morning, 'Baby-Eater'; the Forum buzzes with nothing else. After the escape of the Christians from the prison in the night there is talk of a general hunt. Rumors are flying in my neighborhood; my fellow clerks in the treasury have likewise found their symbols— the cross and the fish—chalked upon their doors, with curses and lewd words. To Jews and Christians the differences between us are obvious, but to the Greeks and the Romans, and the scum that crowd this city like maggots in the belly of a rotting dog, Jews and Christians are very much the same.''

Marcus shivered, knowing the old man was right. He remembered how in the courtyard of Quindarvis last night the two terms had been used interchangeably by the bearers and linkboys. With sudden enlightenment, he realized old Sixtus' anxieties over the dangers to the innocent. Of course, he thought. Sixtus was a soldier, and an imperial governor. There can't be much of the uttermost depths of human brute folly and ignorance that he hasn't seen. He understood long ago what a general persecution would mean to the families of the Christians.

It was on the tip of his tongue to warn Symmachus about

the raid on the catacombs, to tell him to beware. But what, after all, could the frail, bitter little clerk do to protect himself or the other members of his family? And if by some chance he did meet his son that day, it would ruin all hopes for saving Tullia. So he only said, "I haven't seen him, not since he left Timoleon. But if I do, or if I hear of him, I'll tell him you're seeking him."

"Always that," sighed the father, and rose stiffly to his feet. "In my youth I prayed for a brilliant son with an ardent spirit, like a lion that roars and is not afraid. How the Lord, who sees all the future, must have laughed to grant me my desire. Better I had prayed for a son with the brains and the spirit of a willing ass." He moved toward the door, and Marcus was uneasily conscious of how thin he was, how fragile his long clerkish hands, how brittle his body. He looked very breakable. He had seen the rack, in the dark hole under the Capitoline prison. Those old bones would come apart like overcooked meat.

The old Jew went on, "Judah is proud, proud as Satan. After he left Timoleon he would not seek out his friends that he knew there." He sighed. "I must go. With the audits and the changes in the offices of the praetors, we are working by lamplight these nights, even though the men we work for wallow like hogs in wine. If you see my son, tell him that this is where I am."

"All right." The shadows had begun to fold down over that hot little room. Knowing where he would go tonight, Marcus dreaded the thought of meeting Judah Symmachus.

Those dark burning eyes rested on him briefly, curious. "You have left Timoleon yourself, then? I sought you there yesterday and today."

Marcus paused, his mouth open to speak, and then nodded. "Yes," he said. "I've left Timoleon."

Symmachus pursed his lips for a moment, then sighed and took his leave. Marcus heard his footsteps retreat down the hall, stiff and halting and old, as though weighted down by an unsupportable burden of care.

*   *   *

When he crossed the Forum in the last slanting light of the late afternoon, Marcus saw that what Symmachus had said was perfectly true. On the bare rock face above the Silver-smith's Rise someone had painted a rude cross and some obscenities; he had earlier passed a gang of children throwing mud at an old blind Jewish beggar, and had heard them taunting, "Blood drinker! Body snatcher!"

"How did it get around?" he demanded, over a cheap supper of pork and cabbage at an eating-house off Tuscan Street to which he and the centurion had repaired after meeting outside the prison. "If the Christians didn't know we were on their trail before, they sure as Fate will now!"

"They knew," grumbled Arrius, mopping vinegary sauce from his plate with a hunk of bread. "They knew the minute we dropped on them, after tolerating them so long."

Marcus was silent for a moment, watching the shopkeeper across the way putting up the shutters over his storefront with the aid of his wife. They worked like a smooth and well-oiled team while arguing at the top of their lungs. Evening shadows filled the street, but beyond the corner he could see that brightness lingered in the open spaces of the deserted Forum. Then he turned back to his companion. "Arrius, why *have* the Christians been tolerated for as long as they have?"

The centurion shrugged. "The emperor's a just man. He's not going to order wholesale slaughter without proof."

"But everybody knows . . ." He paused, realizing that no philosopher argues from what "everybody knows." "Surely among as many Christians as there are they'd have got some kind of proof?"

"You think so?" One long eyebrow was cocked at him. "There are many different groups of Christians; what's true of one may not be true of others. And it's not as easy as you might suppose to get an initiate to talk about the secrets of a mystery. Have you ever been initiated into a mystery, Professor?"

"Of course not!" Indignation made his raw voice squeaky.

Arrius' back was to the light; the shadows of evening made it difficult to read his expression, but Marcus thought the hard cynicism of his voice had softened. "I don't think there's a man in the Praetorian who'd reveal the secrets of Mithras, even under torture. The bond of a mystery is a powerful one; you cannot understand its power unless you've experienced it for yourself. It's knowledge within knowledge within knowledge; the true teaching at the heart binds the fellowship together. You can't reveal it, or any part of it, to outsiders; an outsider simply would not, and could not, understand. Their partial knowledge could only pollute and distort the truth." And seeing Marcus' surprise and wonder to hear that new note in his voice, he added bluntly, "It's like trying to talk about sex to a virgin."

"Arrius," said Marcus softly, "are you an initiate of Mithras?" He felt that he had glimpsed something whose very existence he had never before guessed, a mystical streak that ran like a buried river under the rock of the man's street-wise intelligence and brutal sense of duty. But he should have guessed, he thought. The army was said to be riddled with the cult of the Soldier's God, the Mystery of the Unconquerable Sun.

The centurion drained his wine cup and pushed his plate aside. "Any soldier," he said thoughtfully, "would push your teeth in for even asking a question like that, but since you're young and dumb we'll let it go. What bothers me is that the anti-Christian feeling has gone far beyond the law. If it runs high enough—which it seems to be doing, between these rumors that are all over town and the news of the emperor's latest defeat in Persia—people may start taking the law into their own hands. If there are any Christians to be killed, I'd rather we did it, after having a chance to question them first."

They crossed the Forum, their footsteps echoing oddly in the deserted wilderness of marble. The only people left there were the public slaves, sweeping the temple porches, and an occasional loiterer outside the shadowy basilicas of the lawcourts. Marcus had spent his last few sesterces on a long, late bath and a massage, and was surprised at how much improvement there was. He still couldn't speak above a hoarse breathy croak, but at least he no longer feared he'd be crippled for life.

A squad of fifty of the Praetorian Guard was assembled in the old public assembly grounds, the Comitium, before the doors of the Senate house. As Symmachus had said, there were lamps burning in the nearby treasury offices. Marcus wondered if the old Jew heard the soldiers assembling, and if he guessed the reason. He felt a twinge of guilt, as though he had betrayed the old man to his death.

At one time the Praetorian Guard had been entirely composed of Italians, but now it was mostly Germans, huge blond men in their bronze mail, their thighs like tree trunks beneath the scarlet hems of their tunics. The few Romans, Spaniards, and Illyrians among them had been chosen to match them in height and build; Marcus felt like a baby among them. These were the shock troops of Empire, tough and hard and trained to a hair. Their influence had boosted men to the precarious throne and slaughtered them upon it. The noise of their arms slapping out in salute was like the single crack of a sheet in the wind.

Watching Arrius as he walked among them in the cool twilight, Marcus found himself wondering how many of them were initiates of the Soldier's God. How many of them had received that promise of life and salvation beyond the blood-edged bronze that any day could stop any of their hearts?

"The thing to remember," Arrius was saying, "is that this isn't an ordinary raid. It's a hunt, and Christians are slippery as ferrets. Like ferrets they're tunnelers, and slick as snakes. We're hitting the old Tomb of Domitilla out on the Ardeatine Way—one of the old Flavian imperial tombs—that the Christians have been using for burials for years. Mithras only knows how far they've tunneled away from the original shaft of the mausoleum. That's one reason I'm taking half a century to round up a dozen or so crazy Jew-Greeks. Hermann . . ."

"Ja?" A big German with a badly bent nose saluted.

"You're in charge of stopping the other earths. You know the Ardeatine Way?"

"Ja. It's tombs out ten, twelve mile from the city."

"I want you to put three men at every major tomb or group of tombs two miles up and two miles down from the one we're hitting. Cover any old shrines or abandoned houses as well. I want them in place before Antares clears the hills."

The man nodded. "Is done."

"Good. The rest of you I'm taking down with me. Take charcoal with you and mark your way. There's no knowing how far those galleries run underground, or what other tombs or cellars they connect up with. If anyone bolts I want them taken alive. Same with the guards outside. I don't want a bunch of dead Christians on my hands. Understand?"

There was a deep-throated rumble of assent, reminding Marcus for all the world of Priscus Quindarvis' lions. Arrius looked around at them sharply, the faint stirring of the evening breeze ruffling at the stiff crimson horsehair of the cross-roached crest on his helmet. With his stride the chain of his mail shirt jingled, the leather of his scabbard slapping his thigh. The last stains of evening light were fading from a sky streaked rose and amber and heliotrope; they put an edge like a knife blade of brightness on the burnish of his helmet and a glint in the watching eyes of the men.

Arrius went on, his voice gruff and matter-of-fact. "There's one more thing. It's after sundown, and we're going to be trespassing on the precincts of the dead."

There was a silence and a shift of those glittering eyes. Marcus remembered the darkness of the trees around the tombs when he'd scrambled over Quindarvis' wall. Even three years rigorous training in philosophy hadn't quite wiped from his soul the tales his Greek nursemaid had used to tell.

"That's why I asked for volunteers," continued the centurion. "I asked for men whose gods are strong— stronger anyway than the ghosts of a bunch of dead Christians. Mithras is the Bringer of Light, and Donar's a match for any ghost that ever walked. And you can bet your next month's pay the dead won't raise their hands against men who've come to avenge the defilement of their tombs. Now let's go trap those ghouls." He glanced sideways at Marcus. "You ready for another walk, boy?"

It was not, on the whole, an unpleasant walk. The Praetorians moved at Caesar-speed, that swift ground-eating pace whose uniformity served everywhere in the empire as a standard of distance, but Marcus found that despite his soreness, once he fell into the rhythm of it he was able to keep pace with them easily. They passed out of Rome over the same way he had traveled behind Sixtus' hired litter last night— through the Naevian Gate and the commercial suburbs that lay beyond it, past a big suburban house or two, into the green darkness of the warm country night. In the ranks no one spoke, but the beat of their hobnailed boots on the stone of the roadbed was a hard steady pulse that worked itself into Marcus' blood. The moon had not yet risen; early starlight silvered the mailed shoulders, tipped the tall helmet-crests and dyed the crimson of their tunics to the blackness of old blood. In time they began to pass tombs: the dovecote columbaria of poor workers' fraternities, the walled little cemeteries where the poor lay under gabled shelters of tiles or simply buried in clay jars, the better-off in brick tombs, shaped like houses or temples, shaded by their trees. The larger ones were surrounded by orchards or boasted a statue or two, glimmering like ghosts in the darkness. The smell of roses, the flowers of the dead, was suffocating on the warm night air.

At the first such large family tomb, three soldiers fell out from the ranks, slapped their breasts in salute, and moved off silently into the trees. Arrius knew his business well, thought Marcus. Two men are too easily separated in the hushed darkness of a graveyard on a moonless night. Three can laugh their fears to scorn. In a distant field a run-down shrine could be seen, dark against the paler grass, a tangle of thorn and overgrown trees, and guards were sent to cover that as well. They passed other tombs, or clusters of tombs, dark brick or white moony marble, sometimes low and square, occasionally fanciful, pyramids, or pillars, or towers. The night was as warm as a spring day. Marcus found himself remembering that in two days was the pagan festival of Midsummer, when Churaldin's people—and probably the relatives of most of the men he marched with, back in Germany—would be binding human captives into their green wicker cages and setting them alight.

Nero, he thought, would have loved it.

They reached the Christian cemetery, a white foursquare tomb that had belonged to some connection of the imperial Flavians and had later come to be used as a catacomb for the Christian community. The marble walls looked cracked and dirty, half-overgrown with vines. The pepper and willow trees that shrouded it looked untrimmed; the little funerary chapel in the nearby orchard, run-down. The silence and blown leaves reminded him somehow of Sixtus' house; a richness fallen upon evil times.

Half the remaining soldiers moved on up the road, to cover the possible bolt-holes farther south. Silent as a panther, one of the men scouted the abandoned orchards and chapel and returned to whisper softly, "The grass has been trampled."

Silhouetted in darkness against the shadows of the grove, Arrius nodded his head.

They waited in silence for what seemed an interminable time to let Hermann get his men in place. Through the dark trees, Marcus could see the stars and recognized when the claws of the Scorpion appeared over the eastern hills. Distantly, only a little south of them, he could see the twinkling lights of Quindarvis' villa and, much closer, the stand of trees that marked his lion pit. He wondered what that suave and cynical family friend would have to say when Varus returned to find his daughter missing. How much of the pity and horror he would express—had expressed—would be real, and how much mere political accompaniment to the father's grief?

He wondered where they'd buried that poor little drunken slave, whom the gladiators had drowned in the fishpond.

Arrius said, "Time."

Marcus looked up and saw the red angry eye of Ares' star glaring balefully above the black line of the eastern hills.

At the bottom of its twelve worn marble steps, the narrow

tomb door opened easily. The smell that rushed forth was choking, a stink of rot, of dampness, of rats, of flesh putrefying in darkness. The centurion took a cold torch from one of his men and lighted it from the closed bronze lantern an orderly carried. The ruddy flickering light spread over the narrow gallery before them, picking out old gilding, tarnished inscriptions, statuary busts befouled by rats. Above them on the vaulted ceilings a fretwork of wreaths and roses announced to the world the wealth of the builders of the tomb, a hollow hymn of forgotten names. On one wall someone had drawn a cross.

Leaving five men to guard the steps, Arrius led the way forward, Marcus and the remaining guards following in silence. Their shadows loomed huge, grotesque giants wavering over the carved sarcophagi that lay in some burial niches, the elaborate ash-chests of metal and precious stones that occupied others. At the far end of the room a shaft had been cut into the floor. The smell of putrescence rose from it in a gagging cloud.

At the bottom of the rude ladder that led down the shaft, a narrow hallway led into blackness. Smoke from the torch brushed the soot-stained ceiling; on either side, niches had been cut into the clammy gray stone of the walls and sealed over with slabs of cheap flawed marble, or with tile. Sunk in the cement, coins glinted, and an occasional, long-dried bottle that had contained perfume. Sometimes names or the symbols—the cross, the fish, the lamb, the cup—had been chalked onto the slabs. The torchlight only penetrated a few yards into the horrible gloom, and beyond its perimeter, wicked little red eyes flashed and winked in the dark.

As they moved along the gallery into the black shadows, doorways became visible, other passages cutting the first at right angles. Marcus fumbled a piece of chalk from the purse at his belt and marked arrows, to guide them back. Some of the soldiers lit torches from the centurion's and moved off to explore the branching corridors; others remained with him, looking about them uneasily in the dark. They passed a doorway where the smell was stronger and found a square burial chamber, sealed niches let into all four walls, and another shaft with a ladder leading down to a level below. Arrius whispered, "Mithras knows how far these tunnels extend," and Marcus replied, "I didn't know there were this many Christians in Rome!"

Leaving a portion of the men on the higher level the centurion took the rest—now only about a dozen strong—down below. The galleries here were exactly the same: low, narrow, damp, and stinking, broken here and there by transverse passages that in their turn led to farther tunnels. By the wavering yellow gleam of the torch Marcus could see the arched doorways marked with signs—a fish, or sometimes a cross—and once, down a branching passage that led away into Stygian darkness, he thought he smelled water and stone.

"Look," whispered Arrius, pausing in the doorway of a square burial chamber and holding the torch aloft. Against one wall lay folded blankets, a cheap wooden bowl, and a jar of water. He stepped inside as Marcus and some of the others crowded around the door, then unstoppered the flask and drank. He came out again and said, "Fresh."

"Sir!" called out one of the soldiers in a hushed voice. Arrius hurried to where he stood, in a doorway farther down the black narrow hall.

A kind of a chapel had been made from one of the burial chambers. More than anything else Marcus was reminded of a Mithraeum, the underground chapels where the followers of the Persian god were supposed to meet. But instead of the carved Slayer of the Bull, the wall above the altar simply bore a crudely chalked cross. The altar itself was simple stone, stained dark with blood or wine, bearing nothing but a cheap clay lamp of the kind that, filled full, will burn for about four hours in summer, or five in winter.

The lamp was just guttering itself out.

On the floor in front of the altar someone had written in charcoal:

And the Lord shall deliver them from the wicked, and save them, because they trust in him.

Hands on swordbelt, the centurion regarded this inscription for a long and silent moment. Then he sighed, "All right, boys, we might as well go on home. Looks like Papa knew we were coming."

XI

These lunatics [Christians] believe that they are immortal and will
live forever, so they do not fear death, and willingly accept arrest.
Deluded by their original lawgiver, they believe that they are all
brothers once they have wickedly denied the Greek gods and
worshiped that crucified Sophist. . . .

Lucian

"Mother of God, Queen of Heaven, you who wander through
many sacred groves and are propitiated with many different
rites . . ." Pure and flutelike, the voices lifted in a fading
wail. Like ribbons of gauze the smoke that curled from the
altar wreathed the serene face of the image of the Holy
Mother and her Child, seated between her pillars in the
massive darkness of the shrine. "You whose womanly light
illumines the walls of every city, whose misty radiance nurses
the happy seeds beneath the soil, you who control the wandering course of the sun and the very power of his rays . . ."

Like a shaken string of golden coins the sistrums tinkled in
the shadows of the heavy columns. From a window high in
the roof a single bar of sunlight turned the floating smoke to a
cloud of powdered diamonds and caught gold glints in the

unbound hair of the woman who lay prone before the high black basalt slab of the altar, her white robe spread about her like a shroud.

Deeper, stronger, the male voice of the tonsured priest rose against the sweet counterpoint of the chorus. ''Mother of Sorrows, Mystical Queen, you understand the griefs of women. I beseech you, by whatever name, in whatever aspect, with whatever ceremonies you deign to be invoked, have mercy on this woman, you who yourself have known sorrow. You who created heaven and earth, law and justice, you who are all that has been, all that is, all that shall be . . .''

From the darkness of the door of the inner shrine, Marcus saw the woman stir, but then she lay still again, her fragile white hands pressed to the black marble of the floor. Turned toward him he could see the sole of one small foot, scratched and still slightly bleeding. She had walked all the way to the Temple of Isis from the Quirinal Hill, she who had never gone more than a hundred feet except by litter in her life.

The chanting of the choir lifted again, words and music winding like smoke among the heavy columns of the shadowed hall. Where the sun touched the statue, jewels flashed in the marble ears.

Perhaps in some cases hope can be greater than knowledge, thought Marcus. *At least she's spared the horrors that knowledge has brought me. The knowledge that tonight is Midsummer Eve. The knowledge that there isn't a thing I can do, there isn't a thing Arrius can do, that none of us knows a thing except that they have her somewhere, and that there's a sacrifice of some kind set for tonight. And unless we can follow Tiridates tonight when he leaves his house—unless we can track them to their place of worship—when Varus returns his rage will sweep Rome like a destructive fire, and consume the guilty and the innocent alike.*

And against that knowledge, the consolation of philosophy was poor remedy indeed. Better, he thought, for Aurelia Pollia to come here and lay her griefs in the hands of Isis. If it did no more to find her daughter than philosophy had, at least she would have the comfort of knowing that whatever happened, whether Tullia was recovered or not, Isis would sustain them all.

Could it be that the same goal is reached, he wondered, *through emotionalistic drivel as through rational philosophy?* Was it enough to know that the gods, as Arrius had said of that strange old aristocrat in his vine-choked hermitage on the Quirinal Hill, knew more about the situation than you did, and would not fail you?

"Marcus," whispered a woman's voice.

He turned, to see his mother standing at his side.

For a moment he was so shocked he could find nothing to say. She was veiled and looked every inch a Roman matron, as her husband insisted that she should. Her blue wool dress bore the stripe of a woman who has done her duty to state and family by bearing three or more children; she wore the massive gold jewelry befitting a lady of her rank. She could not have looked more out of place in that solemn locus of Egyptian worship if she'd come in the saffron toga of a whore.

Then he whispered, "Thank the gods you've come," and hugged her, in spite of the shocked gaze of a passing priestess. "Father doesn't know?"

She shook her head, her eyes sick with trepidation. "That's why I came here," she whispered back. "I hired a chair."

He grinned shakily. "That sounds like you were going out to meet a lover. You'll get a terrible reputation if that one gets around."

And as he'd hoped, it brought a quick smile to her eyes. But it faded just as quickly. "Do you know, I'd almost believe he'd rather it was a lover than the wife of a political foe of his? As though poor Aurelia ever knew the first thing about politics."

She looked unhappily down at her hands, twisting in the fine indigo folds of her veil. Marcus took her gently by the shoulders, and she looked up into his eyes again, almost on level with her own. She sighed, as if ashamed of the tears that tracked down her faded cheek. "I suppose it could be worse," she murmured. "He could flaunt girl friends and pretty dancing-boys all over town, like Porcius Craessius does, or be sottish and spendthrift like so many others. But this—this petty day-to-day viciousness, this spying on me . . .''

"Leave him," said Marcus quietly. "You're not married to him strict form; he doesn't have the legal right to keep you as a slave."

She shook her head in despair. "Where would I go?" she asked. "Your grandfather Pollius married me to him in the first place because he wanted me out of his house. The dowry was barely respectable then and certainly nothing that could be lived on now. I'm certain none of my stepbrothers would take me in." She sighed and put her hand on his arm; they walked together down the narrow corridor, to the massive doors opening out into the shadows of the temple porch. "It is how it is, Marc," she said softly. "I've known it for a long time."

They stood together for a time in the blue shade of the porch, a pillared concession to the proprieties of Roman taste built onto a structure that had come straight out of the Valley of the Kings. The statues that sheltered there were in the smooth heavy style of Egypt, the goddess's homeland: sphinxes of rose-colored porphyry, Osiris and the dog-headed Anubis in black basalt, graven with long columns of hieroglyphics. From the porch a stairway led down to an aisle of more sphinxes and black granite obelisks, leading through the gardens of the temple grounds. Beyond stretched the Field of Mars, with its gardens, its trees, its columned porches and fashionable shops, strollers taking the air along the covered arcades, nurses herding little gaggles of children at play. Though it was still early morning the day promised hot, and in the windless air the noise of the Forum, the riverside markets, the packed hot streets and crowded tenements of downtown hung like the buzzing drone of a hornet-hive. In the bright hot sunlight the seven hills of Rome loomed to the south and east. Even at a distance of a half mile or so, Marcus could imagine that he smelled the stink of the streets.

Somewhere out there, thought Marcus despairingly. *They have her somewhere there, and tonight is Midsummer Eve.* Sunlight beat into the east-facing porch; he felt the sweat running down his arms and back under the heavy wool of the toga. Every informer Arrius knows is out there, poking, prying, searching . . . *Mother Isis, just this once, bless informers in their chosen task . . .*

"What's wrong, Marc dear?"

He shook his head, not willing to tell her what was afoot that night. He gestured back through the temple doors. "It's only that she doesn't deserve this."

His mother sighed. "Poor Aurelia. She may not be much of an intellectual, but she's one of the kindest people I have ever known. Even as a girl, when it is so much more fun to be cruel." She smiled sadly at him and stroked back the uncombed curls from his brow. "It's good that you're so concerned for her."

"If the gods are kind," said Marcus slowly, "she's going to be my mother-in-law."

She was silent for a moment, hiding her hope under downcast eyelids, as she had learned to, living with Silanus. "Your father can forbid it, you know," she murmured. "And he would, too, in spite of the scandal. Even leaving out that Chambares Tiridates is supposed to be still very set on the match, do you think you could persuade Tullius Varus to consent to a marriage that will have to be paraded through the lawcourts first, and may very well have the children declared bastards after?"

"Tiridates," said Marcus through his teeth, "isn't likely to be in any position to interfere. And as for Father, after tackling the entire Christian cult to get her back, I'm certainly not going to let the threat of a lawsuit stop me. If he tries to exercise his legal rights as a father over me . . ." Marcus took a deep breath. "If her father consents, Tullia and I may end up leaving Rome for a time."

Patricia Pollia Cato studied him for a moment, her light brows drawn together, as if wondering about this new young man. She said, "You've changed a great deal, haven't you, Professor?"

He shook his head, and smiled. "Not so much."

"Your father kept saying that you'd outgrow philosophy

and return to being a sober and worthy son like Caius—poor Caius! But you'll never come back to the fold now, will you?''

He sighed. ''I don't think I've outgrown philosophy so much as realized that I haven't grown into it yet. I can't—I can't think too much ahead now, Mother, in fact I can't think farther ahead than tonight, but when this is over . . .''

''My poor darling,'' she whispered, ''none of us can. When Varus comes back to Rome and can put a proper search in order, they'll find her.''

God help us, thought Marcus in despair. *By then it will be too late.*

He stood aside when Aurelia Pollia emerged from the great temple doors, watching as she embraced the tall lanky woman who through childhood had been her closest friend. She had aged terribly in four days, her face thin and ravaged far more than the absence of cosmetics could account for, her hair hanging like a penitent's in a loose mane around her thin shoulders. She was built like her daughter, small and slender; she seemed a girl against her friend's bony height. It was clear she had never expected to see Patricia again—*a logical assumption,* thought Marcus bitterly, recalling the hideous quarrels his parents had had over his mother's friendship with his father's senatorial foe. Aurelia Pollia held to her friend and wept bitterly, like a thin little waif in her sleeveless white linen gown. He saw that his mother wept, too.

A shadow fell over him. ''Well,'' said a cynical, well-modulated voice at his elbow, ''so Caius Silanus Senior has healed his political breaches with the prefect after all.''

Marcus replied, through taut lips, ''Hardly, Praetor Quindarvis. I should appreciate it if none of this got back to him.''

Those dark little eyes rested speculatively upon him, as though asking the reason for the coldness in his voice. But he only said, ''Sits the wind in that quarter, then? Your mother was raised in Cornelius Pollius' household, wasn't she?'' He turned his gaze back, watching the two women standing beside the granite sphinx, clasping each other's hands. ''Your mother has a great deal of courage. Lady Aurelia needs a woman friend she can trust."

Remembering the obscene blonde goddess who had shared Quindarvis' supper-couch the night before last, Marcus only replied, "Yes, she does."

"I've stayed with her as much as I'm able, between the Senate and the games." He folded his thick strong arms; he had clearly come from the Senate house, for he was dressed in his formal toga, its purple borders dark as wine in the banded shadows of the porch. The scent of his perfume could not quite overlay the smell of his body, sour as a man's is when he has drunk too much the night before. "By Jupiter I'm glad the games are over. They went quite well—extremely well-received. The beast-fight between the Persians and the hyenas was a connoisseur's delight. But this—this ghastly business . . ." He shook his head angrily, his face darkening at the thought. "For all that centurion says, anxiety has hung over my head like the sword of Damocles."

Not that it spoiled your supper-party much, thought Marcus. But he only asked, "And when will Varus be back?"

The big man blew his breath out in a sigh. "Four days, five days. As I said, I'm glad there's someone Lady Aurelia can trust. These next weeks will be busy ones in the treasury. This is the time of year we have to settle down with all our mingy little clerks, bless their circumcised little souls, and get everything straight for the elections. It's going to be worse than a circus until September. With this happening in the middle of it . . ." He shook his head again. "The thing is, we don't know whom we can trust. You know they've arrested the physician Nicanor?"

"What?" gasped Marcus, the guilt like the prick of a dagger.

"Seems some Christian whore denounced him—I'd never have thought it. Still, slaves are master dissemblers. I've never met one who didn't lie, given a chance. But betrayal of a man who was as good to him as my poor cousin Varus was . . ."

Marcus felt his stomach turn, as though he'd swallowed

poisoned food. Tonight was Midsummer Eve—Arrius was calling in all his debts. But still . . . The shady cool of Varus' atrium returned to him, the desperate anxiety in the Greek's dark eyes. ". . . If he thought there was it'd be the rack for us all . . ." The darkness under the Capitoline Prison, a woman's hysterical sobbing, naming anyone to save herself pain . . .

Quindarvis growled. "If I was that blamed centurion I'd have that boy Hylas strung out as well. He should never have left her . . ."

"She ordered him away, and she was within fifty feet of her own front door!" protested Marcus indignantly. "She wanted to talk to me in private."

"Blast it, boy, don't you know all good slaves are deaf? It didn't save her, did it? We've suspected all along they had a Christian confederate in the household, haven't we? How else would they have known just when to expect her to return?"

"But—" Enlightenment hit him. He gulped hastily, "I have to go. Excuse me . . ." He dashed to where his mother stood, caught her by the arms, and gave her and the startled Lady Aurelia quick kisses. He gathered up his toga and went clattering down the stairs, hearing the praetor's gruff voice behind him mutter, "Zany philosopher."

He headed for the Forum at a loping trot.

"So you see, he can't know anything." Flies hummed in the high corners of the cracked plaster ceiling. The small officers' room of the prison, facing east across the Forum, was already blisteringly hot. Under his mail-shirt Arrius' tunic was dark with blotches of sweat. "They didn't need a confederate within the household at all. Not if Tiridates set the whole thing up."

"For a philosopher you're making a mighty big leap there, Professor," growled the centurion, turning over the wax tablet he'd been writing on to continue on the back. The wax was dark and soft already with the heat. "Just because they didn't need Nicanor to set up the ambush doesn't mean he wasn't in on it, and isn't a Christian."

"But that woman would have accused anyone! She was nowhere near right about Lady Aurelia's maid!"

"No?" He glanced up from under jutting brows. "But it happens Nicanor wasn't able to account for his whereabouts last night—when we raided the catacombs—or the night before, when the jail was broken. He's refused to talk at all."

Marcus stared. "But—he has to. I mean . . ."

Arrius said dryly, "Precisely." He set the tablet aside and cracked his broken heavy knuckles. "So what about it, Professor? You want the hangman to have a few words with him this afternoon, or do you feel sure enough of his innocence to throw double or quits on tonight?"

In the hot heavy silence the noises from the Forum outside sounded very loud: the flutes of streetcorner dancers, the harsh cry of a Chaldean woman, hawking amulets against the evil eye. From the guardroom beyond the open door a soldier could be heard, cursing the poxy whoreson of a faggot charioteer who'd lost him his money on the races. Marcus thought of what Sixtus had said; that if Tiridates' house had a passage out of the cellar, Arrius and his men could sit all night around it. Even though the men would be scattered, to pick up the Syrian if he emerged some distance from his house, they couldn't cover the whole Aventine. He thought of the rack and of the physician's stiff-necked, unpracticed pleas.

"Let me talk to him," he said.

Arrius shrugged. "You're welcome to try I couldn't make him open his mouth." He stood up and stretched, to unkink his back. "I'm going over to that eating-house down on Tuscan Street. Let our Son of Asclepius know that I plan to have some answers, one way or the other, by the time I come back."

And he strode from the room, deadly and impersonally cruel as a tiger.

Marcus descended the ladder from the guardroom to the smothering darkness of the corridor below in an almost unbearable torment of mind. Justice cried out to him to tell Arrius to wait. Why dislocate every joint in an innocent man's body—or a guilty one's, for that matter—if the night would bring them the proof they sought? Why put anyone through the hideous torment of the rack on the say-so of a prating, cowardly person who had clearly been making accusations at random, especially if they were going to follow Tiridates that night to the rendezvous and the Christian sacrifice, and recover Tullia anyway?

But if they did not, after tonight it might be too late. If they failed—if Tiridates proved too clever for them, as the Christians had twice now slipped through the fingers of the guards—if Tiridates was, in fact, Papa—they would have no further clue. When Varus returned in four days from Sicily, it would be to find his daughter still gone, either dead or a forced participant in Christian rites. Then all of them—Nicanor, and the girl Dorcas, Judah Symmachus and his innocent father—would be consumed by his revenge.

Did he have the right to endanger them all, for a man who might just possibly be guilty anyway?

The guard on the cell that had once held the Christians gave Marcus a half-comical salute, and said, " 'Mornin', Professor. Callin' on our friend here?'' Under the greasy yellow of the torchlight his face looked stupid and cruel, for all its amiable expression.

Marcus straightened the inexpert folds of his soiled toga. "Yes. Please.''

The guard unlocked the door. "Popular fella. Hear he's got afternoon callers lined up, too.'' He held up his torch to illuminate the cramped little hole.

The stink of the place was like mud in the nostrils. Nicanor lay in the dense shadows at the far corner of the cell, his face turned to the wall. He neither moved nor looked up when Marcus entered.

"Nicanor?'' said Marcus doubtfully. He received no response. "Nicanor, it's me, Marcus. I have to talk to you.'' He crossed the room to that unmoving figure in the darkness. "I'm sorry I—'' He stopped. From the door the general stink of the room had overwhelmed it, but this close it was unmistakable. The hour or so he'd spent in the pits of the amphitheater, if nothing else, had taught him the stench of fresh blood.

"Holy gods . . ." He dropped to his knees, turning that hunched and drawn-up body over. His hand came away blazing red, as if he had set it down in paint.

"How'd he do it?" Arrius pushed the plate of bread and stew across the little table at him; Marcus shook his head weakly. Behind them on Tuscan Street, the male whores for whom this district was famous were beginning to parade in their long-sleeved tunics and eye paint, primping their perfumed curls.

"He had a cloakpin. He ripped the veins in his wrists." Marcus shivered at the memory. "The physician from the gladiatorial school was the closest we could reach—the one down by the Flavian. He was working on him when I left."

Arrius finished off his wine and stood up, shaking straight the folds in his red cloak, "So he's not dead?"

"Not when I left."

He paid his reckoning and a little over for the girl who'd served him, who favored him with a big smile from which half the teeth were gone. "You'd be surprised how tough men can be," he mused, as they jostled through the crowds on that narrow street. "I've seen men crawl twenty miles with a broken spear-head in them, then have the camp doctor cut it out at the end of it, and have them wake up and ask for food just as we were rolling them up in their shrouds. Doctors at the gladiatorial schools will tell you stranger things than that." They detoured around a little knot of brightly clothed Syrians, grouped in the doorway of a fortune-teller's shop, their rings flashing with the waving of their arms. "We'll see what we can find out tonight, but if—"

He broke off, as the clamor from a side street interrupted him, a medley of jeers and curses and men's voices yelling, "Murderer! Corpse-eater!"

"What the—"

Halfway down the lane a mob had gathered, flinging stones and garbage at the bent, spiderlike figure of a man crouched against the pink-washed wall of a tall building that ran the length of the block. They were idlers, men out of work for the most part. Men who yesterday had occupied their time at Quindarvis' celebrated games, thought Marcus, and hadn't quite had their fill. But a couple of the local shopkeepers had joined them, a slippermaker in his little leather apron and a man with an ironworker's soot-blackened face. Children crowded the lane, picking up dung from the road to hurl. Cries of "Christian! Jew! Christian!" tangled in the thick hot air.

Arrius snarled a startled curse and left Marcus to stride toward the mob.

The Christian straightened up a little, and a familiar voice screeched over the din of the crowd. "You stone the prophets of the Lord! God made himself manifest as Christ Jesus to smite the abodes of sin, to delve out the taproots of abomination! Oh ye wicked and adulterous generation . . ."

"Abomination yourself, you dirty ghoul!" someone yelled, and a piece of dog shit splattered stickily against the Christian Ignatius' dirty robe.

The shrill voice rose. "Repent of your evils! Cast aside your wickedness and your fornications! God shall smite this city with his fire, and shall shatter it into atoms . . ."

"That stupid little . . ." The centurion began to force his way through the crowd with businesslike brutality. In the crowd behind him Marcus heard one idler mutter to another.

"Serves the little bastard right. Anyone who'd believe the Lord made himself manifest as Christ, rather than merely imbuing the human substance with divine nature, deserves to be stoned."

" 'Specially after it clearly states in Paul's letter to the Corinthians that there was one God and one Lord Jesus Christ."

"You'd know that little bugger'd get it all wrong."

Marcus swung around, but people were pressing up so closely behind him he could not see who'd spoken. All around him mouths were open, men and women howling, "Murderer! Kidnapper! Kill him!"

A bigger stone tore a jagged bruise of red in Ignatius' cheek. He fell back against the wall behind him, shaking his bony fists at them all and screaming, "Neither fornicators, nor idolaters, nor adulterers, nor effeminate, nor abusers of themselves with mankind, nor thieves, nor covetous, nor drunkards, nor revilers, nor extortionate shall inherit the Kingdom of God . . ." Juice from a burst plum trickled down the side of his bald head into the blood in his beard. In the doorway of the house behind him women had appeared, clutching their thin robes about them, some of them shrieking in excitement, others giggling. A bigger rock smashed him in the shoulder, whirling him around, and he fell to his knees in the muck of the lane. Baying, the mob closed in.

"HERE!" roared Arrius, in a voice trained to carry over urban bread riots. "What is all this? Get back, curse you . . ."

At the sight of his armor the mob milled a little, losing their momentum. Some of them dropped the rocks they bore; one man who'd been kicking the hunched little form on the ground gave it a final boot and turned sulkily away, like a child called to order by an unloved older brother. In the crowded doorway of the tall house a woman pushed her way to the fore, her gilt hair dressed in careful curls around a heavily made-up face, her thin tunic and toga of flame-colored silk leaving neither her profession nor her charms in any question. In a face like Venus' her eyes were cold as a moneylender's.

"Take that little pig out of here and keep him from slandering decent people!" she cried, in a voice rich and sweet as Samian wine. "I run an orderly house, and I can't have filthy little troublemakers like him . . ."

The crumpled form in the mud stirred itself; a bloody, angry face was raised, fire sparking from those dark brilliant eyes. "Whore that sitteth on the waters! Scarlet mother of adulteries, drunken on the blood of the martyrs of Christ!"

The red rosebud mouth popped open in shocked distaste. "Well, I never!"

Arrius seized Ignatius by the arm and hauled him to his feet.

"Pig! Devil! Scum!" shrieked the Christian, spitting on the

man's scarred brown arm. "Bloody beast of Caesar! You persecute the servants of the Lord!"

Around them the mob was already losing interest, drifting away down the narrow street or returning to abandoned pursuits. Behind the blonde woman the gaggle of girls still peeked, or else pulled the thin gauze of their dresses tight, so that the rouged tips of their breasts showed through the cloth, and blew kisses to the men who still lingered, as though to say that it was not too early in the day for other matters than killing Christians.

The centurion held his rescued martyr at arm's length and looked up at the madam. "What's our boy here been up to, Plotina?"

"You saw him! Cursing at customers, blocking the doors, ranting that garbage . . ." She shrugged, her big hard breasts shifting like melons under the thin silk. "I've always run an orderly house and I pay taxes to keep it that way. I can't have this kind of thing. My customers come here to relax, have a little decent fun . . ."

A little decent fun like you were having at Quindarvis' supper-party, thought Marcus suddenly, recognizing that round pink face in its frame of too-bright hair. It occurred to him to wonder if she'd helped provide the entertainment, and he felt a kind of sick distaste, as though he'd bitten into something rotten.

Meanwhile Ignatius was striking ineffectually at his rescuer's arm. "Beast of seven heads! Pimp of Antichrist! In the days to come you will be thrown into the fiery pit, and the saints of God shall laugh to hear you scream!"

"Hey!" One of the few remaining onlookers, a big burly fellow in a blacksmith's leather kilt, cuffed him angrily. "He didn't have to save you from stoning, you little Jew."

"What is stoning to me?" screamed Ignatius. "What are the beasts of the arena to me? In rending my body they shall offer me a pure and perfect sacrifice to the Lord . . ."

"Not if you go around preaching *that* heretical drivel they won't," grumbled a retreating voice somewhere behind Marcus.

"Mother of harlots! You are filled with the abominations

of the earth! You shall be made desolate and naked, and the beasts shall eat your flesh while your soul burns in hell!''

"I'm afraid you got that backward, preacher," said Arrius quietly. "You're the one most likely to be cooked or eaten, and what happens to your soul after that is no business of mine. But I have a few questions to ask you, first.''

XII

Though I am worshiped in many aspects, known by countless
names, and propitiated with all manner of different rites, yet the
whole round earth venerates me. The primeval Phrygians call me
Pessinuntica, Mother of the Gods; the Athenians, sprung from
their own soil, call me Cecropian Artemis; for the islanders of
Cyprus I am Paphian Aphrodite; for the archers of Crete I am
Dictynna; for the trilingual Sicilians, Stygian Proserpine; for the
Eleusinians their ancient Mother of the Corn. . . .

Invocation of Isis (from Apuleius)

"And did you get any sense out of him?" Sixtus selected a
date from the bowl on the table before them, turned it over in
his fingers as though searching for a maker's mark, and
consumed it with slow enjoyment, his eyes never leaving
Marcus' face.

Marcus shook his head. In the garden beyond the open
archways of the summer dining room, late sunlight shim-
mered among the embroidered veils of the pepper trees,
making a mingled harlequin of shadows on the worn marble
floor. "Well, when we got back he was taken up with
Nicanor, and then the hangman had left to take his siesta.

Arrius questioned him himself—pretty roughly, I thought—but all he got was ranting."

"Hardly surprising," commented the scholar. "He sounds like a man not easily turned aside from his purposes—certainly not by anything so paltry as life or limb. How's Nicanor?"

Marcus looked unhappily down at the tabletop, a smooth-worn marquetry of fruitwoods and mother-of-pearl. "He's alive," he said quietly. "That's about all that can be said for the present. It's too early to tell. He cut longways down the veins, instead of across."

Sixtus nodded. "He's a physician, he'd know about things like that."

Churaldin came in, carrying a bronze wine mixer; at his heels trotted the little dancer from Quindarvis' feast, well-brushed and well-scrubbed in her plain linen dress, and shy to the point of muteness.

"But why would he do it?" asked Marcus miserably, as the child handed him a cup.

"Possibly he did not wish to be racked. I shouldn't, my-self." He accepted the offered cup from the little girl as though she'd been a table. She was looking at him with worship in her eyes; if he'd spoken to her she'd probably have fled the room.

"But if he was innocent . . ."

"What makes you think he was?" asked Sixtus. "If he was a Christian—or if he had anything else to hide—suicide would be the logical course. And even if he was innocent, you cannot prove innocence by torture—only guilt, or stam-ina. Will you see him tomorrow?"

Marcus nodded wretchedly. "I think a lot depends on what we find tonight."

In the garden outside the light was fading; the evening promised warm and still. Through the tangling vines he could see the gray cat beginning to prowl, green eyes wide with the madness of summer. Churaldin asked, "Will there be any-thing else?" and Sixtus shook his head. "Let's go, Octavia." Collecting her dippers and water jar, the little girl hurried out at his heels. As the shadows swallowed them up, Marcus could see the tall Briton rumple the child's dark hair.

"You bought her from Quindarvis?"

Sixtus shook his head. "No, I simply left with her. Since I contrived to look unspeakably bored during the rest of the orgy, they now suspect me of vices they can only guess at—even our friend Porcius Craessius was tremendously impressed."

Marcus cried, "How disgusting!"

The blue eyes twinkled. "I would far prefer what others will say about me to what I would think of myself if I left her there. I don't suppose you saw more than half of what went on—you left rather early."

"I saw enough," muttered Marcus.

"I daresay you did. Where were you when you were attacked that night? You said close to the circus?"

"Pretty close to the east corner of the circus," he agreed. He was becoming more and more used to the old philosopher's lightning changes of topic. "We passed the Temple of Ceres almost immediately, when those two Christians saw me home. I still don't understand that—"

"Who understands Christians? Would you say the men you were following were headed for the river?"

Marcus nodded. "I thought so at the time. I remember wondering how I was going to track them across the bridges, or through the Tiberside district. If you think the Subara's bad, the streets of the Tiberside are like some kind of Damascus bazaar. Most people over there don't even speak Latin. Once over the bridge they could go anywhere . . ."

"Indeed." Sixtus nodded, folding his thick knotted hands against his chin and staring out into space over the minor mountain range of his knuckles. Then his blue eyes seemed to flicker into focus once again. "And where is Arrius posting his men?"

"Various places on the Aventine, where they know about houses with tunnels or subcellars. A couple of places near the circus, in that warren of slums there."

"Anyone on the bridge?"

"Not that I know of. Sixtus, why do we have to wait? Why can't we just have Tiridates arrested, search his house . . ."

"Who would arrest him?" asked the old man reasonably. "Who would order the search? The city prefect's away. The praetorian prefect might, if he wanted to risk a complaint to the emperor about the way he's fulfilling his duties, but what if he's wrong? What if he can't prove Tiridates is anything more than an extremely wealthy and powerful member of the Syrian merchant community who happens to have a fish tattooed on his arm? The emperor is notoriously hard on secret informers and men who listen to them."

"But it's Midsummer Eve!" cried Marcus. "The sacrifice is tonight! We can't just sit here . . ."

"We're not going to," said Sixtus mildly, standing up and limping to the corner to fetch his staff. "We're going to take a little walk down to the Tiber bridges."

It was just over a mile from the run-down mansion on the Quirinal Hill to the bend in the Tiber where the brown waters divided around the little island of Tiberina with its hospital and its shrine to Asclepius. At this hour—the beginning of the first hour of the night—the two bridges that spanned the stream such a short distance from each other were almost deserted, though later Marcus knew they'd be a madhouse of cart traffic as the small farmers from the slopes of the Janiculum Hill and the Vatican started bringing in their produce to the city markets. The last tints of color paled and changed in the western sky, and degree by degree the hot blue summer sky deepened, from the color of a robin's egg to that of a peacock's breast, through teal, through the ultramarine of the summer Adriatic, to the unearthly blue of fine dark velvet, sewn with stars and dusted with galaxies of light. Sixtus sat on the stone balustrade of the bridge, talking of philosophy or of desert warfare, occasionally dropping a leaf or a twig down into the brown stream, while Marcus watched the pinholes of fire sparkle into life all along the darkness of the thick crowding suburbs on the river's western bank. In the calmness of that warm milky night—or perhaps merely due to the old man's serene personality—he had no sense of wasting time, nor of impatience. He felt rather like a runner somewhere in the middle of a relay race, waiting for the torch to come to his hand, but not about to fret himself until it did.

At about the second hour of the night—for the hours of summer nights are very short—the cart traffic started up again, countrymen leading their donkeys or oxcarts through the deep twilight of the bridge, girls driving herds of swine or gaggles of geese, singing as they strolled through the warm liquid darkness. People crossed from the other direction as well, coming from Rome out to the Tiberside across the river: ladies of the evening in bright silks, Syrians chattering in their own tongue, rattling with astrological amulets, rich men in litters with their little troops of linkboys, clients, slaves carrying their slippers, bound for dinner with friends in the villas out in the Vatican Fields, or on the high wooded slopes of the Janiculum. One of these passed by and Sixtus said quietly, "There's our man," and was moving off in its wake almost before Marcus was aware that he'd spoken.

"How do you know?" he whispered, catching up to the old man as he strolled, calm as any other country traveler in his plain tunic and short traveler's cloak, after the plain chair with its close-drawn leather curtains. Even with his game leg and his staff, it was surprising how light-footed he was. "That isn't his litter."

"No, but at one point in the proceedings at Quindarvis' the other night I made it a point to slip out to the slaves' court and make sure I could recognize his other bearers and linkboys." The chair turned from the main way down a widish street leading northwest, the flickering torches of the two slaves trotting ahead of it winking on the gold curtain rings, throwing a confusion of shadows on the high tenement walls. Away from the main traffic artery into Rome there was little activity. The shop-fronts were heavily shuttered, and few lights showed in the windows of the tenements that rose like black cliffs on either side of the narrow way. A breeze blew down from the Janiculum, bearing on it the country smell of greenery and life.

"Why?" whispered Marcus, turning a corner and starting up the slope that led, eventually, to the hill itself. "You didn't know then that he was a Christian."

Sixtus hesitated a moment before replying. "We don't know that he is now; not for certain," he said at last. "Other faiths than the Christians use the fish as their symbol."

"Yes, but the amulet we picked up when Tullia was kidnapped was inscribed with the initials of the Christos. And besides," added Marcus, with an uneasy glance at the totally deserted darkness of the streets behind them, "he can't have evaded Arrius and his men by accident."

"No," the old man agreed. "No, from the beginning it was clear that Tiridates was involved in something—the only question was, what and how? And it always pays to know as much about a potential enemy as you can. It's clear that he posted bearers and a litter somewhere in anticipation of leaving his house secretly tonight; the other men, the bearers whom you recognized and who recognized you, will have told him that you followed them back to Rome. He's a man who knows himself to be watched. He's taking no chances, the night of the Midsummer sacrifice."

Some note in his voice caught Marcus' attention, and suddenly disquieted, he turned to look at the scarred and time-battered face, all but hidden in the darkness of the stone-walled lane. They had left the crowded mazes of the Oriental town behind. They were among the small private houses—half farms, half hovels—that scattered along its outskirts, each with its vegetable patch and poultry yard, its pigsty and tethered goat. To the north, on their right, stretched the dark flat formlessness of the Vatican Fields. Directly ahead of them the Janiculum Hill rose, an undulant line of trees marked with the occasional lights of isolated villas. The litter was now far ahead of them, an occasional jitter of flame seen through the tree trunks, but Sixtus seemed in no great hurry to keep it in sight.

"You sound as if you know where he's going."

"I know that if he crossed the river, there's only one place he could be going." He took Marcus' arm quickly and drew him into the dense shadows of a little alley between a wall and a shed. After a moment a small group of men and women appeared at the end of the lane from which they had just come, the women veiled in Oriental fashion, the men dark-faced and Semitic, clothed in the rough brown tunics of laborers or slaves. Marcus flattened against the wall as they passed and watched them out of sight up the lane; hurrying, furtive forms lost to sight in the shadows like a random tumbling of blown brown leaves.

After that they proceeded more carefully. As they climbed the lower slopes of the Janiculum, Marcus was conscious of others upon the road; drifting shapes that flitted cautiously among the shadows of the trees, an occasional litter and once a cisium, the little hooves of its pony rattling furiously on the stones of the road, tearing past them at a great rate and taking the corner ahead with its outside wheel all but coming off the ground. Sixtus had fallen silent in the unbroken darkness of the summer night, but once when the trees cleared a little above some rich man's house, Marcus could see by starlight how set and drawn his face looked, and how ageless.

He stopped, tense and puzzled. "Is that music?"

An owl hooted. Somewhere there was a rustling in the thin woodland of oak and birch, as coneys sought the faint gurgle of an unseen spring. As a dog will hear whistling above what a human can detect, so now Marcus thought that he sensed, or felt in his bones, the deep insistent throb of drums. Faint as the pipes of Pan, a drift of flute notes blew among the dark uneasy trees.

"What is it?" he whispered. "Where's it coming from? Is it—is it the Christians?"

Sixtus' eyes glinted in the darkness. The starlight put a flicker of white around the ends of his hair, like a fox-fire halo. "It's coming from up ahead," he breathed. "Go carefully—they'll have posted a guard."

Anxiety seemed to have sharpened Marcus' senses to agonizing brilliance. Past the next turn of the path he saw the white line of a marble roof over the brooding cloudbanks of Stygian trees and heard, like a murmuring response to the elusive music, the cooing of a thousand doves.

"Of course," he said softly. "Of course—it's the biggest deserted building in Rome. It's been shut up for—what did you say, Sixtus? Going on fifteen years?"

"Going on that," murmured the old man.

"If the cult of Atargatis was proscribed in the first year or so of Trajan's reign, and the temple was deserted . . ."

"But it wasn't deserted," said Sixtus, "was it?"

"No—no, of course not. Not if the Christians were using it for their major sacrifices. We can—"

Surprisingly strong, the old man's hand closed on his arm as he started forward. Beyond the trees the music had become insistent, driving, like thinned amber fire streaming through the blood veins; there was an urgency to it, like lust or fear. Sixtus whispered, "Listen to me, Marcus . . ."

He tried to pull away. "They'll have started . . ." It might have been his overwrought imagination, but he had thought for a moment that among the cool scents of vines and water and midsummer night, he had smelled smoke.

"Listen to me anyway." Though he spoke in a whisper, such was the authority of Sixtus' voice that Marcus stopped, as though he were one of the old man's soldiers. A lifetime in the field had given this deceptively frail old gentleman a habit of command that rivaled the emperor's.

Behind the throbbing rise of the music, his voice was low. "Do you remember the story of the Maenads? The worshipers of Dionysus who tore to pieces any who intruded upon their rites?"

"Yes," whispered Marcus uneasily, suddenly aware that as well as being the largest deserted building in Rome, the old Temple of Atargatis was also one of the most isolated. "That was in—in *The Bacchae*—Euripides . . ."

"I'm glad you remember your schooldays," said the old man grimly. "Remember then also that we are greatly outnumbered, and that we are dealing with people who may be in the grip of a religious frenzy. If we make our presence known to them in any way, it may very well be the last thing that either of us ever does.''

In the darkness the flutes twisted, the music seeming to gasp and keen, like the mounting urgency of passion. This time Marcus was sure of it; there was smoke on the air. ''But Tullia . . .'' he whispered desperately.

''You're a philosopher,'' retorted Sixtus impatiently. ''Do you know the difference between what is possible and what is impossible?''

The sudden plunge into elenchus startled him. He blinked for a moment and said, ''Uh—no.''

''Well, I'm a military commander,'' snapped the old man, ''and I do. Now follow me, and we'll try to get in round the back.''

The temple grounds were surrounded by a wall, and as Sixtus had said, there was a man at the gate. But fifteen years of neglect had taken its toll. The wall was crumbling, its stones forced apart by steel-fingered vines, and in places the local farmers had made free with the fabric of it to wall their own gardens. There was neither light nor any sign of life in the woods surrounding the temple precinct, only the occasional hoot of an owl, or the soft continual rustling of the temple doves. Marcus found his eyes had grown used to the dim starlight, however, and his companion seemed to be able to see in the dark like a cat. They found a gap in the walls on the far side of the temple itself. Marcus scrambled through it and helped Sixtus up; then they both dropped to the ground on the other side.

Beyond the dense shadows of the trees that surrounded it, the temple of the Syrian goddess sprawled like a vast white mausoleum, its weather-stained walls half-choked with vines and smeared from the eaves down with a streaky cascade of dove droppings. Darkly gleaming in the starlight the great ponds that had contained the goddess' sacred fish lay like black pools of oil, clogged with weeds and mud. No light shone from the pillared porch that enclosed the front entrance, but in one of the high small windows on the bare dirty flank of the building, Marcus thought he glimpsed a red flicker of firelight. From here the music was clearly audible, a wild obscene wailing against the thrusting rhythm of the drum, and below it, the steady beating of hands marking time. Once he heard another sound that prickled the hair of his nape with horror: the protesting wail of a small and terrified baby.

For one instant his eyes met Sixtus' in the dark. Then the old man was moving off again, light-footed despite his staff, soundless in the deep carpet of matted leaves that strewed the entire precinct. Marcus smelled smoke again, and in the eaves of the temple the doves stirred, fluttering in the darkness.

Marcus felt, rather than heard, the thin swooshing of steel through air. With speed he had never dreamed he possessed he ducked and threw himself sideways, shutting his teeth against a cry of pain as he felt the flesh of his arm open. He saw a man—black and bronze in the shadows of the trees— standing over him as he fell, caught the thin starlight as it flashed on the descending blade. Marcus kicked desperately at his legs, making him stumble and miss; the air burned in his cut arm and his blood felt astonishingly hot against his flesh. His attacker caught his balance, and he had a blurred glimpse, through terror and pain, of a brown Arabian face framed in close-curled black hair, teeth horribly white in a grimace. The sword sheared down and sideways, slicing at his throat.

But the blow never landed. Sixtus had reached them in two swift strides and jabbed straight into the fray with the end of his staff, like a bargeman poling off a wharf. The end of the staff took Marcus' assailant just where the ribs curled up around those rippling stomach muscles, meeting the man's full-speed attack. The Arab's mouth popped open, he made a horrible sound, between a groan and a wheeze, and his arms flipped awkwardly out, like the wings of a toy chicken when its string is pulled. Calmly and with lightning speed, Sixtus reversed his walking stick around the fulcrum of his hands, and its iron-shod foot took the man in the temple and dropped him like the dead across Marcus' body.

The sword fell to the rustling leaves. From the pillared porch of the temple someone called out softly, warily; Sixtus called back in another language and got a satisfied grunt in reply. Then he knelt beside Marcus and whispered, "Are you all right?"

He managed to nod. Sixtus pulled the unconscious attacker off him and helped Marcus to sit up.

"Are you bleeding much?"

Marcus shook his head, feeling dizzy and very ill. Sixtus used the fallen sword to cut a long strip out of the hem of the attacker's tunic. In the diffuse starlight Marcus could see it was the taller of the two Arab bearers, the one to whom Tiridates had spoken on the terrace of Quindarvis' house. Working quickly and calmly, as though he did this every night of his life, Sixtus examined the wound, bound it up, and applied a tourniquet higher up on Marcus' shoulder to staunch the bleeding. Then, while Marcus was still sitting dazedly trying to get his wits back, the old man pulled off the assailant's belt and tunic, bound his hands with the belt, and cut strips from the tunic to bind his feet and gag him. Watching the frail old scholar engaged in this task, Marcus realized that the guard had chosen to attack him first, because he didn't see a lame and white-haired old man as being any threat.

The idea of it made him giggle. "I thought you said Christians were opposed to violence," he said, and Sixtus shot him a startled glance. "What's a Christian doing trying to lop off somebody's head with a sword?"

There was a long pause, while the old man finished up his work, and slung the sword and scabbard at his own belt. He handled the weapon as unthinkingly as Marcus would eat an apple. Then he said, "What makes you think these are Christians?" He sat back on his heels, called out into the darkness in another language—Syrian, Marcus thought, or possibly Arabic. The voice from the temple porch replied; Sixtus went into a rapid-fire string of instructions and was rewarded, a moment later, when two dark forms emerged from the shadows of the pillars and went hurrying away through the starlight into the darkness of the woods. He turned back to Marcus. "Are you well enough to go on?"

He nodded weakly and managed to get to his feet mostly unassisted. "What did you tell them?" he asked, nodding toward the temple porch. "And what do you mean, these aren't Christians?"

Sixtus was already moving out into the open starlight, "I told them I thought I'd heard intruders on the north side of the grounds," he whispered back over his shoulder. "It should keep them busy until we can get in and get out." He moved with a swift scuttling hobble, from shadow to shadow, toward the darkness of the porch, and Marcus, with a quick glance to the right and left, followed. The music was like a drug in his blood, a fever that drew him to its crescendo; it was as though he could feel the heartbeat of the worshipers within the dark sanctuary through the surging beat of their hands.

The doors of the temple were shut, barred with wan starlight and the black shadows of the pillars. Crouching to either side were huge things of marble and bronze, things with eyes and wings, beaks and claws. There was an evil in them that made Marcus shiver as he passed the point where those horrible gazes locked, and he wondered if Sixtus felt it, too. The heartbeat of the drum was louder here, and as the old man pushed open the dark door, he became conscious of another sound, the whining snarl of a whip. The music grew stronger, insistent, like a streak of red in darkness; he heard a man groan and shrill voices chanting. He wondered how they would find Tullia in this place, and how they would get out when they did.

Soundless as cats, they slipped into the pitch darkness of the temple.

After the faint starlight the temple anteroom was chokingly dark, the blackness like a muffling blanket. The room seemed alive, the walls vibrating with the deep groaning of the drum, the air seeming to shiver and flutter with the beat of hands, the drugged sway of the dance. The place stank of blood and incense, of smoke that could not mask the pungent salt muskiness of sex. There was a sickness, an ugliness, to the feel of the place, the insinuation of forbidden things, that turned Marcus' stomach and made his skin crawl with an unspeakable feeling of horror. As his eyes grew used to the deeper darkness, he made out tenebrous shapes of couches, of dragged blankets and scattered pillows among the heavy Oriental columns, of old stains on the floor. A single slit of firelight from the sanctuary doors towered at least twenty feet in the darkness before them, red as blood; the black beating air was rank and living as a rapist's breath in his face.

But he dared ask nothing, only followed Sixtus as though hypnotized. The dark shape limped softly before him, to the cyclopean doors.

As he approached them the smell of smoke grew stronger, and with it the stench of new blood, copper-sharp in the hot air, and the stink of superheated metal. Firelight widened over his face as he touched the door; it moved soundlessly on oiled hinges, to show what lay beyond.

He had a blurred impression of darkness, of pillars, of a double line of black marble phalluses six feet high, gleaming with the red glare of the fire. Beyond them like a mingling of fire and shadows men and women swayed, bodies half-naked and glistening with sweat, heads lolling, dark hair falling over faces drenched as though by rain, over eyes whose white showed in a rim all around dilated black pupils. Gimcrack jewelry and solid gold caught flashes of the light. The eyes were empty of feeling, of knowledge; they were wide with the demon emptiness of madness.

Boneless as the creation of a fever-dream, dancers leaped and swayed in the glare of the braziers. Thin androgynous bodies swayed and whirled, streaked all over with streaming blood. They had sharpened shells and little knives in their hands, ripping at their own flesh and one another's with staring, uncaring, unconscious eyes, and the blood splattered up over the feet of the image, the One for Whom they danced.

She was exactly as she had been in the image Sixtus had showed him, back in his vine-cave of a study. Gross, obscene, but with a horrible fascination in that many-breasted body, her head covered in jewels, her piscine tail resting among the lions crouched at her feet. Her eyes stared out, wide and fixed and hideous beyond description; her hands, reaching out over the flames that flickered in her hollowed lap, glowed already.

As Marcus watched in horror something stirred on the floor among the priests, something huge and gross and glistening, like a mountain of wet leather polished with new blood. It heaved itself to its knees. The whips sang, crossing their weals over the rolled fat of that immense back, and where the welts joined, blood trickled to mingle with the man's pouring sweat. The priests swayed closer, beating him not only with their whips but with their stringy hair, and the face he raised to the glowing idol was transformed by ecstasy almost beyond recognition. Firelight, catching in the jewels in his rings, scattered glittering over his arms; the fish of the goddess, tattooed in the flesh, seemed to swim beneath the surface of a sun-sparkling sea.

The man's voice was the bellow of a dying bull. "Atargatis!"

Pounding, crashing, the beating hands and bodies of the congregation echoed back the cry, "Atargatis!"

"You are the Mother! You are all that was and is!"

"Atargatis!"

"You are the she-goat that suckles us all! You are the ocean in which we all swim!"

"Atargatis!"

"Grant us this prayer, give us this blessing that it is within your unending power to give!"

"Atargatis!" The roar of the voices was like the sea, like a drug or the hideous logic of a hallucination. An emaciated eunuch rose from the stairs where he had collapsed in exhaustion, his body pouring blood from a dozen gashes, even his hair sticky and pointed with the stuff. He stretched forth bony hands and took something from a basket that had been in the shadows at the idol's feet; something that wriggled and began to wail in sleepy protest.

Tiridates extended his huge arms toward the idol, the priest, the glowing fire that heated the red-hot brazen hands of the statue; his voice sounded shrill and stiff, almost like something produced from metal and wind. "Atargatis, I must take this girl to wife! Find her where they have hidden her! Send her safe to us!''

The voices of the congregation rose in a storming echo over the wavelike crashing of their hands. The whips sang, tearing the fat flesh; the thin eunuch came forward and mopped a handful of blood and sweat from Tiridates' gleaming bosom and smeared it over the baby he held so easily in one huge spreading hand. The child began to kick and cry in earnest; a half-Nubian baby, Marcus saw, a boy of less than two months, tiny hands and feet kicking in terror at the noise and the smell of hot blood. The priest held it up for the congregation to see; his grinning skull-face was nothing human. Tiridates' shouting was all but drowned in the roaring of the mob. ''Send her safe!''

''Atargatis!''

''Bless us, your children!''

''Atargatis!''

''Let not the plans of thy most loyal son be crushed by stupid Fate! All-powerful, all-Mother, let this girl be found . . .''

''Atargatis . . .''

The priest was a black shape before the immense gold monstrosity, a skeleton silhouetted in the fire and the blaze of the searing brass hands that stretched over it like a grill. Terrified by the heat, the baby had begun to scream, but the sound barely carried over the clapping, the stamping, the rising chant of the goddess name . . .

''DROP IT!''

Marcus had not thought any human voice could carry over that infernal din, much less that he'd be able to recognize any man's. But Arrius had had experience making himself heard over battle, riot, and storm—Marcus would have known that harsh bellow anywhere.

The priest swung around, startled; like Jupiter stepping from the roil of his thunderclouds, the centurion had materialized from the darkness by the altar. At his words there was a singing of steel throughout the shadows that hid the walls, and Marcus saw, suddenly, as they moved, the firelight on red helmet-crests.

There was a moment of dead, utter silence, in which Marcus could hear the crackle of the fire, and the hot metal's hiss. Then the thin priest whirled, far too fast for one broken suddenly from the grip of the god, and hurled the screaming infant straight into the centurion's arms. Arrius dropped his sword and fumbled a catch, cursing; the priest bolted like a scalded tomcat around the other side of the altar into darkness. The sanctuary dissolved into a shrieking chaos as men and women tried to flee, or threw themselves howling upon the armed soldiers, clawing at the armored bodies of the men who swatted them aside like flies. The priests were not among the Maenads—they dropped their bloodstained whips and bolted like rabbits. Many of the congregation followed—it is the chief strength of Maenads to outnumber their prey. Sixtus pulled Marcus clear of the doorway as the scrambling, trampling men and women clawed past them, pushing for the door.

Soldiers had already converged on Tiridates; the fat man was blinking, dazed, as though wakened from a dream, holding a woman's scarf in front of his privates and streaming with blood, a horrible and ludicrous sight. Two guards came back around the main altar, dragging the biting, clawing chief priest. Sixtus grabbed Marcus by the wrist and hustled him down the mobbed steps, through a dark confusion of struggling forms, cursing men, screaming women, and soldiers, toward the bronze form that stood by the altar, as still as an idol himself in the rose-amber glare of the sacrificial fires. He still held the infant, who was wriggling and sobbing helplessly at the bite of the mail into his soft flesh.

The centurion's greenish eyes were bitter and cynical. "Quite a party," he said.

"We were only pleased you could come," replied Sixtus graciously.

Arrius looked up, his gaze moving slowly around the dark room, to the gaggle of terrified priests under one guard and the bleeding, indignant Tiridates under another. Soldiers from the anteroom brought in a dark, small, pretty woman in her late twenties, clutching her shawl about her shoulders; Tiridates' sister Roxanne, thought Marcus, watching the look that passed between the two. Suddenly he felt sick, and very tired.

"Well, credit me with a few wits," the centurion said at last. "I had two men on the bridge. Neither of them recognized Tiridates' plain litter but one of them, may Mithras bless his beady little eyes, recognized the Professor here from our little night at the catacombs. When he saw you hotfoot in pursuit of a perfectly strange litter, he had the sense to send his partner to fetch us and kept you in sight. Though mind you, we expected to find Christians, rather than"—he gestured around him in disgust—"this." He looked down at the sobbing child. "We'll send word to the watch in the various city precincts to see if we can find this poor little bastard's parents. Somebody's been feeding him good." He poked the child absentmindedly in the stomach. He looked around him. The hot darkness of the sanctuary still stank of incense and spilled blood, but the evil and terror it had held had been broken by the confusion. Looking up at the golden idol, the polished blackness of the huge phalluses, Marcus was struck by how much the whole thing resembled a gigantic stage set, or the scene for one of Quindarvis' banquets.

"At least you've broken the cult of Atargatis in Rome," said Sixtus, by way of comfort.

"Not even that," grumbled the centurion. "They'll just go underground again, as they did before. No, all we've done is lost another day. We could have left Tiridates and his poor silly fishworshipers in peace, for all the good it did us. Because it was the Christians who took her—the amulet we found with the anagram of the Christos proves that much. Tiridates and his bearers and the whole stupid boiling of 'em probably don't know any more about the kidnapping than this brat here."

He sighed, his eyes narrowing with annoyance as he watched the fat Syrian and his sister being escorted from the sanctuary on the heels of the rest of the prisoners.

"I'm sorry," murmured Marcus, aware that it was he who had identified the fish tattoo on the merchant's arm.

Arrius shrugged. "Not your fault. I'm only dreading what

the praetorian prefect is going to say when I tell him I've hauled in the chief of the whole Syrian merchant community on a charge of worshiping with abominations.'' He sighed and tucked the baby under his arm like a fowl. The child had fallen asleep. ''Well, let's go. Party's over for the night.''

XIII

"They are slaves," people declare. Nay, rather, they are men. . . .

Seneca

Despite the centurion's rather optimistic assertion, the doings of the night dragged themselves out until almost dawn. The prisoners were sorted and questioned, one and all denying any knowledge of Tertullia Varia's disappearance. Tiridates was indignant at the question; it was of vital interest for the Syrian community and his own business and political hopes that the girl be found, and that he take her to wife, which he was still willing to do in spite of her having been among the Christians. "Not wishing to be vulgar," he said rather stuffily for a man whose only articles of dress were his shoes and his sister's scarf, "but I should think her father will be glad to marry her off now to a man of my fortune."

"Whatever fortune's left to you after the emperor gets done reading your sentence," grunted Arrius. "And I'm not sure what old Varus will take against more—his daughter being used as a pawn by the Christians or by the worshipers of the Syrian goddess. In any case I don't think you better start buying flowers for the wedding wreaths just yet."

"This is preposterous!"

"So's murderin' babies."

Out in the main guardroom Marcus had his arm bound up by the company surgeon, an ugly little man to whom a slice this small was about as consequential as a summer cold. He ripped off the makeshift dressing casually, washed the wound with water and then wine, and applied a stinging salve; Marcus gritted his teeth to keep from crying out and prayed to whatever gods he thought would listen not to let him faint. The few men on the late-night watch at the prison were tough scarred customers, veterans of every sack from Jerusalem to Germany, dicing in the grimy semidark of the few smoky torches and talking of women and chariot races. He would have died sooner than have them mock him.

The guardroom was nearly empty at this time of night, for it was well past the eighth hour, and outside the city sprawled in deepest slumber. Far off, Marcus could hear the rattling of wheels, the clatter of hooves of construction teams, the distant yelling of roisterers coming home from the brothels, but nothing compared to the cacophony of day. In time the noises seemed to retreat, the guards' voices sinking to a distant buzz, and the gloom of the guardroom seemed to thicken, so that its few torches appeared only as blurred orange spots in soiled brown darkness. He remembered that it was Midsummer Eve, the shortest night of the year; that Tullia's father would return in three days. She seemed to be slipping further and further away from them, with every day that passed, and he wondered why he still believed that she was alive at all . . .

His mind went back to the incense-wreathed porches of the Temple of Isis. It seemed like years ago, but it had only been that morning. He wondered what his father would say when he learned that his wife had flouted his commands and sought out his enemy's wife in such a place. He flinched from the thought, remembering the little man's blind and violent rages. He had enough experience with his father's spies in the household not to deceive himself that he wouldn't find out about it, and wondered if he should go there in the morning. But it would only make the old man's rage worse: at him for defending his mother, at her for turning his sons against their father. He knew his mother had been long ago broken of the habit of fighting back. He shut his eyes again, his head throbbing, and wondered what the old man would say when he asked for Tullia's hand.

"Here, kid." A big gnarled hand caught him as he slid sideways. "Better have some of this." His eyes cleared and he saw that one of the soldiers had come over to his bench and pressed a boiled-leather cup of dark neat wine into his hand. "Good for what ails you."

"Thank you," said Marcus shakily.

In the jumping orange light, the man grinned like a friendly satyr. "Doc says that'll heal up clean, give you a nice scar," he said encouragingly; he must have had a dozen of his own in view and the gods only knew how many more beneath his armor. "Give your dad somethin' to tell his pals about."

Marcus giggled, trying to picture his father clapping him on the shoulder with the words, "The manliest of all my sons." He'd probably think it one step above getting cut in a pothouse brawl.

There was a murmur of voices from the door, and he caught a familiar name. A soldier said, "You got any idea what time it is, honey?" and one of the men dicing in the shadows cracked a lewd joke. Marcus looked up suddenly, to see a woman standing in the door.

Despite the heat of the night she was wrapped in a cloak, more for concealment, he thought, than warmth. She'd worn a scarf over her head, too, and was in the act of putting it back, revealing a face as proud and delicate-boned as an Egyptian temple cat's. Her lips were Negroid but less full than some; her black hair had been braided flat to her shapely skull and ornamented with gold beadwork. Beneath her cloak her dress was amber silk, but there was something in those wary almond eyes that marked her for a rich man's slave.

He sat up and asked, "Why do you want to see Nicanor?"

She turned, startled, and he could see beneath her hard-kept pride the fear in her. Her eyes widened a little at the sight of him—as well they should, he realized, with a rueful look at himself. Dirty, unshaven, bloody and unkempt, he must look like some slave arrested for brawling rather than a highly polished product of the best philosophical schools in the empire. He stood up, only to have his knees betrayed by the wine. He caught the edge of the table to steady himself and said, "I'm a friend of Nicanor's. Maybe I can help you?" He added, seeing her look, "I don't always look like this. My name is Marcus Silanus."

At the name her eyes changed, less apprehensive but even more startled. She stammered, "I—I realize what it looks like, to come here so late . . ."

One of the dice-players hooted. Marcus took her hand and led her to the bench where he'd been sitting. "The centurion Arrius is in charge of the case," he said gently. "I can ask him to let you see Nicanor in a few minutes. What's your name?"

"Hypatia," she replied. "Is—is Nicanor all right? I know they—they arrested him for questioning this morning. He isn't a Christian, I swear he isn't, I have to tell them—they have to believe me. You believe he isn't a Christian, don't you?" Her grave dark eyes were pleading. "He said you wouldn't betray him."

Marcus studied her for a long moment, the beauty of that highbred face, the cost of the gold rings she wore in her ears. The fact that she had come here, alone, at this hour of the night, to see some other man's slave. He said slowly, "Did you know that he tried to kill himself this afternoon?"

From that creamy gold complexion all the blood drained, as though her throat had been cut. For a moment he thought she'd faint, but her eyes never moved from his. She said through lips suddenly stiff and gray, "No, I didn't." Then she swallowed, and said in a more normal tone, "You said 'tried.' " He saw she'd begun to tremble.

"He's alive, but . . ."

She said, "I see." She was looking down, her breathing suddenly thick.

"Hypatia," said Marcus gently. "Who's your master?"

She hesitated a long time before answering. Then she said, "Porcius Craessius," in a muffled voice.

The dapper gentleman, Marcus recalled, who had told Quindarvis so offhandedly to drown his drunk slave in the fishpond. That had been the night of the jailbreak—this woman's master had been from home. If Quindarvis had pressed Craessius to stay at that opulent retreat another night—or even if the dandified little rake had been too spent by his excesses of the night before—she would have been free the night of the abortive raid on the catacombs.

Free to put her life in danger.

For some reason he found himself remembering Quindarvis' private lion pit, with its elegantly appointed pavilion overlooking the view. He rested his hand on her shoulder, as he would to comfort his sister, and felt her muscles stiffen. He pulled it back, blushing. She must have been pawed by so many men that a touch was enough to sicken. It was understandable, with her looks.

"We have no rights in a court of law," she said slowly, "but I'll tell anyone it would do good to know."

"You were with him last night, and the night before?"

She nodded. "My master was at . . ."

"I know where your master was," said Marcus. "And I know what he'd be likely to do to you if it were to come out."

She gave him a bitter sideways smile. "Let's hope not. You're young to know things like that. But I can't let him take it for me." She still did not meet his eyes but kept her gaze cast down, fixed on her long, slim hands drawing the edge of her russet cloak over and over through her fingers. The grubby torchlight spangled her beaded head with fire. Her womanhood was fragrant, like cinnamon and musk.

"Where's Craessius tonight?" he asked softly.

"With Paris. That's his boy. He's starting to tire of me already. We hoped . . ." She shrugged. "But there's not much hope for slaves, now, is there? Maybe Nicanor had the right idea, after all."

"No," said Marcus. "Look at me, Hypatia."

She raised her eyes to meet his, gleaming with tears, though her mouth was smooth and still as cast bronze.

"I'll tell the centurion what you've told me; and I'll tell him why Nicanor would prefer death to questions about his whereabouts on the last two nights. Nothing's come to official trial yet, and nothing will until the city prefect returns."

She sighed, like a child cheated too often of promised treats. "And when he returns?" she asked dully.

"With luck nothing about Nicanor will be brought up at all. There's no need for it." He thought it wiser not to mention that the city prefect, when he returned, might well be half-crazed with grief and fury and likely to punish anyone within reach.

Hypatia lowered her eyes again to her stacked fingers. Her plum-dark lips tightened momentarily, then she said, "So we can go on as before."

"You can choose," he said softly, "what you will do. Would you like to see him now?"

She shook her head. "If he's ill he'll be sleeping," she said. "And he'll be angry enough at me for coming at all. If your centurion doesn't believe you, send for me. I'll come." She stood up and drew her veil over her head. "Life means little enough as it is. I might as well finish it, as Niko's always saying, 'worthily.' " She moved to the door with the grace and swiftness of a lioness and was gone almost before Marcus could lift his hand in farewell. He was left with a despairing sense of tragedy, far beyond the tales of ancient kings.

One of the guards said, "There goes one splendid woman."

And though he knew they spoke only of her body, Marcus could not imagine her better described.

"I am shocked. I must tell you, Marcus, I am deeply shocked." Priscus Quindarvis stared through the latticework of the arbor at the leaping waters of the fountain, the sunlight glittering hard as diamonds on the bronze flanks of the nymph and satyr, caught there in their eternal play. He shook his head, his thick brows meeting heavily over his nose. "One of the chief members of the Syrian community. A man trusted, respected . . .''

"I never trusted him," said Aurelia Pollia unexpectedly. She looked up from the plucked lily she had been turning in her fingers as Marcus gave them an edited version of the night's events. "And I never respected him. I always felt him to be . . . ugly inside."

Quindarvis raised his brows, startled to hear the usually timid and retiring Lady Aurelia speak out on any subject. She looked much better than she had in days. Though she was still pale, her brown eyes sunk back into bruised pits of sleeplessness, a perilous kind of calm seemed to have descended on her spirit. Her hair was brushed, oiled, and fixed in a simple style, and for the first time Marcus had the feeling that she wasn't half-drugged with poppy or some other herb of forgetfulness. Whether it was Isis who had wrought this change or his mother, he was not sure.

The praetor laughed, "He was never any prize outside either, Aurelia. A rolling suet pudding, stuck with jewels . . .''

. . . *whom you thought well enough of to court for support three days ago,* thought Marcus, looking across the hot dappling of the afternoon shadows at the big man's square, cynical face. Yesterday not a man would have mocked him.

"You seem to have plenty of connections in the prison these days, Marcus," said the praetor, after a few more cutting comments on the Syrian's fatness, his bought citizenship, his boys, his audacity at trying to arrange a match with the daughter of the city prefect, just as if he himself had not actively fostered the match to win favor with both sides. "Do you know what will be done with his holdings, at the sell-up? A man could turn a little profit there if he gets in quick enough."

Marcus shook his head. He had not slept well, having not returned from the prison until after daylight, to lie sweltering for hours listening to the din of the streets outside. The time of the noon siesta was past, and by the time he could reach the prison, Arrius would have returned from the baths. His head felt heavy and his gashed arm ached, and Priscus

Quindarvis, broad-shouldered and elegant in his purple-bordered senatorial toga, was the last person he would have wished to meet when he called upon his mother's friend. But he had to answer politely, so he said, "The case won't come to trial until Consul Varus returns. Beyond that I don't know."

Quindarvis sighed heavily and shook his head, but none of them spoke of what awaited the prefect on his return home. Marcus got to his feet and straightened the folds of his rather shabby toga. "I have to go now," he said. "I'll return later if I have news."

The praetor nodded absently. "Very good, my boy."

"I'll see you to the atrium." Lady Aurelia rose. "Excuse me, Priscus, will you, a moment?" She took Marcus' arm and led him along the columned walkway from the arbor into the quiet marble coolness of the red summer dining room, with its stylish black statues and gilded trim. "I just wanted to ask you to tell your mother how grateful I am she came to see me," she said softly. "Tell her I'll understand if it's a long time before we see each other again."

Marcus took her gently by the shoulders. "She knows you will."

Her brown eyes were anxious. "Your father won't—won't be too angry if he finds out?"

Marcus lied, "No." He leaned down to kiss her forehead. "Don't worry about it, Aunt Aurelia."

A smile fluttered very briefly around the corners of her eyes. "It's been years since you called me that."

He held the embroidered curtains aside to let her pass before him into the atrium. Several of Quindarvis' clients who were loitering there looked up hopefully, and though faces fell a little (after all, Lady Aurelia was certainly not going to invite them to dinner), there was a murmured chorus of "Good afternoon, Lady Aurelia Pollia Varia."

She took his hands gently. "Thank you for stopping," she murmured. "Tell your mother to be careful, Marc. And you be careful, too."

He kissed her again. "I'm learning care from the experts," he promised her, and a slave came to escort him out the door.

Care from the experts, he thought wryly: a slashed arm,

cracked ribs, assorted bruises, a stiff leg, and residual head-
aches and soreness of the throat, yes sir. But _nothing_, he
thought, _to what others had to face_. Torture in the lower cells
of the jail, or the more silken, spiteful tortures that could be
performed in some quiet villa outside the city. Or merely the
pain of living with a man you hated, who hated you, who
could, on a whim, send you away from the city altogether to
some dreary estate in Gaul or Africa. He remembered that
once, as children, he and Tullia had found Felix clumsily
trying to cut his wrists after his father had sworn he'd sell him
to the galleys. He'd been eleven.

Marcus made his way down the sloping streets toward the
New Forum, the din of the spice market rising in his ears.
Activity was picking up again after the noontime siesta; a
Thracian barber was yelling his trade and a couple of
Carthaginian acrobats were performing on a blanket, to the
almost total stoppage of all traffic in the narrow lanes. A
beggar's hand plucked at the hem of Marcus' toga; a water
seller jostled into him, wetting his feet; he was surged to the
wall as a litter with six bearers trotted past, pursued by a train
of sweating, toga-clad clients. Where the road curved over
the shoulder of the hill, he glimpsed the curving porticoes and
domed roofs of the Basilica Ulpias, the red tiles of its roof
warmly glowing in the sun, with the slender column and the
emperor's statue rising beyond. He had come down this way
so often, tacking back and forth across the steep streets of the
spice market; he remembered a time when he had lived
between the Ulpias and the libraries, so buried in his books
and his metaphysical speculations that he had not heard of
Tullia's betrothal until a week after it had been publicly
announced.

And that, he thought with a kind of astonishment, had been
only a little more than a week ago.

He thought of the cool marble spaces of the Basilica, of its
clustering columns, and the voices of the philosophers and
their students who met there in the mornings to discuss the
Truth, Beauty, and the Good. An overwhelming nostalgia
filled him, a memory of that distant self still wearing this

same ink-stained toga, sitting on a marble bench in those cool caves of knowledge, watching the sunlight falling through the high windows onto Timoleon's fading red hair, listening to that beautiful voice quoting Plato against the deep harsh tones of Judah Symmachus' questions. He wondered if he could return there now, find his former mentor, and sit once more at his feet.

But there was nothing that he could think of to say.

Like a sudden splattering of mud he heard voices, jeering and obscene. "Christian! Jew-whore!" He heard a woman cry out, and a man's coarse laugh, and the crack of a stone against a wall. From an alley a woman emerged at a stumbling run, clutching her torn dress around her bosom. A band of men and boys surrounded her, catcalling and heading her off as she tried to flee. One of them grabbed her veil, pulled it off, and began waving it like a flag, giggling all the while. She tried to dodge down an alley, and another man sprang in front of her, spreading hairy arms and singing, "Come to me! Oh, come to me!" She veered away, slapping at the hands that snatched at her skirts from behind.

Marcus recognized her at once.

"Hey, Christian, lemme put my finger in your stew!" yelled one of the boys. "Look, I'm a Christian, too!" And he mimed hanging on a cross, his tongue lolling horribly.

"Come on, maybe you'll get me to join!"

"Hey, I wanna be saved!"

One of the men grabbed her from behind, pawing her breasts. She twisted in his grip, gouging with her elbows, the black curly mane of her hair coming loose from its pins to fall over a tear-streaked face. She pulled free and another man grabbed her wrists, shoving her up against the wall. Men behind their shop counters were watching, but the ones who left their work only came closer to gawk; one passerby picked up a piece of dung and threw it, yelling, "Christian twat!" without pausing on his way. Marcus watched in sickened horror the girl's struggles to get free and the faces of the gathering ring of spectators. Clearly no one was about to proclaim Christian sympathies. As she wrenched her face away from the man's greedy mouth and fumbling fingers, it crossed Marcus' mind to fight, and then he thought, *Six of them? Always provided I didn't trip over my toga as I sallied to the rescue?*

And for a Christian at that, who deserves this for what they've done to Tullia?

But he knew Tullia would never have countenanced his walking on.

With a sigh, he took the plunge. In his best imitation of Arrius' parade-ground voice he bellowed, "DORCAS!"

At the sound of her name, the girl gave a cry and looked up. That, and the combination of outrage and authority in his voice, was enough to distract her molesters momentarily. Praying for the best, Marcus strode into the breach.

He roared, "You little whore, how dare you slip away from me?" Without sparing them a glance, he shoved his way through the midst of the men, bristling with righteous wrath. He pushed aside the man who held her against the wall, jerked her brutally forward by the arm, and dealt her two stinging slaps across the face. "When I get you home I'll teach you to make a fool of me!" he yelled, shaking her until her head lolled, her dark eyes staring at him in uncomprehending terror. Her erstwhile tormentors looked on, yielding to his obvious authority and rage without lifting a hand.

Cursing her he thrust her before him; the men stepped aside, bemused and silent. She stumbled, and he dragged her from the muck and pushed her ahead of him, snarling abuse and thanking his guardian gods that he was wearing the toga that was the badge of Roman citizenship, however shoddy it might be.

Behind him, someone called out, "Mister!"

In panic he almost dropped her arm and ran. But he turned, blazing with his father's wrath.

The fat little man who'd snatched her veil held it out to him mutely. Marcus took it with a sneer and thrust it at her. "Not that you'll wear it enough to matter, you little bitch," he muttered in a vicious and audible aside. She accepted it meekly, gathering it clumsily over the rips in her dress, and with downcast lashes whispered, "Yes, master." Marcus shoved her ahead of him up the first alley he saw. With expressions of respect for his manliness, the men and boys watched them go.

They turned another corner, to a narrow street of steps that led down into the New Forum. Glancing at Dorcas from the corner of his eye, Marcus saw the color slowly returning to her face. As she readjusted the pins in the shoulders of her torn dress, he could see the small silver cross, glinting like flame on her heavy breasts. Then she looked up and asked, "How did you know my name?"

"Uh—" How do you explain to someone you have just rescued that you know her name because you spied on her?

"Did they tell you at the prison?"

"Yes—sort of."

Under long lashes her wide brown eyes were grave. "Then you're one of the centurion's informers?"

"No," said Marcus indignantly, "of course not. It's just that—" He broke off, uncertain how to continue, and fell back lamely on, "I'm sorry I had to slap you."

Her smile was startling, like the sweep of spring sunlight on a cloudy day. "No, you were good. I don't think I've seen even"—she hesitated, barely perceptibly swerving from a name—"even an actor in the theater do better."

Instinctively, he knew she had been going to say, "even Papa," and he remembered again that little comedy called wicked uncle that she and Telesphorus had played, to get her safely out of the prison with her message to that powerful and elusive priest. "Are you all such good actors?"

She shook her head. "Only when we have to be."

"And do you often have to be?"

She stood still, studying him for a moment in the shadows of the steep, hot, echoing street. The strong brows drew downward again, the brown eyes turned grave. "As often as the fox has to lay false trails for the hunters," she replied quietly. "We do a lot of it, to protect our own. You saw yourself, back there"—she nodded in the direction of the street where they'd met—"how easy it is to create a totally false impression with very few words."

He abruptly remembered Sixtus at the orgy, acquiring his reputation for unnamed vice, and had to laugh. "Now that you mention it, I've seen a man do it with no words." He grinned. And then, his smile fading, "Does that kind of thing happen often? Being baited that way?"

Dorcas shook her head and shuddered, drawing her veil closer around her shoulders, as though involuntarily seeking to cover herself from the memory of those obscene hands. "It's never happened to me. Even if people know—and many people in my neighborhood do—they mostly let us alone."

They had resumed walking, descending the steep cobbled stairs through a canyon of five-story apartment houses whose projecting upper stories almost met above their heads. Someone far above sang, "Heads up below!" and the two of them flattened against the wall just in time to avoid the subsequent shower. Marcus found himself astonishingly at ease with this girl, in spite of what he knew about Christians. She had many of the qualities that he loved in Tullia Varia—the spirit, the humor, the high courage that had taken her into the prison, the wits that had eluded him in the mobs at the amphitheater. It was increasingly difficult to remember that the puckish, triangular face masked cannibalism, treason, perversion. That this girl who walked so trustingly at his side might very well know where her brothers in Christ had taken Tullia, and what they had done to her.

Maybe she'd been there herself.

She looked up at him again. "You're the man who followed me to the Flavian," she told him simply. "Does this mean I'm under arrest?"

"I'm not sure," said Marcus helplessly.

The smile returned, ruefully amused. "I suppose I ought to thank you even if you had saved me to arrest me, but it wouldn't be very sincere thanks in that case. But thank you, whyever you did what you did. As I said it—it's never happened to me. Sometimes boys will follow me, or call me names. But this . . . Since that girl was kidnapped I've been afraid to go out. Not because of the soldiers, but because of ordinary people in the street."

"This Papa I keep hearing about should have thought of that," said Marcus grimly, "before he had her kidnapped."

Dorcas whirled on him, bristling like a bating hawk. "Papa never ordered it!" she cried fiercely.

Her very sureness took him aback. "But if he's the head of the Christians, he'd have to have known," he pointed out.

"It's a lie!" she said. "The Christians would never have done such a thing."

The street debouched into the New Forum. The pillared porch in which they now walked was almost empty, a cool shaded forest of white marble occupied only by occasional strollers and a fortune-teller half-asleep on a blanket-load of cut-rate amulets. As if in a sunlit clearing, the gleaming bronze statue of the emperor himself shone in the open spaces beyond the porch.

Marcus retorted, "Not even if her father had had their friends thrown to the beasts?"

Dorcas paused, her full lips tightening, and in a moment the sparks of anger faded from her brown eyes. "No," she said softly. "I suppose you could call that the bone in the throat about Christianity; or one of them, anyway. Revenge— Well, we're taught that if someone strikes you on your right cheek, you should turn the other one to them so they can strike that, too. No reproach intended," she added, with a quick flicker of a smile. "Or that if someone steals your cloak, to give them your coat as well. It's very hard to return good for evil," she concluded. "And I'm not very good at it, myself, yet. It was even harder when I was a slave."

"Are you a freedwoman, then?" His stomach turned suddenly at the thought of this pretty, courageous girl in the power of someone like the dissolute Porcius Craessius, or even of a man like his own father.

She must have read the pity and disgust in his eyes, for she said gently, "It could have been worse. I had one horribly bad master, and one who could have cured anyone of hatred of mankind."

"And yet you became a Christian in spite of him."

The dark heavy curls swung against her cheek as she raised her head. ''You don't understand.''

He could have said that he did. A week ago he would not have—a week ago it had been inconceivable to him that anyone would have indulged in bizarre rites, in wholesale treason, in a vicious sect whose brotherhood was deliberately designed to undermine social order. But a week ago he had not known about Hypatia and Nicanor, nor seen a human being drowned simply for a man's amusement at the way the words ''Drown him'' rolled off the tongue . . . A week ago he had not understood what comfort lay in the illogical assurance that someone—Isis, Atargatis, Christ, or Papa—had all things in hand, or what evil could lurk behind the most smiling of facades.

Looking down into those grave dark eyes, clear and simple-seeming as a woodland spring, he reminded himself that by her own admission this girl was versed in the foxlike art of laying down false trails, of seeming to be what she was not.

The longer he spoke with her, the more difficult it was to believe.

''If you Christians don't even agree on whether your god was a god or not, how can you agree on what he taught or didn't teach?'' he asked her. ''There might be a branch of you who believe in returning vengeance for wrongdoing, against the enemies of the Lord.''

''Papa would know,'' she insisted quietly.

''How would he know?'' Marcus cried.

She took a step back from him, holding her veil about her, her puckish face troubled by the vehemence and misery in his voice. Then her dark brows lifted. ''It's you,'' she said. ''You're the girl's lover—the girl who was kidnapped. Papa told me . . .''

And when she broke off into silence, he demanded, ''Papa told you what?''

''Papa told me that the lover of the girl who was kidnapped was seeking her. That's how you came to follow me, isn't it?''

''What does Papa know about it?'' cried Marcus furiously.

He strode toward her to seize her wrist, but she backed from him, dodging among the pillars. "Who is Papa?"

In the shadows her eyes flooded with compassion. She whispered, "I'm so sorry." He lunged at her and she was gone, her footsteps light and swift on the marble of the pavement. He plunged after the sound, but the forests of columns baffled him. Despairingly he cried, "Come back here!" and his only answer was a disapproving glare from a couple of aged senators, walking in the porches in the quiet of the afternoon, who plainly thought little of young men who played catch-me with pretty girls in the colonnades of the imperial basilicas.

Angry, disgusted, and perplexed, he turned away, making his way down Silversmith's Rise to that small ugly building on the flank of the Capitoline Hill.

He found Arrius there, still in the same faded red tunic and chain-mail shirt he'd worn last night, writing up a report on wax at the warden's desk. There were big blue smudges under his eyes, and his unshaven face was lined with fatigue; standing in the doorway watching him, Marcus was uncomfortably aware that if he'd got any sleep at all in the last twenty-four hours, it had probably been on the bench at the back of this room. He glanced up as Marcus came in, his greenish eyes hard and cold as a hunting cat's.

He said, "We've got them."

Marcus blinked at him stupidly. "Got who?"

"The Christians who had Tullia Varia."

The room, the world, did one slow, deliberate spin. Then he cried despairingly, "Had?"

The centurion tossed something across the desk to him, something that tinkled softly on the wood. "We found this in their meeting place."

It was a bronze earring, shaped like a lily, snagged with a single strand of brown curling hair.

XIV

"The usual thing," reported the centurion in his dry, uninflected voice. Marcus followed him into the dingy twilight of the guardroom, his head buzzing and the ache that he had felt before returning to his whole body but mostly to the wound in his arm. "An informer told us about a meeting this morning, down near the circus. We surprised half-a-dozen Christians in a cellar they've been using regularly for a meeting place. We found this on a blanket in a corner."

"Papa would know," Dorcas had said.

Well, maybe Papa had known. And maybe Dorcas had, too.

Marcus felt like a child who has been robbed by a kindly stranger.

"It lets your friend Nicanor and his lady off the hook, anyway," continued Arrius, climbing down the ladder ahead of him. "But it'll be hell if these characters turn stubborn."

224

Even outside the cell, they could hear the voices raised in acrimonious conflict.

"I don't care what kind of self-deceitful arguments you spout! The fact remains that it's God's grace and the holiness of Christ that make a sacrament efficacious, not how pious the priest is! It says in the Book of the Twelve Teachers . . ."

"You heretical drunkard, you wouldn't know God's Law if it came up and bit you!" screamed the familiar voice of Ignatius. "By that argument the city hangman could preside over the Supper of the Body and Blood! You'd have the priests of the Church no better than a bunch of thieving rascals, like the priests of Cybele—no better than yourself, I daresay . . ."

"I suppose we should all be as perfect as you are!"

"Neither the fornicators, nor the lustful . . ."

Arrius threw open the door with a crash just as a big muscular woman in the short tunic of a farmwife shoved the two would-be combatants apart. Typically, not a Christian in the room turned his head.

Around the massive peacemaker's muscular arm, Ignatius continued to jeer. "A man who is as bound as you are to the sins of the flesh has no business meddling in the affairs of heaven! You should put aside your wife . . ."

"I'll give you the priests of Cybele, you little . . ."

Another woman chimed in. "Anyone who would believe in the coequality of the human nature of Christ with the Divine—"

Arrius roared, "Silence, all of you!"

Neither of the two combatants over the purity of the priesthood so much as paused for breath; their peacemaker, moreover, plunged into a long misquotation from some neoplatonist philosopher on the subject of essence and accidents.

Marcus yelled into the rising din, "Shut up! I've heard enough! Does it matter how many natures your god had?"

Ignatius broke off mid-curse and whirled on him. "Of course it matters, you stupid idolater! How can anyone be saved by faith, if their faith be false and crooked? Only pure faith, and purity of the body . . ."

"No, it isn't faith alone that'll save a man from sin!" cried another woman, leaping to her feet. " 'A tree shall be known by its fruits . . .' "

"That filthy heresy was disproved by—"

From a corner a young man's voice yelled, "Shut up, Ignatius! Your logic is as shoddy as your manners!"

And Marcus recognized the voice.

"Judah!"

The young man who had spoken rose from his place with the lithe powerful movement that Marcus remembered, and came to the patch of light that fell, grimy and yellow, through the open doorway into the fraught darkness of the cell.

"Marcus," he greeted him quietly.

Timoleon's two erstwhile students faced each other in silence, groping for words and finding none. It was as if bars of mistrust, and the threat of death, had been lowered between them. It is said that the saved cannot speak with the damned.

It was Judah who broke the silence. "I see you've turned informer."

It was the second time in as many hours that this charge had been leveled at him, and Marcus cried out perhaps more vehemently than he need have, "I'm not! Dammit, I'm only trying to find Tullia!"

Judah's dark brows knotted. He studied him for a moment, sweat gleaming on his dark breast, the silver fish that hung there flashing like a chip of fire.

Marcus cried, "Where is she? What did you do with her?"

Something changed in Judah's eyes. "You're arguing ahead of your facts, Silenus."

"They found her earring in your damn cellar is all the facts I know."

He made an impatient gesture. "I should have expected something like that from you. What Roman citizen would ever admit he doesn't know what's happening?" He flicked Marcus' toga with a scornful finger. "The whore that sits upon many waters—but it won't be her adulteries that bring her down. It'll be her damn certainty that there's nothing beyond what she already knows." He stared bitterly at Marcus. "I'm a lying Christian, remember? You believe what you believe."

Marcus was silent, carefully telling over the letters of the alphabet. At *F* he said, "I don't know what to believe, Judah. I'm sorry I—I argued ahead of my facts."

The Christian looked down his high-bridged nose at him, bleak scorn in his dark eyes. "I'm sorry, too," he said coldly, "that your rotten little informers haven't anything better to do than persecute the servants of the Son of man. But the Lord will look after his own. Vengeance is mine, saith the Lord . . ."

"WHERE IS SHE?" shouted Marcus.

"Judah?" A hesitant voice spoke at Marcus' elbow, and he turned, startled, as Isaac Symmachus hobbled diffidently into the grimy cell.

Judah swung around savagely. "And I suppose you're going to ask me about the stupid little bitch as well?"

Symmachus hesitated, then said, "No, son."

"Or beg me to recant? Join you as a nice civil slave in the treasury? Hold your pens for you while you audit the books, like I was taught? It's a little late for that, O patriarch of my house."

"It is a little late for many things, my son," replied the Old Jew quietly.

"It's a little late for the whole damned world," said Judah, his voice quiet but its scorn and strength filling the cramped darkness of the cell. "The Lord will come in judgment; the vessels of his wrath have broken, and their fire will pour over this filthy empire that's even now drowning like a man in a sewer in its own crap! And when it happens you'll still be fetching and carrying for the Romans, auditing the books and wiping the arse of some fat jumped-up tradesman's son of a Roman hog, who spends a million sesterces on his dinner and then doesn't even bother to digest it! You're worse than the German barbarians! They were raped, at least; you were only paid."

"I may have been paid, my son," said Symmachus, and his voice shook suddenly with suppressed fury, "but by the God of Hosts I was paid in a whole house, and live children instead of dead ones, and time to hand on the teachings of the Law and the prophets . . ."

"The Law and the prophets! That's a book that's been rolled up like a scroll—yea, a scroll in the hands of the angel of the Lord! You've sold your honor and your god for bad coin. A man shall forsake his father and mother . . ."

"You cannot forsake us!" cried the father in fury. "By the God of Hosts you will drag us with you by your heedless pride and destroy us all!"

Marcus turned away, unable to listen further. There was a strange humming in his ears as he climbed the ladder to the guardroom, a hot restless weakness in all his muscles. The voices followed him up from below.

". . . kiss the feet of your filthy praetor!"

". . . may not have honor but I and my family are alive!"

". . . Book of the Acts of John clearly states that the Christ could appear in any form that he wanted to, from a youth to a bald-headed old man . . ."

". . . lower and a higher element; his spirit is of divine origin, locked in an exile in a fleshly body until the coming of a divine messenger . . ."

"Driveling Gnostic!"

"Heretical jackass!"

He leaned his head on his hands, seeing the guardroom through a blur of weariness and fever. The baking heat of the day was beginning to pass off; outside, the street was deep in shadow. The guardroom torches were again lit. At a table in the corner the men of the day watch were sharing watered wine, laying bets, and joking; by the door the bored bursar was paying out silver to a short sturdy man in the brown tunic of a slave or a day laborer. Someone called out a joke—the man looked around and grinned, his teeth flashing whitely in the dark tangle of a beard, gleaming in the twilight like the gold ring he wore in his ear. A man jostled past him, his shadow blocking the dimming outdoor light, and Marcus recognized the massive form of the city hangman. *They will argue about the nature of their god*, he thought, *while the hangman heats up his little tools.*

He frowned suddenly, as something snagged at his memory. Some memory, he thought—perhaps a dream. He couldn't remember it clearly, or why it troubled him. He knew now that his wound had turned feverish; many things looked dream-like in that blue-shadowed room.

From below, since the trap had been left open, Judah's voice could be heard in a fury of shouting. "Son! You never in your life wanted a son! You only wanted a name, and if you could have found a dog who'd father acceptable grand-children he'd have done as well!"

"Vengeance is mine, saith the Lord." That's what Judah had said, and, presumably, Christ or Paul or some other Christian notable before him, since these people seemed to talk largely in quotes. But in the forest cool of the columns of the New Forum, Dorcas had said, "Turn the other cheek . . ."

Was it possible to have two wholly opposite doctrines within the same faith?

". . . but Jesus abandoned his earthly body when he said, 'Woman, behold thy son,' and a moment later his heavenly part ascended into the hands of his Heavenly Father . . ."

"And reunited, I suppose, for dinner on the road to Emmaus?"

Hadn't some Christian said, "With faith, all things are possible?"

Did the possibilities of faith include a likable, grave-eyed girl like Dorcas hiding the knowledge of abominations behind her sunburst smile? The shadows of the guardroom seemed to deepen, the voices of the guards growing fainter. The old dream returned to his waking eyes, Persephone struggling in the tender green of the river reeds, white hands pushing helplessly against the brown strong chest, the laughter in the death-god's dark grinning bearded face . . .

He opened his eyes, knowing suddenly whose face it was.

Not Pluto's. Not the face of the god of money and the dead.

A brown face with a black beard and one gold earring, grinning at him as they struggled in the dark street.

He scrambled to his feet, almost falling over his long legs as he stumbled across the room. The bursar was putting away his little box of silver pieces and preparing to go home to the Praetorian camp outside the city.

"Who was that man you were paying off just now?" demanded Marcus breathlessly. The soldier looked up at him in blank surprise.

"Who, the informer?" He looked to a couple of the drinkers for confirmation. "Lucius? Lucian? Centurion'd know. He's the man who put the kiss on our talkative friends downstairs."

"You're sure?" Arrius drew a careful, deliberate gridwork of lines on the corner of the wax tablet on the table before him, then just as carefully smoothed them out with the blunt end of the stylus, making the dark wax as blank and uninformative as his unshaven face.

"I'm positive!" insisted Marcus. "I saw the man, he was as close to me as you are now!"

"When was he that close?" inquired the centurion. "Just now, or in the street?" In the blurred brownish twilight of the warden's office, his green eyes gleamed like a beast's. Flattened and straggling from his helmet, his hair was like a beast's pelt as well. From beneath long curling eyebrows he studied Marcus' face with a hunting cat's impersonal intentness.

"In the street, when Tullia was kidnapped! But I'm not mistaken, I'd know him anywhere. Don't you believe me?"

"Oh, I believe you, Professor." Arrius' mouth drew together, thin and hard as the lines he made with his stylus on the wax. "I'm fast reaching the point where I'll believe anything about Christians. The little turncoat scum," he added. "You didn't recognize any of the others down there?"

Marcus shook his head. "But I'm not sure that I would. He was the only one of them I saw clearly."

Arrius cursed and rubbed at his eyes as though they ached. "He never said he was one of them," he growled. "Damn the man, if he was going to get scared and sell out, the least he could have done was tell us where they were likely to take her. And like a fool I never thought to question him. He only said he knew where they were hiding; I didn't ask him how he knew it."

"He wouldn't have said," said Marcus, disconsolately.

The centurion sighed and ran a knotted hand through his hair. "No. They're slippery as eels, and from what you've told me at least a few of them—that Dorcas girl for one—are geniuses in the art of misdirection. She acted her way in and out of here and got word to this Papa of theirs; I should have had my suspicions about Lucius—if that's really his name—when he gave a false address. But a lot of informers do that. It's a stupid kind of pride, considering."

"But why would he have sold them out?"

Arrius shrugged. "Who knows? Maybe they didn't like his opinions on the writings of Paul and kicked him out, and he did this to get even. I don't know."

A soldier entered, carrying a couple of lamps that emitted more smoke than light. Doubled shadows reeled across the cracked plaster of the walls as he hung them from an iron bracket. "Will you be back working tonight, sir?"

Arrius thought about it a moment, then shook his head. "No. I'll finish up here and go back out to the camp. I haven't slept in a bed since I don't know when. I'll be back sometime tomorrow."

The man saluted. "Very good, sir."

The centurion rubbed at his eyes again, the swaying lamps making his mail glitter like the scales of a bronze fish. "I've given them all a preliminary questioning, for all the good that did me. I couldn't get any of them to stop quarreling long enough to make sense. The only connection with Nikolas and the group that were executed three years ago is that crazy little monkey Ignatius, and I haven't figured out whether he's completely insane or the most skilled actor of them all."

He stood up, stretching his back like a digger after a long day shoveling. "That arm bothering you?"

"A little," Marcus admitted. "I think it's turned feverish."

"Have the surgeon look at it before he goes. Then I'd advise you go by the baths, get a good rubdown, go home and have a good meal, and go to sleep. By tomorrow evening the hangman and I should have got something out of that gang downstairs besides metaphysics and abuse.''

But though Marcus obeyed all of these instructions, when he returned to his dark and oven-hot rooms in the Subura, it was long before he could sleep. The incessant rattle and voices in the streets outside kept him awake far into the night, and when he finally slept, they followed him into his dreams. The clattering of the cartwheels transmuted itself into the banging of a hammer, as a tall Jewish carpenter put together a marriage-bed for the goddess Persephone.

"He ain't in."

"Isn't in?" Marcus stared down at the tubby little kitchen slave who'd answered Sixtus' door, startled and aggrieved. "Is Churaldin in, then?"

The slave shook his head. "Which isn't to say they won't be back later, Professor. That is—I think the old man's gone out to the baths, and maybe the gods know where that tomcat Churaldin is, but I sure don't. Will you come in and wait a spell? We can find you some wine, I'm sure."

Marcus shook his head. "No, thank you. I'll be back later."

Disappointed and vaguely troubled, he took his leave, wandering slowly back through the sunlit afternoon dust of the street.

It was about the middle of the seventh hour, the time when the shops reopen after the noon siesta, and men wake up from their naps and start thinking about exercise and baths. Marcus had slept off his fever, waking still rather tired but clearheaded, and had gone out to the baths early. On his way down the stairs one of the girls who lived on the first floor of the tenement building had told him that his family had sent word to him sometime yesterday evening, but Marcus had decided that if his father wanted to dress him down for encouraging his mother in her disobedience, he could wait until dinnertime to do so. The athletic trainer at the baths had changed the dressing on his wound and kidded him good-naturedly about staying out of tavern brawls. He had thought about going back down to the prison, but had decided to fill Sixtus in on events first. At heart, he did not want to be there for the questioning.

He had just decided to return to the prison after all when he caught a glimpse of Churaldin, crossing the street in front of him. In spite of the intense heat of the afternoon, he wore a dark cloak pulled close around his shoulders; he seemed to be carrying some kind of a bundle under one arm. Curious, Marcus followed him as he ducked into an alley between two shops. He turned left around somebody's garden wall, right through a deserted pottery-yard, moving swiftly, as though to avoid pursuit. Marcus lost sight of him for a moment, then walked a few steps farther and saw him in a narrow alley, hurrying down a flight of steps to the sunken door of the cellar of a deserted building. As he watched, the slave turned the key, pushed open the door, and slipped inside.

Intrigued, Marcus followed him. He found the door locked and knocked at it, only wondering after he had done so if the place weren't some kind of rendezvous-point between the Briton and some neighborhood girl.

The door was pulled open. "Churaldin," said Marcus quickly, "I won't keep you, but—" He stopped. The slave was wearing the scarlet tunic of a member of the Praetorian Guard, the outline of the breastplate he'd just removed clearly visible where the garment was plastered to his body with sweat. "What the . . . ?"

The slave reached out quickly, dragged him into the cellar, and shut the door.

"What are you doing here?" he asked in a low voice.

"Why were you in armor?" countered Marcus. The rest of the armor was there, helmet and swordbelt in a bundle, thrown down on top of the dark cloak and the red cloak of a soldier as well.

The cellar was dimly lit by a window looking out onto the stairwell and another one, high up in the wall at the far end. It smelled of clay and a faint sewery stink; cobwebs wreathed the brick pillars of the foundation of the house above. "A little masquerade," said Churaldin briefly. "It isn't important. Were you looking for Sixtus? He'll be home later, he's at the baths now. Come back this evening, at about the second hour—"

"Churaldin, I've seen one of the men who kidnapped Tullia!"

The slave was already hustling him back toward the door; his hand was on Marcus' arm, and through the hard fingers he could feel him startle. But he only said, "Tell us about it this evening."

Marcus struggled to free himself. "Wait a minute, what's going on here? You're not supposed to be armed. Sixtus wouldn't have gone out alone."

"Harpalos went with him."

"Harpalos just talked to me at the door! If there's anything wrong, if either one of you is in trouble . . ."

Sharp knocking sounded on the cellar door. Churaldin hesitated, his dark eyes flickering in the gloom. "There's a stairway over in that corner that'll take you up through the building," he said tersely. "Why don't you go out that way?"

The knocking thundered, urgent.

"I'm not going anywhere until I know what's going on. Are you in trouble? Is Sixtus—"

"Sixtus doesn't know anything about this."

Another furious battery of knocks. Churaldin strode quickly to the door, unlocked it, and pulled it open. Framed in the light from the alley outside stood Alexandros, burly as a bear, also armored in the uniform of the Praetorian Guard. With him were Dorcas, Telesphorus, and Ignatius.

Alexandros was saying, ". . . now the epistle general of James the brother of Jesus clearly states that Christ *is* the Lord God and therefore . . ." and Dorcas, hurrying through the door with her arms full of blankets, said, "These were all I could come up with on short notice, Churaldin, but they'll do until—"

Churaldin shut the door behind them and turned to face Marcus, who stood, dumbfounded, in the center of the cellar. Quietly he said, "If you tell Sixtus about this I'll break your neck."

XV

There is little point in expecting much of your own projects, when
Fate has projects of her own.

Petronius

Telesphorus' harsh eyes flickered over him once. "It's the
centurion's little clerk," he said.

"I am not one of his informers!"

Dorcas had gone over to lay the folded blankets beside
Churaldin's discarded armor. She straightened up. "Of course
you aren't," she said warmly and brushed back the thick
curls of her black mane from her face.

Like a man speaking around the pain of a wound, Churaldin
said, "Why don't you go, Marcus? Sixtus knows nothing of
any of this. It kills me to deceive so good a master —so good
a man —but he wouldn't understand."

"You could get him killed," whispered Marcus. "If you
were caught . . ." He looked over at Alexandros, enormous
and awkward in the white light of the slit window. It came to
him suddenly why the other servants had worked so hard to
give him the impression that the young Briton was a
womanizer—a reputation he had never quite understood. What

better reason for those nightly excursions, he reflected bitterly. A game, a fakement, like "wicked uncle." In despair he cried, "Is the whole household Christian?"

"Yes," admitted the gardener, and in the same breath Churaldin said, "No." They looked at each other.

"If there's a general persecution, they'll never believe he didn't know!" pleaded Marcus. "He's offered you your freedom more than once, he told me that. The least you could have done was take it!"

"We could have," said the Briton carefully. "But—it was an extremely good cover."

"You would kill him for the sake of your stinking cover?"

Someone else knocked. Alexandros crossed the room to open it. Churaldin faced Marcus in hopeless silence, like a man caught *in flagrante* in the worst type of sin, with no possible justification—which was, in fact, the case. Marcus remembered what Sixtus had said—that he had known people suspected of being Christians. He was a man who understood truth; it wasn't that he hadn't suspected. But once Varus returned to the city, once the mechanism of persecution ground into operation, no one, not even men like Arrius who had served under him, was going to believe in the old man's carefully engineered innocence.

Marcus had the despairing sense of having been surrounded, meshed in a far greater conspiracy than he'd known. Then he turned and saw Judah Symmachus and the other Christians from the jail quietly enter as Alexandros closed the door behind them. Belatedly, he understood what Ignatius' presence should have told him from the first.

"You broke them out of jail!"

"You always did have a fine talent for the obvious, Silenus," commented Judah acidly. "You should be in the civil service, you and my father would get on famously."

"You're going to have the Praetorian Guard combing the city!"

"And finding nothing," insisted Churaldin. "By nightfall they won't be in the city. There's nothing to fear."

"I won't run from any Roman dogs!" snapped Ignatius

savagely. "I fear nothing of the beasts of the arena! The rending of my body—"

"Well, since the games are over you'll probably end up being sentenced to work in the marble mines," Churaldin shot back at him. "It isn't death and it isn't life, and you'll have God's own time getting yourself martyred there!"

"You barbarian scum! Anyone who would believe in the coequality of the two natures of Christ *would* take that attitude . . ."

"Shut him up," whispered Churaldin through his teeth.

". . . no better than a Persian fire worshiper . . ."

"Now, you can't speak that way of coequality," began Alexandros reprovingly, and another one of the Christians sailed in with, "And in any case the dualistic nature of God . . ."

Under the rising bicker of their voices Marcus said, "You were behind it all along, weren't you?"

"Yes," said Churaldin quietly.

"Are you Papa?"

It had never before occurred to him that Papa might be a man of his own age. The slave hesitated, as though debating his answer, and Ignatius shot scornfully, *"Him?"*

Goaded from all sides Marcus caught Churaldin by the shoulders. "Then who is Papa?" he demanded.

A sudden, unprecedented hush fell upon all that clamorous congregation. Churaldin raised his eyes, looking past Marcus' shoulder. Marcus whirled.

Sixtus seemed to have materialized out of the rear wall of the cellar.

"Papa," said the old man, gathering up the folds of his toga to pick his way down from the junk-littered dais that fronted the length of the wall, "seems to be the informal title of the Bishop of Rome. Papa, Pappas, Pope . . . The central priest to whom all the other priests, whatever their opinions on the date of Easter or the coequality of the nature of Christ, owe allegiance. Really, Churaldin"—he looked about him mildly—"one does find the most extraordinary things when one investigates the secret passages in one's cellars. And yes,

I've known about that passage for years." He studied him for a moment longer, in his eyes the mingled disappointment and reproof of a nurse who finds lewd drawings in her charge's bedroom. Then he looked mildly past him, to survey the flock of the Children of Light who were, for once, absolutely silent. His eyes returned to his slave's, and he shook his head in sorrowful regret.

Churaldin burst out unhappily, "I didn't want you to know."

The old scholar made no reply to that, merely continued to look around the cellar with interest. His gaze paused on Alexandros, and the big man flinched. Sixtus shook his head sadly, and his eyes moved on. Finally he said, "Well, in any case I now understand how you could be so sure of it when you swore to me that the Christians could not possibly have had anything to do with Tertullia Varia's abduction."

"I couldn't tell you how I knew," said Churaldin hastily.

Sixtus raised his eyebrows. "Evidently not. But I never believed it was the Christians, even before your so-well-informed assertions. I knew from the beginning that the amulet was a plant."

Marcus gasped, "WHAT?" Nobody else said anything. All eyes were fixed upon the old man, with mingled startlement and hope.

Serenely unconscious of his audience, he turned to Marcus. "Have you the amulet still?"

He produced it in silence. Sixtus limped over to the shaft of light that fell through the window and held it up. Its fellows dangled on the necks of at least half the persons there. "It is pure silver," he said, "and quite soft. Look, here's the nick I put in it that first day with my thumbnail." He looked around. "Come here, Judah."

As Judah crossed the room to him obediently, Sixtus continued, "I said before that the chain it hung upon might be instructive—its absence is even more instructive." He touched the amulet that lay on Judah's hard bronzed chest. It was clearly of the same manufacture, a small fish pierced through the head with a hole, through which a ring had been threaded, to hold it to the silver chain. "See how it's attached?" the old man pointed out. "If I were to pull it free, it would involve either breaking the chain, breaking the fish, or breaking the connecting ring. Now, you said yourself, Marcus, that no chain was found on the scene. But neither is there any mark of the soft silver around the hole being so much as scratched, let alone broken. Inference?"

"If the ring were broken it could easily be lost in the mud," said Judah, glancing down at the frail old scholar.

"But any force enough to break the ring would have scratched the metal around the hole," pointed out Marcus. "You mean, it was dropped?"

"Palmed, presumably. And dropped at the last moment, to prevent it from being trampled into the mud during the fight."

The big countrywoman asked, "But why would anyone want to throw the blame on us?"

Sixtus shrugged. "After Nero, the precedent is impeccable."

"The Children of This World hate the Children of Light!" theorized Ignatius shrilly.

"Anybody got a rag?" grumbled another one of the Children of Light.

"Spawn of Lilith! You seek to gag—"

"Ignatius, be quiet," snapped Telesphorus. "Is there anyone else who would want to kidnap this girl? Other than this young man, who would, I believe, do almost anything to prevent her from marrying a Syrian?"

Marcus swung around with a gasp of indignation. A calming hand was laid on his shoulder, and Sixtus answered, "Considering that Syrian is a devotee of Atargatis and has, in fact, been sacrificing children, I find Marcus' reluctance to see her wed to him understandable. There remains, of course, the question of the earring that was found in your meeting place, Judah."

"I swear I never knew it was there," insisted Symmachus. "Not that anyone would believe the word of a Christian. But it was a satanic lie, a plant . . ."

"Of course it was a plant!" cried Marcus. "The informer who led the soldiers to your place was one of the men who kidnapped Tullia in the first place! He must have planted it himself beforehand . . ."

"Since he was the one who picked it up," said the massive woman, "he didn't even have needed to do that."

"It's all of a piece!" screamed Ignatius. "The Evil One seeks to destroy us, and his minions are everywhere. Many will be martyred to the greater glory of Christ . . ."

"They will be if that girl isn't found before her father returns to the city," said Telesphorus grimly. "Be quiet, Ignatius—"

"You bunch of cowards!" shouted the little man furiously. "You run this way and that, you escape, you break one another out of prison, whereas you should run to the lions of the amphitheater with open arms! You should seek the glory of the rack and the wheel, the everlasting splendor of the stake! The rack is but a gate, the fire a robe of glory, and beyond lies the sure and certain welcome into the Lord's heaven! Cowardly, puling . . ."

"It isn't suffering for my faith I mind," rumbled Alexandros. "It's suffering for some other man's convenience that puts my back up. I don't think any of you has been called to recant our faith, have you?"

"Precious little good it would have done if we'd offered," grunted the big woman.

"Bah! A heretic Greek's prevarication! It matters not why we die, but only that we welcome it in the name of Christ! You're cowards, all of you, to flee from a simpleminded scheme—"

"Shut up, you flea-bitten little . . ."

"You would run from glory because you were scared by some whore's earring!"

"She is not a whore!" Marcus launched himself at the Christian, hands outstretched in blind rage, and Ignatius ducked behind Telesphorus, his voice mocking, biting as a gadfly.

"She is a whore because a whore gave me this!" He pulled something from his robe and threw it at Marcus' feet; something tiny and metal, which tinkled like a little bell on the rough stone of the floor.

Marcus stared at it, as though transfixed. "Where did you get that?" he asked, his voice barely audible, stiff and strange to his own ears.

Ignatius slid from around his protector, stared scornfully at him as he bent to pick it up. "From a whore."

It was a bronze lily, delicate as a real flower on its tiny wire. Marcus grabbed him by the robe, as though by force he could wring the answer from that twisted little saint, and Ignatius threw back his head and stared at him with hot black furious eyes.

"Where?" Marcus shouted.

The Christian shrugged. "Rome is full of them."

"And you go visiting them all, don't you?" yelled another voice from among the Christians.

Ignatius twisted like a cat to face his new challenger. "Mocker!" he shrieked. "False Christian! 'The scorner is an abomination . . .' "

"Ignatius!" Sixtus' deep voice filled the hall like thunder. The little man flinched as Marcus let him go, cowering back from Sixtus, his dark eyes flashing defiance. Sixtus came slowly forward to him, holding his gaze as if with a chain of iron. "Where did you get that earring?" asked the old man quietly. Ignatius seemed to grow smaller, shrinking away from that frail awesome form like a yapping dog faced with its master. For a time his eyes burned in sullen anger. Then they dropped.

Into the utter silence of that dim stone room he said, "It was thrown down to me from a window the afternoon I was arrested." He looked up with a last flash of defiance. "The window of a whorehouse."

"Plotina's," said Marcus.

Sixtus' gaze flickered to him. "You know the one?"

"I was in the crowd," he replied in a stifled voice, sick with the thought that she might have been trying to throw it to him. How many days ago had that been?

"That's just fine," snapped Telesphorus scornfully, "I can just hear the news in the Forum now: 'Christians Arrested Raiding Whorehouse . . .' "

Sixtus ignored him. "Would Arrius take his men in?"

Marcus hesitated. "Maybe. But Plotina's well-connected. I've seen her dining with some of the most influential men in Rome. If we're wrong . . ."

"Yes, it would make for some awkward explanations. Especially since, thanks to various members of my household, I seem to be in a rather ambiguous position myself." He glanced across at Churaldin. "You haven't converted Octavia yet, have you?"

The Briton looked sheepishly at the floor. Sixtus sighed.

"I could go in and have a look at the place," said Dorcas quietly, "and see if she's there."

Sixtus met her eyes. "That isn't necessary," he said softly.

"It's all right," she replied. "I'll go in the morning, before the place is open for business, when most of the girls are sleeping or having their baths. The sister-in-law of a neighbor of mine works as a cleaning woman in one of those places. She says cleaning people go in and out all the time. I won't be noticed."

He went to her, laid gentle hands on her shoulders, his voice barely audible to the others in that still, underground twilight. She was a tall girl, her wide brown eyes on level with his blue ones. "I don't want to see you hurt, child."

Just as softly, she replied, "I'll certainly be hurt, if there's a persecution. And so will you. If Churaldin was right, we haven't more than a day or two before Varus returns to Rome, and after that it won't be a simple investigation." She put her hands over his wrists, where they lay on her shoulders; it occurred to Marcus that, like Churaldin, Dorcas was already a friend of the old man's, possibly a former slave who had taken his offer of freedom. The look that passed between them as they stood together in the shadows was not the look of strangers, but, as with the Briton, the look of a father and an adopted child.

"God guard you, then," he whispered and, leaning forward, ceremoniously kissed her forehead. Then he looked around at the others: at Churaldin in his red military tunic, at Alexandros, whom one of the other Christians was trying surreptitiously to help out of his armor, at Marcus, watching him with uncertainty and anxiety, suspicion and confusion mingling in his soul. "As for you others," he continued in his usual mild voice, "you are welcome to remain under my roof—for this *is* my roof—provided you behave yourselves. I presume your deacon here"—he shot an accusing glance at Churaldin—"has made provision for feeding you, and I don't wish to be told where you will go and what you will do after you leave. One thing only I ask." He limped to the center of the group, that serene blue gaze suddenly hard, like a knife stripping bone and soul. "I remember hearing somewhere that the founder of your faith enjoined that where two or three of you are gathered together, there would he be also; so I beg you, do not disgust him by quarreling in his presence. Come along, Marcus, I'll show you out the front door . . . it's only a step or two down the secret passage here, through a short neck of the municipal sewers and past my wine cellars. Churaldin, I want to see you when you're finished."

"Yes, sir," said the slave stiffly. Sixtus turned on his heel and led the way to the jumble of broken boxes and disused furniture on the dais, which half-hid the entrance to an ancient tunnel. Not a Christian moved or spoke, any more than the old man's legionnaires would have; Marcus half-expected them to salute.

"I have had my suspicions about Churaldin's activities for some time," continued the old man quietly, as they ducked their heads under the low entrance. "But as I believe I said once before, there are things that it is more convenient not to know." They turned a corner, and the dim light from the cellar behind them faded. They groped through what seemed to be a bricked-up section of another cellar and down a short ladder through an old dry drain in the floor. The sewer was disused but clammy; Marcus shuddered, wiping his hands on the hem of his toga, and almost ran into the foot of another ladder that led up to a low-roofed cavern of blue twilight and dust, which turned out to be Sixtus' wine cellar. The old man limped to a corner, where his staff leaned against the wall among the stone wine jars. "I'm afraid I'm going to have problems enough trying to think of a convincing story to tell our friend the centurion that won't too badly violate my philosophic commitment to truth," he added, brushing cobwebs from his shoulders. And, in a gentler voice, "I shall send you word as soon as Dorcas returns."

Marcus looked at him curiously, a white ghostly shape in the gloom. "She was your slave, wasn't she?" he asked. "She said something to me once about having had a master who would cure anyone of hatred of mankind. I should have known she meant you."

"A hard cure, in her case," sighed the old man. "At fourteen she was as tough and nasty a little urchin as ever stole from her master's guests. But she's as fearless as a gladiator, and clever as a thief. If Tullia is in Plotina's brothel, Dorcas will find her there."

They climbed the steps to the pantry, a ramshackle closet built off the tiny kitchen. Through one arched doorway could be seen the dirty flagstones and matted wall of vine and thorn that had overgrown the pillars of the arcade around the garden. Through another, the drift of spices and vinegar blew, and with them Harpalos' voice telling Octavia a hideous tale of vampires that rose from their graves in the night to bite the noses off their victims, to the little girl's breathless delight. Marcus followed him, exhausted, into the shadowy corridor of jungle, his mind groping to assimilate the repeated shocks of the afternoon.

"I don't understand it," he said at last. "Why would they have stolen her in the first place? If they were going to turn her into a whore, it would be too dangerous to keep her in Rome. Somebody would be bound to recognize her."

Sixtus shook his head. "They didn't kidnap her for anything of the kind," he said quietly. "There are far too many girls in Rome who are pretty, and helpless, and cheaply come by, to run that kind of risk to take an unwilling one. No, the choice of victim, of method, and of witnesses were all deliberate—they have to have been. And very clever by the way: who'd look for a missing girl in a brothel?"

"You're probably right," whispered Marcus.

"Marcus." Sixtus laid a hand gently on his arm, halting him before the half-ruinous cave of a splendid summer dining room, whose archways were so choked with vines as to make the room inaccessible from the gardens at all. Green dappled light mottled his toga, checkering his lined, enigmatic face with wan brightness. "If they're holding her in Plotina's, which is after all a semi-public place, they're not about to run the risk of any kind of violent disturbance. In a place like that it would be too easy for word to get about."

"You mean rape makes a lot of noise," concluded Marcus for him bitterly, daring him to deny that it had been in his mind.

Sixtus returned his defiant stare with one of quelling calm. "Yes," he replied. "Even in a brothel."

"Thanks for the comfort." He turned away.

The old man followed him, not at all put out. "And she had her wits about her enough to pitch one of her earrings down, on the off-chance that someone would see it and recognize it. So she was able to get about. And more important, her spirit wasn't broken, if that means anything to you at all."

Marcus swung around, an angry retort flooding to his lips. But it died unspoken. He wondered why he fought so to keep the hope from his heart. He whispered, "It's so close."

"It's hard to trust," said the old man gently.

In the atrium the sunlight had narrowed and focused itself to a two-inch slit of molten gold, cutting the shadowy faded frescoes of the east wall like a burning wound. They paused beside the dark flickering waters of the pool; from their depths Isis regarded them, veiled in her long green hair.

"Thank you," said Marcus quietly. "For everything."

Sixtus smiled and dismissed the thanks with a shake of his head. "I'll send you word— if that pack of fanatics I've been feeding for the last several years ever returns to bear it— tomorrow morning at your family's home."

"What?" Marcus halted, startled, in the act of turning toward the door. "How did you know I'd got a message from my family?"

Sixtus frowned. "But it's all over the city," he said. "I heard the criers myself in the Forum."

"What?" He stared at him, uncomprehending. "What are you talking about?"

The old man saw that he did not understand and laid a blunt scarred hand gently on his arm. "I'm sorry," he said quietly. "I didn't know you had not heard. Your father is dead."

XVI

A life honorably lived reaps its rewards of authority to the end.

Cicero

Marcus stood for a long time in the doorway of his mother's summer bedroom, looking down at her unconscious form on the sleeping-couch. Someone had bound up the wound in her temple; the bruise on the jaw was livid, but small. In the diffuse twilight that filtered from the garden beyond the covered walk her eyes looked bruised and swollen with weeping.

He asked, "How did it happen?" aware that his voice sounded very distant and offhand; aware that if he didn't fight to keep it so, he would break down and weep. His father had always called it unmanly. One couldn't, he supposed, offend the old boy now.

Caius said, "Her maids said they quarreled. She had been gone all day and returned home late in the afternoon, after he had come back from the baths." His voice sounded bitterly disapproving in the hushed heat of the afternoon. As well it might, thought Marcus, turning quietly away and letting the curtain fall back to cover the doorway, lest the light awaken the woman who slept within. He walked back along the breezeway, feeling hot and sticky in his heavy toga and oppressed by the silence of the house.

"That was the day she went to see Aunt Aurelia at the Temple of Isis," he said quietly.

"That was the day before yesterday," replied his brother. For a moment their father's voice crept into his tones, as though the old man himself were reproaching his son for hearing of the event so tardily, and from strangers. They passed through a graceful triple arch of pillars into the drawing room, which had been curtained off from the atrium but where one could still hear the professional grief of the hired mourners. Caius sat down in a carved backless chair. "I do not know where she had been, for I have never made it a practice to question my parents' affairs. Priscilla—one of her maids—said that she heard angry words coming from Father's office across the court. She was frightened—naturally—for Father was in a terrible passion, the sort of blind rage in which he might do anything. She says that she heard a scream, and a blow, and the sound of furniture falling. She dared not go in until she heard him leave, and then she ran in, and saw Mother"—his thoroughly controlled voice wavered a little—"lying unconscious beside the desk. She was naturally shocked and turned to see Father storming across the garden in one of his black rages. She says that he stopped beside the fountain and half-turned, as if to come back; then he passed his hand across his eyes and suddenly doubled over, as though he had been struck, though there was no one nearby or, in fact, anywhere in the garden at all. He was dead when she reached him, his face bright crimson, almost purple."

Marcus ran his hand along the carved edge of the room's ebony scroll case. "Sounds like a burst blood vessel."

"That is what our physician said."

"Had he ever struck her before?"

Caius was silent a moment, looking down at his hands resting among the white folds of the toga in his lap. He had already had the family barber crop his hair, and looked austere and disapproving: his father's expression in his mother's wide brown eyes. But it was not his father's bitter callousness that answered.

"Since you left us, Marcus, to choose your own paths, Father was more and more given to this kind of rage. When we were children he might order a slave beaten, but he would never do it with his own hand. It was almost a sickness in him."

"A sickness," repeated Marcus quietly. "Or maybe just a rage at Fate, that our kind are not what we were. He was right, of course—the old families and the Senate aren't ruling the empire anymore. The ones with the real power are the emperor's freedmen—former slaves from who knows what background—and people with money, like Tiridates. We're only valuable because of the prestige of our names, so that people whose fathers made their fortunes in trade like Priscus Quindarvis can have themselves adopted into our class. The Silanus family is one of the oldest in Rome, but Father was never more than an aedile."

"That is still no reason," said his brother thinly, "to strike our mother because she thwarted his will."

"Whom else could he strike?"

Caius' face seemed to grow longer with the lengthening of his upper lip. Marcus prowled over to the courtyard door, stared bleakly out into the carefully trimmed garden, with its white and pink lilies and its sweetness of mint. On her pedestal beside the fountain, a bronze Macedonian nymph glowed like gold in the last of the sunset. "In some ways I think anger was almost a luxury for him," he said after a time. "He enjoyed being angry. Maybe people do ask for the deaths they get."

"Maybe," agreed his brother in a thin voice. "But it does not become you to speak ill of a man whose spirit has not yet departed this house."

Out in the atrium the mourners' wailing droned steadily on, breaking rhythmically every now and then as one of them beat on her breast. Above it rose the wailing of the double flute. "Sorry," murmured Marcus. "I'm sorry." He looked around at the small formal room, with its marble bust of his mother as a young girl, its scroll cases and painted pillars on the wall. "Where's Felix?"

"In his room." Caius' tone could have chilled wine. "You will be staying the night, of course. The funeral will be tomorrow, at the sixth hour . . ."

"Tomorrow?" All thought of his father vanished from his mind as though wiped with a sponge.

"In this heat it would hardly do to delay," stated his brother stiffly. But Marcus hardly heard him, his mind racing ahead to Dorcas, and when she would bring back word . . .

"I trust you will take time from your affairs to attend?"

He ignored the ponderous sarcasm and murmured, "Yes, of course." He wondered desperately what he would do. If Dorcas returned with word that Tullia was in that place, he couldn't absent himself from the rescue-party. He had to see her, to speak to her before she spoke to anyone else, to reassure her and to be reassured himself. But like the Furies that punish impiety, the voices of the other side of his soul rose up, crying that he could not forsake this last duty to his father. His philosophy had taught him that a man's body, after death, is of no more consequence than an empty wine jar. But he had been raised in the family cult; not to attend the funeral, for whatever reason, would bring a guilt that would haunt him as though he had struck down the old man himself.

In a sore torment of mind he left the drawing room, crossed the evening shadows of the garden toward the bedroom that had been his as a boy. The house seemed hushed, the noises of mourning in the atrium very distant. As he passed the open door of Felix' bedroom, he paused, hearing from within the soft sounds of drunken grief and catching the smell of the place, like the breath of a tavern. From within a boy's voice whispered, "Who's that?" And as Marcus turned, "Oh! Master Caius, sir, please don't be angry with him . . ."

"I'm not Caius." In the dim evening light, wearing a plain white tunic and toga, he realized how easy it would be to mistake them. "Is that Giton?" He stepped inside, peering through the darkness to identify the pretty young boy who'd poured out the wine at dinner.

He was sitting at the foot of Felix's sleeping-couch, wearing only a little loincloth in the heat of the stuffy room. A clay wine jar was cradled against his bare side. Four others lay empty, amid lakes of spilled dregs, on the parti-colored marble of the floor. Felix himself was stretched, sobbing bitterly, face down on the couch.

At the sound of his brother's voice he rolled over, his long perfumed curls plastered to his cheeks with runny, half-melted unguents. His eye paint had run too, streaking his face with black and purple. He forced a drunken smile. "Ah! Professor! Sorry 'bout all this. Silly of me, an' all. Maudlin in my cups, you know. Always was." He held out his hands to his brother, tears shining on his blotched cheeks. "Fancy it, cryin' for that old hardfisted roughneck." His voice cracked grotesquely, and he sobbed, "Give m'brother wine, kid."

Giton looked questioningly up at Marcus, who nodded.

"It's all right," said Marcus after a moment, as the boy fetched another cup from the sideboard. "Thank you," he said softly, and the boy nodded, a little absently. He was watching Felix, sorrow and concern in his intelligent, hyacinth-dark eyes.

Felix pawed at his eyes with his long fringed red sleeve, making the mess worse. "Pious, an' all," he said. "Caius'd approve. Oughter call him in."

"No," said Marcus.

Felix nodded owlishly. "Unmanly," he agreed. "Still . . ." He flung his cup down, the dark wine spilling like blood across the floor that was already awash in it. "I hated the old bastard!" he cried, his voice breaking with sobs. "Never gave nothing but pain—Mother, Aemilia, and you. Don't even know why I'm cryin'." And he sank back on the cushions, gulping, his body shaking with renewed grief.

"Maybe because it's possible to love and hate the same person at the same time," said Marcus softly. "You hated him at closer range than I did. You knew him."

"An' to know him is to love him," he choked, with drunken sarcasm. "Kind of a messy theory for a ph'los'phr, frater mine."

"Life's messy." He drank off the wine and handed the cup back to the boy. "Will you stay with him?"

Giton nodded. "He'll be better after the funeral," he predicted quietly. "He didn't learn about it until the morning after it happened; that's what hurts him, I think." He walked with Marcus out into the breezeway, slender and effeminate-looking and diminutive, but with those bright, unsurprisable violet eyes. "In a way it's too bad," he continued, glancing toward the doors that led into the atrium, through which the sound of wailing had died away as the mourners packed up to go home, their day's work done.

"What is?" asked Marcus. "That any man would make himself so hated that his own sons were avoiding his house at the time of his death?"

The boy glanced up at him, those long painted lashes throwing soft curved shadows on the alabaster cheeks. "That he was that unhappy. It's very difficult to change the way you are." The boy looked as though he would have said something else, but changed his mind. A moment later he slipped back into the stifling darkness, and as he walked away, Marcus could hear the murmur of his voice and Felix's sobbing, drunken replies.

The mourners had left the atrium by the time he returned there. The only light now came from the four lamps on their tall bronze stands, set at the corners of the bier, making his father's face look like something wrought clumsily of wax. Despite the heavy wreaths, roses and asphodel mingled with ripe fruit and colored ribbons, Caius was right about the necessity for a quick funeral. As he came from the quiet alcove into the main room, the woman at the foot of the high couch looked up and smiled lopsidedly. "Hello, Professor."

"I thought you'd be asleep still." He leaned down to kiss her unbruised cheek. "Caius and I went by to see you."

"Did you, dear? That was kind." In the uneasy saffron light her face looked worse than it had earlier, drawn and exhausted. Her hair, loosened for mourning, was visibly graying.

"Are you all right?"

"Oh, yes," she smiled. "All the notables of the Senate have been in and out of the house all today and yesterday, including that horrid Garovinus man who's still under the impression that he's going to marry your sister. I couldn't very well come to look at him then, not looking like a gladiator's moll—not that any of them would have been so ill-bred as to ask, of course," she added, with a faded smile. "But I feel that I owe it to him, to mourn beside him tonight."

Marcus rested his hands on her shoulders. "You don't owe him a thing, Mother."

She sighed and shook her head. "I owe him the outward form of grief, since I feel none within. And even that isn't strictly true." Beyond the indigo curtains in the drawing room they could hear Caius moving about, giving orders to Straton in a low voice about the funeral banquet and wreaths for the pallbearers. At the foot of the bier, incense hissed in the burners, the clouds of it soft and blue and sweet-smelling over the oily smoke of the lamps. "I've been his wife for twenty-seven years, Marc—quite a record, these days. And I can't remember ever being happy, or feeling anything but trapped by it, and helpless to get out. But still—it is twenty-seven years. One can't just put it behind one without a backward glance."

She turned from him and rested her big soft hands on the curved foot of the bier, the four torches touching her face with their multiple shadows. "I don't know why I should feel there was something I could have done differently, some way I could have kept him from finding out ."

Marcus shook his head and put his arm around her waist. They stood almost shoulder to shoulder; standing as he had used to, the top of the dead man's head would have come to his son's chin, and to his wife's lips. "If Caius was right, and it was a kind of sickness in him," he said softly, "you could have done nothing to prevent it. One or the other of us would have provoked his wrath; if it had not been this, it would have been something else, quite soon."

Her glance slid sideways, asking; then she smiled wanly

and turned her head to kiss his cheek. Between Patricia Pollia Cato Silania and her sons there had never been much need of words.

With an odd sort of peace in his soul, he returned to his room and slept, for the first time in years, in the walled-in and expensive quiet that only the rich in Rome could afford.

It was as well that he did, for the morning was hellish. Marcus' attempt to slip quietly away after a bite of breakfast was thwarted by his older brother, and he found himself involved in a bitter, sordid quarrel about funerary arrangements, the order of the procession, Felix's drunkenness, and his own random and irresponsible life-style. As he so often had with his father, Marcus cried, "How can I make you understand?" and Caius retorted, pinch-lipped, "I hope I shall never be so lost to propriety as to understand how any man, no matter what his feelings toward his parents, can put a mere woman before his duty toward them. I hated our father as much as you did, but I respected him, something I fear neither you nor our drunken sot of a brother ever did. Since I am now the head of this family—"

"You may be the head of this family, but you do not have a father's power over me!" Marcus shouted at him, losing his temper in his anxiety to be away. "My father is dead and I owe him nothing."

"You may owe him nothing," yelled Caius back, "but by Capitoline Jupiter you owe it to our house to remain here and to our mother not to desert her at such a time! If you will not do your duties to the House of Silanus, then depart from it and never look to us for another scrap of bread or another sesterce of silver as long as you live!"

"You can keep your filthy money if that's all that matters to you!" cried Marcus, by now in a towering rage. "I don't care . . ."

He was saved from further escalation of the quarrel by the entrance of Straton into the drawing room, crop-haired and wearing the ash-streaked white of mourning. "A visitor to see Lady Patricia," he announced quietly, and with a withering glare at Marcus, Caius got to his feet and strode stiffly into the atrium. In the shadow of the vestibule Aurelia Pollia stood, her veil drawn over her head, looking timid and very small in the presence of the man who in life had so detested her husband and herself. Like a grave guardian, Priscus Quindarvis stood at her side, wearing, like her, plain white clothing, and Marcus took the opportunity to slip quietly away. Since the night of the banquet he had had badly mixed feelings about the praetor. As he let himself out a side door like a thief, he heard the voice of the time-slave calling out, "It is now the beginning of the third hour! It is now the beginning . . ."

There was not much time, he thought, to effect a rescue and get back in time for his father's funeral.

He broke into a trot.

"I tell you anything could have delayed her!" Sixtus limped to the corner of his shadowy cell and turned like an old white fox, driven to bay among his watching baals. From the green tunnel of the overgrown walkway Marcus could hear his voice, even before he stepped into the room.

"Anything!" spat Telesphorus harshly. "You send a chaste young woman into a brothel and you say 'anything.' "

"Don't be an ass, cleaning women go in and out of those places all the time!"

"You'd know best about that," snapped the priest. "I say she should never have gone."

"Who else would you have sent? Arete? That Quartilla woman, who'd start preaching about fornication and adultery the first time she glimpsed a naked bum? Dorcas is clever, and she has the courage of a soldier, she'd——"

"What's happened?" asked Marcus quietly from the door.

Priest and philosopher both turned. They seemed equally at home, Telesphorus with the green cavelike room with its litter of scrolls, inscriptions, and unknown gods, and Sixtus with the presence of the Christian. Marcus had the impression they'd been arguing doctrine and elenchus since breakfast.

It was Telesphorus who spoke. He folded his big callused

hands on his bony knee. "Dorcas hasn't returned from Plotina's brothel."

"When did she go?"

"Shortly after the first hour of the morning," replied Sixtus. At this time of the year, the daylight hours were very long.

"Is the place open now?" asked Marcus after a moment, and Sixtus nodded.

"But you'd be about as inconspicuous as a black cat in a roomful of laundry. I'm having the place watched."

"By whom?" asked Marcus, and the old man looked embarrassed, as if he'd been caught in a social solecism.

Telesphorus' eyes glittered maliciously. "Once a general, always a general," he purred. "The habit of command dies hard." He cocked one chill gray eye up at Marcus. "Christians, of course. You don't think Rome isn't meshed over with a net of Christian intelligence? The Children of Light may be in bondage to the Children of This World, but slaves, as has long been known, know all things before their masters. Some of them are silly, and heretical, and believe wrong and foolish doctrines, but at least they believe something. They may haggle over it like market women, but at least they aren't busy numbing themselves with booze or the sight of other men's spilled blood. And whatever their doctrinal differences, they—we—are all of us bound together by the baptism of water and fire, an invisible baptism as strong and binding as that dunking in animal blood that holds together the followers of the Persian god. God sees all, and what God does not"—and he flashed the first wry smile Marcus had ever seen out of that austere priest—"the Bishop of Rome certainly does."

Marcus was silent for a moment, looking down at that tall rawboned man, who leaned back against the wall like an angular spider. "Are you the Bishop of Rome?" he asked softly, and then remembered the scene in the jail. "No, of course, you couldn't be."

"And if I were I certainly wouldn't let a centurion's clerk know it," remarked the priest. "No, Papa's a far cleverer man than I, despite his woolly-headed doctrinal errors. Far too clever," he added spitefully, with a sharp accusing glance at Sixtus, "to have sent a girl on a dangerous mission, as our friend here has done."

"When would be the earliest I could go there?" asked Marcus, looking from Telesphorus to Sixtus. "Tonight? After dark?"

"Second hour of the night. That's when the crowd will be the biggest."

"You'll fit right in," sneered the priest, "with that funeral-crop of yours, smelling of sacrificial incense."

Marcus felt himself flushing to the hairline, not so much because he contemplated a trip to a brothel directly following his father's funeral, but because he scarcely had remembered that it would be so.

Sixtus' deep voice cut into the burning silence. "Yes," he said gently, "he will. It's very common, I believe. After the awareness of death, one seeks the act of generation. So the illusion will pass, provided," he continued, "you are willing to go through with it. If you aren't, we'll contrive something else."

"No," said Marcus, "no, I'll go. At this point I don't know who Arrius suspects, but any one of your people might be recognized. And Plotina's is expensive. If Alexandros or Churaldin is suspected, someone might wonder where slaves got the kind of money it takes to go there."

Sixtus limped back to his desk. "Thank you," he said quietly. "It's a point well taken. Arrius was here this morning, furious over the disappearance of the Christians from the prison, but whether he suspects Churaldin, or Alexandros, or the whole household including myself of carpenter-worship I don't know, and I'm not certain that he does, either. What will your family say if you do this?"

Marcus shook his head. "My family's said all it's going to," he replied in a hard voice. "I'm sorry it has to be this way, but I'm not going to kill the living to honor the dead, and if they've captured Dorcas, they'll know someone's on their trail. We haven't time to waste." He turned to go. "The funeral's at the sixth hour; I should be back before the sun's well down. I expect my mother will save me a cake from the banquet afterward.''

In the doorway he was stopped by Telesphorus' voice. "Although it hardly does to say so to someone entrusted with a mission of this sort in such a place," said the priest, in that same hard, half-mocking tone, "go with the grace of God, my son.'' He raised a hand, to sketch a holy sign in the air between them. "Heaven knows that the Son of God himself saved people from worse places than that.''

The House of Silanus was an ancient one; its tombs lay in a great private garden beside the Appian Way a mile or so beyond the gates of the city. As he bent his shoulder under the weight of his father's bier, Marcus looked about him at the other members of the funeral cortege and knew that the old man had been right. There were few enough trueborn scions of the ancient houses in evidence, and the ones there were, were men like Porcius Craessius: highborn, wealthy, and appallingly dissolute, who poured out an eternal stream of money in a vain attempt to fill the emptiness of their lives. More of them were like Garovinus—who'd had himself adopted into a minor branch of the Cornelius family—or Quindarvis, whose father had made his money in speculations in Egyptian wheat. They both wore the purple-bordered togas of their senatorial rank and walked with bowed heads in silence among the mourners. There were a great many of the Senate in the procession. The music of tubas, of cithara and bagpipes, the wailing of the flutes and the keening of the hired mourners reverberated from the walls of the basilicas and temples as they crossed the noon hush of the Forum, and rang among the tall buildings of the circus district, as they crossed toward the Appian Gate.

The funeral moved slowly, the pace and the dirge weaving themselves together into a lugubrious whole that drove all other thought from his mind. Stiff-backed with outraged piety, Caius bore the other front corner of the bier; just behind him, Marcus could hear Felix's agonized whimpers at every crash of the cymbals. After two days of continual drinking, his brother looked in worse case than the corpse. Over the wailing of the mourners, he listened for the sounds of his mother's or sister's voice, but perhaps the music drowned them. In any case, by the laws of the old republic, such outcry would have been thought unseemly.

Sweat rolled down his face beneath the muffling folds of his drawn-up toga. The few passersby, loitering before the siesta hour, stepped respectfully aside, but at this hour even the city seemed hushed. Marcus wondered if, wherever she was, Tullia could hear the faint strains of the music passing by.

The garden in which this branch of the family had its tombs was unwalled, a quiet and well-kept place, redolent of citrus trees and myrtle. His father's tomb lay some distance in, near the columbarium of the family freedmen and slaves. It had been built some years ago; the young plane trees planted earlier were already taller than its corniced roof. His father had always said that he would wall the garden—no traveler, he had declared, would use *his* tomb as a privy—but like so many other things, it had never been got to.

They laid him in his sarcophagus, wrapped in his shroud and already starting to smell. They sealed the tomb, being sure to leave the little tubes down which offerings could be pushed or poured at the Feast of Families; killed the lamb they had brought and poured out blood and wine. It was late afternoon by the time it was over, the clear crystal light softening the faces of those who stood around the tomb. Seemly things were said; his mother put back her veils just enough to drink a little of the wine. The rest of it was poured through the tube that led into the sarcophagus itself, the final drink shared with her lord.

Then they returned in silence to the city.

It was close to sunset when they reached the house. The slaves were already stirring about, making preparations for the funeral banquet. His father's associates and longtime clients were hanging about the atrium, talking over the funeral, or the emperor's campaigns in the East, or discussing the games. Marcus slipped away as quickly as he could and crossed the garden to his own room, moving swiftly to avoid Caius. Even without his own concerns that evening, he had no desire to be trapped into a funeral banquet.

His room was almost dark, facing northeast into the court. He threw off his white toga and tunic and pulled from the chest the clothes he'd cached there earlier in the afternoon: a dark-blue dinner suit he'd stolen from Felix's room, the hems of tunic and mantle embroidered alike with a delicate line of tiny bullion stars. Absolutely the latest thing, Felix had assured him. Marcus, regarding himself in the long mirror of polished brass, with his cropped hair and knobby knees, thought he looked like an ass in it.

If Caius sees me, he thought as he slipped down the breezeway toward the atrium, he really will kill me.

From the drawing room he heard his brother's voice, welcoming a late-coming guest. ". . . such an arduous journey, to return to such grief. We are honored at your presence. For all your political differences, I know that our father always respected you as a man." *(Another politic lie, thought Marcus. Of the precious few men their father had respected, none had espoused politics that differed from his.)* "We would be honored to have you at our board."

· "No," replied a rich, mellifluous orator's voice that brought Marcus' heart up into his throat. "Caius Silanus Senior and I were old enemies. I would not do injustice toward his feelings about me by eating at his table, even after his death." Marcus glided to the curtains as silently as he could, nearly tripping over a footstool in his stealth. Through a fold in the curtains he could see Caius, tall and pompous in his white dinner suit and plain house slippers, standing in the ocher lamplight beside the vestibule doors. The man before him was shorter than he by half a head, dark, middle-aged, wearing the purple-bordered toga over a dark tunic smutched with the dust of travel. His handsome face was drawn with fatigue and grief, but he held himself like a man supremely used to command. He went on, "It has been, as you say, an arduous journey, to a most bitter homecoming. I am here only to fetch my wife, and to speak with my cousin Quindarvis, if you will be so good as to let them know that I have returned.''

Caius bent his head in respect. Straton came in with a lamp; the flicker of its oily topaz flame threw shadows over the guest's face and drew a deep glint of long-burning anger from the dark eyes. Caius said, ''Straton? Will you go to Lady Aurelia Pollia and tell her that her husband, the prefect Varus, has returned and is looking for her.''

XVII

When you are going to take any act in hand, remind yourself what kind of an act is it. If you are going to bathe, place before yourself what happens in the bath; some splashing the water, others pushing against one another, others abusing one another, and some stealing: and thus with more safety you will undertake the matter, if you say to yourself, I now intend to bathe, and to maintain my will in a manner conformable to nature.

Epictetus

Plotina's brothel was built above and behind the Baths of the Golden Swordsman, and Marcus spent a long time simply lying in the warm tiled pool, watching the play of the steam before his eyes. In spite of imperial edicts requiring the closing of all baths by the eleventh hour of the day, at the second hour of the night these showed no signs of emptying. The high arches of the ceiling rang with giggles and raucous laughter; rose and amber lamplight sparkled on the waters of the dark lapis pools. Through the skylight, stars blazed in a warm black ocean. Marcus stared straight ahead and thought of Tullia and Dorcas, wondering if he would find them after all, or whether they would simply retreat again, dreamlike, as

Tullia had done from the catacombs, and from the temple on the Janiculum Hill.

The warmth of the water swirled around him. With barely a splash, a woman had slipped down to sit on the underwater bench at his side. She offered him a cup, dark wine, unmixed and smelling of the vineyards of Chios. "Wine sometimes helps sadness," she said quietly, her eyes dark as plums in a fine-boned, angular face.

"Thank you," he said and drank—cautiously, since he hadn't stayed for the funeral dinner. The woman watched him, but said nothing, and in his heart he thanked her for her undemanding silence. After a time she leaned her head back against the tiled rim of the pool and like him seemed content for a time merely to watch the antics of the bathers. But he felt her awareness of him and, every now and then, the touch of those dark eyes.

It was the first time Marcus had been inside one of the fashionable baths-cum-brothel; for a while he only looked around him, at the expensive marbles, the mosaics on the tessellated walls, the giggling riot of wet gilded bodies and splashing water. It was as different as possible from the only other time he'd ever visited a brothel.

The memory of that first visit still scalded him with shame; it had been, he supposed, part of the reason he'd given up the gladiatorial games. For Sixtus had been right, of course; death, or the closeness to death, is a terrible aphrodisiac. For a boy of fifteen the sight of men trapped hopelessly between the threat of torture and the certainty of death in battle, the sight of women screaming under the claws of leopards worrying at their white, blood-splattered throats, brought a pain to his loins that nothing would satiate. The blowsy woman who'd picked him up as he'd stumbled, taut-legged, down the ramps had doubtless seen a million boys and men come walking out of there in that fashion. The brothel had been black as a pit and stunk like a vomitorium, and had left Marcus feeling shamed, filthy, and violated. When he'd discovered the next day that he'd traded his virginity for body lice, he had seriously considered suicide as an alternative to asking Straton for a remedy.

He had avoided Tullia for days, out of sheer shame.

The Golden Swordsman, however, was an entirely different matter, a world removed from the stinking cribs that lined the arcades of the arena. Golden lamps in the shape of nymphs hung low over the water; music pervaded the rooms. The place was redolent of perfume, bath oils, and women. Pillars of pink marble, veined and mottled with white and black, threw a kind of rosy reflection over everything, and on the arched pediment above the main entrance to the lobby, a voluptuous Leda twined in amazing embraces with her feathered lover.

Marcus found himself wondering what the rest of the place was like.

He looked quickly sideways, to meet those dark painted eyes. She sat close to him, her arm just brushing his beneath the rippling surface of the warm silken water. Her hair, piled in loose coils on top of her head so as not to get wet in the pools, looked tousled, the tendrils of it that hung about her face sticking to those high cheekbones.

She asked simply, "D'you want to come upstairs with me?"

He nodded, suddenly unable to speak for the dryness of his mouth.

He left the money on the table, near the floating light of the alabaster lamp. The sum had been written on the door as they'd gone in, along with her name, which was Antara. As he was putting on his clothes, she looked up from the pillow and smiled her slow lazy cat's smile. "Will you stay for a cup of wine?"

Marcus shook his head. "I—I can't."

She seemed to accept this, held out her hand to him, and kissed his fingers softly. In the heat she was covered only by a thin sheet of gauze and by her long hair, which had come undone. "Will I see you again?"

He felt himself blush, a comprehensive effort that started

from the navel, and hastily pulled on his tunic. She watched him uncritically, though her smooth lips tucked up a little at the corners. "I don't think so," he managed to stammer, his eyes wholly engaged by his belt buckle, and the tucks deepened.

"You're a sweet boy," she said inconsequentially. Marcus blundered first into the doorpost, and then out into the hall.

Above stairs Plotina's was clean, but lacked the opulence of the baths. Frescoes and paintings on the walls depicted the loves of the Olympian gods in an awesome wealth of detail, but the rooms themselves were small and furnished sparsely. There were some two dozen of them on this floor—the one directly above the baths—laid out like the rooms in an apartment building along a wide central corridor. At one end a great stairway of worked chalcedony and lapis led to the baths, and the sound of them drifted upward like a breath of warmed perfume. At the other end of the hall a less elegant stairway led to the floors above.

For the moment, the hall was deserted.

The next floor up seemed to be laid out the same way, only the rooms were smaller. It had the smell of use, but as Marcus slipped down the hall like a thief, it appeared more deserted, quieter, and much darker. He paused before a shut door, hearing within the hissing whine of a whip. Tullia leaped to his mind, in a welter of anger and shame and guilt; then he heard a man's voice whimper within and plead, "Again."

Gilded nymphs cavorting in warm water, he supposed, were not to everyone's taste.

He moved on cautiously up the stairs.

This floor was deserted, and hot as an oven after a baking day. It was lightless but for the wan reflection of moonlight that leaked through the big square windows at either end of the hall, and it smelled of dust and mice. The doors he paused beside were silent; opening them, he found most rooms empty, though one or two at this end showed signs of not-very-recent habitation by maids or slaves. One, horribly, turned out to be a punishment room, its bare blood-stained couch scarred all over with the cuts of whips and decorated at the four corners with chains. He crept silently on, the floor squeaking under his feet, sick with apprehension and not daring to picture who might have occupied that room.

There's no reason they would hurt her, he told himself desperately.

But there's no reason they would have kidnapped her at all! The whole thing's senseless, a vicious, filthy, meaningless act of terrorism that only fanatics could perpetrate!

He pushed open a door near the end of the hall and saw that it bore not only a lock, but metal bolts on the outside. For a moment he thought it was another punishment room, but he saw it was only a kind of cell, the window boarded over, the darkness almost absolute. It smelled and felt of use, of recent habitation, but its smell was of neither sex nor blood. His groping hands encountered a sleeping-couch, a stand with a basin for water on top and a chamber pot beneath, and a kind of little stool. Nothing further—no evidence of who had been here, or why.

Then a stray sliver of light caught on something bright, like a coin in the shadows under the couch. He bent and picked it up, and saw that it was a silver cross, still fastened to its broken chain.

He thought, *Dorcas.*

And then: *Where did the light come from?*

He hit the door in a desperate rush barely in time to prevent its being slammed to. Weight greater than his own shoved against it, skidding him back; he braced his feet and fought, worming to get an elbow or knee into the crack. Lantern light bounded crazily through the gap, and he glimpsed a brown bearded face and the glint of a gold earring.

The man yelled, "Crescens! Pugnax! We got him!" He was drawing in his breath for another bellow when Marcus slammed his weight on the door, off-balancing him. He thrust hard and slithered through the crack. The kidnapper Lucius swung at him, a blow that would have felled a donkey, and he ducked and was satisfied to hear the man's fist crack against the doorframe. Then he was running for all he was worth down the hall, the shorter man pounding at his heels.

Two shapes, one massive and the other more massive, loomed against the light from the stairs. Torchlight flickered on edged steel. He dropped to his hands and knees, felt his pursuer's shins collide briefly with his side as the man's momentum somersaulted him into the arms of his friends. They were still tangling when Marcus ploughed his way past the whole melee, hearing his cloak snag and tear. As he plunged down the narrow stairs he heard men yelling, "Thief! Thief!" and footsteps pounding at his heels.

Doors were opening all along the darker hallway of the floor below, white frowsty faces peeking out. He clattered down the stairs and was halfway toward the main staircase to the baths when he saw the shadows of men racing up from below with torches. Other people were running into the hall now, men clutching bedsheets and dignity inadequately about themselves, women wearing nothing but paint and jewels, all of them giving tongue like the hounds of Hades. Marcus flung open a door at random, dived through, shut it behind, and gasped, "Beg pardon . . ." as he fled for the window, hoping for a shed roof or, at worst, a nice soft midden below.

The window was barred. Men were yelling in the hall, women screaming, fists pounding on doors. The woman in the bed sat up with a gasp of indignation, clutching the sheets around a magnificent bosom with somewhat inappropriate modesty. The man with her blinked at him, startled, in the dim light of a gold glass lamp, and said plaintively, "B'Castor, they're right! Y'are a thief. That's my best dinner suit you're wearin'."

"Felix!" gasped Marcus.

His brother sat up, his shorn hair making him look crumpled and rather pathetic. His eyes were red and puffy with weeping. "Here," he complained, "what're you doing here, Silenus?"

Outside in the hall doors were slamming, voices yelling. Among them Lucius' was recognizable, cursing like a gladiator. Marcus gasped, "Felix, you've got to switch clothes with me."

"What? Are you drunk?" Marcus was already stripping.

"This's a fine way to comport yourself on the night of your father's funeral!"

"As the pot said to the kettle. Put these on, get out there, and run like blazes, and when they catch you, tell them I've already left—tell them anything. I'll get out a window . . ."

"There's a back stairs two doors down from this room," said the girl, vastly interested, leaning back against the pillows and forgetting about the sheet. "My name's Xaviera, if you're ever back this way."

"Uh—pleased to meet you." He finished slinging Felix's elegant Persian silk cloak around his shoulders, fastening it with long ornamental pins. Felix was shaking his head as he struggled into the dark-blue tunic. Fists hammered the door across the hall, a man yelled, "He's got to be in here somewhere . . ."

"Y'know, Marcus, Caius might have been right when he said all that philosophy addled the brain."

"Just get going!" He thrust him squeaking toward the door.

"Got a minute?" inquired Xaviera, with an inviting wriggle.

"Another time . . ." He watched through a crack in the door as Felix went tearing down the hall. As he'd expected, every tough ex-pug in Plotina's employ pelted at his heels, yelling for him to stop. Felix must have had more brains than any of them had given him credit for (Well, reflected Marcus, he could hardly have less), for he ran waving his arms, yelling, "Stop thief! Stop thief!" like a gawky rabbit at the head of a pack of slavering mastiffs who were also bellowing, "Stop thief!"

The whole melee went pouring down the stairs in a noisy cataract. Marcus straightened his twice-borrowed silks, cast a quick look up and down the milling crowds in the hall, blew a kiss at Xaviera, and walked down the back stairs.

As he passed through the baths he saw the group gathered at the foot of the main staircase. Bristling with indignation, Felix was being held against the wall by three armed bodyguards; in front of him were ranged Plotina, like a jewel-encrusted idol under at least ten pounds of gold ornaments, and Lucius, who sported a black eye. Lucius was snarling, "That isn't him, you unprintable jackasses!" and Felix protesting in his highfalutin voice, "Flamin' balls of Jupiter that's what I'm tellin' you! It's m'cousin! Looks just like me! Stole my clothes, beat me up—gone berserk, I tell you! If this's the sort of place you run, madam . . ."

Marcus tipped the bathman handsomely as he walked through the lobby. Felix's purse was far better lined than his own.

He waited for him in a discreet wineshop on the corner. Felix emerged from the baths a short time later, trailed by the faithful Giton and fulminating over the rip in his cloak. "B'Castor, you've torn it," he accused, aggrievedly, as Marcus got to his feet and fell into step with him.

Marcus looked at the slash. "I was lucky that wasn't through my belly," he said grimly. "That's too clean for a tear. It's a sword slash."

"Is it?" Felix examined it again, with renewed interest. Then, "Dash it, Professor, what were you doing messing about with swords? And why were they after you, anyway? Really, Caius has no call at all to say *I* get myself into stupid scrapes."

"This isn't a stupid scrape." They turned the corner of Tuscan Street, and along the New Way, the shadows of the torch sprawling drunkenly along the walls on both sides and the narrow archways overhead. "And where on earth did you get this outfit in the first place? I feel like somebody's bedboy."

"Well, whoever it is has dashed bad taste," sulked Felix. He skirted a particularly noisome pool of garbage. "Not that Caius'll ever speak to either one of us again, after tonight," he added as an afterthought. "Leaving him there with all those wretched mourners, and all."

"We'll have to go back there," said Marcus quietly, gathering the thick silk of his robe in one hand to keep it out of the mud. "We'll have to talk to Priscus Quindarvis."

"Quindarvis? What d'you need that sleek brute for? And listen, Professor . . ." He pulled something from the purse at his belt. "I respect your philosophy, an' all, but if you've turned Christian, Caius really *will* kill you.'' He held up the silver cross on its broken chain and regarded his brother with earnest, worried, sheeplike brown eyes.

''No,'' Marcus assured him gently. ''No, I haven't turned Christian. Listen, Felix. Tullia was up in that place, held prisoner in the attics. I think she's been there all the time. But this morning a girl—a Christian—went snooping around and discovered her there, and I think the kidnappers took fright and took her someplace.''

''A Christian?'' said Felix querulously. ''But I thought she was snatched by the Christians? Only this evenin' Consul Varus— You know Consul Varus is back? He said . . .''

''The Christians didn't take her,'' insisted Marcus.

''How d'you know? Stands to reason they would.''

''They just didn't. Shut up and let me talk. That's why I need to talk to Quindarvis. I know he's—he's a friend of Plotina's. He might be able to learn something, to give us some kind of clue—something he's heard . . .''

''Friend!'' hooted Felix. ''Holy tits of Venus, brother, what rock d'you philosophers hide under? Quindarvis *owns* the wretched place.''

Marcus stopped dead. ''What?''

''By Castor, yes. In fact it's one of his chief sources of income—that and his office, I bet. I mean, there's a difference between making money off a praetorship and havin' your hand in the till, and I ain't saying Quindarvis doesn't know what it is, but . . . Well, if there's ever an audit of his books he may find himself taking a quick trip to Gaul. Man's been all to pieces for these two years gone. Don't know how he coughed up the tin for the games.''

''Yes, but that doesn't mean . . .'' And Marcus' voice trailed off. He felt as though his eyes had been smitten by an enormous light, and stood blinking, gazing into darkness of the narrow street. ''Felix,'' he asked quietly, ''who audits the praetors when their term of office is over?''

His brother shrugged. ''Dashed if I know. Some Jew or other on the treasury staff, I suppose—half the staff's Jews, y'know. They're everywhere. That's why there's all this shifting from an eight-day week to a seven-day—blasted confusing, tryin' to figure out whether you're on a sabbath or not. I made up a little chart, once, for use with my moneylender, but dashed if I didn't lose it . . .''

Marcus whispered, ''That bastard.'' Certainty and rage poured into his veins like fire. ''That callous, calculating, vicious, coldhearted bastard.''

''No,'' protested Felix, ''quite a decent fellow, for a moneylender.''

Marcus swung around on him with startling fury. ''Quindarvis knew it!'' he raged. ''He knew what would happen if there was a general persecution of Christians! That if Varus' daughter was kidnapped it'd be the amphitheater for every Christian they could find *and their families* . . .''

''Well, of course,'' argued Felix reasonably. ''I mean, stands to reason. If you're going about eating babies, you can't hide something like that, y'know.''

''They do not eat babies!''

'' 'Course they do,'' protested his brother, laying a soothing hand on his arm. ''Everyone says so. You look a bit fagged, brother. Tryin' day, and all. Here's a wineshop, by midnight the old farm'll be cleared out enough that we can cut on home . . .''

''You go home,'' said Marcus quietly, resisting his brother's well-meaning tug on his mantle. His rage had turned suddenly to ice within him. ''You go home, and if someone comes demanding to see Quindarvis, delay them. Do whatever you have to, but keep Quindarvis from leaving Rome for as long as you can.''

''Here, are you all right?'' twittered Felix, feeling his hands for fever. ''What's Quindarvis got to do with it all, anyway?''

''Everything,'' said Marcus softly. ''Everything. Listen to me, Felix. You're Priscus Quindarvis. Praetor of Rome. Friend of all the aristocrats, in with the richest, the most socially prominent. It's an expensive crowd to run with—parties at a million sesterces a night, a villa that would make Nero's Golden House look like a shed. Pet lions. Dancing girls.

Your wife lives apart from you and you can't touch her wealth, but your father made a fortune from trade.

"But things haven't gone so well for you. You're living above your means. You can make money off your office, but if you lose that you're in over your head. So you make a bid to win popularity by giving the most fantastic games Rome ever saw. They're expensive, but the investment is worth it—and besides, it isn't your money anyway. All right?"

"All right," agreed Felix, puzzled, his soft eyes completely sober now, and grave.

"So you've got a clerk, who works with you, handling the treasury side of your affairs. A little Jew you despise, but he's smart. He knows money, and he's going to know when they run the general audit in July that the books don't balance. You know it's only a matter of time, but people have already begun to talk. Everyone in Rome knows you've been all to pieces for the last few years. If this little Jew should happen to choke to death on his Chanukah-fish or get beaten up by toughs in the street, maybe someone would think your ill will had something to do with it."

"Well," agreed Felix uneasily, "it doesn't do to rub folks' noses in things."

"No," said Marcus, "it doesn't. Especially if people have already begun to talk. But you happen to know your little Jew has a son. And his son's a Christian. And a lot of people aren't very clear anyway on the distinction between Christians and Jews—I'm not, myself, except that Jews don't scream at one another over their theology like Christians do. But the real distinction between Christians and Jews is that you can't be killed simply for being a Jew. Your whole family doesn't come under suspicion of treason simply because you're a Jew. Are you still following me?"

"Marcus," said Felix quietly, "I don't like this." In the jumping light and shadow from Giton's torch he looked ill.

"So what do you do?" pursued Marcus softly. "You might just kidnap the daughter of a powerful man who's once run spectacularly afoul of the Christians, which he could hardly help doing, being city prefect. Kidnap her in the presence of her mother and leave a Christian amulet on the scene. You don't even have to leave it, you can just palm it and pretend to pick it up from the mud yourself. You start rumors . . . You wait for Varus to come back to town . . . and his first morning back in town—"

"Marcus, stop it!" cried his brother, horrified.

There was an ugly, momentary silence in the lane, broken only by the clatter of cart traffic in the markets and the singing of a drunk two streets away. Then Marcus said softly, "Go back home. See if someone doesn't try and talk to Quindarvis."

Felix swallowed. "All right."

"And thank you. Thank you for everything."

Felix turned and pattered off down the lane, the gold stars flickering in the light of his slave's torch. Then he turned, seeing Marcus starting off up the rise to the Forum of Peace, and called out, "Brother?"

Marcus halted. "What is it, brother?"

"Where're you going?"

"Looking for Christians!" he yelled, and vanished at a run into the night.

XVIII

All things are lawful unto me—but not all things are expedient.

Saint Paul

"As I thought." Sixtus came limping back to the silent group that waited in the shadows of the dark elms by the road. "They're watching the wall, all the way along here." In the darkness of the trees, his toga and silvery beard gave him the moonlight glimmer of a ghost, a spirit risen from the tombs that lay like scattered bones among the groves on either side of them. "They've already been panicked. We're going to have to slip in among them without their knowing if we're going to get the girls out alive."

No one, Marcus noticed, had asked if the old man had a plan. After this long it was something one took for granted.

Telesphorus asked, "Are you sure they'll still be alive?"

The old man hesitated. "I think so. Quindarvis didn't know when Varus would be returning to Rome."

"This is madness," whispered Judah. In the Roman helmet his brown face looked stark, somehow stripped to its bones and very severe. The roached red crest stirred in the breeze as he moved his head to scan the dark countryside between them

274

and the park wall. "If anything goes wrong, if that girl is killed, with Christians raiding the place, we will have precipitated the very thing you've been fighting to avoid."

"Hardly." Sixtus leaned on his staff. "The die has already been thrown—it was thrown the moment Varus walked into Caius Silanus Senior's house. We can only hope to delay the consequences long enough to disarm the trap." He glanced from Judah to the other three soldiers in the company— Churaldin, Alexandros, and Anthony, whom Marcus had encountered on the night of the jailbreak. Word had evidently gone out—some twenty Christians had been mustered from groups all over Rome. Only their universal awe of Sixtus kept them from a major doctrinal showdown on the spot.

"You think this'll work?" inquired Anthony, unworriedly.

"It stands an even chance. Faced with authority, Quindarvis' slaves might not be so willing to lay down their lives for their master, particularly if they are under the impression that he has already been arrested. There's a handful of toughs we may have to worry about, ex-gladiators mostly, but they'll all be down watching the road."

"Yes, the road," sneered Ignatius. "Or are we all going to disincorporate the coequal portions of our bodies and spirits and pass among them unseen?"

"We will use deeper means than that," replied Sixtus serenely, while from the half-seen posse the tall woman's voice hissed, "And in any case only a heretic would think that kind of disincorporation possible, since the divine spark—"

"—is too extensive a topic to be discussed now," finished Sixtus for her. He turned to the others, mostly men and boys but including two women, the gigantic Hebe and Anthony's tough little wife, Miriam. "You all understand what you must do?" he asked them. "We're searching for Dorcas and another girl, a thin girl of sixteen with curly brown hair. If she isn't found—or if she's found dead—we're finished, and the Church of Rome with us. We're not here to fight, and we're not here to prove anything. We're here to clear the Church of a hideous charge and to save everyone—family, wives, children—from being wiped out in a general persecution. The men we run into may be armed, so by all that's holy, if you can do it, run. We'll regroup at the catacombs when Betelgeuse rises, fall back at the old Mithraeum at dawn. All right?''

There was a murmuring among them—Marcus thought he saw the woman Miriam grin and slap a little piece of steel braided in rawhide into her palm. Judah growled, ''Thus shall the unrighteous be smitten by the hand of God,'' and Sixtus retorted, ''Since the unrighteous are going to be extremely well-armed I'd advise you to be careful about whom you smite.'' He gathered up his toga and set off up the bank, scrambling through the long rank grass with the Christians following like a border patrol behind him. An owl hooted somewhere in the night. Rather like an old white owl himself, Sixtus led the way toward the pale bulk of a tomb, set apart in its little orchard.

Marcus recognized it at once, the dirty marble walls, the overgrown pepper and willow trees. It was the old tomb that had once belonged to some member of the Flavian family, the entrance to the Christian catacombs. He whispered, ''Sixtus?'' The old man, engaged in hanging a lantern on the end of his staff, glanced over at him curiously. ''You aren't . . . ? What you said to them, about the Church of Rome . . . ?''

''A good general always gives his troops a pep talk before the battle,'' smiled Sixtus.

''But you said that the Church would perish 'with us.' You—you aren't a Christian yourself, are you?''

''I shall certainly be executed for one if Churaldin and Alexandros are gathered in.'' He led the way down the worn marble steps, the iron foot of his staff scraping on the slick stone. It was only then that Marcus realized how they were going to enter Quindarvis' private parklands. He noticed also that Sixtus, like the Christians he'd spoken to by the Tiber bridges, had not answered his question. He was beginning to realize that Sixtus very often didn't.

With a muted rattling of panoplies, their four counterfeit Praetorians followed them down the long gallery, the little lantern throwing immense shadows on the sealed niches and plasterwork garlands of the walls. Rats fled squeaking, red eyes gleaming balefully from the shadows; Sixtus limped ahead as though he were crossing the atrium of his own house. Looking behind him, Marcus saw the shadowy faces of the Christians like ghosts in the dark: Telesphorus with his black dog Ignatius at his heels, Hebe and Josephus arguing for all the world like a shopkeeper bickering with a stingy customer over the price of turnips, until you caught phrases like " . . . but if you don't have the knowledge of the perfect gnosis, the divine emanations . . ."

For the rest of them, they looked like the worst scum of the streets, dirty, uncouth, and ignorant. At least two wore the metal collars some masters put on slaves. If they were opposed by their faith to violence in any form, for some of them it didn't look like a renunciation of long standing. As Sixtus scrambled down the ladder to the mazes below, Marcus heard the soft quibbling whispers. ". . . Well what does your priest know about it? Ours says a priest has to be pure before he can consecrate the bread and wine!" "Who says?" "Our priest says!" "Well it stands to reason that . . ." "You fleabitten heretic, there is no reason in faith!"

Sixtus led the way unhesitatingly through the dark windings of the first level, turning and twisting through narrowing galleries with their gray sealed wall niches, until they reached a ladder going down. Marcus didn't think it was the same ladder Arrius had found on his former visit, but in the damp, clay-smelling mazes it was hard to be sure. From the darkness below the smell of water came to him, and the wet slipping of furry bodies. Out of the black corridors behind, Ignatius whispered viciously, "Anyone who thinks they can buy their way to salvation by good deeds is a fool! The emperor does good, after his fashion, the prideful, maggot-eaten idolater! In faith, and faith alone, lies salvation . . ." "That's a pile of horse-dung! Who gave you the authority . . . ?"

"How did you know about this?" hissed Marcus, as Sixtus climbed nimbly down the second ladder to the black stinking seam of the lower level. "Don't tell me this comes under the heading of research into eastern religions!"

"Not directly," returned Sixtus evenly, holding the lantern

aloft to light his feet as he descended. "But as we found in the case of Tiridates, Rome is a honeycomb of tunnels; the Christians aren't the only ones who use them. In my research I've come across whole conventicles of Black Gnostics who haven't seen daylight in years and can travel underground from one end of Rome to the other, although personally I've always thought that a respectable appearance and a sufficiently authoritative manner can take you much farther."

Later Marcus calculated they could not have been underground for more than half a summer hour. But at the time the darkness seemed to go on forever. The stinking catacomb was succeeded by a repulsive tunnel roofed in ancient stone that had once been part of an Etruscan sewer, foul with ancient mud and alive with rats. This in turn gave onto the underground galleries of some other forgotten tomb, its roof half caved-in, the thin topaz gleam of Sixtus' lantern dancing like a demon's eye over broken slabs of carved sarcophagi and scattered, grinning bones. The stench of dust and water and decay filled his nostrils; the constant, fitful murmur of the Christians bickering trailed them like the chittering of ghosts. At times the tunnels grew so narrow that his vision was limited to a splinter of deep rose light edging the white hair of the man before him and the red glint of eyes in the dark. Once the tunnel was half-flooded in several inches of noisome water; he whispered, as they hopped over it, "Was that the Styx?" and Sixtus whispered back, "Certainly. I hope you have no objections to three-headed dogs?" "No, one of my mother's lapdogs had three heads . . ."

Then they ascended a makeshift ladder, and he felt dusty air open up all around him, warm and close. Only a thin chink of light escaped the lantern; he felt Sixtus' hand on his sleeve, drawing him out of the way as the others emerged.

"Where are we?" he whispered, hearing his own voice rebound from hard walls and a low ceiling.

"The vaults below the little temple in Quindarvis' gardens," replied the old man softly. "It was built on the foundations of a much older and larger shrine."

"That filthy bag of abominations would take to his use the

haunts of demons,'' whispered Ignatius' shrill voice out of the darkness.

"How far are we from the main house?'' inquired the ever-practical Anthony.

"Not far—twenty yards or so. Soldiers with me. Civilians fan out, stay low, search as much and as fast as you can. Keep as quiet as you're able. God knows when Quindarvis is likely to return. Your charming brother may be a doughty fighter, Marcus, but presumably he can't hold him in Rome forever. Even if he went to the officials, I'm not sure that Arrius—if he could find him at this time of night—would respond to a complaint against so prominent a citizen on so little evidence.''

Marcus caught the edge of his toga as they started toward the worn and ancient steps just visible as Sixtus uncovered his lantern. "You do think I'm right, don't you?'' he whispered anxiously. "About Quindarvis?''

His strange old commander raised white bristling brows. "They're certainly guarding the road against someone.''

After the fetid dark of the tombs the night was a scented paradise, a bath of sweet-smelling oils and tepid water, redolent of roses, honeysuckle, jasmine. Like a Persian carpet, starry darkness stretched overhead; against its hem the hills of Rome glittered like a border of goldwork and gems. On such a night, Marcus thought, it was possible to believe that the stars sang.

"Lights up in the villa,'' whispered Churaldin.

Sixtus nodded. "With me,'' he said softly. "We'll see how long we can bluff them. Light the torches.''

They clattered up the terrace steps, four Praetorians in their crested helmets, a cold and haughty citizen with the bearing of a consul at least, and a gawky overdressed clerk in a gay Persian cloak and swirling robe at his side. The noise brought them running, the fat majordomo in his scarlet tunic, the flock of house slaves, none of whom appeared to have been in their beds, and two grim ex-gladiators with muscles like wet shining rocks in the torchlight. The torches they'd lit from Sixtus' lantern threw a brilliant circle of gold around them on the inlaid marbles of the pavement, gleaming on the burnished armor and incidentally blinding the eyes of everyone there to whatever movements might have been seen in the darkness beyond.

Churaldin barked, "Clietos, slave of Priscus Quindarvis?" Sixtus had evidently learned the name of the majordomo on the night of the banquet, a circumstance that the slave found tremendously disconcerting. He approached cringing.

Sixtus said, "In the name of Tullius Varus, consul of Rome and prefect of the city for His Imperial Majesty, Emperor Trajan, I place you under arrest on charges of kidnapping, rape, and conspiracy to do murder, and for these same charges you will be detained for questioning with regards to your master, the said Priscus Quindarvis."

The taller of the two gladiators rasped, "I don't know what you're talking about," in the same moment that Clietos cried, "We never laid a hand on her!"

The gladiator drew his sword and struck in the same movement, a belly rip that somehow snagged in the voluminous folds of Sixtus' toga as a dog's teeth will snag in the loose skin of a twisting cat. In the instant it took for him to drag it free for another cut, Sixtus hit him and tripped him at the same time; the crack of his skull striking the marble was audible even above the general confusion of the fight. Panting, Churaldin and Alexandros threw the other armed man to his knees and took his sword, while Judah caught Clietos by the scruff of the neck and the majordomo wailed, "She was never here! I never knew anything about it! They made me do it!"

"Where is she?" demanded Marcus furiously. The rest of the slaves who'd come flocking to the terrace stayed where they were in a scared huddle. Two of them had attacked Anthony in the general melee, but the one of them who was still conscious was sorry he had done so.

"I don't know! I don't know!" the miserable butler was sobbing.

Judah shook him like a rag doll. "Is she in the house?"

"No! She isn't anywhere! They took her away! She was never here in the first place!"

"Search the house," snapped Sixtus, turning with the gladiator's sword in his hand. He faced out into the cricket-crying darkness beyond the torchlight. "Surround the villa!" he called out. "Kill anyone who tries to leave." All the slaves on the terrace cowered and tried to look as homebound as possible. Sixtus limped back, caught Clietos' tunic in a rough grip, and stared at him with the cold imperiousness that had terrified two generations of frontier legionnaires. "Where's the girl?" he asked quietly.

"I don't know! They took her away from the house . . ." He almost choked himself on denials.

"Is there a fire still in the kitchen?"

"Yes, sir, of course—I mean, no!" he gasped, realizing belatedly the intent. "It's gone out, I don't know anything, don't—"

"You." Sixtus pointed to a cowering Syrian boy. "Go light it and put a poker and a handful of coins and some tongs in the coals."

The boy raced off like a little hare, pursued by the majordomo's despairing screams. "Lock him up," ordered Sixtus offhandedly. "Tie these two and lock them in the cellar. Judah, Anthony, keep guard over these scum"—he flicked a scornful glance over the slaves—"Marcus, come with me."

"You aren't really going to torture him?" whispered Marcus in a horrified undervoice as they swept from the terrace into the house.

"Of course not. I'm almost certain the man knows nothing. But I've managed to terrorize the rest of them without lifting a hand."

Telesphorus and Hebe met them in the atrium. Around them the house was in confusion, slaves running this way and that, shadows slipping through other shadows. The bobbing of lamps and torches threw eerie racing gleams over dark pillars of porphyry and lapis, the sparkle of gilding and the cool green malachite floor. "This place is enormous," complained the priest. "It stinks of effeminacy, of fornication and idolatry. We've searched the lower floor . . ."

"They wouldn't keep her in an inhabited part of the house, would they?" protested Marcus, and Sixtus gave him a sharp sidelong look.

"What slave of Quindarvis' would have nerve enough to tell anyone if they did?"

"Miriam went through the attics," continued Hebe. "Martin and his group took the stables; Dio, Narses, and Josephus are going through the other wing of the house."

"There's a little temple kind of place farther out in the gardens," added Marcus. "There're supposed to be grottoes, too, down in the water gardens below the terrace . . ."

Telesphorus groaned, "We haven't got all night."

"No," agreed Sixtus, "and it's only a matter of time before one of the household slaves decides not to believe my convincing remarks about the house being surrounded. You check the temple—can it be seen from the terrace? Marcus, we'll look through the water gardens . . ."

From the distant terrace Judah's voice bellowed, "We have guests!" and the richly painted walls suddenly echoed with the pounding fury of hobnailed boots as Quindarvis' private troop of tough-guys effected an entrance from both sides of the villa at once.

"Drat," said Sixtus. "Can you handle this?" He handed Marcus the sword he'd had from the original gladiator.

"No! I've never touched one of the things in my life!"

From an adjoining drawing room a wild shrieking cry rose, "I will smite the Philistines in the name of the God of Hosts!" accompanied by a splintering crash, and the cacophonous rattle of an armored body hitting the marble.

Sixtus grabbed Marcus' cloak and dragged him toward the triumphal arch that led into the hallway. Gladiators poured into the atrium, drawn swords flaming in the ruddy glare of the few lamps, scarred ugly faces offering no hope of quarter. Half of them bore down on Telesphorus and Hebe, only to have the two Christians duck aside at the last moment to reveal the impluvium in the shadows behind them. As half-a-dozen men hit the water in a foaming wrath of shining muscle and armor, the Christians and their allies faded like wraiths from the room.

"Which way is it to these grottoes?" asked the old man, dodging into the first door they came to in the darkness of the corridor.

"We're not still going to search them?"

"Certainly we are. The guards were expecting force—they haven't the slightest idea what's happening. They'll storm through the house for a good twenty minutes looking for someone to fight." They hastened across the lapis floor of a small dining room, Sixtus' staff clicking on the inlays, and slipped through heavy curtains into a courtyard redolent of jasmine and rustling plane trees nourished on wine. Like a cat, another shadow faded into being beside them, Marcus startling at the sight of armor. Churaldin's voice said, "Nowhere in the house."

"Kitchen wing?"

"Just came from there. Cellars, too. Great Llyr!" he cursed, backsliding into momentary paganism as a sudden scarlet flare leaped in the windows of a room across the court. A moment later the dark yellowish flicker in the room next to it strengthened suddenly to hot springing orange.

"Just as well," said Sixtus callously. "We can search the outbuildings in some kind of peace." Greedy light illuminating other dark windows marked the fire's spread; if a large lamp had been knocked over, thought Marcus, spilling oil would carry it everywhere. "Are those two thugs in the cellar?"

Churaldin shook his head, flame sliding on the edge of his burnished helmet. "We left them tied on the terrace."

"Good. Their—" He looked up suddenly, startled at some sound, and over the growing roar of the fire Marcus heard it, too. Hooves clattered wildly beyond the walls, and with them, the careening scrunch of wheels on the gravel on the drive.

They exchanged one fast, horrified look, and Marcus said,

"Quindarvis. He brought Aurelia Pollia to the funeral in a cisium . . ."

"He'll go straight to her." Sixtus was already headed for the doors that would take them through to the terrace, Marcus and Churaldin catching up behind. Firelight from the opposite windows banded his toga with blood as he crossed through the shadows of the columns. "He has nothing to lose now and he knows it."

The younger men broke into a run, leaving Sixtus limping behind. Marcus flung open a bronze-bound door that he recalled led into the great dining room, and found himself staring into an inferno of blazing curtains and couches, the wild illumination rippling and spreading along the painted panels of the ceiling. Churaldin yelled, "The whole wing's burning!" wrapped his face in his short soldier's cloak, and ran like a madman through the blaze. After a split-second hesitation, Marcus followed. A burning rafter fell between them; he leaped over it, seeing as he did so a fire-framed tableau of two slaves at the far wall, trying to wrest a pair of enormous gold-and-ivory sconces from their bolts. The Briton kicked open the doors to the terrace, and he and Marcus plunged through the flaming curtains into the safety of the outer air.

Blazing red light poured onto the drive, throwing into stark relief the light open cisium with its two stamping, terrified horses. It was surrounded by armed men, the gladiators shouting, waving their arms, fire and shadow dyeing them red and black like an ancient vase. Marcus saw Quindarvis' face, set with rage and horror and that cold hard look men have when their plans come to grief and they seek a way to salvage what they can at any cost. Turning to follow the praetor's gaze he saw the reason: The whole villa was one great pyre, sheets of flame like a waterfall streaming upward from its roof. He heard him curse and shout an order to his driver, saw the heads of the horses wrenched brutally around, and the black-snake lick of the whip. The carriage bounced high on its two wheels as it hit the rough stones of the drive, then vanished into the darkness.

"Follow them!" yelled Marcus, and started to race along the terrace. The roar of falling beams echoed from the dining room behind him, and with a hoarse cry he swung back, remembering Sixtus' slower, limping steps.

Every curtain of that room was blazing; beyond the archways was nothing but a wall of searing flame, as though he looked into a furnace. Black against the unbearable brightness, Churaldin was dragging his master, who was choking on inhaled smoke and struggling to get free. As Marcus came running to them, Sixtus managed to get breath enough to snap, "Don't just stand there gawping, which way did they go?"

"Down the road, toward the woods."

The old man wrenched his arms free irritably and started to limp along the streaming firclight of the polished pavement. "What's in that direction?"

Marcus and Churaldin caught him up between them, half-dragging him with their swifter strides. At the end of the terrace they dropped off into a wall of myrtle and scented shrubs, the smell of roses surrounding them like the summer ocean. Firelight poured over them bright as day, but beyond, the night seemed the blacker for it. Over the bellowing roar of the blaze, the shouting of the slaves, the gladiators' curses, Marcus strained his ears to catch the wild retreating clatter of the carriage.

And distantly, he heard another sound over the blowing confusion of the night, a bass booming echo, deadly and feral.

It took him a moment to realize that it was the roaring of lions.

The little pleasure pavilion glowed in the darkness like a lighted lamp. The richness of its interior that Marcus had only been able to guess at before showed up like an illuminated window: the worked marble of the floor, scattered with carpets of Persia and the East; the lampstands of nymphs and chimeras bearing their soft glowing flames. The cushions of the couches were white, embroidered with red flowers—at this distance they might have been stippled with spilled blood.

But all this Marcus saw as a hideous backdrop, like the painted scenery on a stage, behind the struggling figures between the columns that supported the pavilion's roof. As he broke from the woods to the narrow clearing around the rim of the pit, he heard Tullia's voice, choked and inarticulate over the some fifty feet that separated them, and then Quindarvis', clear and hard, saying, "You silly bitch, I haven't got time for your stupid tricks." He saw the praetor silhouetted against the rosy glow from the little dining room, gripping a small thin form that struggled determinedly, kicking at his shins and fighting to free her arms. He knew with a part of his mind that there were other men in the pavilion, but those two only he saw, fighting as the big man dragged her to the rim of the gilded floor, and the twelve-foot drop, the lions stalking back and forth below. Quindarvis cursed as she bit his arm. Marcus moved toward the distant bridge, then froze in horror as the man shoved her between the pillars. For an instant they rocked on the brink, the girl fighting for balance against his greater weight and strength; there was a crashing, a man's voice cursing, in the pavilion behind. Time seemed to stand still; he was aware of Churaldin racing along the brink of the pit for the bridgehead, and equally aware that he would never reach it in time. In a sort of detached slow motion he saw Tullia's feet slip, saw Quindarvis shove her outward, and the white flash of her limbs in the tangle of her pale dress as she fell.

She hit the ground hard at the foot of the wall, the lions startling back. In the next second a great slopping drench of fire fell from above, thrown outward and down, hitting the ground in a rough semicircle in front of where she lay and blazing up brightly against the darkness. From the pavilion there was a ringing clatter of a falling lampstand, men cursing, and the meaty slap of blows. Two men in armor shoved another woman forward, her black curling hair falling thickly over her bleeding face. Down below the lions were shying back from the blaze of the spilled lamp oil that lay between them and Tullia; Quindarvis was heard to say, "You whore-sons should have stopped the little slut." He caught Dorcas by the back of her dress with the gesture of a man shoving his way impatiently through a crowd, and thrust her unceremoni-ously out over the edge.

She was conscious enough to grab at the edge, but missed it and fell hard. The lions were circling, snarling; she crawled weakly for the protection of the fire and Tullia scrambled on her hands and knees to drag her behind it. The darkness all around them seemed to be alive, a moving ripple of tawny fur, and the jeweled flash of eyes.

The whole could not have taken more than ten seconds.

"Marcus! Churaldin!" It was the voice of the hunter who calls his dogs, and like trained dogs they returned to the man who could command. Sixtus was already stripping off his toga. "There's six of them in the pavilion, the footbridge can be defended by one. Give me your cloak, Marcus."

He fumbled with the long ornamental pins that held the folds to his shoulders, pricking his fingers and cursing. His eyes never left the two girls, sitting against the rough wall of the pavilion's base. Tullia got cautiously to her feet, moving with the slow grace of a perilous dancer; in a chorus the lions growled, watching her beyond the sinking wall of the flames. Slowly she glided to the bronze door that was set in the rough stones, tried its handle, pulling as hard as she could without making a sudden movement. Two lionesses began to circle around the end of the puddle of burning oil and the rank sparse grasses and weeds that had caught, and Tullia slipped hastily back to Dorcas' side. Her dark hair hung down in a mane over her back. Against the short, unbleached slave's tunic she wore, her arms were like peach-colored silk, bur-nished by the light of the flames.

He shouted "Tullia!" and she looked up, her face flooding with joy.

But she called out to him, "There are men in the pavil-ion." The practicality was so typical of her that he would have laughed had the danger not been so terrible. In danger, he thought, it was like her to warn him first, and thank him after. It would take more than lions to break courage like hers.

He called back, "I know." Close by, he saw Churaldin cinching the end of a rope of knotted cloth around the bole of the beech tree at the precipice's edge: his scarlet soldier's cloak, Sixtus' toga, poor Felix's beautiful green-and-bronze peacock silk. Between the girls and the lions, the wall of fire was sinking as the oil burned itself out.

Movement caught his eye, and he swung back, hearing a soft *thunk* and the violent rustle of bodies hitting the leaves. He ducked and felt something slide by his ear, turned and rammed forward with his head into something armored that nevertheless gave back with a gasped "Woof!" Hard fingers clawed at his throat as he was rolled and spun down into the leaves. Marcus clutched at them, managed to get a final squeaking gasp of air, and rammed his knee up as hard as he could between his assailant's legs, nearly breaking his kneecap on the hard-boiled leather of the man's codpiece. Above him he saw the white glint of teeth in a tangled beard, as he had in the darkness of the street outside Consul Varus' house, a little over a week ago. Thumbs dug into his throat, elbows curving outward to block his flailing hands. His ears roared, and he felt his struggling muscles slack. He rolled, trying to shake off the death that pinned him, and felt something jab his ribs on the ground. It was one of the long brooch pins that had been in Felix's lovely cloak.

The man above him was armored, but through his blurring eyes Marcus could see the gleam of sweat in the exposed hollow of the brown throat. It took his last strength, but he felt skin, muscle, windpipe puncture, and Lucius' weight rolled back from him, his eyes staring and his breath whistling in horrible gasps as he pawed at the knot of jewels sticking out of his flesh. Marcus heaved him off, gagging himself on returning air. The man tumbled thrashing into the leaves, and when he tried to rise, more from instinct than anything else, Marcus kicked him with all his strength in the side. The man shot backward . . . and fell.

He heard one of the girls cry out, and a sudden bass snarling roar from animal throats. Someone dragged him to his feet, shoved a torch into his hand, thrust him stumbling through a world that dipped and spun. The dragged hem of his ridiculous Persian robe tripped him as he stumbled, and a heavy hand pulled him upright. The ringing in his ears occluded sound; then he became aware of a deep urgent voice saying, "Do you hear me? Marcus? Can you do it? Marcus?"

He nodded, gasping, as the world slowly came into focus and the darkness around him became once more cool and open, instead of black and close and beating. He whispered, "Yes," and felt the pinch of his cracked ribs again.

"You're sure?"

Sixtus' face was scratched and bleeding, close to his; farther away Churaldin lay among the leaves, blood spilling over his slashed face, close by the body of a dead gladiator whose cut throat had sprayed the surrounding trees in gore. The night stank of blood, the roaring of the lions filling his ears as the beat of his own heart had filled them a few moments before. He gasped, "Yes. Yes, I can." He saw two other men unconscious on the ground and remembered the old man's deadly facility with his hardwood staff.

The strong grip half-supported him, half-thrust him toward the makeshift rope. "Quindarvis and one other are still in the pavilion, I believe. We could force our way in, but it would take more time than we've got."

It was no easy task to scramble down the knotted cloth and keep one hand free for the torch. The lions were still horribly busy, tearing and snarling; their lashing tails and tawny backs made a dark knot in the moonlight. There were more of them than he'd thought—eight or ten. Some of them looked up with dripping muzzles as he stepped away from the cliff, their eyes like amber mirrors in the torchlight.

Something fell from above, the lions all startling and backing. Looking down he saw it was Sixtus' staff. With a ringing clank a sword was dropped as well, and before he could protest, the old man came sliding nimbly down the improvised rope.

"You're crazy," he gasped, and Sixtus said, "Move! Go

slow and smooth, and for God's sake don't startle them. They have their taste of blood now.''

Dark-muzzled as though they had been drinking wine, the lions circled them. The ammonia reek of their urine, the dusty fetor of their pelts, and the rankness of carrion filled the air of the pit. Marcus could feel his own blood hammering in his veins, life and terror burning in him as he edged his way across the rank deep weeds to the shorter grass near the pavilion; saw how the lions were already prowling back to the dying glow of the spent lamp oil. Dorcas and Tullia had got to their feet but were standing perfectly still against the wall; only the glint of their eyes moved in the growing dark. A shift in the night wind rippled in their garments, outlining their bodies where the cloth stuck to them with sweat.

Dorcas said, "I knew you'd come. Did you torch the villa?"

"You're going to give me a worse reputation than I have already," murmured Sixtus, holding out his hand for them. A lioness crouched to spring; Marcus took a step toward her, thrusting with the torch, and the circle of cats broke a little, snarling and flashing their stained dripping teeth. The girls came slowly, their eyes wide with fear but untouched by panic, barefoot and smooth as dancers in the sparse stony grass.

They moved from the wall, and like sharks around a slave galley, the lions moved with them. Marcus swung the torch and the circle widened again; he felt his every nerve strained to the cracking point, conscious of each movement in that dense hunting darkness. They picked their way over the stones, the girls pressing close to his back, Sixtus moving behind with his sword. Every now and then the lions would prowl too near, and he would slash at them with the fire; to his keyed nerves the world narrowed to the tiny ring of amber light, the black dark just beyond it, the touch of a small cold hand every now and then on his shoulder, the hungry hate of the gleaming eyes, and the thick panting breath in the darkness.

And thus he didn't see Priscus Quindarvis until it was far too late.

Tullia gasped "Marc!" at the same instant he thought he heard a wasp buzz close by his ear—only wasps do not fly at midnight. He felt her stumble against him, clutching at the slippery silk of his fringed sleeve, and turning saw the red gash on her arm and, beyond her, Sixtus crumpling slowly to his knees. Tullia cried out, and from the darkness the lions closed in. With a desperate yell of fury he lashed about him with the torch, blindly concentrating on one thing at a time, and when he looked up, the makeshift rope lay like a heap of old clothes at the bottom of the cliff, directly below where Quindarvis stood.

He had a bow in one hand, the arrows lying on the ground at his feet. Sweat plastered his white tunic of mourning to his heavy body, and his face gleamed in the light from the pavilion, sticky with unguents from the funeral banquet. His mouth was a taut black line of anger, not a personal hate, but the enraged frustration of a businessman whose plans have been thwarted by malign fate.

He said, "You stupid meddling boy."

Behind him Marcus heard Sixtus whisper, "Get away from me. Get under the cliff, he can't hit you from there." Glancing back he saw the old man propped on one arm, the arrow standing in his right shoulder and blood running down the shaft to drip from the saturated feathers to the grass. The lions were growling, scenting the blood, and Marcus stepped back to stand over him, slashing at them with the torch. They backed, but not nearly as far as before; they were hungry, and the blood drew them.

Marcus turned to yell, "You'll never get away with this!"

The praetor didn't even bother to reply. He stooped to pick up another arrow, his cynical eyes hard and angry, choosing his victim. It occurred to Marcus that he knew his plans were shattered beyond repair. Instead of running, he had stayed to take his revenge.

He was nocking the arrow as he straightened. Marcus wondered if he would shoot him first or the girls. The torchlight against the darkness made them all splendid targets, and at this range he could hardly miss.

Then a voice screeched like a wildcat from the darkness,
"DEATH TO THE BEAST OF A THOUSAND NAMES!" and Ignatius—
small, vicious, and wholly unexpected—slammed into Quindarvis' back like a bolt from a catapult, swinging hard little
balls of fists and screaming apocalyptic curses. Balanced on
the very edge of the precipice Quindarvis staggered, tottered,
his hands clinging to the bow and his mouth opening in
horrified shock. Dirt crumbled under his sandals; the arrows
showered down around him like falling twigs while the little
saint screeched with vindictive triumph on the pit's edge.

The lions swung, snarling, toward the sudden movement as
the praetor hit the long grass at the base of the cliff. But
Quindarvis had a speed and a kind of hard grasping strength
that Marcus had hardly credited him with. He flung himself to
his feet in a long rolling dive and launched himself at Marcus
in a flying tackle, his hands grabbing for the torch. The
impact of his body threw them both backward; Marcus felt
knees jab into his broken ribs, a powerful grip wrenching and
twisting at the wood in his hands, and he held to it with the
blind certainty that to let go would be death indeed. His
mouth was full of sand and rocks and long dry grass. He
rolled, clinging to the grappling body, smelling the sweat and
dirt and smoke mixed with musk and cinnamon perfume,
hearing the lions roaring in anger and confusion all around
them. His hand was slammed down, beating on some rocks.
His fingers opened, empty.

Quindarvis tried to free himself in a flopping dive and
Marcus clinched his arms around that hard thick body in a
death-grip. Past the man's thick wet shoulder he could see the
torch lying in a patch of stony sand, smothered and flickering
its last. Dorcas caught at it, her tense pointed face blanched
even in the warm light; touched the last of the fire to the
raked bundle of dried weeds she held in her hand.

The light exploded into the faces of the lions. They sprang
back like startled cats as she waded toward them, swinging
the knot of fire; Marcus had a blurred vision of Tullia tearing
at the weeds, winding them in a ripped piece of her dress as

Dorcas had done, to protect her hand. Then Quindarvis' weight rolled across him, and he was shoved brutally aside.

The big man was gasping, his hard face clotted with fury under the sticky mess of perfumed dust. He glanced quickly around, as if gauging his flight, knowing there was none. The torn weeds burned with a hot clear light, but they burned fast; those in Dorcas' hand were already dimming, where she stood with her feet braced over Sixtus' body in the blood-stained grass.

Marcus whispered, "You stinking coward."

Quindarvis seemed hardly to have heard. His eyes were still traveling around the dark wall, the locked pavilion, seeking an escape. Marcus realized that he himself was as incidental to the man's scheme as the Christians, or Tullia, or her mother's hideous grief had been. Like the little dancing-girls at the banquet, they'd been part of the background; like so many thrushes, killed and plucked to make a pleasant meal. The man's whole-souled self-centeredness had made no distinction between them at all.

"You murdering bastard!" he shrieked, more to get his attention than anything else, to get him to look, just once, at one of them as a human being instead of as a step toward the goal.

But the praetor's glance held only irritation, as though a lobster had nipped his fingers from the pot. "You don't know anything about it, boy," he muttered, and swung around as Dorcas slashed with her improvised torch at the nearest of the advancing cats.

Like the blade of a sword, light touched them, a gold slit pouring through the door at the pavilion's base. The darkness opened, like the gates of heaven; framed within the doors Marcus glimpsed Telesphorus' bald shining head, the burnished gleam of the armor Alexandros wore, the crowding shapes of the rest of the Children of Light. With only a single guard left they must have forced the pavilion doors in silence.

Later, when he thought about it, Marcus thought Quindarvis should have known better. But whether he had got drunk at the funeral banquet of his colleague Silanus, or whether he had grown careless with despair, or whether from where they all crouched in the sparse wiry bloodstained grass, among the closing lions and the dying fire, it had looked to be a better gamble—Quindarvis made a run for the door.

Judah Symmachus told him afterward that they could hear him shrieking as far away as the villa, even over the noise of the fire.

XIX

One should not believe in conspiracies until they have attained their goal.

Domitian, emperor of Rome

"Mad?" Felix critically inspected a sliver of lobster held delicately between two fingers, then popped it into his mouth. "B'Castor, I'd be half-mad, too, if I'd had a villa that cost as much as his did, and came back to find the whole thing in flames. D'you know what that place must have cost him?"

"Close to ten million sesterces," replied Arrius equably, "at a conservative estimate. But of course, he didn't pay for it all."

"Didn't he, by Jove? Who did?"

"Your father, for one," replied the centurion, holding out his cup for Alexandros to pour the wine. "And your brother Caius, and myself, and every other person in this city who's ever paid taxes. You were right, Marcus. Old Symmachus started on the audit today. If word of that had got back to the emperor, I'd be surprised if our friend would have come out of it with his head."

"He would not have." Varus moved slightly on his couch,

the gems of his rings flashing in the dappled light that came through the wall of vines. In that handsome face his dark eyes were brooding and angry. "His Highness may be a soldier, with a soldier's tastes and crudities, but he is hardly a barrack-room emperor. He has striven to make Rome as clean, as upright, and as honorable under his rule as it was in the days of the ancient republic."

"I pray Isis he will succeed," murmured his wife, and lifted her cup in a small gesture of libation, which her husband ignored. She glanced sideways at her daughter, who sat, as all good Roman daughters should, at her parents' feet. Her thin face glowed, and she added softly, "For I know truly now that Isis answers prayers."

"By Jove I hope she'll answer that one," twittered Felix. "Don't think I could stand another night like that one. Let's have the mustard, O frater mine."

"You acquitted yourself like a soldier," smiled Sixtus, reclining on his couch at the head of the table. He reached stiffly for his winecup, and Dorcas, who sat at his feet, handed it to him. "Tell me, just out of curiosity. How did you contrive to delay Quindarvis' arrival at the villa? You gave us the time we needed; had he arrived any sooner it could have been extremely embarrassing for us."

"Maybe I should leave," offered Arrius, making as if to rise. "I'm not sure I ought to know this."

"No, no! Perfectly decent—well, classical, anyhow. Fact is, it's just about the only thing I remember out of my schooling. Some Greek or other used it to fox a chariot race. You pull the linchpin out of the wheel and stick a wax one in the hole instead. Works just fine till you get going, then slam! You're on the pavement. Not surprised he was annoyed. Dashed dirty trick. If you whittle it down a bit a candle works just fine. Pass the mustard, Professor."

"He was an evil man," said Aurelia Pollia quietly, "and I cannot say that I'm sorry that he came to the end he did."

"It was merciful," said Varus dryly, "compared to what it would have been."

"What is hard to believe," she continued, running the

embroidered edge of her shawl through small fragile fingers, "is that he knew. I don't understand someone like that; who comforted me, all that first night and all the next day; who cared for me; who stayed with me at a time when I was so distracted I think I would have lost my mind."

"I suspect," said Sixtus quietly, "that he stayed with you chiefly to make sure that you did not start asking yourself questions, such as, with the whole route from the Aventine to the Quirinal Hill to choose from, why did they decide to kidnap her on her very doorstep? And why would a man spend the day before the games he was sponsoring—the day when all the business of them has to be settled—loitering around the house of an absent patron, as Nicanor tells me he had from the eighth hour onward."

There was a long pause. Then Lady Aurelia said, "I feel very badly about Nicanor. He was so good, and so helpful to me that night; and then to do that to him."

"Well, y'know, slaves have to expect that kind of thing," reasoned Felix brightly. "I mean, if they get on the wrong side of the law . . ." He glanced hastily around at Churaldin, who with a perfectly impassive face under the whiteness of a bandage was bringing in a basket of dates. "Well, there's slaves and slaves, of course." He wriggled in embarrassment. "Dash it, Professor, if you won't pass me the mustard on the third time of asking . . ."

Marcus and Tullia hastily surfaced from drowning in each other's eyes and looked around, startled, at reality. "Uh—oh, yes." Marcus handed him the salt. Felix rolled his eyes heavenward in disgust.

Varus said, "I will make it up to Nicanor. Fate did him a terrible injustice, and he met it with great courage. A man deserves his freedom for that." He glanced across at Marcus. "Who was the woman?"

Marcus hesitated, then said, "A slave of Porcius Craessius'. Her name is Hypatia."

The prefect nodded. "I will speak to him in the morning." He looked down the table at his daughter, who was blushingly attending to her untouched food. "And what would

Quindarvis have done," he asked quietly, "had not you and these mysterious friends of yours intervened, Sixtus?"

The old scholar glanced at Tullia, his brows drawn down in concern, and she met his eyes calmly and turned to look at her father.

She said quietly, "I knew from the first they planned to kill me. Plotina made them stop talking about it in front of me. They—they hadn't done so to torment me, I don't think; it was just as if I were a lamb or something. I was nothing to them. I think that was more frightening than anything else."

Her mother, who had been reclining beside Varus, sat up and clasped her hands, her face suddenly wrung with compassion. Tullia gave her a bright, close-lipped smile, denying that the horrors had any aftermath of nightmares or fears. Varus was enough of a Roman to look down his nose disapprovingly at the display of emotion, and his wife quickly returned to her position on the couch. Tullia gave her a sideways glance of understanding connivance and pinched her ankle to let her know she understood.

"It's an apt comparison," said Sixtus after a moment. "He thought no more of you as a person, my child, than he thought of those poor devils he purchased from the courts to fling to the bears at his games. In a way it was staged like the games, a deliberately planned crescendo of pathos and horror. Had we not been on his heels, he might have waited a day or two after your father returned to the city to let public sentiment and your father's horror and anxiety work itself to a fever pitch, secure in the knowledge that no matter how many Christians or supposed Christians were questioned, none of them would have the slightest idea where you were. Then I suspect your body would have been found under dramatic circumstances. The deaths of Judah Symmachus and his father, who was the real target of this murder attempt, would pass virtually unnoticed in the ensuing slaughter."

The deep mellow voice ceased; there was silence, as Varus looked down into the darkness of his wine. "It is my shame," he said quietly, "that you are right."

"It is an easy matter," returned the former imperial governor, "to get at a man through his child."

"As Quindarvis knew," the prefect replied. "And since I had thrown those poor silly Christians to the beasts without any more thought than he showed, it made the accusation all the easier to believe."

There was an embarrassed pause in the conversation following this remark, as Dorcas, who had sat in almost unnoticed silence, glanced up suddenly and met his eyes. The prefect reddened. But she only said softly, "At least you acted out of your own conviction and the law, rather than for personal gain."

"No," said Varus softly, looking down at his hands, smooth and unworked around the chased gold rim of the cup. "After this long, I really cannot say what my motives were. But I suspect that the fact that I was sponsoring games affected my judgment." And he raised his head, staring down the hastily averted gazes of astonishment from his wife and child. "If there is divine justice," he continued stiffly, as an old man does when he uses muscles long inactive, "I can only say that I am thankful that I received less than my deserving."

The silence that followed this admission was so painful that out of sheer tact Sixtus stepped gracefully in and changed the subject by asking, "By the way, prefect, what will be done with Plotina? She was in this thing up to the neck, of course."

"Will they kill her?" asked Tullia unhappily. "It wasn't that she was kind to me—she wasn't—but she did keep the men from abusing me. I'm sure it was simply to keep there from being any uproar, but I owe her that."

"If it were not for Plotina," added Dorcas, "the man Lucius would undoubtedly have killed me when he found me outside Tullia's room in the brothel." She glanced across at Arrius, her brows drawn together in concern.

Varus said dryly, "I don't think we need worry about Madam Plotina. Too many people will be interested in keeping her from trial; I expect she'll merely find herself invited to leave Rome and never return."

Sixtus remarked, "There are worse fates," and drained his

cup. "And with Quindarvis dead, I doubt that any of this is going to come to trial—or, indeed, to public notice—at all. And in a town like Rome," he added in a kindlier voice, as Tullia's cheeks flushed a bright vermilion, "you'll find that there is so much gossip that one scandal very quickly chases another. In a year very few people will know, or care, where you were."

Stealthily, Aurelia Pollia reached to grip her daughter's hand. "What surprises me," she said, with a timid glance, as though for permission, at her husband, "is that they would dare to keep her in town at all. Wasn't it terribly dangerous?"

Arrius shrugged. "What's one more girl in a place like that?" he asked. "It was only chance that connected Plotina's place with Quindarvis in Marcus' mind at all. And they had no way of knowing you'd have the wits to throw down your earring that way, Tertullia."

Tullia smiled wryly. "It was the only thing I had that was small enough to fit through the crack I'd made," she said. "The window was boarded up, you see. I worked—days I worked—to chip a hole in the corner of one of the boards. It was stupid, because the only thing I had to work with was a hairpin, but it was the only thing I could think of to do. I knew from the street sounds I was several stories up, and fairly near the Forum. I thought if I could just throw something down, someone might recognize it. I suppose in a city the size of Rome that was a terrible long shot."

"Here, don't speak ill of long shots," protested Felix. "Only the other day I backed the scrawniest little chap in the arena you ever saw, couldn't have weighed any more than you do, Tulla, and by Castor he killed his man, at fifty to one." He looked across at her for a moment, as though trying to reconcile this slender girl in soft rose-colored linen, her hair smoothed neatly back in the old-fashioned republican style her father favored, with the hoyden who'd gamely followed him and his brother in and out of trouble in their early days. For a moment he seemed to struggle with untoward leanings to serious emotion and thought. Then he said,

"Y'know, Tulla, it's good to see you safe. I thought poor Silenus was going to fret himself to death there for a while."

She met Marcus' eyes, and he colored to the roots of his shorn hair.

"And yet you did not, as your brother says, fret yourself to death," said the city prefect slowly. "You acted with courage and tenacity for which, knowing your philosophic antecedents, I would hardly have credited you."

He felt the prefect's gaze going through him like a hot probe, as though sizing him up and gauging his manhood. He swallowed hard. "No, sir," he said. "I would have given up, or failed, or done something stupid, if it weren't for my friends—Sixtus, Arrius, Felix, Churaldin—Dorcas—the Christians. Without them I could never have even begun."

"Indeed," said Tullia's father, and folded his elegant hands. "So tell me now, Silanus, do you propose to return to the life of philosophy?"

In the long silence that followed, the sounds of the quiet evening came to him, singly and clear: the trickle of the moss-choked fountain, the rustle of the gray cat among the jungles of vines that blocked the walkway, the evening quarrelings of the birds. He found himself acutely conscious of the girl who sat at her parents' feet, watching him with wide brown eyes filled with hope and dread, and of Arrius, like a lean tawny lion next to him on the couch. For a moment he did not know what to say.

Finally he stammered, "Well, the thing is, philosophy isn't a life. It's a mode of living, like—like a religion, or an ethical system, can be. But you can't just be a philosopher. Not unless you're a genius, which I'm not."

"You may not be a philosophic genius," said Arrius after a moment, "but you do have a flair for looking into things. Things that maybe we wouldn't trust a paid informer with. You have the advantage of education and a gentlemanly background, as well as wits, Professor. If you're looking for a life to replace that of a philosopher, come see me at the praetorian prefect's office in the morning. I think he'd like to talk to you."

Marcus fought to suppress the surge of illogical delight that broke over him like a wave. It was stupid, of course. Any reasonable man would have run shrieking from the prospect of making a living at the kind of thing he had been engaged in for the last week or so. His smarting shoulder, cracked ribs, and aching throat all winced in protest as he said, "Do you think I'd do for it?"

"Marcus!" cried his brother in horror. "Caius'll have a stroke!"

Arrius thought it over and said, "With a little training."

"Mother'll faint! No," Felix added after a moment, "dash it, knowing Mother . . . But anyway, you can't turn into a—a paid police informer!"

Across the table, Tullia was signaling *Say yes!* her eyes sparkling like stars. *The hoyden!* thought Marcus, who had no idea what his own eyes looked like.

"He won't be a paid informer," corrected the centurion equably. "He'll be a regular junior civil servant, on a civil servant's salary. Nothing excessive, but—sufficient."

Marcus looked from Tullia to her father, who preserved his stern judgelike countenance and betrayed no thoughts of his own. His mouth felt like wood as he asked, "Sufficient—to keep a wife on."

"If she isn't picky," said Arrius brutally.

As though he had drunk several glasses of neat wine, a warmth of deep delight rushed through him, brightening the twilit room like an all-encompassing halo. A sound like the ocean seemed to roar in his ears.

"Dash it, Professor, you don't need their piddling salary!" protested Felix, a peripheral twitter on the edge of a world bounded by the brown depths of Tullia's singing eyes. "You can't do it! You're a rich man, you can't . . ."

Marcus swung around, startled as if his brother had flung ice water over him. "What?"

"I said you don't need their money," said Felix plaintively. The wreath of hyacinth he wore over his shorn hair hung askew, and he pushed it up indignantly. "The old paterfamilias never got around to making a will. The three of us inherit as a consortium. Even settin' aside a whopping chunk for Aemilia's dowry, that leaves us all buttered on both sides. You'd have known that," he added, "if you'd stuck around at the banquet, instead of—well, instead of leaving."

"And when were you at the banquet?" retorted Marcus.

"Later," said his brother hastily, "after you'd torn m'cloak for me, rot you. And went and ruined my bronze silk."

"If we inherit as a consortium," purred Marcus, "you're rich enough to buy another bronze silk."

"Well, I will. Fact is, I already have. And I'll buy another, to wear to your wedding."

Varus said, in a stiff disapproving tone, "Owing to the recentness of your father's death, it is unseemly to discuss such matters for the time being. When the nine days of mourning are past . . ." He paused, feeling himself the center of all eyes, particularly his wife's and daughter's. He sipped his wine. "We shall see."

The meal was over. Sixtus lifted his cup, and said, "To the God of Long Shots," and Arrius, and Varus, and Felix rose to go.

"See me at the praetorian camp in the morning, Professor," said the centurion, as Alexandros handed him his cloak. Even out of armor, in his dress tunic of scarlet wool, he had the air of danger. He was a storm trooper to his bones. His slow firm tread retreated across the atrium, accompanied by Felix's high nattering voice complaining about "Leadin' m'brother astray, an' all . . ."

Varus held out his arm, and the burly gardener draped his cloak with the confidence of a master. "We shall be on our way as well, Julianus. Our thanks for the supper. It has been my privilege to dine with a man whose name has been little more than a legend for the last fifteen years. And our redoubled thanks for the part you played in our daughter's rescue. Tertullia," he added austerely, "as I wish a word in private with your mother, I beg you grant us a few moments' leave."

The prefect and his lady stepped into the shadows of the hallway. Marcus heard their footfalls recede to the dusty reaches of the leaf-strewn atrium, but if they were having a word in private, it was wholly inaudible. As Sixtus seemed to be absorbed in what sounded like a theological discussion with Dorcas, he rose and went quietly to the couch where Tulla still sat, cradling her empty winecup between her hands.

"I know it's unseemly," he said softly, "but because of mourning I won't be able to see you for nine days. I can't stand it for all that time, not knowing." He took her by the hand and raised her up, her brown eyes looking up into his. The evening sun had left the garden, and the little summer dining room was almost dark; he led her gently to the narrow door Alexandros had hacked in the vines, to give access out into the dappled cave of the walkway beyond. "I have to know," he said simply.

She looked down for a moment at his big hands clasping hers and said, "You know my father. I have nothing to say in the matter."

"That might have been true before . . ."

"And besides," she added, her eyes suddenly bitterly ironic in the semi-dark, "it isn't likely that there's another man in Rome who'd have me."

He gaped at her, hurt as though she had struck him.

"I'm sorry," she said, tears of contrition flooding her eyes, "I shouldn't have said that."

"It doesn't matter! I swear to you."

She reached up, gathering a handful of toga in one hand and laying the other gently over his lips. "I know perfectly well," she said softly, "that half the people of our acquaintance are going to be saying—to my face, even—what a noble gesture it was for you to ask for my hand, 'All things considered.' And what the truth is will have to remain in trust, between you and me.

"I thought about it, days and nights, lying upstairs in that stinking place. Listening to the noise downstairs. Never knowing what was going to happen next. Listening to them outside the door, talking about killing me. Hoping they would, before I ever had to come back and face the way people would look at me, that awful contemptuous pity people have for victims.

I thought I'd rather die than have you ask for my hand to save me from—that.

"But in the midst of all that, in those awful days and nights, you know, I never stopped chipping at that silly board in the window. Even when I thought I'd rather die, I kept on fighting to live. I don't know what I thought I'd do afterward, but it wasn't come back. And then Dorcas came. She said you were combing the city, searching for me—not just waiting for me to be found dead or alive. She said that Papa knew where I was, that Papa would help you get me out somehow."

In the gray evening light her eyes flooded with tears at the memory. As though frozen by a spell Marcus dared not speak, dared not break the train of her thoughts, but he reached out gently to wipe the tears from her face.

"You know," she went on softly, "hope is about the worst torture there is?"

"I know," he replied, remembering Sixtus' words about the comforts of despair.

She reached up, putting her arms around his neck. It had always been a long stretch, and she smiled at the familiar awkwardness between their two bodies. "Marc, if I can trust you—if I can trust the truth of your feelings about me—the opinions of a lot of people I barely know are so much less than that. Can I?"

"Papa?" said Dorcas softly, watching the tall awkward form in the white toga stoop to embrace the small thin shape of the girl. Their shadows blended in the liquid twilight; in the dining room, Alexandros had begun to light the lamps.

Sixtus glanced over at her. "Yes, child?"

"Do you think he knows?"

"I'm sure he's being very careful not to," replied the old man calmly. "We're all skating on very thin ice, my children—my deacons—and getting closer to the edge all the time. He understands as well as we do the need for care." He looked gravely from her young, serious, triangular face up into the dark scarred face of Churaldin, and smiled, to make them smile. "Not that I didn't fully expect to end up thrown to the lions in the end, mind you."

"It isn't a joking matter." The Briton seated himself at his master's feet on the end of the couch, his dark face solemn under the white bandage. "It's only a matter of time. Some may be willing to take it on trust that the mystery of Christ's fellowship isn't evil, though it may be secret from outsiders, but most people hate what they do not know. The emperor's been very tolerant, but he's not going to live forever, the way he's going—and he has no heir. What will happen when someone else takes the throne? What if the next emperor is a monomaniac like Domitian? Or outright insane, like Caligula?"

The Bishop of Rome flexed his injured shoulder gingerly and considered his two young deacons, sitting at the foot of his couch. For a moment something very close to grief seemed to pass across the back of his eyes; then he smiled. "If I seriously wanted to avoid violent death," he said thoughtfully, "I wouldn't have become a Christian at all at my time of life, much less a priest; and I certainly wouldn't have agreed to be answerable for a pack of quibbling lunatics like the Church of Rome. But the future is the future; it is not time as we know it, but a wholeness in the mind of God. And in any case, Christ never said he had been assigned the task of making our lives on this earth more comfortable and pleasant. He came to rip us from our complacency, to shove us—violently if need be—onto the nasty, hard, tedious, confusing, and quite possibly fatal path to God. And beside that, all else, my children, is quite peripheral."

He looked up, to see Marcus and Tullia standing handfast in the hacked-out archway of vines.

Tullia came forward without speaking and, to Churaldin's surprised embarrassment, took his face between her hands and kissed him. Then she turned and embraced Sixtus like a father. "Thank you," she whispered, "thank you all." She reached out and clasped Dorcas' hand, and nodded toward her prospective bridegroom. "*He's* going to be mewed up for the next week, but if you're free tomorrow, Dorcas, maybe we can meet?"

"All right," smiled the older girl, "I'd like that. I'll introduce you to my son, if you're interested," and Tullia laughed.

"If you don't think the Professor here would be jealous."

"He might," decided Dorcas, after giving the matter judicious thought. "My boy's a real charmer."

Tullia frowned suddenly, as another thought crossed her mind. She glanced up at Marcus. "Didn't you say a few moments ago that you'd never met Papa, the Bishop of the Christians? Because Dorcas told me that you had."

Marcus regarded the three of them for a moment: Dorcas in her plain dress, her strong curling black hair already working itself loose from its confining pins; Churaldin with the slave brand on the side of his face, sitting so familiarly at the feet of that frail enigmatic old man—philosopher, scholar, soldier, former imperial governor of Antioch, and perhaps other things besides.

"If I did," he replied, "no one ever told me who he was."

The blue eyes met his, startlingly young under white brows. "For one reason and another, people may have worked to mislead you, my son," he said kindly. "But I have never told you a word of a lie. And I never will."

Marcus considered him for a moment in silence, meeting the challenge of that calm, heavy-lidded blue gaze. Then he smiled. "I'll consider myself warned." He put his arm around Tullia's shoulders and led her out into the shadows of the hall.

AUTHOR'S NOTE

In writing this book I am attempting merely to entertain, not prove any kind of historical or theological point. The only two characters in it with even a remote claim to historicity are Sixtus and Telesphorus, about whom only their names, and the fact that they were the sixth and seventh popes, are known. Otherwise all persons and situations in this book are totally fictitious, and not meant to resemble any modern-day persons, groups, or events.

Even a cursory reading of the writings of the early church fathers will indicate that the early church was a theological battleground. The width of the spectrum of opinions, and the vituperativeness with which the Fathers defended their own opinions and attacked others', is almost unbelievable to present-day Christians. It is recorded that the Gnostic Christians accused the Catholic Christians of evading martyrdom if they could; but it is likewise recorded that hundreds of Christians in the province of Bithynia flocked to the new magistrate of the province requesting to be martyred. (He sent them away in disgust.) I have attempted to portray the Christians not as plaster saints, but as the upper-middle-class Romans must have viewed them—alarming and incomprehensible.

Most Christian catacombs date from the third and fourth

centuries A.D. Only two or three of the oldest (including the catacomb of Domitilla) were in use at the time of this story.

When the Temple of Atargatis on the Janiculum Hill was excavated, numerous charred infant skeletons were discovered in its cellars.

Tacitus and Suetonius both refer to the Christians as a sect of the Jews.

All quotes given at the chapter-headings are contemporary.

About the Author

BARBARA HAMBLY was born in 1951 and grew up in Montclair, California. She holds an M.A. in Medieval History from the University of California, Riverside, and a black belt in karate. She is the author of a fantasy trilogy, TIME OF THE DARK, THE WALLS OF AIR, and THE ARMIES OF DAYLIGHT. Ms. Hambly lives in Los Angeles, California.